Before the First Snow

BOOKS BY WALTER M. BRASCH

A Comprehensive Annotated Bibliography of
 American Black English (with Ila Wales Brasch)

Black English and the Mass Media

Cartoon Monickers: An Insight Into the Animation Industry

Columbia County Place Names

The Press and the State:
 Sociohistorical and Contemporary Interpretations
 (senior author)

A ZIM Self-Portrait

Forerunners of Revolution:
 Muckrakers and the American Social Conscience

With Just Cause: Unionization of the American Journalist

Enquiring Minds and Space Aliens:
 Wandering Through the Mass Media and Popular Culture

Social Foundations of the Mass Media (senior author)

The Joy of Sax: America During the Bill Clinton Era

Brer Rabbit, Uncle Remus, and the 'Cornfield Journalist':
 The Tale of Joel Chandler Harris

Sex and the Single Beer Can:
 Probing the Media and American Culture

America's Unpatriotic Acts:
 The Federal Government's Violation of
 Constitutional and Civil Rights

'Unacceptable':
 The Federal Government's Response to Hurricane Katrina

Sinking the Ship of State: The Presidency of George W. Bush

Fool's Gold: The Government's Data Mining Programs

forthcoming:
Betrayed: Death of an American Newspaper

Before the First Snow:
Stories from the Revolution

by Walter M. Brasch

Greeley & Stone, Publishers
Sacramento, California 95834

LCCN 2010914056
ISBN 978-0-942991-19-2

Greeley & Stone, Publishers, LLC
4000 Alan Shepard St., suite 150
Sacramento, California 95834
www.greeleyandstone.com

PRINTED IN THE UNITED STATES OF AMERICA

Dedication . . .

. . . to Rosemary R. Brasch, my beloved wife and friend, who has helped me to better understand love, and whose help and mental stimulation allows me to reach higher than I ever could.

. . . for my children, Jeffrey and Matthew Gerber, who, in their own way, also provided mental stimulation, but also love and friendship.

. . . to my sister, Corey Ellen Brasch and her daughter, Terri Pearson-Fuchs; to my aunt and uncle, Jeanette and Walter Haskin, and their children Clifford and Kenneth. For my "Detroit Family"—Charles and Eva Brasch, Birdie and Philip Dworin; Leon and Gertrude Brasch; Charlotte Tessler, Joel Dworin, and Linda Freedenberg. And to some special family— Harvey Freedenberg, Gary and Barbara Michael, and Warren and Rachel Tessler.

. . . And, especially, to my parents, Milton Brasch and Helen Haskin Brasch; and my grandparents, Fannie Haskin Frieden, Samuel Frieden, and Morris Haskin, all of whom helped shape my life.

. . . And for the Apryl and David that reside together within some of us.

Acknowledgments

Because writers don't exist in isolation, the only honest answer to the question, "How long did it take you to write this book?" is "All my life." This is especially true for *Before the First Snow*.

So many places, events, and people influenced me that it would be impossible to include them all. During my lifetime, I have met thousands of people; most were acquaintances, professional contacts, or colleagues. A few became close friends. They know who they are, and that's what matters.

I am thankful for the friends from my school years, and the places I worked; for Thursday Night, the students and professionals of Beach Blanket Journalism, and almost 350 people who were on the staff of *Spectrum* magazine between 1987 and 2010. They all hold a special part of my life.

I appreciate and acknowledge the hard work of key staff of Greeley & Stone, Publishers, notably MaryJayne Reibsome, Rosemary Renn, and Diana Saavedra, who provided innumerable suggestions and assistance throughout the development and subsequent publication.

"There is in every true woman's heart a spark of heavenly fire . . . which kindles up, and beams and blazes in the dark hour of adversity."
—Washington Irving, *The Sketch Book*

Contents

Prologue   1
1/ Precipitous Beginnings   7
2/ 'So Tired I Can Not Read to Her':   37
     Farm Workers on March to State Capitol
3/ The Whatever Room   43
4/ Decisions   49
5/ Transitions   54
6/ The Nature of Fear   62
7/ Statistically Insignificant   66
8/ Lines of Emptiness   86
9/ Isotopes of Change   88
10/ Glazed Eyes Penetrating a Soul   103
11/ Patriotic Dreams   110
12/ 100 Injured in Chicago Riot;   126
     Humphrey Blasts Police Tactics
13/ Full Frontal Assault   131
14/ Voices of America   139
15/ Waiting for a Bus on Morrissey Boulevard   151
16/ The Company Spirit   166
17/ Snarls of Determination   171
18/ The Monday Night Football Game   187
19/ Questions Without Answers   192
20/ Sounds of the Concrete City   200
21/ Revelations and Curiosities   204
22/ The Cost of an Education   221
23/ Interlude in A Flat   223
24/ The Soul of a Fisherman   228
25/ 'A Spark of Heavenly Fire'   231
26/ Land of the Preferred Address   265
27/ The Amazing Stone Mill   267
28/ The Azalea Bush   283
29/ Hidden Truths   286
Epilogue   295

Prologue

There was nothing distinguished or distinguishing about Bill Drumheller.

Ask ten witnesses to describe him to a police sketch artist, and most will agree he was average. Average height and weight. Average looks. No marks.

Maybe sandy brown hair, cut just about right. Not too short. Not modishly long. No mustache or beard. He may have had hazel eyes. Maybe brown. His brown suit was probably from Sears or Penney's. Shoes could have been from any Wal-Mart.

There wasn't even anything about his voice patterns or dialect anyone could remember. Just seemed like everyone else. Not Southern. Not from the Bronx. Not from New England. And, definitely, not from any foreign country.

If anything, they would remember him as helpful. Friendly. Always with a smile and a story. But that's about it.

This afternoon, he was having lunch with Annie Fenstermacher. The first time they met, she didn't want him in her house. Couldn't be too sure who he was, or why he really wanted to meet with her. So, they met on a bench outside the township library. Just to get acquainted. For a few minutes. Just so he could explain why he wanted to meet with her.

The next time, a couple of days later, they met at Nikki's Café. At a table right there near the front window on Market Street. She still wasn't too sure, but she liked him. Liked what he said. That he wanted to build a summer cabin near the river. Near where his grandparents grew up. Wanted to get away from the city. Wanted to enjoy the land and nature. But more than

1

anything, she appreciated that he was a teacher. Teachers are good people, she thought. They care about children. And they have college degrees.

Annie Fenstermacher didn't have a college degree. She did graduate from high school. Third in her class of 56. That was farther than most girls in the area went in the pre-war years. But, she didn't go to college. There was no need to. She was needed on the farm, and that was that. But, most of all, she appreciated that Bill Drumheller was a veteran of the Vietnam War. Not like those hippies who protested it. The ones who raised their voices against the President of the United States. The *President*! The ones who shamed the nation. Her husband, rest his soul, was a veteran of World War II. Infantry. Corporal with Charlie Company, 22nd Infantry Regiment, 4th Infantry Division. Wounded twice. Came home from Europe with medals and a leg brace.

Yet, almost every day, he worked the 20-acre farm. Early morning when it was dark. Late evening when only the light from his John Deere 50 tractor showed him the fields. Oats, barley, and field corn in the spring and summer; winter wheat and hay in Fall. Machine and farm maintenance through the winter. Worked the fields and farm almost every day, usually with the help of his three children, almost from the time they were 6 until they moved away to find their own jobs and spouses. They knew farming wasn't in their future; it wasn't in most people's futures. Large corporations were moving in, taking over the operations, changing how things were done, changing the economy, changing a lifestyle and culture that went back more than three centuries. But, Jake Fenstermacher wasn't going to go quietly. For almost 30 years, after a couple of hours in the fields, he showed up at 9 a.m. every Monday through Friday at Liberty Ford, where he worked in the parts department. Precisely at noon, he ate the bag lunch his wife prepared; at 3 p.m. he left for the day. Thirty hours a week, minus the 15 minutes a day for lunch. A dollar an hour above minimum wage and no benefits. Always a dollar an hour above minimum wage. When the minimum wage was 75 cents an hour in 1950, he did quite well; when it slowly rose to $3.10 an hour by 1980, that dollar an hour bump wasn't so lucrative. No matter what minimum wage was, he always got a dollar above it. With good financial management, he and his wife could pay the bills.

Could keep the bank from foreclosing.

But now, even with the land barren, Annie Fenstermacher held onto it, for reasons she no longer understood. Just as her husband and her parents and their parents held onto it. She hoped her children would farm the land, maybe even build houses and find jobs locally. She knew it wouldn't happen, but she hoped.

And now came a stranger. A teacher. And all he wanted was just two acres. Not many. Just enough to build a small vacation home and pond, maybe to grow herbs. Maybe tomatoes. Perhaps plant a truck patch. Half-acre. Maybe even a full acre of something. He didn't know what just yet, but something. Enough he could harvest, put into a pickup truck, and take to market. Certainly not enough to feed a family, but something. For those two acres, he was going to pay her $2,450 an acre, slightly more than the assessed value. If he paid her too little, he'd be cheating her. If he paid too much, every Realtor and land speculator would not only be trying to figure out what he was doing, but would also artificially inflate all the other land prices, probably bringing others into the area. What Bill Drumheller didn't want was anything more than normal real estate activity.

For their third meeting, Annie Fenstermacher had invited him into her dining room. She apologized for it being a bit cluttered; it's not always easy for a 73-year-old widow to always be putting things where they once belonged. But she knew what was in the pantry and where the kitchen utensils were, and could fix the finest chicken and dumplings in all of northeastern Pennsylvania. Learned how when she was a child. Every potluck, every fundraiser, that's what everyone wanted. Not her chicken pot pie or her meatloaf. Not pork and sauerkraut, scalloped potatoes, or applesauce. Chicken and dumplings. The best there ever was. And that's what she was serving for dinner early on this crispy Monday afternoon in February.

That afternoon, after dinner—no one discusses business at dinner—Bill Drumheller took a sheaf of papers from his briefcase. More papers than Annie Fenstermacher had seen in quite awhile. But everything was carefully prepared. Neatly typed out. She looked them over. Read almost every word. The polite teacher said nothing about all the time the farm wife was taking. Most people just glanced at the papers, signed them, and took the money. But, Annie Fenstermacher looked at them.

Thought about them. And then agreed it was time to visit the Realtor. Before a notary, Annie Fenstermacher and the Realtor signed the forms; she never noticed that the nice, polite teacher never signed anything. But, she did notice that he was going to pay for the land. Two acres. And so she and he went to the bank. He took $4,910 from his savings account, and handed it to her. Cash. Not a check. Not a money order or a promissory note. Cash. The kind the government guarantees. She didn't have much in her own savings account; she didn't know how a teacher could have so much in his savings account. Figured he probably saved it over a few years. Maybe got a loan. She looked at the cash, but didn't count it. Bill Drumheller—the teacher and war veteran—was a decent man. An honest man. One who took his only personal day that semester to come all the way to Madison Twp. in Marshfield County to close the deal. Besides, she was just going to put it right back into her own account.

Bill Drumheller drove Annie Fenstermacher to the Courthouse, filed the paperwork, and then drove her back to her home. Hugged her, and then left. It was the hardest he ever worked to get just two acres.

That evening, he put on a pair of work boots, changed into a pair of Levi's and a denim shirt. He was driving out to see a woman in Fisher's Ferry, an hour or so away. She owned 40 acres in Marshfield County, in Jefferson Twp., not far from the two acres he had just bought from Annie Fenstermacher. And *that* land was more than an hour from where she lived. Mostly timberland with a stream running through it, and the Susquehanna River nearby. He knew she didn't farm it. Didn't even live on it. Didn't know what she was doing with it. But he knew she was a musician. Musicians always need money, and he figured it wouldn't be too hard to get her to trade her land for some money. Buy her a nice dinner somewhere. Flash her some "serious consideration money" and make sure she knew she would get the rest in cash. Probably more money than she ever saw at one time. The banks and the Courthouse would be closed. Even if she agreed on the spot to sell her land, he'd have to wait until the next morning to close the deal. He didn't like to do that. It always gave people time to think. And he didn't want them to think too hard. But, these 40 acres were crucial, and they could be the easiest buy he ever made.

There was just one final thing he had to do. He taped two of his fingers. Just in case this musician asked him to join her for an impromptu jam session. He'd plead he'd like to, but just couldn't. Broke his finger on his right hand just the other day. Not only couldn't he play the guitar for awhile, more important it kept him away from the kiln, and from the clay sculptures he made.

That night, with a Just for Men dye of black in his rumpled hair, Bill Drumheller became Roger Davis.

1/

Precipitous Beginnings

It was 10 o'clock on as bleak a Sunday morning as I ever saw in May. Not only was there no sun, I had serious doubts there ever would be any sun. The only questions about the forthcoming rain were when—and how much. But there I was, sitting behind two eight-foot brown folding tables placed at right angles in the middle of Victory Park in the middle of the Rites of Spring Jamboree, Marshfield County's annual mid-spring transition from winter to summer, and just about everyone's excuse to clean their houses.

Along the Susquehanna River in northeastern Pennsylvania, it was just me and 200 others hawking their wares. Rather than call it junk from the attics, they chose to call it arts and crafts, antiques, and near-antiques. For me, it was books. My job was to smile, say a few appropriate words, and autograph books, which hardly anyone cared about. It was just about the last thing I had wanted to do. But here I was, one stop on a cross-country book promotion tour.

"It'll be fun!" a 24-year-old Radcliffe English lit graduate, now masquerading as a corporate publicist, had proclaimed more than two months earlier, shortly after my first book was published. "You'll do 12 major cities in two weeks. New York. Philadelphia. Washington—"

"Boston," I said. "I'll do Boston. Nothing more."

"Boston, yes, but we need you in other markets. You're a journalist. You know the power of media hype."

"Because I'm a journalist, I despise media hype." I imagined my arrows tearing out her clueless soul. I could advance dozens of arguments against my proposed book selling tour, but this publicist was determined to spread me out like liver pâté on stale crackers.

"Think of it as a two-week vacation away from the office. A chance to meet people. To get to the heartbeat of America."

"Boston."

"Boston first, then Hartford, New York, Philadelphia—"

"Boston!"

"Sam Weissmann," she said, stopping me cold. "Sam thinks it's a great idea."

I had been a young newspaper reporter at the *Tule River Tribune* in central California in mid-1967. As a bonus for not complaining about unpaid overtime, my managing editor had sent me on a three-day limited-expenses trip to Oakland to do a "home-towner" about the embarkation of some local soldiers on their way to Vietnam. With a few extra hours before I needed to take the train back, I followed the music into the Haight-Ashbury section of San Francisco and saw a different kind of White culture, one I had trouble understanding at the time. My editor splashed my 1,200-word story and pictures of soldiers about to go to war a half-continent away across page 1, with a jump inside, and spiked my 950-word profile of the youth culture. Said it just didn't "seem to fit" into a family newspaper. Elated by the page 1 byline, furious at what happened to the profile, I rewrote it and sent it to five or six magazines, all of which rejected it.

Sam Weissmann thought it had potential. He had just founded *Century* two years after management had killed *The New York Herald Tribune* where he had been national correspondent. *Century* would be his voice not only for social activism, but also for what he thought journalism could be at its best. He took my profile, forced me to endure innumerable rewrites, subjected me to even more of his editing, and published a much stronger 2,700 word article/profile in the March 1968 issue, which had all of 9,000 circulation and not many advertisers. With my three comp copies came a $125 check, $20 more than my weekly salary at the *Tribune*.

Like Art Buchwald and Tom Lehrer who humorously stripped away presidential veneer and society's pretensions and stupidity, and Paul Krassner who co-founded the Yippies a few years after he created the *Realist*, I had wanted to be a satirist, but the establishment papers considered satire to be subversive. Like Lafcadio Hearn, John Hersey, Damon Runyan, Tom Wolfe, Truman Capote, and Hunter Thompson, I wanted to fuse literary fiction and journalism to better understand society, but the core of newspaper journalism at that time was the inverted pyramid structure, to throw as many facts as possible into the first couple of paragraphs, a practice that had begun in the Civil War and had not changed in a century. Like Jacob Riis, Upton Sinclair, I. F. Stone, Seymour Hersh, Noam Chomsky, Mort Sahl, Pete Hamill, Stanley Sheinbaum, and dozens of others, I wanted to be a modern muckraker, to expose greed and corruption, but which the establishment media considered subversive gadflies to be swatted away. With the newspapers I was with, I knew better than to write anything more cutting than police reports about mothers who stole from the PTA or a company that was cited for not paying its taxes. Now and then, whenever a story wasn't quite right for my newspaper, I would send it to Sam who blue-penciled it until it bled, fired innumerable questions at me and became the best editor I ever had. Ten years and three newspapers after he had published my first magazine article, I became one of his associate editors. Three years later, I became executive editor of just about the only general circulation magazine in America that didn't publish articles about diets, exercise, sexual fulfillment, and the latest Hollywood scandals. Of course, I often thought of boosting sales by writing a blockbuster article, "How to Be Your Own Best Friend While Baking Diet Pornographic Cookies to Sustain a New Relationship With an Actor." I would do anything for Sam—except, maybe, subject myself to a promotion tour.

"You checked with Sam? Short, mustachioed, roly-poly fella with 10 pounds of black-gray hair that's trying to escape? *That's* who said it'd be a great idea?"

"Said it'll get you out of the office; refresh your mind. Said we should do whatever it took to promote the book."

"You *sure* Sam O.K.'d this?" Sam wasn't much for PR, but he understood it. He even tolerated PR people who had once been journalists. But now there was a newer trend. The anti-war outrage of the 1960s and early '70s, followed by the Watergate era, led young journalists to believe they could help improve society by exposing the problems of poverty, of government and corporate corruption, of worker exploitation, of any of a thousand things that ambitious journalists could uncover. As with any social movement, that era was over; now at the beginning of the 1990s young clean-cut freshly-minted college graduates who could barely write a sentence went not into journalism but into PR because they "liked to meet people," or because they lusted for the lure of being "event planners," a rising specialty, and hanging with corporate executives and celebrities. This young publicist, who was never a reporter, had given every indication she liked meeting people, loved setting up media events—and knew nothing about what it felt like to chase stories.

"I didn't talk with him directly," she confessed. "Milt Steiner did."

"*Your* publisher conspired with *my* publisher?"

"Conspired wouldn't exactly be the right word."

"No? Try these. *Scheme. Plot. Connive.* Want more? *Manipulate. Jerk around.*"

"I also have a couple of words," she replied sweetly. "Paragraph 19."

Paragraph 19 of my contract, she reminded me, requires authors to undertake all reasonable requests by the publisher for promotion. Trapped by 94 words of eight-point type, I reluctantly agreed to the tour, with one of the Sundays being a day of minimal demands. At least I knew the publisher would promote this book and not let it die as so many do.

"Don't worry," she assured me, "you won't have to do anything. It'll all be done for you."

"Would you mind terribly writing your name on this poster board?" one of the ladies of the Marshfield County Historical Society apologetically asked, handing me broad-tipped red and black Magic Markers. "Just write something simple, like 'Meet David Ascher, *Century* executive editor.' I'm afraid that your publisher forgot to arrange for signs."

"Also forgot to arrange for the books to be here," another added. The two dozen books on the table were there because members of the Historical Society had called the five bookstores in a 40 mile radius and charmed each of their managers to split their 40 percent commission, allowing the Society to sell books at full price and still reap 20 percent. I tried to pay for the books, and for the Society's gas and expenses, but the ladies politely refused, assuring me that although theirs was not a society blessed with large fortune, they weren't stupid. "We have every intention of billing your publisher for the cost of books," the treasurer gleefully noted. "Less the commission, of course."

I was thankful for their help, but furious at my publisher's apparent ineptness. Nevertheless, I did admire the publicist's perverse sense of justice in setting me up in a public park in the middle of nowhere in order to comply with my demands for a quiet Sunday with nothing much to do. She had to know that after a full day on Saturday, followed by a day of rural boredom, I'd be pleading for 15 cities in 11 hours. On what was probably a beautiful Sunday somewhere in the suburbs of New York, I could hear the staff of a book publishing company, each of them quietly relaxing at home, reading the Sunday paper, maybe watching TV or mowing the lawn, chuckling about how they got me to spend a rainy Sunday in a park in the middle of nowhere so I could promote books that no one would be interested in, while I took the "heartbeat" of America.

This particular heartbeat was in a rural county of 55,000, a friendly confederation who appreciated the relatively unpolluted streams and air, didn't lock their houses and cars, greeted you at the store and asked how the fishing was, read a local newspaper that ran pictures of orange-clad smiling hunters with their deer kills, and would tell anyone, politician or stranger, how proud they should be of their country. But, it was also a county where unemployment was running 13 percent, more than anywhere else in Pennsylvania, where houses sold for much less than their value, if they sold at all, where Big Government had forgotten them and Big Business had stormed in to mine the people and resources, and then deserted them faster than a gigolo deserting a plain rich girl for a plain richer one.

The coal and copper mining companies had already stripped the earth in the southern part of the county; lumber companies had tried to denude the northern part. More than two decades earlier, Glenco, the region's largest industry had escaped. Just quietly packed its bags onto a hundred or so moving vans and fled in the middle of the night, leaving twenty-five hundred people without jobs. Oh, they were told they could apply for new jobs in South Carolina where the company relocated because it could pay its workers less and not worry about union security and benefits in this "right-to-work" state.

After Glenco pulled out, the Jamison Corp. and Dart Industries, both of which had supplied materials to Glenco, laid off most of their workers. Houses were boarded up, stores were closed, the daily newspaper saw its advertising plummet, and the school district saw its tax base erode, while the banks began their systematic foreclosure of people's lives. But, still, the people of Marshfield County endured. They may not have been residents of the ZIP codes that entice national advertisers, but they were comfortable with their lives, secure in their isolation from what urban America had become, and proud to make sure everyone knew that.

For the past 41 years, the first Sunday of every May, Marshfield County holds a Spring Jamboree to thank God for the end of winter and to express their joy of life, but most of all to welcome a rebirth of its spirit.

And so it was that on a table in Victory Park sat two dozen books, surrounded by Historical Society brochures, pamphlets, flyers, commemorative spoons, postcards, and jewelry boxes, all available for sale. Folded over a laundry rack, standing on the ground at the end of a table, was a hand-sewn blue-and-white wedding ring quilt donated by one of the members and worth, maybe, $500. For a buck a chance, all proceeds going to the Society, someone would win that quilt in two months at the county's Independence Day extravaganza.

People, no matter where they live, are not revolutionaries, nor will they tolerate the few among them who are willing, often at great risk, to speak out against social, economic, and political injustice. On the eve of the American revolution there were more Whigs and Tories than Radicals. But it was the Radical journalists who, sacrificing their personal liberties, relentlessly brought forth issue after issue, forcing the people to look at injustice.

Voices of Revolution: America's Radical Journalists wasn't supposed to be a book. Unable to find anyone willing to do yet another routine "America Celebrates" article for the July issue two years ago, I had decided, amid much good-natured ridicule, not only to do it myself but also to make it the featured article. Three months and 4,000 words later, *Century's* 325,000 subscribers and 50,000 one-issue-at-a-time newsstand buyers read about Sam Adams, propagandist for the Revolution, and of John

Gill, Benjamin Edes, Thomas Paine, Isaiah Thomas, and the other Radical journalists, most from the Boston area, without whom the Revolution could never have been sustained.

They read not of patriots defending liberty, but of anarchists determined to overthrow an established and legal government. They read of threats, of the destruction of Tory printing presses, of biased reporting filled with lies. More important, these readers of a left-of-center publication had learned from a *Century* survey that most Americans would flunk a basic civics class; more had guessed it was the Communist Manifesto than the Declaration of Independence that stated, "Whenever any Form of Government becomes destructive . . . it is the Right of the People to alter or abolish it."

It was a controversial article, drawing more than 500 letters, about a third from readers righteously indignant about what they believed was a deliberate distortion of history. But, as any capitalist publisher knows, in controversy there are sales. Within a month of publication, three book publishers had contacted me, each with the original idea to do a series of articles about revolutionary journalists, colonial to contemporary. And so began a series of vignettes not only about the colonial journalists of the Revolutionary War, but also of radical journalists and social reformers of other eras. Of Thoreau who protested the Mexican–American War. And of the Chicago 7 who protested the Vietnam War. Of human rights leaders Frederick Douglass, W. E. B. DuBois, and Richard Wright. Of Heywood Broun, the rumpled giant of a man who founded the Newspaper Guild and used his national column to speak out for social justice. Of Jacob Riis, Emma Goldman, Eugene V. Debs, Upton Sinclair, Lincoln Steffens, Rachel Carson, George Seldes, I. F. Stone, Betty Friedan, Gloria Steinem, Paul Krassner, Noam Chomsky, Robert Scheer, Grace Paley, Howard Zinn, and dozens of others whom most Americans had never heard. To make sure there would be controversy, on the book cover the publisher had married the images of Malcolm X, his fist raised high, over the ghosted image of the jovial but equally militant Benjamin Franklin.

Being in Boston aided considerably; having a $2,500 advance against royalties, with another $2,500 advance upon completion of the manuscript, aided even more. Not much by what publishers pay celebrity tell-all authors, but enough to keep me interested. In a little more than a year, I collected the second part of the advance. A year after that, I was on tour.

Although controversy draws readers, publishers usually don't send mid-list authors on book promotion tours, especially one that includes bookstore appearances. It's too expensive, too much trouble, and produces too small a response. Nevertheless, between the 10 to 15 sales during a two-hour period, authors exchange small talk with minimum wage clerks, hoping they will tell their friends and customers about the book. But while history and social issues don't sell, historical romance does.

During my research, I had bumbled into a few shreds of unconnected trivia. I had been fascinated by the revolutionary writer known only as "Willow," one of the most vitriolic journalists of the pre-Revolution and for the first two years of the war. Only a half dozen Radicals had known his identity. Journalists, historians, and academic types for the next two centuries had suspected "Willow" was a Royalist, but they had also believed—often in print—it was any of 50 others, including many of the greats and not-so-greats of the Sons of Liberty. By the time I had finished chasing down the leads, I had determined that Willow was really the Duke of Gloucester, illegitimate son of George III and an English peasant woman. He had been given riches and property instead of a room in the Tower of London, and then sent to the Colonies in 1773 by the Hanover monarchy to get both him and his fertile father out of scandal in England. Within a year and a half-dozen trysts, the Duke met a Colonial seamstress, herself a Revolutionary spy, fell into a bad case of lust, and was unwittingly trapped into becoming a spy for the Colonists when she threatened to expose him not only to his father but also to Sam Adams and his Sons of Liberty, who had been manipulating the whole affair. Now, for the first time, we knew the secret identity of the Duke of Gloucester, and why he became not only a spy but also a leading voice of revolution; his story would become the most salacious, and undoubtedly the most read, of my 29 chapters.

The quality of writing, connecting the American Revolution with contemporary American problems, even my connections to many of the nation's major media markets hadn't justified the tour. What did justify it, what guaranteed me air time, ink, and—alas—bookstore and Jamboree appearances—was sex.

Looking around Victory Park, I doubted anyone had any

sexual urges. I just hoped someone would have the urge to buy a book, or at least bring a long day to a quick climax. And so I sat, waited, made small talk to the ladies of the Historical Society, watched clowns and magicians and children and adults and squirrels of every kind scamper among the tables. Two Little Leaguers, their blond hair falling out of blue baseball caps, their uniform shirts proclaiming them to be Lions, came begging for money so their league could prosper and grow old, and they could grow up to be Babe Ruths. They got two bucks from me, as did the Mental Health Association and, for all I knew, the Association of Widows of the Unknown Soldier.

Every now and then someone would stop at the table, thumb through the book, say something like "Nice book," or "How much is it?" and then buy a historical postcard or a commemorative spoon or a chance for the quilt. Unwilling to let overpriced historical postcards grab sales from American history, I tried promoting the book as a historical romance, figuring the women of Marshfield County would escape into a world of slash-and-burn tanned and buffed pirates. For my efforts, I was constantly rebuffed. Even the dogs—there had to be at least five or six dozen dogs, all on leashes, all guiding their humans through the maze of crafts, antiques, and junk—didn't stop. It was embarrassing and humiliating. I like dogs. Dogs like me. And, today, they didn't even want to sniff me out.

Behind me, a slightly plump gray-haired grandmother figure, obviously put there by Central Casting, was selling multicolored pipe cleaner butterflies. By the end of the day, she would probably have sold enough to make that month's payment on the Ferrari. To the right of me, an antique dealer had just sold a 40-year-old Lionel train set; near him, a Coca-Cola platter brought in $35. More passersby. Probably rushing off to buy buck-fifty *Reader's Digest* anthologies; four novels in the binding of one; 37-1/2 cents a novel, a price impossible to beat anywhere else.

Don't worry, the Historical Society ladies assured me, *the crowds usually don't come until after church. We'll sell lots of books*, they said, believing every syllable, while I remembered sitting for nearly two hours nearly alone at bookstores in Boston and Hartford waiting for the masses to smile and pass by. Occasionally, they'd stop, ask a pertinent question or two, such as, "Is it on the Best-Sellers list?" or "Can you tell me where the

Children's Book section is?" Switching from author to carnival barker, I tried another technique. "Hey, how 'bout a book? We have a lot here!"

"Yeah, thanks," and she walked on. That one didn't work, but the next one might.

"Great book! Only a few thousand are left!" A smile, and a passerby.

"Fantastic writing. Great plot! I've even read it myself!" No reaction.

"It's about the writers who helped give us the Revolution!" Still no reaction. "It makes a great gift!" . . . "It's less expensive than taking your family to a movie! O.K., how about less expensive than a Cadillac?" Are they deaf? "It contains the secret recipe of safe sex!" The excuses why people didn't buy books in Boston, Hartford, and New York were no different from excuses I encountered in Marshfield County—"I don't have any money," "I'm just looking," "I'm just here to meet someone," "I'll be back later," "I'm sorry, but I only read self-help books."

Yeah, I'm sorry too. Now and then, one of my spiels worked and someone would stop, pick up a copy, and chat awhile. Two high school girls asked for my autograph. They didn't buy the book, but got some nice comments on 3-by-5 cards. Maybe they collected autographs. Maybe they needed it for extra credit or because they thought they could sell it for a dime somewhere. But so far, in a park in the middle of a celebration, there was a lot of interesting chit-chat, a lot of worn-out clichés by both sellers and potential customers, but no sales. I really didn't expect many, but at least I was checking for heartbeats.

Twenty yards away, the first of the day's seven bands had begun its 50-minute set. Sales were non-existent, and I had no doubt that Jumpin' Jerry Jerulsky and the Pennsylvania Polka Dots wouldn't do much to spur sales of a book about radical journalists. I doubt anyone, including Jumpin' himself, knew why a polka band was scheduled for 10 a.m. On the other side of the park, someone was playing a flute, a syncopated 4/4 up-tempo jazz beat of soprano notes floating over the 2/4 polka beat in a strangely harmonious dichotomy. Near her, playful, alert, and providing an occasional counter-harmony, was her dog, a shepherd mix of some sort, her gull-wing ears as much at attention as they could be. Elsewhere, people were sitting, talking, moving. But there I sat, author, journalist, executive editor of a major national magazine, arrogantly expecting the public to crawl all over me, alone except for ladies of the Historical Society who tried their best to make me feel comfortable—when they weren't liquidating their inventory.

Sometime between the "Beer Barrel Polka" and "The Clarinet Polka," I barked out to a 50ish lady that the book would help her learn more about journalists from our Revolution. She stopped, looked at me, pity I assumed, looked at the cover, and then quietly said she didn't want to make her husband mad.

"For reading a book?" I asked jokingly, thinking she didn't want to spend the money on a book when there were other things she or her husband may have needed.

"I . . . I just daren't do it," she said.

"Reading is bad?" I hadn't meant it to be as incredulous a statement as it sounded.

"It's not a book he'd approve of," she said with no hesitation.

A half-dozen responses, none of them civil, flashed through my mind, but I had been ordered both by Sam and by my book publisher to be polite. So in my most polite incredulous voice, I asked, "He doesn't approve of the Revolution that founded our country? He doesn't approve of Sam Adams and Ben Franklin?"

She saw this as a challenge, and firmly informed me that her husband was a war veteran, both of them were Christians and patriotic Americans, and I should be ashamed for putting such loyal Americans as Ben Franklin in the same book as that Black militant Muslim Malcolm X who had tried to destroy the very country she loved. And then she huffed off.

The next encounter was with a gentleman, probably in his mid-30s, whom I later learned was an agronomist for the Soil Conservation Service. He bought five chances for the quilt, and then informed me he wasn't interested in radicals who were "so . . . so . . . *un-American*" I was about to be resigned for an instant replay of the previous discussion as I reminded him that our own country was founded upon one of the greatest revolutions in history.

"That was different. That was for freedom and justice. All you journalists do is stir up people. Write about all the bad, never any good. It's all that liberal bias." The media are part of the establishment, I pointed out, part of society but never at the cutting edge. Briefly, we discussed revolution and journalism, neither of us changing the other's opinions of dissent or the

press, while the Historical Society ladies were the perfect host-
esses, now and then interrupting our conversation to mention
about the great food available for lunch. My hunger could wait.
In fact, it had to wait.

"Did you know that the Army invaded Marshfield County
and wiped out a band of revolutionaries?" I wasn't paying much
attention, thinking about the gentleman who recently left, of
the strength of his beliefs, of the hundreds who would walk
past, and the black German Shepherd mix who just nuzzled my
arm. "There's no need to apologize, David. We all have our own
worlds." Around her neck was a Nikon F-2, two lenses attached
to a neck strap. Also around her neck was a large peace symbol,
probably brass or copper, attached by a leather strap. A multi-
hued tie-dyed headband kept her long black hair from flying
into her face on this cool, windy morning. She wore an off-white
peasant blouse and a paisley-print skirt of yellows, reds, browns
and purples. On her feet was a pair of lilac-and-white checked
high-top rainbow-laced funky sneaks. Her skin was dark, more
pigmentation than sun, I reasoned, since she didn't seem to
have any sun-dried wrinkles. I couldn't tell if she was 30 or 40.
A hippie? In 1990? "I'm Apryl," she said, extending her hand,
but it was her eyes, large, blue, and full of life that said "hello."

"I'm David Ascher. I'm executive editor of—"

"I know who you are. I subscribe to *Century*." She paused a
moment, but before I could question her—the usual questions—
Did she like the magazine? What are her favorite sections? Any
memorable articles? What would she like to see that we aren't
doing now? Does she have a heartbeat that I can record?—she
again asked if I knew that this valley was invaded. I said I didn't
doubt it since Pennsylvania was one of the original 13 colonies.
She laughed at my intellectual naïveté and abruptly cut me off,
brightly informing me that it wasn't during the Revolution that
the county was invaded. In the heart of the Declaration of
Independence, where Sam Adams, Thomas Jefferson, and Ben
Franklin plotted to overthrow the government of the mightiest
nation in the world, this hippie photographer told me that at
the beginning of the Civil War a band of Confederate sympa-
thizers had created their own newspaper. "They didn't even
have guns. All they were trying to do was give the Confederate
side of the issue. And do you know what the Army did?" I didn't.
"They sent in a troop of Union soldiers under the command of a

general. Destroyed their newspaper. Killed the resisters and arrested the ones who wouldn't die. There's a statue of the general on horseback. You know, the one over by the parking lot."

"I assume you're from the South."

"Oh no," she smiled. "I'm a Yankee. But, isn't it interesting how the establishment always tries to destroy dissent and shred the Constitution in the guise of protecting our security?" Before I could agree, she quickly changed the subject. "There aren't many photos in your book."

"Talk to my publisher," I suggested, explaining that the lack of photos was a business decision.

"Maybe the day will come again," she said, "when publishing decisions will be based upon the art and craft, and not what lawyers and businessmen think." I agreed, but still planned to drop a "truism" like, "a publisher with no income is no longer a publisher," when she cut off my thought. "Mainstream publishers have enough for promotion, but very little for editorial. Like this, for example."

"Like what, for example?"

"*This*," she said, waving her arms. "Your publisher is paying me well to shoot you in the park, but— "

"My publisher is *what?*"

"Paying me to shoot you in the park. Anyhow, the problem with publishers—"

Apryl Greene, as I was to learn, had little concept of linear logic. When I could stop her thought process, I learned she was a freelancer who occasionally got assignments from newspapers, magazines, and book publishers, but mostly was the official photographer, often for expenses and little or no pay, for unions and social service agencies in Pennsylvania and surrounding states. But now, on a Sunday morning, she had driven more than an hour from Fisher's Ferry, which I learned was right near Herndon, which was still nowhere near anything else, in order to get a half-dozen stills of an author in a park, for what use neither she nor I knew, and was being paid $100 plus expenses. Everything that was right with this hippie was wrong with publishing. The 24-year-old Yuppie publicist couldn't get books to the most boring afternoon I ever spent, but she could arrange for photo coverage. Go figure.

"Shoot away," I commanded.

"I already did. Got some good stuff of you at the table with a couple of people. May get some more later in the day. Have to be off. Got to collect money for a school I'm building. Got more people to shoot." And with that, she was gone.

A '50s/'60s cover band, which replaced the polka band, was now replaced by a mutation that looked like an acid-rock/heavy metal punk band, complete with black leather costumes, spiked wrist and leg bands to match their spiked rainbow color hair, and $20,000 worth of sound equipment—two dozen speakers, monitors, and a 12-channel mixer, drawing 125 amps of screeching power, all of which had been carefully placed on a $300 wooden stage four hours earlier. More than anything, I hoped they would soon stop tuning up. It wasn't long before I realized they weren't tuning up. A county of conservatives, fueled by eclectic music, made as much sense to me as a liberal at a park table pushing books of revolution.

A few feet from the bandstand, the funky photographer, now surrounded by at least a dozen children, was bouncing, gyrating, swaying to the music, her peace symbol bobbing and flopping to the beat, a black ebony flute with polished silver keys clutched in her left hand held high as a drum major's mace, her camera and lenses in a case on the ground.

Tired of sitting, tired of being ignored, I wandered around, looking and touching antiques and junk, nostalgic pet rocks from another time, and recently-made clay wind chimes, wooden wine racks, and metal jewelry, chatting with sellers and customers, monitoring their heartbeats. A state trooper and his school teacher wife were hawking hand-made $40 silk banners; a couple of tables to their right, a paralegal displayed bulky-knit sweaters; a grocery store clerk was selling custom-made leather belts, all at bargain basement prices. Several tables displayed lithographs, oils, or watercolors; others displayed hand-sewn plush animals, hot pads, and mittens. At one booth, a folk artist sold mailboxes, 12-inch circular saw blades, and three-foot buck saw blades, each one with a different farm or town scene painted on it. One ingenious family—she an admissions counselor at a local college, he a machinist, their three children spread from the seventh through eleventh grades—presented gourds, painted with delightful comic faces, shellacked and available for only $3 each. At another booth, a husband-and-wife team cut, welded, and sold stained glass wind-catchers. A family, dressed in late 19th century clothes, sweated over a black kettle hung by leather straps to a tripod of tree branches, boiled a concoction of liquids, poured, cut, molded it, and sold it as soap, all for less than a buck a bar. An iron worker, sweat pooling on his ash-covered face and arms, with bellows and a portable furnace, fashioned souvenir horseshoes and wrought-iron ornamental flower pot holders, five feet tall and suitable for any backyard.

Red label and blue label 78s made of acetate-coated shellac in the pre-oil crush days, the kind that feel like they have substance to them, were bringing in as much as $5; postcards of historic scenes, sent by one-cent stamps, were worth as much as $8 each. Four or five booths had reproductions of century-old bowl-and-pitcher sets that, if original, would have sold for as much as $300, but were "on special" in their brand-new look-old look, selling for only $25 a set. An empty bottle of Warner's Safe Diabetes Cure fetched $42, but an empty bottle of Warner's Safe Kidney and Liver Cure was priced at only $16. It wasn't worth the effort to think of the significance. Around me was Depression glass; bowls, plates, and saucers; ashtrays, pitchers, and candy dishes. Amber, blue, pink, green, and milky white. Patterns called Princess and Queen Mary, Patrician and Old Café. Prices from a couple of dollars to a hundred or so. There were stories all over the park. But first, lunch.

A half-dozen food stands, each sponsored by a non-profit organization, were competing for my stomach. I wondered if there would ever be a booth to raise money to improve the sanitary conditions in booths selling food at fairs. Since everything has bacteria, and I have a great health plan, I stopped by the Mental Health booth. For $2.95, I got a cup of lemon tea, crisp fries, an air-filled hotdog covered by Mystery Sauce in an emaciated bun, and the inalienable right to fight the flies for custody of the chopped onions, relish, ketchup, and mustard from nearby bowls. I dribbled sauce and onion onto the dog, thought about the 342 cases of tea the Radicals dumped into Boston Harbor, and walked back to the tables.

The chances for the quilt were going fast; spoons, calendars, and postcards were selling well—and the Historical ladies had even sold two books while I was gone. It's much easier to digest a non-profit hotdog when your books are selling. I figured I might just stay around awhile longer, but the euphoria wouldn't last.

The skies became darker, and sent forth a few drops of rain, scouts for the main torrent. By two o'clock, drops had turned into intermittent drizzle, but three copies of the book had been sold, and even some of the lookers had read *Century*, although most preferred *Field & Stream, Family Circle*, and *Reader's Digest*.

"You don't think I'm crazy, do you?" Her blue eyes smiled with mischievous delight. Apryl, who had popped out of no-where, had again caught me unprepared. "I have a proposal for a school," she bubbled. "It'll be a place where people can come and think, and talk about the great social issues of today. Or, about nothing at all. There will be all kinds of things to learn. And every weekend there will be a crafts festival, and there will be plays and concerts, and writers and actors and artists of every kind can get together. And more than anything else, it will teach peace."

"A noble thought," I replied.

"More than noble! Necessary! In Georgia, the Army trains soldiers of Latin American dictators about counterinsurgency, psychological warfare, and combat," said Apryl, her voice as fiery as her eyes. "Less than two hours from here, in the state founded by Quakers, the Army has a War College on what was a school for Native Americans. It sits on land where this government forced the Indian youth from hundreds of miles away to live after it forced them to leave their families." She told me how the government cut the students' hair, usually against their cultural and religious beliefs, made them wear trousers, purged their languages, and then told them they were being trained for service industries because they weren't intelligent enough to do anything else. I had known about the Carlisle Indian School, where Jim Thorpe had lived and trained. I also knew about how the government forced segregation and then assimilation into a race of people who had lived on the land that an invading cul-ture had seized for its manifest destiny, but Apryl filled in the details before quickly morphing into another topic. "If you were in the army, no matter if it was to massacre Native Americans, to protect Americans from the Nazis, or as a desk jockey in Kansas, people say you served the country," Apryl declared, "but we never say that those who were in VISTA or the Peace Corps, no matter how many hardships they faced and no matter how much good they did, *served* the country. That tells us more about our priorities than anything else!" In the moment I was about to say something, Apryl looked into my eyes and made it clear. "This will be a School for Peace. For all children. It'll be like a populist Swarthmore, but for the children!" A breath. Nothing more than a swallow of air, accompanied by a gleam in eyes that once were about to shed their tears. In that one moment, it seemed as if her blood pressure had dropped, replaced by a quiet, perhaps even joyful, determination. "Chairman Mao said that an army without culture is a dull-witted army, and a dull-witted army can't defeat the enemy."

"I believe Chairman Mao is in decline at the moment."

"Makes no difference. His words are what are important. But when our revolution comes, the creative people will fight it! Not with guns but with love. An army led by writers and artists and musicians and people who care about people. And some of the generals will be Quakers, and everyone will be welcome to enlist! The fluids of change are in the fountain well." She paused a moment. "I'm going to write a story." Sure, I thought, just like Chairman Mao. "It'll be an important story." Why not you? Everyone else thinks they're writers. Easiest thing in the world. Just sit right down and write. Anyone can do it. Write a few pages, call it an article, and sell it to *The Atlantic Monthly*, *Playboy*, or even *Century*. It doesn't even have to be true. Call it a short story and sell it to *Redbook*, *Home & Garden*, or *The New Yorker*. Write a few hundred pages and sell it to the major book publishers, all of whom will bid in the high six figures. At parties, lawyers and doctors casually mention that they would like to write a novel if they only had time or, maybe, when they retire. Maybe if I had the time, I'd do brain surgery.

"It's going to be about a princess and a knight." It's got best-seller written all over it. Throw in a fire-breathing dragon and a castle and the world will pay you royalties until the day when Disney begins marketing triple-X films. "I don't know what it's about yet, but I know it'll be interesting." Sounds mesmerizing already. "I want my princess to be real." Yep. Hard-hitting non-fictional journalism. "My princess will live in a world no longer possible, but she'll be the vehicle to help all of us experience life. To make people happy and to liberate their minds. That's very important." She looked at me, her eyes searching for a solution to a problem I didn't understand. "It's harder to write a novel or a children's book, isn't it?" she asked, answering her own question with a reason. "Because although you have to base it upon reality, everything has to come from within you."

"I don't know. I don't do novels or children's stories," I said trying to be polite. Some other time, I might have been friendlier, might have spent several minutes, maybe even an hour, with this person, one of the few liberals I had seen all day. But, I was tired. Physically and mentally.

"You could write a novel," she said as if possessed with divine wisdom. She wasn't even bubbling enthusiastic about it; it was just a matter-of-fact statement.

"I don't do windows and I don't do fiction," I repeated, hoping she'd let the matter drop. She didn't.

"You'd probably write a pot-boiler. It'd move fast, one thing after another because that's what your life is like." If I were to do a novel, it wouldn't be a pot-boiler. It'd be character-driven. Probably start slow and deliberate. Set a base. Introduce the characters. Hold back the plot. Readers wouldn't even know where the story was going. Probably more exposition than action, something editors and readers don't appreciate. They may even become frustrated with just looking at people. There would be a lot of facts, just lying there, quietly embedded. A word. A phrase. A sentence or two. Innocuous but powerful. Waiting. Just waiting to explode. The reader would have to wait. Wait for the plot to develop. Wait for the obligatory sex scenes that agents, editors, producers and, unfortunately, readers demand in fiction. It wouldn't be anything at all like journalism where everything is revealed in the first few paragraphs, and the last few lines could be lopped off to save space or included if extra space was needed to be filled. This book would require people to think. Read between the lines. Make connections. Get revelation from finding threads carefully woven into the fabric. Maybe they'd even have to read it two, three times to understand—*Hey, wait! I'm not writing a novel. I don't do novels. I'm a journalist!*

"I don't do novels." I made sure she heard the force of every syllable, but then confessed I often committed literary journalism, using the novel form to drive the journalism.

"You could combine both fiction and nonfiction," she said, her eyes smiling.

"How could I do that?" It wasn't a question as much as a statement of disbelief at her naiveté.

"How would I know!" she retorted, catching me unprepared for the edge in her voice. "I take pictures for a living. You're supposed to be the writer." A moment of silent rage was punctuated by a mischievous smile. "Tell me about your writing."

Not then, and certainly not now could I explain my writing or anyone's writing. You have to read it. Explain the sun or the grass or even a cow; how do you explain something that shouldn't be explained? Besides, the markets for vignettes and satire are fewer now than ever, decreasing in proportion to the increase in myriad how-to and self-help articles and books targeted for the me-generation, and celebrity tell-alls targeted to the . . . well, just about everyone. "I don't know how to describe my writing. "I suppose that's for someone else," I replied, dismissing her question, but ego-pleased that someone cared.

"Do you always know who your characters are before you write something?"

"Since I write nonfiction, I have a good clue. Sometimes, it's easier to understand fictional characters than real people." She smiled.

"Did you do much writing?—I mean when you weren't an editor?" Yeah. Lots of writing. Thousands of stories. For every drop of rain and all that crap—"Do you remember everything you write?"

"For about a week. Maybe if you really immerse yourself into it, you'll remember some for a few months. After that, it's just excess baggage. You have to move on, clean your memory. I can't even remember what I did yesterday."

"Maybe you wrote about me," she said, her eyes teasing me.

"Not likely. *You*, I would have remembered." A smile countered her words.

"You would have probably forgotten me," she said quietly, "just as you have forgotten your own life." Quickly, before I could respond, she changed the topic. "You looked like you were composing an article out there by the bandstand," she said, catching my surprise. "Didn't think I noticed, did you? You were trying to figure me out. Others didn't see, or thought I was nuts, but you were writing."

"I wasn't writing. I figured you were playing a flute and dancing."

"Brilliant observation. No wonder you're a big time editor. Great insight into character."

"O.K., so I was curious. You're up there prancin' around in a park in the middle of nowhere, surrounded by a dozen or so yipping children, waving your flute to the gods of imposing thunder, and celebrating their role in a world of mediocrity."

"They're trying to make music," she said sharply. "They're trying to make some kind of a statement."

"The Polymer Pterodactyl is not music, and the only statement they have is probably overdue."

"You *sure* you're an editor? Isn't *Century* supposed to be liberal? You didn't inherit the magazine, did you? You write of revolutionary journalists, but are you a revolutionary journalist?"

"I'm a journalist," I said throwing off her question. "I write about many things."

"Journalists never experience life; you just report it. But no matter how long or how hard you observe, you'll never meet the most important requirement of good journalism."

"Which is?"

"You won't be able to participate."

"If all journalists were expected to be what they write, there would have been no stories about the space program. Nothing about AIDS. Tell me one reporter who has the Jarvik-7 heart."

"Artificial, David. That's what it's all about. Without feelings, your journalism isn't real. It's clinical. When's the last time you wrote of the Movement? Of the struggle?"

"I write about the struggle," I said, defensively and with some anger. I briefly told her of my articles for the *The Light, The Phoenix*, and Art Kunkin's *L.A. Free Press*, like the *Village Voice* on the East Coast, that were at the beginning of the social revolution, much like the underground newspapers of the 1760s and 1770s. She told me you couldn't write about the struggle without being a part of it. I told her to fuck off. O.K., so I didn't exactly say it in exactly those words, but I let her know that she didn't even know who the heck I was and she shouldn't be doing pop psychology. I reminded her that the leaders of revolution are often journalists. Sam Adams. Ben Franklin. Upton Sinclair. Abbie Hoffman. I recited a list of names.

"And they participated in the struggle."

"My book is about the struggle!"

"As history it's important, because knowing your history gives you insight into the human condition," she said. And then she changed the direction and attacked my editorship. "You're an editor. You're no longer part of the working class; you're management. It's hard to be radical when you're fiddling with Profit-and-Loss statements."

"I'm the executive editor of a *liberal* magazine."

"You're the executive editor of a magazine. Makes no difference if it's *Forbes* or *Century*. Makes no difference if you're the CEO of GM or the director of a Salvation Army rehab unit. You're either a worker or management. If you're a worker you're part of the oppressed; if you're management, you're the oppressor." I had no intention of letting her know I agreed with her. A chance to spar with someone—anyone—is always more exciting than watching park grass grow.

"When you open your School for Peace, who'll run it? Someone from the Fairy Godmothers Union? You'll push paper, and worry about finances. There'll be licenses and permits, supplies and roads that close in the winter. You'll manage staff and handle complaints, take unpopular stands, and wipe little Johnny's nose and worry if some idiot parent will get upset and sue you because she doesn't want little Johnny's nose wiped." As quickly as she started the argument, she shifted. Maybe I had hit a nerve. Maybe she just wanted to change topics. As short as I knew her, as long as I might, she fluttered around arguments as easily as she did life.

"Were you a part of the Movement? Did you participate?" she again asked, bouncing back to the attack.

"I've supported my share," I countered. "Maybe even more than you."

"A score card!" she said, pleased with the observation. "Everyone needs a scorecard. That's so we know who wins and loses. The establishment has score cards! We have sex and drugs and rock and roll, and no one keeps score!" I smiled at the sarcasm. Again, she was right. "Cynicism is harder than laughter, isn't it?" she asked, somewhat amused that she had been able to get a sparring partner. She wasn't finished. "The journalists, all they do is try to find leaders, but the Movement wasn't of leaders. But you guys—" *Us guys?* "—needed to find leaders; it's something in the media's personality. The media are always looking to find someone to quote, so we'd all get together and say, 'You're today's leader; talk to the man.' Made no difference who it was, as long as it was someone." It was a point I had repeatedly made for many years, but few in the establishment press ever listened. But, I wasn't about to let go of a discussion—*any* discussion—even if I was mentally and physically exhausted from my job, from the book tour, which still had a week to go, and from the seeming boredom of a rural town park.

"You haven't read my writings; we weren't all like that. Some of us still have our roots in the social movements."

"You may have roots in the '60s but the leaves say '90s."

"We have to live in the time we're in. We can't go back, no matter how much we want to."

"We can take it with us!"

"It's dead, Apryl! Don't you understand! We killed it. It won't be back no matter what we do. The best we can do is to remember."

"It's not dead, David. It's just in a coma. There will once again be a time for joy, a time for a better economy and a concern for social issues." She again paused. Just a moment. Nothing more. "And there will be a time for darkness. A time when we will again have to rise up to protest. A time to defend our rights and civil liberties." If there was again to be such a time, I knew she'd be there. I hoped I would be.

Rumblings from the clouds now rose into thunder. Hawkers and vendors, buyers and lookers calmly prepared for the imminent storm. It finally came, hard and furious, trying to destroy everything it touched.

Beneath one of two dozen semi-porous picnic shelters, Apryl and I talked about the idealism of our youth, of levitating the Pentagon in an anti-war protest, and teasing America with idle threats about sending the country on a psychedelic high from acid-laced reservoirs. We remembered Ken Kesey and the Merry Pranksters, the Hog Farm, and the hippie who became known as Free. We agreed that Paul Krassner's *Realist* may have been one of the more outrageous publications, but in its outrage and what Krassner called "investigative satire" was truth. We argued about the Polymer Pterodactyl, and remembered the folk music of the '60s, of Tom Paxton and Tom Lehrer; of Pete Seeger, Bob Dylan, and Phil Ochs; of the Smothers Brothers, Simon and Garfunkel, and Peter, Paul, and Mary. Of Dick Dale, the Beach Boys and Surfer Music. Of Sgt. Pepper, the "White Album," Allen Ginsberg, and the Panhandle—not the ones of Oklahoma or Florida, but of Golden Gate Park, San Francisco, where the Movement called home, where the Jefferson Airplane and the Grateful Dead occasionally gave free concerts, where Apryl first learned tie-dying and where I had gone a couple of times while on assignment. It was the Summer of Love. The media swarmed in and gave the Movement credibility. For me, a young reporter planning to become the editor of *LIFE*, it was an awakening of the spirit of freedom.

A year later, I was in Chicago for the Democratic convention. Twenty-three years old and two years out of college. My paper, in the form of a 40ish managing editor, told me that if I was so all-fired determined to be in Chicago, I could get an advance on my vacation time, but I'd have to get there on my own money and do the reporting on my own time. Although the *Tule River Tribune* wouldn't be able to run anything from Chicago—it was still a "community family newspaper"—there would be no objection if I marketed stories elsewhere, as long as it wasn't within a 50-mile radius and I didn't identify myself as a *Trib* reporter.

A magazine article and an announcement in March had helped me determine that I needed to be in Chicago. The article was the first 90,000 words of Norman Mailer's *Armies of the Night*, first published in *Harper's Monthly Magazine;* the following month, *Harper's* published the last 30,000 words almost simultaneous to publication as a book. Not only was *Armies* a powerful depiction of the march on the Pentagon by 200,000 people the previous October, it extended the new journalism, a literary journalism forged by Tom Wolfe, Ken Kesey, Truman Capote, Hunter Thompson, and Jimmy Breslin. Mailer had fused fiction and nonfiction into a powerful narrative to tell the truth of America and of the anti-war movement. At the end of March, probably little influenced by *Armies of the Night*, Lyndon Johnson shocked the nation with his late-night announcement that to concentrate on critical issues, including the war in Vietnam, and to not allow personal politics to play into his decisions, he wouldn't run for a second four-year term as president. The announcement threw the nation into even greater chaos. Anti-war and civil rights riots increased, while Robert Kennedy, Eugene McCarthy, George McGovern, and Hubert Humphrey increased their jockeying for position to be the Democrats' presidential nominee. By the Chicago convention, Kennedy was dead; McGovern was only a minor candidate, McCarthy's campaign was no longer at its zenith, and Humphrey, the liberal smeared by a vice-presidency of a war that America could not win, would become the nominee in a riot-torn convention. But in August 1968, reporters only knew there was going to be a war of beliefs and, perhaps, a war in the streets. Not many realized that Chicago would also be what led to the election of hard line conservative Republican Richard Nixon as president, slightly aided by his appearance the following month on Rowan & Martin's hip, irreverent "Laugh-In." Chicago had become my baptism by fire, pushing me to develop my reporting skills under intense deadline constraints. I wouldn't be able to match Mailer, Wolfe, and the others, but I was determined to get close.

A year after Chicago, a half-million others took up temporary residence on a soggy farm in upstate New York. While they were high on life, I was covering city council meetings and the courts. By then, I had moved on to my next paper, one that actually believed in enterprise reporting. It would be another year, a few months after covering the Kent State killings on my own time that I would finally write about Woodstock.

Apryl and I didn't talk about Woodstock. She might have been there, grooving on the music of Country Joe, Joan Baez, and Janis Joplin. Even if she wasn't there—less than one-quarter of one percent of the whole country attended—she and I were children of Woodstock. Like Chicago, Woodstock was an awakening, a celebration of life.

After Woodstock came Altamont, originally billed as the West Coast version of Woodstock, but which became the Movement's lowest point. The Rolling Stones had hired the Hell's Angels to provide security for a free concert. In a drug-induced time warp of some sort, it might even have made sense. The Angels had been at the Be-In, and provided "security" at other venues. No one was going to cause trouble around a gang of anti-establishment, drug-induced sexist, racist, and homophobic thugs. But, at Altamont, by the time it was over, the Angels had killed one spectator, injured others, and sparked a full-scale riot. Altamont marked the beginning of the Diaspora of the counterculture. Some became Crazies, believing in revolution and violence just for the hell of it; others mixed love and militancy to raise their voice so that society could hear and see what they were doing to the world; and others blindly charged into the tunnel of the "Me Generation." The music industry, once a vital part of cultural history, a time when most groups—good, bad, and struggling—could get an agent or be heard by a music publisher, was dying into mediocrity like the print media, both of which were dictated by a new bottom-line mentality, and executives who had little understanding of the creative process.

I continued doing stories about the counterculture, working evenings and weekends with splinters of the Movement, disguising my beliefs from my editors on general circulation establishment papers, and developing bonds with a re-emerging alternative press. Richard Nixon was elected president in 1968 by a fearful public that believed he could restore law and order to a nation they were sure was being overtaken by the marauding hippie culture. Shortly after his inauguration, Nixon unleashed COINTELPRO, the government's oafish way to suppress dissent, and claim it was protecting America from whatever spooks were trying to destroy us and, thus, avoid the glare of truth by making the people believe they were better off losing their freedoms in exchange for their security. Like my stories of poverty and injustice, none of what I wrote about the government's invasion of Constitutional rights was published by the establishment press.

Mostly, I wrote routine stories from the police, courts, and government beats, ocasionally mixed with a few investigative stories of local corruption and scandal. I was on a fast track, moving from newspaper to newspaper, each one larger than the previous one, staying just long enough to become discouraged and find another venue for my voice, a young man trying to mix idealism with journalism. There were Pulitzers to win, editorships to earn, and soon no time for counter-anything.

"David? . . . David! Rain saturating your brain cells?"

"Just thinking."

"Do you know we're near the heart of the anthracite coal region?" I didn't, but then again I knew more about the sweat shops of Massachusetts and New York City than the coal fields of rural Pennsylvania. Not far from here, I learned, was the site of the Avondale Massacre, which showed the brutality of the mining bosses—and where the fiery compassion of Mother Jones still lives. "In the mines," said Apryl, "five- and six-year-old boys worked as trapper boys, sitting in dark passages, ready to open and shut the mine's trap doors to regulate the air. Boys of 10 and 12 dragged out the tubs of coal. They'd go to work at 6, 7 a.m., work all day in the cold and dark for a buck or two a week because their families needed the money. They never got a formal education and they and their families were relegated to lives of working for the robber barons." I looked at her; tears were pushing against her eyes, trying to escape. "I have to build the school. It's important, David. When we understand the world, we won't ever have to hurt anyone."

"Do you have a place for this school?" I asked, wondering why she was telling me all this, and with so much passion. Journalists are snoops, but much of the time we merely collect facts, never learning truth. The Yuppie crowd of the "Me Generation" would have said, "Thank you for sharing."

Her blue eyes reflected her wonderment with life and of her own special kingdom. "I have the land. It's a beautiful tract along the Susquehanna, just north of here. Everywhere you look you can see hills fencing out the industrial revolution. There's so much here, so much that could be done. Instead of reading about plants and animals, we'll see them and talk with them and learn about life! It has all kinds of grasses and flowers and plants. And there are trees! Lots of trees! Maple and oak and chestnut and some of them have been there forever and there are trees that have just been born; and there are all kinds of animals. Frogs and chipmunks; even insects; yes, millions of them, some so small that you can't even see them, but you know they're there, and they know you're there, too; there's black bear and deer; lots of them; and they're safe from the hunters because I don't allow any hunters on my property! Dogs! We'll have dogs. All kinds of dogs. You can't have a life unless you have dogs as your companions. It can even be a refuge for abandoned dogs. Yes, that would be nice. A place where thrown-away dogs can have love. And give love." She paused just for a moment to briefly pet her dog lying quietly at her feet, and then bubbled forth. "A creek! It's so clear that you can see stones on the bottom and the ferns look like they grow in the water and you can see the fish swimming among them and in the river and there's even a falls maybe a mile away that's 30, maybe 40 feet high and—"

"It sounds like a wonderful place," I said, cutting her off at the exact moment she again came up for air."

"It is! Oh, David, it is! And a mill! There's an old stone mill on the land. It's been abandoned for years, but it can be fixed up, and it can be the school. And it can be where creative people come to sell their belts and pottery and paintings." As wonderful as it sounded, Apryl still had a reality to face. I learned she was three months behind on payments, with not much in her trust fund for the building of the school, but her enthusiasm and energy were infectious.

"I have friends who might want to invest. Maybe—"

"Don't dangle a carrot!" she said brutally. "Don't patronize me, and don't tell me you can do anything for me! In fact, don't even *do* anything."

"Sorry I offended you," I stammered, not knowing why I should apologize for her rudeness. "I was just suggesting—"

"Don't even *suggest*! You have no business even suggesting!" At that moment, not one person in this shelter, or any of the dozen others nearby, would have suggested anything.

"Look, ma'am—"

"The name is Apryl, David. Remember?! Apryl. Apryl Greene. It's not 'ma'am!'"

"Look, Apryl Greene, I'm standing here in a shelter that doesn't work very well, on a miserable day listening to every kind of music known to mankind and one band that probably isn't, in a park guarded by some God-damned put-the-star-on-my-shoulder-and-I'll-lead-you-anywhere general, hundreds of miles from my home on a Sunday not selling books to people who don't buy books but who criticize my magazine, and then you show up and shoot me and now you're freaking out on me, and I haven't done a dang thing other than try to make conversation with you!" A breath. More than anything *I* needed a breath. The fire left her eyes as quickly as it had come.

"In your own misguided way you were trying to do something nice." I said nothing, just looked at her—and those bright vibrant eyes that hid three, maybe four, decades of life. "My whole life, people dangled carrots in front of me," she said, tears again about to leave her eyes. "Bosses. Schools. Lovers. People I didn't even know. And all of them knew how cheap carrots were, and they all knew I wanted that carrot." She choked back tears, "And they all used it to exploit me, and . . . and—O.K.! So I yelled at you! Big deal! I'm sorry! O.K.? . . . Friends again?"

"Yeah. Sure."

"David, please don't hate me."

"I don't."

"I'm doing it for the children." The world doesn't need one more altruistic spirit floating in the haze of war and corruption. I felt guilty thinking it. But I meant it. "The children are the most important people we have. They're the ones who will make war or peace. They'll be the ones who make sure our environment will survive."

"That's true." O.K., so I didn't have anything more brilliant to say. She did.

"Did you ever go to a museum?" she asked, didn't give me time to answer her question, and then continued. "Go to a museum, but don't look at the art or the sculpture or the stuffed animals. Look at the children. Wait for a second grade class. Makes no difference who they are or what their backgrounds are. Every one will be in awe of what's in that building. It's new. It's different. They'll listen to their teacher. They'll ask questions. A few years later, they will have lost that sense of discovery. That sense of wonderment." She paused for a brief moment, long enough to grab a breath, not long enough for me to say anything. "People are always hurting the children. It doesn't make any difference if it's prescriptive teachers with iron lace mentalities or exploitative bosses." She paused again. I said nothing. "The wars are fought by the children. They're the ones sent to die for whatever glory there is in dying." She said it not with the fire in her soul, but with the sigh of the reality of history. "Camus said that all children suffer. He also said we can lessen the number of suffering children, but if we can't do that, who can?"

"I guess that's right," I said, filling space, while more people had moved into other parts of the shelter, or even other shelters, giving us a wide buffer.

"David, we're all children of this life. That's the most important thing. Please remember it. We're all God's children. And we are all very fragile." Her eyes lit up again. I wondered how one person could have so many mood shifts in so short a time. I wondered what her history was. Hell, I wondered what mind-altering drugs she was taking. "Well, I'm off," she said brightly. "I think I can get some groovy close-ups of the tulips. I'll be back." And with that, she hugged me, flashed a peace sign, and she and her dog danced away into what was left of the rainstorm.

About 20 minutes after the fury had begun, the rain moved on, releasing several hundred from their sheltered prisons. The ground looked like a swamp, but everyone was back, taking plastic covers off tables, merchandise from boxes. Once again, it was time to sell dishes and phonograph records, metal jewelry, sand candles—and books. Even the sea of emptiness between the Historical Society tables and the rest of the swamp would soon be filled.

An elderly gentleman floated up to the table, said little, but left with an autographed book. An elderly lady, maybe 70, maybe 80, talked to me about how she loved books, used to read two or three a week when she was younger, but couldn't see well enough any more. "My children used to read me the newspaper," she said, "but I guess that was too much of a bother. They just tell me things now."

Sale of the chances picked up, at least a dozen more people took home Historical Society souvenir spoons, and the sky was now sporting gray not black clouds.

"You've just got to meet someone. He's also creative, and he makes beautiful animals from wood. Really nice things. All kinds of animals. Like bear and deer, and sometimes even people." From out of nowhere there was Apryl. Her black hair was drenched, hanging limp against a tanned face that looked even thinner; her lilac-and-white sneaks were tied together and hung over her shoulders. "Would you like to meet him? I know he'd like to meet you. I told him all about you. A writer and a woodcarver! There's got to be a story there!" If she didn't quit bouncing around on a soggy field of grass, I would become seasick.

Why did she want me to meet him? What did he want out of this? What the heck, there wasn't much else happening in the two hours before Rolling Thunder would play the last of its nasal-twanging country notes, or whatever it was that it played, thus ending my adventure in a park. I didn't have to wait long. In moments, Apryl was back with the woodcarver. Introduced him as Ronnie Soifer.

Judging from Ronnie Soifer's expression, he was just as doubtful, just as confused, as I. And, yet, here we were. Two people making small talk, brought together by a bouncy, happy-go-lucky hippie who likes books and carved wooden animals, and who thought we should meet each other.

"Do you do this full time?" I asked.

"No. Work in construction during the day. Stone mason."

"Ever want to chuck masonry and be a carver full time?"

"Think about it all the time. Can't make a living from it. Got a wife and three kids. Just do this for a hobby. Besides, masonry is what I'm trained for." Apryl was still there, absorbing every word, delighted that she had brought two people together. Or, maybe, she had some other idea. I didn't know.

By the time the woodcarver and I finished small talk, Apryl was gone again. Maybe she was out in the mud trying to unite a watercolor painter with a musician, or an artist and auto salesman. Maybe she found some children to play hide-and-seek or Frisbee with. Maybe she even found some union leaders or social activists and was shooting them. . . . Who knows? What I knew is that I would probably see her again.

2/

'So Tired I Can Not Read to Her':
Farm Workers on
March to State Capitol

by David M. Ascher
Special to The Light

Well, I was born one morning
When the sun did shine.
I picked up my clippers
And walked to the vine.
I loaded sixteen crates
Of the winemaker's grapes
And all I got
Was pains and aches.

*[Music copyright by Merle Travis. Lyrics by Rachel Greenberg and the
California Student Social Welfare Association, 1966, public domain]*

DELANO, Calif., March 17, 1966—With posters proclaiming *Huelga!* (Strike!) and *Viva La Causa*, about 150 farm workers and supporters left Delano early this morning on the first part of a 25-day 340-mile march that will end Easter Sunday at the state capitol in Sacramento. More than 2,000 migrant families are expected to participate in the march, which unites the largely Latino National Farm Workers Association (NFWA) and the primarily Filipino Agricultural Workers Organizing Committee (AWOC). Several hundred students, civil rights workers, members of the clergy and others are expected to walk part of the way in support of the movement. Sen. Robert F. Kennedy (D-N.Y.) had come to Delano to support the workers.

Staff members and a young photographer from *El Macriado*, the union newspaper, and a handful of student, alternative, and establishment news media are recording the protest as it moves single-column behind American and Mexican flags, a large banner of a thunderbird against a red background, the symbol of the NFWA, and numerous picket signs raised high against a clear sky. Plans call for the marchers to leave Highway 65 and continue along back roads.

Led by Cesar Chavez, the 38-year-old charismatic NFWA executive director, the marchers hope to convince the state to enact legislation to aid the estimated 500,000 persons, most of them migrant laborers, who work in California's $6 billion industry.

Delano police blocked the road and told Chavez that because he didn't have a parade permit the protest was illegal. The intervention of several members of the clergy and the local business community allowed the protest to continue after about an hour.

The marchers are scheduled to reach Ducor tonight and Porterville the next night, a total of about 35 miles. They are carrying no food and have no plans for shelter. Chavez says that farm workers will feed and house the marchers along the way.

Each evening, a four-page "Plan of Delano" will be read in Spanish. Part of that plan declares, "This is the beginning of a social movement in fact and not in pronouncements . . . Because we have suffered, and are not afraid to suffer, in order to survive, we are ready to give up everything, even our lives, in our fight for social justice. We shall do it without violence because that is our destiny. [We suffer] for the purpose of ending poverty, the misery and the injustice with the hope that our children will not be exploited as we have been "

Arturo Herrera, 41, Nogales, Ariz., says that most migrant families live in shacks provided by the growers, "but we pay them rent." Among the problems he cites are unreasonably high rental costs, poor ventilation and heat, toilets and sinks that don't work, and floors that are often rotted.

Margarita Montoya, 27, Chino, who has worked the fields for 15 years, says, "The growers, they promise tutors for our children. We see no tutors. They go to public school month here, month there. We teach them ourselves."

Juan Fernandez, no address, says the reason the children, some as young as 9 or 10, work the fields is because families cannot live on what the parents earn. "You try to feed wife and three children on $50 a week," he challenges.

Herrera, Montoya, and Fernandez are bilingual. Many have learned English, but most haven't, except for a few words and phrases; they need only to provide sweat for growers who don't speak Spanish.

At each campsite, marchers will participate in the *Teatro Campesino*, a multi-event "people's theatre" that includes short satiric sketches, many written by Luis Valdez, formerly of the San Francisco Mime Company. The protest has the support of the California Migrant Ministry, a largely Protestant organization; the Catholic archdiocese of San Francisco; and several Jewish organizations.

> Well, some people say a grape
> Is a mighty small thing.
> But to us in the valley
> The grape is king.
> We work it in the morning
> And we work it at night
> But if the laws don't change,
> You'll harvest alone.

In 1959, the AFL–CIO had created the AWOC. A strike by lettuce pickers had failed in early 1961, partially because the Mexican–American laborers did not trust the Anglo leadership, and suspected that the union was organized primarily, as one NFWA official said, "to get dues from our brothers to support the industrialized unions that have traditionally barred ethnic minorities from membership." It was during this strike that a serious division was created, separating the Mexican–American and temporary Mexican workers from the Anglo and Filipino workers. That division is beginning to dissolve because of the efforts of Bill Kircher of the AFL–CIO and Chavez.

In 1962, Chavez formed the NFWA after serving 12 years with Saul Alinsky's Community Service Organization (CSO), which had provided significant assistance to the migrant farm workers. Last Sept. 8, the AWOC began a strike of the grape industry in the San Joaquin Valley, considered to be the richest farmland in America. A week later, the NFWA, with more than 1,000 families, joined the strike.

The growers retaliated by importing workers from Texas, Arizona, and Mexico. The Mexican workers—almost 30,000 of them—came across the border because of special regulations enacted by the U.S. Department of Labor in response to the strike. More than 125 NFWA pickets were arrested for allegedly harassing the non-union workers, most of whom were never told they were replacing striking workers. There were also several instances of growers spraying insecticide on the pickets. No arrests were reported.

Chavez, like the Rev. Martin Luther King Jr., a disciple of Gandhi's non-violent protest tactics, responded by organizing information centers and church services for all workers, union and non-union. During the next few months, thousands of students and human rights activists responded to Chavez's challenge to help their "fellow man." The volunteers picketed stores selling grapes and table wines. Secondary boycotts, however, are illegal under California law.

Principal targets of a potential nationwide protest are the DiGiorgio Fruit Corp. and Schenley Industries. DiGiorgio, the largest grower in the Valley, owns four vineyards totaling 20,000 acres, and employs almost 1,500 workers during peak harvest season. Schenley, the second largest grower, employs about 500 workers during peak harvest season.

> When you see us marching,
> Better step aside.
> A lot of growers didn't
> And a lot of grapes dried.
> A decent living wage,
> A home of our own
> Better working conditions
> Or you're on your own.

The growers have maintained that the strike is "an unimportant wildcat walkout" that is not affecting production. They point out that during the past season fewer than 500 of the 30,000 acres were left unharvested. However, inexperienced labor caused severe damage to many of the grapes that have been harvested, and the additional cost of importing workers has cut into the growers' profit margins. A representative of the NFWA says he hopes the growers will "soon recognize the democratic principles of worker representation, and allow the formation of a union," but says he has "no hope of that happening until such a time as agribusiness sees its profits dropping significantly." Chavez has repeatedly said that the protest march, based upon the successful civil rights march in Selma last year, is to make people more aware of the plight of migrant workers, and to force the growers "to recognize their responsibility" to those workers.

"My family, many family, we came to Lindsay one day we were told to be there," recalls Henry Zavalla, 52, no listed address. "We were ready to work. Owner he say no work. Come back in week, he say. We have no work, we tell him. We have no place to stay. He say come back in week. No work now." Like hundreds of other migrant workers, he often slept on the ground, protected only by a bedroll. "Just like hippies," he says, breaking a smile.

The workers currently receive $1.20 an hour, plus 10 cents a box as incentive pay. The NFWA wants the growers to pay $1.40 an hour, and 25 cents incentive pay. Minimum wage in the United States is $1.25 an hour. The NFWA is hoping the state will begin to enforce regulations requiring maintenance by the growers of adequate sanitary conditions for workers in the field, and to respond to such things as laws regarding work breaks.

"I work 10, 12 hour a day," says Celeste Garcia-Mata, 23, Ontario, "as long as there is light. I want to take break. Foreman he say 'No, Celeste. Not now. Later.' . . . So tired when I leave field. Cannot read to my child." She pauses a moment, and then sadly says she is even too tired to read the newspaper or watch TV news. For Garcia-Mata and the other workers, the billions of dollars spent on the space race and the war in Vietnam, and the billions that are not being spent to help the poor and the underclass, are irrelevant. No one is going to make the owners pay better wages or treat people any better. And so, she lives hour to hour, day to day, hoping to earn enough to send some home to her parents, perhaps to save a few dollars so she might buy a nice pair of shoes for her daughter.

For decades, the growers have brought in Mexican nationals to help work the fields, claiming that no Anglos wish to "bend over." The bracero program, which allows Mexican nationals to work the agricultural fields of the Southwest and California, has spurred charges of racism. The low wages have eliminated many Anglos from jobs, while encouraging Mexicans, who often have a lower standard of living than Americans, to cross the border to work a few months in deplorable conditions, and then to return to their families. More than one grower has said that it's a symbiotic relationship; the owners get cheap labor, and the workers return to their families and live like kings the rest of the year, at least so the owners say.

For Cesar Chavez and his followers, racism isn't the main issue. "It's the rights of the workers," Chavez has repeatedly said, forcefullly noting, "It is their right to organize. And it is our responsibility to make sure that the state does not continue to allow these deplorable working conditions to exist."

Public opinion and the state legislature will now have to decide if it wishes to allow these conditions to continue, or if it wishes to make sure all workers, no matter who, are entitled to basic human rights, including decent wages and adequate housing.

3/

The Whatever Room

About a half-mile off Route 3A, on Beach Avenue paralleling Quincy Bay, 12 or so miles south of Boston, Sam and Ruth Weissmann bought their first and only house, a two-story, four-bedroom colonial that was doing its best to succumb to the saltwater air. To others, it may have seemed to be a foolish, perhaps eccentric, purchase since Sam was an unemployed journalist, Ruth was a struggling artist, and neither had the slightest idea what it took to fix up a house that had been inhabited but neglected since the Korean War.

For their entire lives, Sam and Ruth had lived in apartments, whether as children, singles, or adults. It made no difference if it was brownstones, row houses, walk-ups, or garden apartments; efficiencies, one-bedrooms, or their parents' two-bedrooms; roach-infested or cleaned and freshly painted. They were all apartments, owned by someone else who could raise the rent or throw you out just about anytime for just about any reason.

Sam and Ruth could have bought a house when he was first hired at the *Herald Tribune*, his third newspaper. A decade after World War II ended, housing developments were popping up like weeds in a garden, and there was no excuse for anyone not to be able to afford a house. But what Sam and Ruth did was move into another apartment, this one in the Bronx, not far from where Sam had grown up. When Ruth had her first major gallery showing, a 10-day hanging at the Whitney Museum, they could have tried to buy a house, but they didn't since they were comfortable where they were. And that's where they stayed, through the birth of their only child in 1960; through the 114 day strike in 1962 and 1963 when Sam's income dropped from almost $325 a week, well beyond the Newspaper Guild's top minimum, to the strike-fund payments of $50 a week, supplemented now and then by the sale of one of Ruth's paintings.

By now, Sam was a national correspondent with a limited expense account but almost unlimited freedom to pick his subjects. He was riding high, and turning down job offers. And, he could use his full byline—Samuel A. Weissmann—not S. A. Weissmann, as might have been required by the *New York Times*, a Jewish-owned liberal-leaning newspaper that was trying to reduce its identity by requiring its Jewish reporters to use initials, not that anyone was fooled into thinking that Abraham M. Rosenthal, now known as A.M. Rosenthal, was an evangelical Christian or a Buddhist monk. No, the *Herald Tribune*, politically conservative, socially liberal, and WASP-owned, didn't have to worry about public reaction to too many "Jewish-sounding" names. And, if some of the *Herald Tribune* staff may have been at odds with some of the editorial policies, at least they knew that their newspaper would lead the others in pointing out and analyzing social problems that could be unraveling the country.

The *Herald Tribune* was a twentieth century merger of the *Herald* and the *Tribune*, two populist newspapers founded in the early 1840s. The *Herald*, under James Gordon Bennett, had established the framework for the present-day newspaper; the *Tribune*, under crusading editor Horace Greeley, gave journalism its soul and became the most influential antebellum newspaper in America. By the early 1960s, the *Herald Tribune* was dying, strangled by management greed, editorial inflexibility, and staff lethargy that left the newspaper, at one time one of the most aggressive and best-written newspapers in American journalism, waddling in the wake of the other New York City dailies. The statue of Minerva, Greek goddess of wisdom, which adorned the old Herald Building at 34th Street before it was torn down, was not a part of the memory to this corporation.

While others were jumping off, Sam stayed, believing that great reporters, with renewed vigor, no matter what obstacles management put in their way, could keep a great newspaper alive, giving it back its dominance. Unfortunately, the loyalty he had for the *Herald Tribune* was not the same kind of loyalty that publishers have for their employees. The publishers had avariciously tried to merge three newspapers, descendants of six once-great newspapers, combined all operations and cut the staff by almost half, forcing another strike by the Guild and other unions. The publishers' response to that bit of treason was to maliciously kill the *Herald Tribune* after innumerable promises that it would continue to be the morning newspaper.

Because Sam had seniority, the new corporation, a monolithic monstrosity called World Journal Tribune, Inc., the *WJT*, which New Yorkers derisively called the "Widget," would have had to keep him employed. But such was not to be; the company cared too much about profits and had thrown down a new contract that robbed the workers of what little power they had, and Sam cared too much about his integrity and his profession to keep working for the new corporation. April 24, 1966, the last day of the *Herald Tribune*, was also Sam's last day as a full-time newspaper reporter. Moments after walking out the front door for the last time, he turned, looked up at the corporate offices on West 41st Street, shouted just one word, "*Genuk!*" and walked away from newspaper journalism. He had enough of the corporate lies. Enough of deception. Enough of incompetence. And, most of all, enough of a large corporation treating reporters, the soul of a newspaper he believed, as if they were nothing more than a necessary annoyance and a financial drain upon the right to make whatever profits the corporation could squeeze from its income. Samuel A. Weissmann, one of the best reporters on a daily newspaper, simply had enough. He took his 22 weeks severance pay, two for every year he was on the *Herald Tribune*, a benefit negotiated by the Newspaper Guild, and left. With a bitterness that left him closed to alternatives, and refusing to go into public relations, which he knew was the Dark Side, Sam and Ruth packed everything into a rental truck and moved to Arlington, Massachusetts, to the two-bedroom apartment of her parents. There, they lived only three months until finding the "just-needs-a-little-work" dream house, his *kholem*, complete with a six percent 20-year mortgage of $124.25 a month, co-signed by Ruth's parents.

Sam and Ruth had never worried about money, for they always assumed that God would provide, and if He didn't provide, they reasoned, it wasn't worth having. And *this*, the four-bedroom Colonial dream house, with just the slightest bit of work, maybe some painting and fixing up here and there, at least that's what the Realtor said in so many words, seemed like something a mischievous God thought they should have. But to friends, relatives, and journalists of all kinds, it was just about the dumbest thing Sam and Ruth could have done, especially since four bedrooms were probably two bedrooms more than necessary—and why would only two people need two and a-half baths? To the skeptics, Sam easily explained the purchase as buying nineteenth century workmanship and twentieth century sweat.

Because they always lived in apartments, Sam and Ruth never needed to know much about maintenance. That's why they only owned a hammer, two pairs of pliers, and three screwdrivers between them. And now, in their own house, shrouded by almost every house repair and restoration book they could buy or borrow, they were hopelessly lost. Not just Boy Scout lost, but Bermuda Triangle lost. That's where it would have stayed had not some amused employees of Renn Construction taken pity upon them. In exchange for unlimited free cold beer, and Ruth's kugel and knishes, the workers snuck tools, boards, and miscellaneous we-don't-know-where-it-went fixtures, as well as unlimited free advice, and even some "bootleg" assistance while they were supposed to be building six new Capes a quarter-mile away.

Sam and Ruth worked awhile, cursed, reworked, stopped, waited for more income—he from freelance articles, she from her paintings—worked awhile longer, stopped again, cursed, and redid, sold more articles and paintings, and continued, becoming rather good at restoration. Soon, they could effortlessly resist every aluminum siding salesman, even the one promising eternal life for the house and all its inhabitants—*hallelujah*!

During the next two decades, one of the extra bedrooms, the ones that everyone thought were two rooms too many, became a permanent guest room for the *mishpacha*, the extended family. Not just relatives who might come by for a short visit, but for friends. And friends of friends. And people they barely knew who needed shelter for a few hours, for a few days. Another room, all 203 square feet of it, became the permanent "Whatever Room," dedicated to whatever project Sam or Ruth were working on. At various times, it was a sewing room, a weights room, or a nautical room. For awhile, a plush stuffed seal won at the Brockton Fair sat contently in the Whatever Room, transfigured into Ruth's campaign headquarters for the New England region of Save the Seals. At other times, the Whatever Room overflowed with civil rights and anti-war literature, flyers, pamphlets, notes, memos, and letters, as Sam and Ruth led crusade after crusade to integrate Boston's schools, while also opening their house for meetings and as a staging area for several protests by Another Mother for Peace. Yet another file cabinet was squeezed into the room when Ruth became the president of the state's NOW chapter.

For six months, it had been a combination art studio and wine cellar, created when Ruth needed more space than her downstairs studio provided, and Sam came home with the remainder of two cases of wine, the grand prize in a press club raffle. Of the 24 bottles, Sam had stood before his fellow journalists, and proclaimed he would not now, not ever, *schlep* home products from non-unionized fields. To a mixture of delight, horror, and hoots by the reporters who hadn't won anything, Sam smashed all but the five bottles from unionized wineries, giving each a eulogy suitable for a scab. When he got home he knew there was only one place in the house to put the remaining bottles of non-California wine. The fact that the wine room would be on the second floor, not in the basement, had only briefly crossed his mind, but he reasoned that only the truly rich or the truly snobbish would put wine in a wine cellar. Besides, there wasn't room in the basement. That's where he kept the 1935 O-gauge American Flyer train set, his woodworking tools, some unused for more than five years, and myriad boxes. Boxes of junk and boxes of books, boxes of correspondence and boxes of kitchenware containers, yellow and brown newspaper and magazine clips, and income tax files. Boxes stacked upon boxes. Boxes in boxes. Even boxes of Christmas boxes, for Sam and Ruth always make sure to buy, wrap, and deliver Christmas gifts not only to their friends, but also to the Salvation Army, Boston City Hospital, Rosie's Place for Abused Children, and dozens of other charities; it was always done quietly, always done anonymously.

Now, had someone thought the wine bottles could have been stored on the first floor, stacked somewhere inconspicuously, Sam would have pointed out that what was left of his grand prize would have detracted from his 1934 Avalon pinball machine; certainly, wine shouldn't share a writer's den or an artist's studio, all of which were also on the first floor of the house almost everyone said was too big. No, there really was only one place to put what was left of the grand prize.

For now, the wine was sharing space with Ruth's overflow art supplies in the Whatever Room. It was the same room that in May 1967—the same month the *World Journal Tribune* finally killed itself and the U.S. began incessant bombing of North Vietnam—had become the first office for a grossly undercapitalized magazine Sam named *Century*.

4/

Decisions
by David Ascher

You figure this is something you'd hear about from Mississippi or Alabama or Georgia. From those Southern bigots. The ones whose grandpappies and great grandpappies fought for the Confederacy. For cotton and states' rights and slavery. The kind who drank mint juleps and barred their Negro neighbors from drinking from the town's water fountains. The kind who now drive pickup trucks with shotguns attached to racks on their rear windows. People who cut up white bed sheets and burn crosses—and homes and churches. But, those are just images. And images aren't always reality.

This isn't the South, and in a few years Southerners are going to come further than their Yankee cousins in civil rights. They will soon realize there is nothing they can do but to live with the decisions being made in Lyndon Johnson's "Great Society," to improve the lives of all people, no matter their color, religion, or beliefs.

No, this story is not about sit-ins and voter registration drives, about marches, riots, or forced integration. This story takes place in the North. The civil rights North. Where everyone says they respect everyone else and they all express outrage at the violence in the South. It takes place in a nice community in Pennsylvania, home of the Declaration of Independence. The Keystone State where the founding fathers declared that all men were created equal. But it could have happened any time in any Northern community.

The cast of characters includes an unmarried 20-year-old

Caucasian, Rachel; her three-month-old daughter, Rebecca; a professor of economics whose investments include apartment houses; and a lot of people who grew up in town, share the same basic values, and have little respect for Negroes. And that's where this story begins. Rebecca's father is a Negro.

For almost a year, Rachel had been moving around the country, from California to Missouri, then to Georgia, and now back to Pennsylvania where there was family. When the father of your child is at the bottom of the Army's pay schedule, it isn't easy just to stay put and set up house, especially if you wish to be with him. First she would find housing, then a job, and then take one or two classes a semester. A few years later, working and studying nights and summers, and adding up the credits she earned from her first year at Berkeley, Rachel figured she'd have a degree; she didn't know in what—maybe music, maybe photography. But we're getting ahead of our story. Right now, Rachel needs housing.

So, she looked at the classified ads of the local newspaper, found several listings, learned that most were already taken— after all, housing goes quickly in a college town. Finally, she found one that was still vacant, and telephoned the manager.

"You're not one of them beatniks are you?" she demanded.

"No, ma'am," Rachel politely answered, amused at the thought. She had been in Berkeley when Mario Savio led a student power demonstration to demand the constitutional rights of free speech, only to have police flip lighted cigarettes at him, while they arrested dozens of others for peacefully handing out flyers. And she had been one of a thousand or so persons who formed the chorus when Joan Baez sang "Blowin' in the Wind" at the university's Sproul Hall. She may have been a liberal, she may have believed in the civil rights movement and opposed the war in Vietnam, but she wasn't a beatnik, a hippie, or a firebrand. She was just a 20-year-old mother with a small bank account who wanted to get a job and a college education.

"Well, if you are one of them kind, we won't rent to you. They don't do nothin' but drink and smoke those drug cigarettes. Trouble! That's what they are! Nothing but trouble!" The manager paused a moment, changed her tone, and recited a litany of the apartment's features. "Furnished. One bedroom. Living room and kitchen. Bath. Drapes. Trash is collected every Thursday. Rent's due on the 15th of the month. Every month.

Not the 16th or 17th. No loud noises. No loud parties. No free love or drinking. You follow the rules and you'll like it here."

Leaving her daughter with a friend, Rachel went to the apartments. The manager, a middle-aged woman who had grown up in town, showed Rachel a small, somewhat dirty, overpriced apartment—after all, it was in a college town. But it had one major feature—it was available. So she agreed to meet the owner, the associate professor of economics who personally talked with every finalist for an apartment. It would be nice to live in an apartment owned by a professor, Rachel thought; at least he'd understand the problems of students working their way to earn a degree. Maybe he could even help her find a job; she heard there were a lot of jobs available on campus and in town. Besides, it would be comforting to know that the professor would probably make sure that the apartments were always cared for, even if they were small, dirty, and overpriced. Well, who are we to tell her how to think?

After a ten minute discussion, Rachel signed a form, agreed to follow the rules, and gave the professor a check for the first month's rent, the last month's rent, and a cleaning deposit, most of it willingly provided by her father. She now had $23.65 left in her checking account and a small monthly check from Rebecca's father who sent everything he could from his pay as an Army PFC.

Early the next morning, Rachel, Rebecca, and their friend, Kashonna, who had given them temporary lodging, always had a meal available, and time to baby-sit, packed everything into Rachel's '55 Chevy Bel Air and went to the apartment. In just a few moments, the manager came by, just friendly-like, just to say "Howdy!" and welcome Rachel into the neighborhood. It was about that time that Kashonna brought Rebecca into the living room. Now, Kashonna is a Negro, and the apartment manager hadn't seen many Negroes in the neighborhood for quite awhile. And, certainly, none of them were ever residents.

"She your friend?" Kashonna knew something wasn't right, and the manager knew something wasn't right, and Rachel just thought that here were three nice people just getting acquainted. Because Rebecca was in Kashonna's arms, it was just natural to assume it was Kashonna's daughter. Until Rachel finished the introductions, that is. And that's when the manager dropped anchor and just about sank into the floor. Sputtering a "Nice to have metcha," she left.

"Think she's alright?" Rachel asked Kashonna, concerned that maybe the manager didn't feel so well.

"Ain't worth no difference," said her friend. "Come on, girl, let's get this barn cleaned. "Two mornings later, before Rachel went to work, before she left Rebecca with Kashonna for the day, the businessman–professor called and said, in a rather haughty voice, that he "got calls." He never said how many. What he did say was that he was not pleased. He wanted to meet Rachel— again. Not at the apartment. Not at his house. Not even at his office on campus. No, he wanted to meet her that evening at the Lantern, an out-of-the-way tavern populated by Townies.

At the Lantern, the businessman–professor began his lecture by pointing out that most of his tenants didn't even cause him one call, and now in a little more than one day, she had caused him several calls. He said he had been told that she was on drugs, that she was a loose woman who probably doesn't even know who the father of the child is.

This isn't real; this can't be happening to me, Rachel thought. *It's just a surreal dream*, she figured; *maybe I'm on "Candid Camera,"* she hoped, knowing better.

The lecture continued, the businessman–professor becoming more patronizing. "You can't continue with this lifestyle. I see nothing but a bad life for you if you keep this up." The lecture became sharper. "You seem bright. Why'd you have to go off and have that kind of kid? Pretty girl like you could have had a White father for your child." It was then she became frightened. Naive she may be; stupid she isn't.

The businessman–professor then evaded the law—the one known as the Fair Housing Act. "I have a business to run," he declared. "I can't force you to move out,"—his voice became colder— "but it can be awfully difficult for you, and I don't need problems."

Rachel wanted to lecture this professor, to make sure he understood that Alan Shepard rode Freedom 7 into space, that Gus Grissom rode Liberty Bell 7, that John Glenn rode Friendship 7, and that none of their capsules were named Hate 7. But, it really didn't matter. Americans were seeing the world from space, not from the hatreds bubbling within its core. And so when she said nothing, the businessman–professor, apparently thinking she didn't understand, repeated himself. "I don't want problems. You understand." She did. She wished she didn't, but she did. The lessons that Martin Luther King Jr. and the civil rights movement were teaching and the hope for social justice that Bobby Kennedy and Cesar Chavez stood for apparently circumvented this northern city. "I have other apartments closer to the college," the businessman–professor said, giving Rachel just the brightest glimmer of hope before he again shoved an eclipse onto her spirit. "But they're already filled. For the entire year. They go quickly. There's no room. Maybe next summer, but not now." He paused a moment. "Besides, you don't want to live in places where people don't like you, do you?"

She wanted to yell and scream. She wanted to bring in the courts and the police and the National Guard if she had to. But what she did was to agree with him. She had a child to raise, a job to find, and a degree to pursue. And all he and the manager—and God knows how many more—had were their prejudices. So, she agreed that it would be better if she looked somewhere else for housing. Intolerance knows no bounds, and fear has no limits.

The businessman–professor gave her back her first month's rent, the last month's rent, and the security deposit—minus $20, which he kept, as he put it, "for my inconvenience." The next day, the apartment was once again empty.

On this unusually cold August morning, you could see a relieved businessman–professor, a happy apartment manager and her friends—whoever they were—and a mother and child who would stay a few months and then return to California to face the rest of the '60s with hope not frustration, with love not bitterness.

5/

Transitions

Because we're a monthly, we don't do "deadline reporting." The dailies and electronic media can jump onto a breaking story better and more efficiently than we can. However, because of a longer lead time, space availability for long-form journalism, the use of copyeditors whose primary job isn't to push through as many stories with quickly-written heads in as short a time as possible, and the use of fact checkers and proofreaders, all of which are becoming obsolete on newspapers, magazines can present in-depth perspectives that most newspapers can't. Although we publish numerous features and a liberal dose of satire, it's our in-your-face investigative journalism for which we're known. Unlike most editors, Sam gives his staff and correspondents the time and resources to dig into the social issues that the establishment press either can't or won't report.

In one of his first issues, Sam went in-depth to report the January 1968 march of the Jeanette Rankin Brigade, 5,000 women from several peace groups who were trying to convince Congress to end the Vietnam War. Most media didn't cover the march, and the few that did had sent either inexperienced or secondary reporters whose idea of social issues coverage was to report what clothes covered the women, and how younger women were in the minority in a minority protest. Although not a pacifist, for more than two decades Sam makes sure his readers know *Century* opposes war, but that at times war is inevitable. The American presence in the War in Vietnam was not. *Century* was a young publication when Sam first wrote against the war in Vietnam. For his reporting and commentary, a large part of

America not only called him unpatriotic, but also branded him a traitor. Those attacks continue to this day.

Under Sam's direction, we put our editorial muscle into stories about discrimination of all kinds. For more than a decade, Whitworth Reed was our primary editor/writer for stories that looked at all forms of bigotry, but he was most energized when he dug out sexism, homophobia, and anti-Semitism in government agencies. Like most of our staff, Whitworth left after a few years. Some go to other media, some enter other professions. Whitworth took a huge drop in salary and an increase in the discomfort level to become a Peace Corps volunteer. He was replaced by Megan Prescott, a Renaissance editor who can work with every kind of writer and story. Megan is an animal rights activist who, in keeping with Sam's belief that editors must be writers, drops her red pen three or four times a year to write features about animals, and to conduct investigations into animal cruelty, embedding in stories her disgust with government and the courts that treat animals as chattel. Whitworth's stories helped our readers increase their outrage to the system; Megan's stories bring tears.

After a few dribblings in the daily press, *Century* broke the junk bond scandal wide open, and in doing so forced Congress not only to look at the shady future of savings and loans, but at their own ethics. We had sent Brandi Domenico into Central America for two months, and when she got back, we not only had a scoop of DEA and CIA complicity in dictator Manuel Noriega's looting of Panama, but also a major exposé that had forced the CIA to admit that it had mined Nicaragua's harbors. Danielle Shea gave us a 3,000 word gut-twisting story about the life and family of one of the Marines who died when terrorists bombed the U.S. embassy in Beirut. With reprint rights, she and *Century* made more from that story than any other—all of which, except for a bonus to our correspondent, Sam put into the military's widows and orphans fund, and then added another $5,000, as he put it, "just because." We sent Dena Karsons into Washington, D.C., and the nation's major airline hubs, and she came back with a two-part series that showed our readers that not only had the major airlines committed significant safety violations, but also that terminal security was not all that secure. Jon Varner, one of the best of our special correspondents, against deadline pressures no dailies faced, gave us a two-part 9,500 word report about the chemical disaster at Bhopal, India, in December 1984 that killed almost 4,000 and injured about 200,000. Instead of just reporting facts, he tied together the U.S. oil industry and the government with political complicity and greed, an area few media had touched. During the past decade alone, we had on-site coverage of the strike by the air traffic controllers, major stories about terrorist activities in Ireland and the Middle East, retaliatory strikes by the U. S. against Libya, a couple of stories about chemical and biological warfare, the refusal of the nation to accept two Supreme Court nominations, the "conglomeratization" of America as we covered one buy-out after another, and the invasions of Afghanistan by the Soviet Union, and Grenada by the United States. I even had some fun with the Grenada invasion, doing a 700-word "back-of-the-book" spoof about how the military awarded more medals for a two-month unchallenged "invasion" than it did for all of the Vietnam War, in which almost 60,000 Americans and a million others had died.

We continuously attack the deplorable states of health care and education, the problems of the homeless and of American farmers, and discrimination against the handicapped. We run innumerable stories about workers and worker rights, and received both heavy heat and praise when we uncovered plans by General Motors to close 11 plants and throw almost 30,000 people out of work. We reported about the deaths of Mexican nationals who suffocated in a boxcar while they were being smuggled into the United States, and ran a subsequent two-part investigation that showed that although border-town Americans didn't want the undocumented Mexicans to live near them, they were more than willing to pay them substandard wages as maids, factory workers, and crop pickers, and force them to exist in substandard housing.

At *Century*, we abhor all forms of evil, even if it comes from the political Left. The Left praised us for our investigations into the American Nazi Party, and then condemned us for supporting their Constitutional right to hold public rallies and distribute literature as long as they didn't incite violence. Although we were at the forefront of reporting about the feminism movement, and even countered the widespread urban myth that feminists were burning bras to protest establishment policies, we took heavy flak from feminist groups after a major investigation disclosed they not only used shock tactics to stop publication of books and magazines they disagreed with, but were actively stealing and burning publications they thought were degrading to the image of women. We didn't think much of some of the magazines, but when it came to First Amendment issues, Sam was an absolutist—the Founding Fathers said all views must be heard, and that's what they meant!

Of course, there are quite a few stories that just lay there, moaning, place holders wrapped in a tangle of their own ink. But there's no need to discuss them, is there?

Nevertheless, for our efforts to keep the nation informed, we were investigated, intimidated, lied to, and even threatened with extinction when several leaders of the banking community, upset with what they thought were too many attacks upon American business practices, secretly made plans to cut off our credit by threatening our printers and distributor. Credit is the lifeblood of publishing, and *Century* would cease to exist if it couldn't pay its printing bills, even if the printers were always paid within 60 days.

But, there were stories we missed or under-reported. The one story all of us wished we had done better was the coverage of AIDS. Sometime around the end of 1981, two young Med students brought in a scientific article about a newly-discovered virus known as "gay pneumonia." Although they were passionate about why we should look at this newly-discovered disease, we decided there wasn't any solid news value in what they were trying to tell us. We thanked them and moved to other stories we thought had far more importance and impact. We weren't alone in our thinking. The two Med students, we later learned, had gone to more than a dozen publications, all of which to varying degrees thanked them and then did nothing. In mid-1983, we ran a two-paragraph short that the nation's blood supply may be tainted by AIDS. It was more an informational item than any great revelation. Finally, in 1985, during the Reagan years when we finally figured out that AIDS was a politically-sensitive social problem, we ran our first major story. The people, and especially the politicians, believed AIDS was just a problem among gays, but they used names other than "gay"; many religious leaders believed it was God's curse for the wages of sin. In the first four years after the AIDS virus was identified, the nation's media—1,700 dailies, 20,000 magazines, and innumerable TV programs—had published fewer than 4,000 stories, many of them the same wire stories; most were about the blood supply problem or that movie hunk Rock Hudson was dying of AIDS, probably not contracted from tainted blood. Coverage peaked around 1987 when the FDA approved the use of AZT to help control AIDS symptoms, with many media incorrectly calling it a "cure," much like the media jump onto any cancer drug as a "cure." But in the three years since then, AIDS coverage has diminished. In the nine years since the AIDS virus was first identified, the number of cases has increased from a few dozen to more than 300,000 in America, and possibly several times that in the Caribbean islands and in Africa. We always wondered what if we and the other media had run more stories in the early '80s; what if we weren't so blinded by our own biases to think it wasn't a greater social problem, that it was confined to a small class of people? Sam, more than all of us, was especially hard upon himself, even after we had run three "shorts" and a feature. It simmered—a comment here, a nuance there.

The lack of coverage of AIDS crept into our thoughts and discussions now and then, often influencing us to disregard the budget and pursue stories others shunted into oblivion. Because of this sensitivity, we were at first concerned, and then openly hostile, when Sam refused to allow us to report the arrests of Abbie Hoffman and Amy Carter. In November 1986, the co-founder of the Yippies and the former president's daughter, along with about 150 others, had decided to "seize" Munson Hall at the Amherst campus of the University of Massachusetts to protest the presence of the CIA recruiters. The police marched in and arrested a few dozen for trespassing, but only Abbie, Amy, and 11 others were held for trial. Their defense would be that since UMass allowed only companies that didn't violate the law to recruit on campus, the CIA should not have been allowed on campus. In what became known as the Iran–Contra scandal, the Reagan administration had apparently skirted federal law by selling weapons to Iran, an enemy of the United States, in exchange for money that was used to fund the right-wing Contras in Nicaragua who were trying to overthrow the Sandinistas, a left-wing government. Although Reagan himself may not have known the details, his vice-president, George H.W. Bush, former CIA director, certainly did.

The arrests in Amherst, the same month that a Lebanese newspaper broke the story about the CIA connections, were themselves developing into a major story that would reach from rural Amherst into the Congress and White House. However, as expected, most newspaper editorials sided with the right of the CIA, an all-American patriotic organization, to recruit college students. Sam told us the dailies and TV media were all over the story, even if they didn't get all the facts right, even if their stories tended to slant against the protestors. He reinforced a media maxim that a monthly magazine just can't jump onto hard news like a newspaper can, although we had by then broken several hard news stories the dailies overlooked or refused to pursue. We grumbled for about five months, even begged to run something—*anything*—about the arrests and the upcoming trial, again reminding Sam about what happened when we ignored the AIDS story, but he just told us we needed patience, and to work on other stories.

Two weeks before the May book was due on the stands, Sam called a meeting of his senior staff, told us to open another signature. Sixteen more pages. No advertising. Just 16 more pages to be dropped into the center. Not one person thought he was serious—we had pretty much locked up everything the first week in April, and the magazine was only five days from going to the printer. But, Sam was serious. To everyone's protest, he said he had something that needed to run. Something that would run, no matter what it took. He put onto the conference table a 3-1/2 inch floppy disk with a file that would check out at 8,200 words, and a hard copy printout. On top of that, he placed more than 50 photos, most of which he had taken. He told us to pick what photos we wanted, but not to touch the copy. No structural or line edits. Typeset it, proof it, put it into a good design, but run it untouched. And then he left. We didn't know where. We didn't even try to find out. We suddenly had raw copy, pictures, and more problems than a printer with a dry inkwell and paper breaks during a deadline production run. Amid our complaints and mumblings, which Sam didn't hear, we looked at what he gave us.

"Holy shit!" or some sort of acknowledgment was the first thing Sylvia Bachman, *Century's* managing editor, said when glancing at the pictures. Within moments, all of us were fighting to look at the photos and read the manuscript. What we saw were never-before released photos of Abbie, Amy, and other protestors, informal shots of former U.S. Attorney General Ramsey Clark who was testifying for the defense, of CIA recruiters, and of Americans dressed as soldiers—Sam spared us the research by labeling them "CIA advisors in Nicaragua."

Two days before April 15, 1987, when a jury would find the protestors not guilty of trespassing, Sam had given us the most comprehensive analysis that any reporter could have written. It was not merely the *facts* of the trial, which included evidence that the CIA had committed atrocities and innumerable times violated federal law, but of the *meaning* of the trial. Sam's hook was a quote that Abbie delivered in final summation. Because the trial was still in progress when Sam gave us the copy, we couldn't figure out how he knew what Abbie would say—or even if this was accurate. But, within hours, Abbie Hoffman would tell the jury two things that would be the base of Sam's article. First, Abbie readily acknowledged that a minor wrong, trespassing, was no crime when it corrected a major wrong. But, Sam's focus, what he hung his story upon, was that 50-year-old Abbie was passing the torch to the 19-year-old Amy Carter, a fresh voice of the revolution. Following an extended lead was a quote from Thomas Paine that Abbie gave at summation. "Every age and generation must be as free to act for itself, in all cases, as the ages and generations which preceded it," wrote Paine slightly more than two centuries earlier. "Man has no property in man, neither has any generation a property in the generations which are to follow," Paine told us.

As we would soon learn, Sam's observations and analysis were based upon access no other reporter could have had, and upon Sam's own genetic code of revolution for the betterment of society. Some of us knew that Sam and Abbie were friends— we never knew how deep it was. Although Sam was a bit older than Abbie, they had near-identical childhoods They had grown up in Worcester, attended Temple Emanuel, graduated from Brandeis, and both became journalists for the same reason, although Sam's path took him into the mainstream media while Abbie's took him more into the counterculture. What we didn't know until years later was that "Barry Freed," a highly-praised environmental activist who often hung out with Sam and Ruth during the late 1970s, and even visited us at *Century* a couple of times, once showing us yo-yo moves that should have gotten him a job with Duncan Toys, was really Abbie Hoffman during his seven-year escape from the law.

The effect of Sam's brilliant reporting was that half the nation reasserted its call that *Century* was a left-wing Pink Commie pile of sludge that didn't deserve to exist, that the trial was nothing more than a bunch of college kids getting arrested for violating the law and then sweet talking their way to acquittal. They completely overlooked the story that one generation of radicals was passing the torch to another.

Two years after Abbie's victory, he was dead. The medical examiner ruled it a suicide, but Sam and many others believed it was an accidental overdose by a man whose demons had again temporarily overtaken him. And so Abbie Hoffman joined Dinah Washington, Billie Holiday, Dorothy Dandridge, Jimi Hendrix, Janis Joplin, Jim Morrison, Charlie "Bird" Parker, Andy Gibb, Lenny Bruce, Elvis Presley, Sylvia Plath, and Ernest Hemingway, all of whom had their own demons, all who died from accidental drug overdoses, medical conditions intensified by drug or alcohol abuse, or by suicide. The media, establishment and counterculture, gave Abbie respectable obits, but not one had the power and truth of what Sam had written at the end of the trial in Northampton, Massachusetts. This was the kind of story that made *Century* different from most newspapers and magazines.

Naturally, that's why *Century* is just about the only place most of us could now work. And, naturally, that's why we would soon become involved in one of the biggest stories in our journalistic history.

6/

The Nature of Fear

SPECIAL COMMENTARY BY DAVID ASCHER

[EDITOR'S NOTE: This is the first commentary by David Ascher, a young reporter on a Central California newspaper. We anticipate publishing many more contributions by him.]

Americans have always lived in fear of someone or something. It's a part of our national heritage, like apple pie, baseball, and racism.

In the beginning, it is written in the grammar school history books, the Colonials came here to escape religious persecution. It was, after all, unfair of England to declare that it had the one true religion when the first Colonials knew they had it all along. Naturally, to preserve peace and freedom, they had no choice but to banish the non-believers to the undeveloped colonies of Rhode Island and Maryland.

And, speaking of heretics, when we arrived on this continent, we were afraid that the Indians, who preceded us here and who we called savages and heathens, might actually want to stay on the land they had cultivated. Worse, we were afraid they might even want to *co-exist* with us. Since we had muskets and they had bows and arrows, we declared ourselves superior, and built forts to make sure the Indians didn't try anything stupid, like move into our neighborhoods.

Then came the French, who hated the British, and soon we could fear Indians *and* French. Naturally, we went to war. When that got to be boring, we became fearful of the British, had a tea party, survived a riot in Boston we called a massacre, and eventually declared our independence.

We could now fear each other, so the Federalists of Washington, Adams, and Hamilton (who now were allied with England) launched campaigns against the Anti-Federalists of Jefferson and his ilk (who now were allied with France). Soon, we were slandering and libeling anything that moved. The result was the alien and sedition laws that were more oppressive than even the British could have imposed. We soon had another war, which we dubbed the War of 1812, which, ironically, began two days after England lifted the naval blockade that was a reason why we went to war.

Having once bought Manhattan from the Indians for $24 in trinkets, and a wide chunk of what became our Midwest from France for about $15 million, we now thought Texas might be worth having. By the time that war was over, we owned a large part of the Southwest. And we didn't have to fear Mexicans ever again—unless they, like the Indians and Blacks, were stupid enough to think they might want to live in our neighborhoods.

While many in the North cried for abolition, the reality was that America had divided itself by far more than the slavery question. When it was finally over, there was a permanent stain of blood on both our flags.

Then, there were those pesky Indians who again tried to keep us from our Manifest Destiny, our westward expansion. Couldn't they just save us the time and cost of ammunition and kill themselves? At least we put them on reservations so we wouldn't have to fear them actually living near us or talking with us. And then we destroyed the reservations.

When we were through fearing what the Spanish *might* do, we added Cuba, the Philippines, and the inalienable right to dig Teddy Roosevelt's ditch across the Isthmus of Panama.

And those "uppity colored people"? Wasn't there that Constitutional Amendment? Didn't it release them from slavery? Didn't we even give them "separate but equal" status so they wouldn't be tempted to become doctors and lawyers and teachers—and reporters—and possibly drink from our drinking fountains, eat in our restaurants, move in next to us and marry our sisters?

With the massive increase of immigrants, we were afraid of losing our jobs to "foreigners"—or worse, having to live with them. They were, after all, *different*. Those Irish fleeing famine. The Italians and eastern Europeans looking for a better life.

The Jews fleeing political and religious oppression. We had to make sure they knew their place, 'lest one of them thought that becoming a physician in America might be a better calling than selling vegetables off a cart in New York City. So, we imposed quotas on college admissions, and carefully explained that Irish had to be cops, eastern Europeans had to be coal miners, and Jews were supposed to be tailors and entertainers.

We feared the Germans so much in World War I that we wouldn't even eat sauerkraut, frankfurters, and hamburgers—it had to be victory cabbage, hot dogs, and Salisbury steak. We feared the Germans again in World War II and added Japanese and Italians, even if they lived in the United States for generations. Into "relocation camps," we resettled Americans of Asian ancestry. Into separate but certainly not equal military units, we put the people we still called colored soldiers while all of us proclaimed we were fighting for democracy.

After the war, we feared the Cold War and godless Communism, and in our fear of the unknown, like we had during the witch trials, went searching for Communists under our beds.

During the Civil Rights wars of the 1960s, northern Whites proclaim how unjust racism is. Some just say it. A few, however, are going into the South to help with the sit-ins or to register Blacks to vote, and are facing fire hoses and snarling dogs unleashed by the misnamed civil authorities. However, in the tolerant but hypocritical North, Whites are moving out of their neighborhoods as fast as Blacks move in.

Because we fear ideas that aren't what we believe, we continue to ban and burn books, forgetting that our nation was founded upon a libertarian principle that *all* views should be exposed to the marketplace of ideas.

We proclaim our individuality, but try to look, act, and think like everyone else, 'lest someone label us "different" or, worse, "radical." In a nation that values appearance over intellect, we are so afraid of looking different that we openly hate any man with long hair and a beard, spend billions for makeup and prescription creams to cover blemishes and wrinkles, go to surgeons to augment breasts and reduce fat, and spend close to what has to be the national debt to go to spas and gyms to "tone up our flab" because we are so afraid that we won't be accepted in what is becoming a rubber stamp society.

We don't hire the handicapped, the short, the tall, the fat, the skinny because they're "different." We fear homosexuals, who we call "fags" and "queers," because they're different—or, we hope, different from the rest of us.

We are so afraid of not being "cool" that we allow advertising to dictate what we wear, what we eat and drink, and even what we drive. We are so afraid that someone else will get something more than we have, so we buy larger Hi-Fi systems, more expensive cars, and bigger houses.

We convince our children to go to college because we're afraid they won't get a good job so they, like us, can spend 40 years on that job, afraid to do anything different or creative, afraid to speak out for fear of displeasing someone who might fire us.

We buy guns so we can blow away burglars, murder people whose views are different from ours, or to warn neighbors not to take short-cuts through our back yards at night.

We fear workers getting a piece of our pie, so we swallow it whole to make sure no one else can get any. We attack teachers because they get the summer off and we have to work. We attack the news media because they don't report what we want to hear—or believe. We attack unions because we're afraid they're getting more for their members than we're getting for ourselves; they're "greedy," we sob, when we should be attacking ourselves for not fighting for equality for all of us in the workplace.

Franklin Delano Roosevelt said that the only thing we have to fear is fear itself. Perhaps it's now time to take responsibility for ourselves and say that the only thing we need to fear is ourselves and our insipid bigotry.

7/

Statistically Insignificant

We called him Doc, not because he had a doctorate—an Ed.D. in something relatively harmless—but because on even his best days he sounded like the tuberculin dentist-gunslinger Doc Holliday, just wheezing and hacking and coughing from a chronic overdose of unfiltered Camels. When he talked, which he did frequently, he made a noise like a spoon caught in a garbage disposal. *Cough. Cough. Grrrind.*

At Bradstreet College, where this *nebbish* taught some innocuous education courses, being addressed as Dr. Boone or Prof. Boone set him apart from the rest of the nascent Philistines who constantly bumped and shoved him on the Orange Line, putting wrinkles into his gray or blue or brown three-piece suit, scuffing his black alligator shoes, scratching his genuine imitation leather briefcase. Being *Dr.* Boone put him in the league of those other famous doctors—Einstein and Fermi, Spock, Seuss, and Salk.

But, unlike those other doctors, he was apolitical. Almost vegetative when it came to social issues. Sit-ins and Freedom Riders, Chicago, Woodstock, and Earth Day all passed him by. He had read the headlines of the murder of Israeli athletes in Munich during the 1972 Olympics, but barely talked about it among his colleagues. And, like most Americans, Doc didn't read the first stories in the counterculture media, and then the early reports in the *Washington Post* in 1972 about the Watergate links to the White House or the truth behind the Pentagon Papers.

What he did believe in was PONG, the first commercial video

game that debuted the year of Munich and Watergate. Not only did he buy one of the first games, while in grad school he became one of the East Coast's largest distributors. By the end of 1973, Israel had retaliated and crushed an Egyptian invasion, *Roe v. Wade* put abortion into headlines, *The Godfather* ushered in a new kind of popular movie, the Vietnam War, which would cost more than a million lives, almost 60,000 of them American, was still two years from ending—and Doc had already made more than $100,000 selling PONG. The next year, Richard Nixon resigned and received a controversial pardon from newly-inaugurated Gerald Ford who also issued limited pardons to the Vietnam War protestors and draft dodgers; the Little League finally allowed girls to be on teams; Hank Aaron beat Babe Ruth's all-time home run record and received both cheers and racial slurs—and Doc made even more money from a two-player game of batting electronic images back and forth. But then the market collapsed and the newly-minted *Dr.* Boone returned to the academic life, where his transcript, filled with education, computer, and statistics classes, was almost as respected as his ability to make money from consumer demand.

Shortly after the Altair 8800, probably the world's first PC, debuted in 1975, Doc bought one, took what was left of his PONG profits, and bought dozens more, selling all of them for a profit to hobbyists. With that profit, he bought Apple I computers that almost anyone could figure out in a few hours. The revolution begun by Steven Jobs and Stephen Wozniak, nerds with a streak of the hippie culture, would be about the only revolution that Doc cared about. A couple of years later, he bought an Apple II which could run VisiCalc software, allowing him to begin a career in numbers crunching.

During the next few years he read, occasionally discussed but never cared about, the building of the Alaska pipeline, the Iranian students who seized the U.S. embassy, the beginning of Reagonomics and the decline of the Cold War, the rise of Jerry Falwell's right-wing Moral Majority, and the near meltdown at Three Mile Island. He knew almost nothing of the Black musicians who had created the base for rock and roll, little about Elvis, and had no clue why Michael Jackson's "Thriller" was important. Surprisingly, three decades after the '50s, he was hopelessly devoted to "Grease," loved TV's "The Wonder Years," and could run a one hour discourse on any of the subplots of either one. He scanned the headlines about the wars that Saddam Hussein with U.S. backing launched against Iran for oil rights, and Argentina's invasion of the Falkland Islands. He was thrilled about the first space shuttle, lamented the Challenger exploding, barely cared about the labor strike by the air controllers, missed seeing who shot JR on "Dallas," saw TV images of John Hinckley shooting President Reagan and Jim Brady, briefly mourned the John Lennon and Indira Gandhi assassinations, and the deaths of Princess Grace, John Belushi, and the Equal Rights Amendment—and had missed the birth of Pac-Man. He just didn't have any interest in games any more. He didn't miss the first DeLorean, however; he paid cash for one, while still teaching four classes a semester to potential teachers.

By 1982, Doc had a Radio Shack TRS-80 and one of the first IBM PCs, upgrading it whenever Microsoft or IBM upgraded. Although most professors had no clue what a PC was, Doc's students quickly saw the advantage of the new technology. While they were playing video games, Doc was surreptitiously teaching them how to manipulate numbers, carefully explaining how school officials could paralyze school boards with just the "right kind" of numbers.

Elliott T. Boone, A.A., B.S.(Ed.), M.A., Ed.D., first came to *Century* three years ago at Sam Weissmann's invitation. Not that Sam had any desire to buy a numbers cruncher, just that he had a greater desire to keep peace with his own board of directors.

"We need a director of research," the banker from Scarsdale proclaimed.

"All the major media companies have in-house staffs. We don't even have one researcher," the elementary school teacher from Quincy declared.

"Circulation has plateaued, and we need better consumer marketing to put your editors back in touch with what the public wants," noted the owner of Philadelphia's largest plumbing supply house.

"The day is over when editors can fly by the seat of their pants," the owner of a chain of supermarkets observed.

"We really aren't maximizing profits as well as we can," the lawyer from Boston emphasized.

As chairman of the board, chief executive officer, editor-in-chief, and publisher, but most of all as owner of 60 percent of the voting stock, with his employees holding about 30 percent, and with no one else holding more than one percent, Sam Weissmann could have declared that a director of research and the necessary supporting staff was a frivolous waste of his time and the company's money, that the magazine would continue to farm out its research studies. He could even have announced he might consider any of a dozen serious offers from corporations to buy *Century*, leaving him financially comfortable and without the headaches of management. But he didn't. Even with all the headaches and meetings, Sam loved what he was doing. More important, he loved why he was doing it. So, Sam, the egalitarian who believed that power must be shared just as ideas are shared, didn't protest. He wasn't going to "maximize profits" by laying off anyone and then hiring this numbers-cruncher who knew how to program COBOL and FORTRAN. If the Board was so determined that a director of research was necessary, and was willing to see it come out of corporate profits, then Sam wasn't about to waste any more time than the hour the Board just wasted.

Sam didn't even think enough of the position to put an ad in the *Globe* or *Herald*, and certainly not the trades. No, for this hiring, there would be no effort or money spent on a national search. One media researcher was worth just about what any other media researcher was worth. Put all their inconsequential studies together and you have one inconsequential monument to triviality.

And so Sam Weissmann, continually buried in paperwork, took the advice of the school teacher from Quincy who had Dr. Boone for a class at Bradstreet College, interviewed him, had him talk to the circulation and advertising directors, and then hired him. On the spot. Not even a background check or an "I'll get back to you."

Since the college administration allowed him to take a leave without pay for a year, Dr. Elliott T. Boone, with his degrees, papers, and computer studies, became director of research for *Century* magazine. He was given a small budget, a few supplies, a non-descript office with a non-descript assistant, which he had to share with a systems manager, and told to do whatever it was that researchers do.

It wasn't long before we realized he was on staff; you could hear that incessant coughing from two halls away; it was a lot better than putting a cowbell on him. When Kathy Steck, an assistant editor freshly graduated from UMass, decided to call him Doc, for Doc Holliday, the name just stuck. He even seemed pleased, ignorant of its etymology. Being called *Dr.* Boone now set him too far apart. And, just being called "Elliot" seemed too informal for a man with an Ed.D. *Doc* was a nice middle ground, sort of like kindly old Doc Adams, *Gunsmoke*'s resident saw-bones. After a year at *Century*, he was confident enough to ask for an extended leave from Bradstreet College, which allowed him to retain tenure as long as he taught at least two courses a year, and was willing to waive all benefits.

Every now and then, he'd deliver a well-bound package of data and analysis to Sam for distribution to the senior staff. Every now and then, someone read at least part of his study. Every now and then, someone found something useful in all the numbers, even if he was a few symbols short of a full equation.

We had tried to be polite, informal, pleasant, but one by one we gave up, hopelessly dooming him to his forced exile as direc-tor of research for a company that didn't really care to be a part of the Yuppie-business media conglomerates, with their teams of marketing researchers who were holding them in a death-grip of bottom lines. For the most part, Doc was on the staff, but not a part of it.

"I'm sorry that I can't be with you right now," said Dr. Elliott T. Boone, his voice and image projected from a 19-inch Zenith perched on a portable typewriter table in one corner of *Century*'s bleak conference room. "I'm at a conference on tech-nology in Denver. Thanks to AmeriSat, which is trying to sell us the S43-dash-11-dash-WS portable system, we have been given one hour free satellite time. This is so we can test the system to see if we like it or not. The costs to *Century* are only for the charges from AT&T." It was what the senior editorial staff feared the most—remote-controlled-researcher. *Cough, cough, wheeze.* "The system permits continual downlink. The tele-phone on the table is connected to a portable uplink. You can ask me questions, and I can answer them. All you have to do is push the green flat button to activate the phone speaker. The red flat button will temporarily terminate the uplink from Boston until the green flat button is pushed again. I will be able to downlink to you continually. Remember, the green button lets you talk to me; the red button temporarily terminates the uplink." Two-way remote-controlled researcher! Earlier that morning, we had seen Sam and two outside technicians scurrying around, but thought nothing of it. Sam is always scurrying around.

"We're testing this *mishmosh* out," Sam told us, explaining the system and its capabilities to the executive staff, glancing now and then at Doc's flattened image and disjointed voice while Doc himself was listening on his own two-way system to Sam's explanation. "O.K., Elliott, let 'er rip!" Sam commanded. He turned down the sound and pushed the red button, saliently announcing, "Let's get today started."

None of us ever understood why we had to have meetings. Even Sam never understood why we had to have meetings. But, we had meetings. Small semi-intimate meetings. Medium-sized meetings. Full-staff meetings. Meetings of the advertising staff. Meetings of circulation and distribution staffs. Production and graphics meetings. Meetings to plan things. Meetings to unplan things. Meetings to announce and unannounce things. And, of course, meetings to critically review the published issue.

"Most important," Sam announced, "there's a party at my house early Sunday afternoon to whenever. Spouses, lovers, children. I'll provide food. You bring the rest. Next, which of you wants to be Interim Secular Anti-God Commie Fascist Humanist?"

"Joseph quit?" I asked. "I leave town a few days and we lose our ombudsman and letters editor?"

"Saw the shit coming down the slide," Sylvia Bachman sarcastically pointed out.

"Day after you left—two days after the June book hit the stands—he came up to me," said Shane Kistler, one of *Century*'s three senior editors, "said he couldn't work without your guiding beacon, even for a few days, then defected."

"To?"

"Hortense Corporation out of L.A.—"

"The *Hortense* Corporation?" I asked, "What kind of a name is that for a company?"

"I don't make these things up," Shane replied. "They're into aerospace. Handed him some kind of PR job with a company car."

"No two week notice?"

"Said he could stay on another month to train the replacement, but I knew he'd be useless in Boston while dreaming of surfing at Redondo Beach," Sam declared. Sam hated it when corporate America raided the nation's news media to take some of the best journalists and turn them into mouthpieces-in-suits. But, he also knew that the managements of corporate news media, eager to improve their bottom lines at the expense of news, wouldn't improve salaries, working conditions, or benefits for their reporters. Sam, a reporter first who grew up in the working class, took care of his staff. On one of his bookshelves was an antique shoemaker's pliers to remind him that in 1648 the shoemakers of Boston organized the colonies' first union; on his office wall was a picture of Horace Greeley, editor–publisher of the *New York Tribune*, the nation's most influential newspaper during the antebellum and Civil War eras, who passionately argued for abolition, for the rights of women to vote, and who defied accepted business practices and founded the first newspaper union to make sure that his employees were treated well. But Sam also knew that the lure of corporate life, with a more regular schedule, complete with a tidy office and a secretary, was often enough to draw away some of his best younger staff. He didn't like reporters crossing over to the dark side. He understood it. He didn't have to like it. "I gave him a month's pay, threw him a party, and sent him home to contemplate if someone could really live in the city of angels with only 29 percent more than we paid him."

"He'll use that up in gas alone," Sylvia fiendishly pointed out, recalling her 12-year life working for Southern California newspapers.

"Whatever he uses it for, we still need a Reader Services editor," Sam pointed out.

"Both Allison and Fite are due," Sylvia suggested. "Either one can handle it." Allison was a music graduate, Fite combined poetry and art. Sam hired staff on the basis of intelligence and enthusiasm. It was a lesson he had learned from Henry Luce.

In the 1930s, when he was developing *Fortune* magazine, Luce hired Margaret Bourke-White, one of the best photographers in the country, and several nationally-known writers and poets, including Archibald MacLeish, James Agee, Alfred Kazin, and Dwight McDonald. His senior advisors were concerned, some were even have been appalled, that the creative arts community could do anything for a magazine that was focused upon reaching the upper levels of American management. Others merely thought he was crazy. But Henry Luce knew more about journalism than they suspected. He told his critics he could teach poets to do accounting, but he couldn't teach accountants to write.

Allison and Fite were perfect for promotion. But not right now. "Right now we need an experienced editor," said Sam. "I'm downwind of the fan that sucked in all that crap, and more's coming in every mail delivery." Some months you get a warm glow from all the praise; some months the warm glow is a fire-fight.

As executive editor, Sam's top assistant, I'm responsible for organizing the in-house staff; contracting with freelance writers, artists, and photographers; and maintaining some control over the budget. However, my major responsibility is long-range planning, not only working on future issues, but also responsible for the direction the magazine should take in the next five years. The special issue on religion in America had begun about a year earlier when Erica Stark, one of our newly-hired assistant editors fresh off the Temple University campus, came into work her first day, proudly bearing a hardcover book she had received from the Krishnas at the Philadelphia airport. "They're free!" she announced, proud as a cat with its first mouse. "I even gave them a donation." None of us had the heart to slam her perky enthusiasm. But from idle chatter about gullibility and naiveté came discussions about the nation's blurring distinction of church–state separation.

During the next few months, the *Century* staff began working on what would become 14 major articles, one of which was to be 10,000–12,000 words, a back-of-the-book essay, more than two dozen sidebars, shorts, and "news notes," all related to the theme of religion in America. And, as is the nature of journalism, I couldn't afford to make this a pet project, to work on it exclusively, because there were other mouths to worry about. Two dozen puppies were all trying to feed off a half-dozen teats. Sometimes being an editor can be a real bitch.

Meanwhile, Sam loosened budget restraints, while business manager Frank Mitchell, pre-approvals and innumerable forms genetically embedded into his MBA soul, fumed about a breakdown in financial accountability. A few weeks later, Sam notified Production and Circulation to plan for at least another

15,000 copies—the number would keep fluctuating until one month before publication—upsetting not only Circulation but Production and Advertising as well. Two months from production, I passed the issue off to Sylvia Bachman for day-to-day details, but still kept an active interest. Six weeks later, Promotion began pushing out one press release after another, all of them extolling the upcoming issue, emphasizing that some of the nation's top writers were in that issue. But, just in case readers didn't care about good writers—after all, how many people know the byline of even one magazine writer?—Sam made sure that a score of religious organizations saw, by only a couple of days, advance copies of the magazine, got their criticism, and then fed it to the media—which, of course, gobbles up any controversy and spits it out under six-column Jesus type, headlines reserved for the "second coming," but used by page designers and editors when they want to scream something at their readers. Sam loved every minute of it, knowing that controversy sells magazines. But, still, it was taking up time.

"A lot of *shtuss*, that's all this is," said Sam. Turning to me, he again asked, maybe for the six thousandth time in the past few months, if I was absolutely, positively, without question, sure that we could stand behind every article. Once again, I assured him we had cleared everything with fact checkers and lawyers, but both of us knew that we may still have problems with what some call objectivity.

Objectivity is the Big Lie in journalism. We all pretend that we're objective, but none of us are. No matter how hard we try, we're bound by our own values and worldviews. Each of us perceives, selects, orders, and analyzes facts differently. We pick and choose who we wish to interview, not from some divine wisdom but from our own gut feelings of who would be the best sources for a particular article—and even then we don't report everything they said or have omniscience to ask all the right questions and sort out the accuracy. Send a dozen people to a routine city council meeting, and there will be a dozen different stories. As any good journalist knows, it's possible to have a story with absolutely no factual error—yet miss the truth. Nevertheless, I had no hesitation in defending my staff.

"It's as solid a book as we've ever had," I again said, more to support the staff than to ease Sam's mind. "Added two fact checkers. Lawyered it twice. I'll stand behind it."

"Perhaps," said Sam, "you would like to do your standing before a bunch of *shlugs* from Falwell's Moral Majority. They've been around—what?—a decade? You'd think they'd mellow out by now. Then there's Religion is Fundamental. They would like to fire a volley in your direction. Not to mention the Birchers, the Nazis, the White Citizens Council, every fringe group in America, a bunch of scattered clusters from the left who think by giving any space to anyone but them casts us as right-wing reactionaries, and a few dozen citizens who had nothing better to do the past few days, so they kept the Post Office, Ma Bell, and the God-damned Western Union wires humming! May they all be resurrected as centipedes with ingrown toenails!" He grabbed a breath. "I love it! This is *journalism!*" He even had Security hold a delegation of about a dozen blustering harpies— "May God give them all shingles, and then have an elephant scrape its toenails on their arms"—heating up in the lobby long enough for the local TV stations, alerted by an "anonymous tip," to dispatch camera crews. The protestors did everything they were supposed to do when confronted by TV lights, while Sam made sure his carefully framed comments about a free press and unrestrained religion were recorded.

"Now, you must remember that gamma is a very sensitive test, and in this instance . . ." came the disembodied and unanswered voice from the tube. Sam turned the sound down even more on the remote satellite, keeping it as a low-level white noise hum, but Doc was still clearly audible, loquaciously prattling his spiel to what could have been a universe-wide audience of housewives, newspaper editors, department store kingpins, Soviet spies, or alien life forms if they had been unfortunate enough to be in the proper band width at a most improper time. Whatever it was that Doc was doing wasn't as important as crisis intervention.

"Sounds good, Doc. You have figures on cost effectiveness to modem usage for field correspondents?" Sam figured it'd keep Doc busy another five minutes. He punched the red button and then sighed. A heavy deep sigh, something he frequently does from being overworked, mentally exhausted, upset, frustrated, or just because that's what he does a lot. Sam looked up from his notes. "We knew it would offend some when we began it."

"They're all jerks!" MaryBeth Martinez, our senior editor for graphics and design, could never bring herself to swear. Not even an "asshole" crossed her lips. But, her deliberately cool and refreshingly sweet demeanor was often betrayed by her left ear. When she was nervous or upset, mad, furious, or frightened, her left ear, never her right one, would turn red. The redder it got, the more it betrayed her coolness, her aloofness. There is nothing she can do about it. It just happens. At the moment, her restored candy apple red '34 Model A would have been pale pink in comparison.

"Any circulation falloff?" she asked.

"Atlanta office reports tremors. L.A. and Chicago are OK. We'll defuse whatever they throw at us." For Gretchen Peron, there are never any problems, only challenges. She was always working a plan, always juggling myriad problems and personalities. If she said she'd defuse problems, she'd defuse problems. Circulation wasn't a problem. A few cancellations. But since 86 percent of the magazine's circulation was individual subscriptions rather than news stand sales, something advertisers liked because it showed stability, by the time their subscriptions came due most of the angry subscribers would have been iced.

At most media, ad salesmen often make more than reporters, with the "independent press" proclaiming a strict separation of Editorial and Business operations, while genuflecting to corporate America. Why else would newspapers have entire Business sections, but no Labor sections? At *Century*, Editorial runs the show, while Sam Weissmann remains faithful to his ideals if not his business sense.

"We always get praise. Even Bush's people sometimes find something nice to say." Dahn St. Michaels, our deputy managing editor, looked around the table, hoping to hear something that would allow him to leave the meeting content, able to continue fighting off his own editorial crises without having to leave the building to buy more gallons of Swiss-lemon flavored Maalox. It's another maxim of journalism—criticism runs on a thousand feet, praise hobbles with a cane.

"Most memorable," recalled Sam, "was a call I got yesterday from a lady in Pennsylvania." At *Century*, unlike most national magazines and metro newspapers, we answer our own phones and quickly reply to our readers' letters, no matter how many threaten to fill dumpster-sized in-boxes. Our "open-door" policy also leads to an assortment of characters who just wander into our offices, some with stories, some with personal problems, but

all with a reason to talk with us, even if it is just curiosity. No
guards keep out the factory workers or secretaries, electricians,
plumbers, corporate executives, and the homeless. Even against
death threats and deadlines, we take time to talk with anyone
who wants us, needs us. It may not be the brightest business
decision, especially since we are constantly overrun by the
loonies and, for all we knew, the ghost of the Boston Strangler,
but it has kept us grounded into why *Century* exists. And now
Sam was telling us about yet another of our guests. "Fifteen,
maybe 20 minutes we talked. Said she read every word in the
magazine and thought we were on target. Said it was the best
issue we ever published."

"What's her name?" asked Porter Dennison, *Century*'s combination senior copyeditor/senior fact-checker.

"A woman of class and intelligence," Sylvia mocked.

"Tell her to write a letter to the editor," suggested Karlen
Aruian, our senior editor for the arts.

"Didn't get her name," Sam confessed.

"You talked a half hour with a reader and—" Sylvia bluntly
stated.

"Fifteen, 20 minutes at the most," Sam corrected. "She was
interesting."

"Whatever. You didn't get her name, and all you remember
was that she was interesting?"

"Interesting is more important." Sam puffed himself up, and
proudly said that this caller claimed he sounded just like her
father—sweet, kind, and "twinkly."

"Anything else about this mental case?" Sylvia teased.

"Photographer. Maybe musician. That's about it."

Apryl? Nothing Apryl Greene did should have surprised me.
Very likely, she really had read every word of the magazine.

"A demented reader with time on her hands," Sylvia caustically claimed. I said nothing.

"A *lady*," said Sam quickly, the timbre of his voice sharply
rebuking anyone who'd question him.

"So," interrupted MaryBeth coolly attempting to break an
unneeded confrontation between Sam and Sylvia, "what do we
have from the Left?"

"Regional counsel for ACLU sent two pages. ADL called.
Said we did a great job but some of our statements about organized religion could be interpreted by others as anti-Semitic."

Yeah . . . Sure . . . we each thought. "A minister here, a rabbi there, each taking the time to call or write. Couple of them even suggested some areas we should have explored but didn't. Lot of it was congratulatory. Even the flack for some archdiocese out in California called to say we did a good job, and to let me know that the Church doesn't burn books."

"At least not the same way it used to," Karlen muttered.

"We have warm and fuzzy feelings, and we love controversy," Sylvia said, "so what's the problem?"

"Just the usual *meshungina* who tried to teach me things I could do to my anatomy that would have pleased Torquemada and his merry band of inquisitors," said Sam somewhat unconcerned. To most of the evangelical Christian Right, we were the crazy people, not them. They were methodically building their membership into what they hoped would be a political machine. We were the ones whose liberal views would break holes in the brick that was America and would destroy the foundation of all that was glorious and great—*hallelujah!*

"*Naturally, if the F test shows an F value larger than the critical value, this would, of course, be accepted as significant. We would, as we have in the past, want to run the Neuman-Keuls, unless earlier variants indicate . . .*" Doc was like background music, mostly innocuous but always droning, always there. A question from Sam now and then would recharge Doc's battery, allowing him to ramble another five minutes.

"Why you taking all the heat, Sam? We're a team here," Dahn emphasized. "Spread it around. We'll each take a little pile of crap so the whole field isn't in your lap. We'll all become Secular Humanist Letters editor for awhile."

"At the top of the masthead is my name." Sam didn't have to say anything more.

"*Correlating the population sample of owners of blue Buicks who attend North American Baptist churches with owners of blue Fords who attend Southern Baptist churches, and then correlating it to readership of conservative versus liberal magazines, we used a modified Pearson Product Moment, showing a z score in Area C of minus oh-point-three-two . . .*"

"TV preachers drawing the most heat?" Karlen asked.

"Strongest letters opposing it are coming from the rural areas. Some scattered praise, but overall there's not much response on that one. It's been a dead issue for awhile now."

"Probably quiet because we unloaded all our ammo when we broke it the first time years ago," Shane observed. Almost every week for two years, there was some revelation, pro or con, about the latest scandal. If it wasn't *Newsweek*, AP, or the *New York Post*, it was *The National Enquirer* pulping forests in order to let all America know about the sex and financial lives of tele-vangelists. When the tabloids ran out of material, they snooped around and came up with favorite recipes of televangelists, favorite books of televangelists, and psychic premonitions of tel-evangelists. Even if you were illiterate, the networks beamed the print media revelations into your lap just after dinner. How-ever, after shooting off their mouths, the media and the public had become narcotized by the presence of TV preachers, and had begun exploring other media-induced fads.

"We still had to do the story," Dahn noted, somewhat defen-sively, somewhat territorially.

"It didn't just have to lay there, though," I argued. "There was no zing in it. Not like the first time."

"You, me, Shane—we all worked with Polly Yannes on it," Sylvia replied. "She's a damn fine writer, even if she's too sweet for her own good. Then, there were the checkers."

"Drip-dried and sanitized," Shane pointed out.

"We may have stripped it while trying to be responsible," Dahn conceded, "but it's still a damned fine piece." We mur-mured lame agreement, continued to argue what was in first place for reader invective, while Sam smugly watched our dis-comfort and annoyance.

"*. . . while using disproportional stratified sampling, as well as tests on measures of central tendency for grouped data to break down quartile deviation . . .*"

"They probably went after Wicker's piece," said Sylvia.

"We've actually been getting far more praise on that than damnation," said Sam, "but even then, there hasn't been all that much response." That came as a surprise since we figured there was enough controversy in Joel Wicker's lead article to bring about another 10,000 sales—and cement our reputation as a fearless leader of insightful but disputatious reporting. Joel's investigation had shown that while the gentrified upper crust were still too involved in themselves, their jobs, and their play things to go to church, synagogue, or mosque, their chil-dren were leading a wave of religious conservatism that was sweeping through America's middle class. If the sequel on TV evangelists and the return to religion was safe, what wasn't?

"Street preachers in third," said Sam, "but may be pushing second." At the time we planned it, it seemed like an innocuous 1,000 words about the people who ran store-front churches. A month before deadline, we bumped it to 2,500 words when we saw the first photo proof sheets. "Most seem disturbed that we wasted our space on them at all," said Sam. "Claimed that by reporting on them we were legitimizing them."

"Using phi *to correlate the dichotomous variables of church attendance with color of pickup trucks, then running a one-way analysis of variants . . ."* said the unheeded voice blathering on.

"Problem with credentials?" I half-heartedly noted.

"Established religion doesn't like free spirits," Sam replied.

"Didn't they read about the homeless?!" Sylvia was spitting venom. "Didn't they read that when some of the establishment churches didn't want to touch the homeless and the sick and alcoholic because it might soil their upper-class lily-white congregations, the street missions took them in?! Sure, we'll give you money, they promise, but don't make us get our hands dirty. What a bunch of motherfuckin' hypocrites!"

"That's probably what upset them; facing their own image," said Shane Kistler. "I'd be scared witless if I were them and had to look into the mirror."

"Even got flak from Billy Joe Hargis," said Sam who knew and liked the former fighter pilot, now a pacifist and the leader of a 2,000 member congregation in New Orleans. The article had quoted Hargis as saying that the church must first worry about souls before it worried about bodies, about getting money before distributing it. He said it, we had it on tape, but in print—taken out of context Billy Joe claimed—it did make him appear to be just another uncaring businessman–minister.

"He gonna sue?" I asked.

"Nah. Gave me a call. Just to let me know he read the piece. Said next time he's in Boston I buy dinner. Half Billy Joe's congregation are street people. He doesn't need to defend himself."

". . . with the Type I error indicating a false rejection of true values as opposed, of course, to the Type II error which indicates a failure to reject a false hypothesis . . ."

It had been 28 years since NASA launched Telstar, which allowed Walter Cronkite to broadcast the news live to Europe, and forever changed the nature of television journalism. At this moment, most of us were ready to blame Walter, NASA, AT&T, and Europe for what had mutated into Doc's Discourse.

"In second place!" Sam announced jubilantly, a sweep of his hand proclaiming the truth, "is the Beaver!" None of us had seen it coming. None of us could believe that a bouncy retrospect of one of America's most popular SitComs, one of four articles we ran that month that didn't fit into the special section on religion, an article we thought of as our monthly pablum-for-the-masses reporting, would cause any controversy, let alone vault it into second place, not when we had innumerable articles that dripped controversy. The hardcore Beaver fanatics were offended by 230 words—a third of it quotes from a UMass sociologist—that the show, like *Ozzie and Harriet, Father Knows Best,* and other family SitComs, reflected an unrealistic America, and by doing so trivialized the problems facing the 1960s America. Our readers—more of them had marched against the war and for civil rights than the readership of most magazines wanted to have the hope that the traditional family structure would survive; they wanted to believe that problems could be solved in 30 minutes. Heck, they even wanted to believe that a talking horse on TV knew more about life than his architect owner. If we wanted realism on TV, argued many of our readers, we should have 24 hours of *Sunrise Semester.*

"If it wasn't our shot at the Beaver," MaryBeth Martinez playfully asked, "what topped the hit parade this month?"

"And stop playing with us!" Sylvia demanded.

"How many guessed book burners?" asked Sam. We all had, of course, but didn't figure it'd be number 1. We expected the usual letters and phone calls, but to have topped the charts? "Still early in the returns," Sam noted, "but it's drawing most the response. At least 3-to-2 against."

"What the hell can Gunnell and his gang complain about this time?" I demanded. "Sylvia's article too accurate? Her pen draw too much blue blood? We hurt their self-righteous indignations?"

"Halle-*lujah!*" Sylvia Bachman shouted, standing up, scanning the room for sinners. "I done seen de light! Burn *all* de trash. Round it up and get it outta de schools and into de fires of *hell!*" We let her continue her Billy Sundayesque sermon until she ran out of breath. Sylvia, juggling her role as managing editor with one she occasionally took on as investigative reporter, had done what we thought to be a brilliant job of reporting the problems of religion and books. She brought forth not only the libertarian arguments for a "marketplace of ideas" with no prior restraint, but also the authoritarian concepts of protecting the public from words and ideas that could be destructive to society.

"So far," said Sam, our own guiding light and all-around Buddha, "the preliminary letter from the Big Dick's legal team claims defamation, invasion of privacy, false light, intrusion, libel, and a few civil and criminal acts I didn't know existed. Only thing they didn't charge us with was bestiality, and that's only because we're too damned fucking busy to find any farm animals! Their lawyers can tie us in knots for months. And with the Supreme Court, who the hell knows what the First Amendment is any more."

We were resigned to such threats. It came with the territory. Whether or not we were meticulously accurate and somehow managed to record impenetrable truth, rather than just a series of facts, people would still complain, and some would sue or threaten to sue. Whether or not their complaints had any merit, it would still take time, energy, and money to defend our stories. Every threat caused a chip to fall from our corporate rock. Enough chips and all that remains is microscopic dust. Every lawsuit, no matter how frivolous, has a chilling effect. No matter how careful or courageous we are, we'd always be hearing footsteps, looking over our shoulders to see what was gaining on us. But we accept it as just another expense of doing business, and brush off the "what if" concerns. Not all editorial staffs have the privilege of working under such principles. Not all staffs have as courageous a leader as Sam. "It would be the greatest *tzedaka*, the highest order of charity, if we rid the earth of that piece of *dreck*," said Sam. It was only a moment before he quickly corrected himself. "No, that *schmendrick* deserves to get his *meshugge* arguments before the public as much as we have that right."

Sylvia agreed it wouldn't be right to kill the bastard, but suggested we could just maim him a little, and stuff down his throat a copy of the Constitution, something he probably had never read.

"We knew there'd be heat on this one," I said, but it's still as solid an analysis on contemporary religion and literature as anything that's appeared the past ten years. And that includes all those fucked-up number-crunching sociological studies that have been pouring out of the colleges."

"*. . . a correlation of point-three-five, except in cases when there was more than two inches of rain the previous 24 hours, and . . .*"

"David's right!" said Shane. "Years from now, people are still going to be talking about this issue. It's the most comprehensive analytical work we've ever done, and we shouldn't be taking this bullshit."

"*Now, when we run both the multiple regression to predict the one single dependent variable of level of political activity against our series of independent variables, and taking into account the previous correlation matrix we ran using a Spearman, with split-half technique on reliability, we note that homeowners who are second generation Americans, and who are aged under 30 years of age, living in rural areas at least 20 miles from any city larger than 30,000 population, who have a median income of $22,600, an average formal educational level of 12-point-2, tend to go deer hunting at least three days a year . . .* hack, hack, cough . . . *who buy primarily red gift wrap for Christmas, own golden retrievers, usually listen to polkas on Wednesdays and Sundays, but country and western on Saturdays, drive a . . .*"

"Shut that joker off!" Sylvia commanded to cheerful applause. "Keep the satellite and dump *him*! Better yet, send him into space to find signals. We're saving humanity, and that asshole is sitting around telling us about red paper and polkas!"

"Ice for Sylvia!" Dahn ordered.

"Okay, so we keep the little weasel," Sylvia said, a smile breaking her lips, "but that doesn't solve the problem of our readers. We should be winning awards not worrying about why we're the main course in a shish-ka-bob buffet."

"You don't have to convince me," Sam reassured us, perhaps reassuring himself in the process. "

Puckish Sam, who lived the Biblical pronouncement that joyfulness prolongs life, was now quiet, a sad kind of quiet, bringing an eerie quiet upon the room.

"People," he said sorrowfully, idly glancing around the room, carefully composing his thoughts. We knew we were about to endure one of Sam's eternal monologues. And, we knew when he got through winding and weaving, ranting and raving, we would not only learn something, but be ready for the Second Half Kick-off. "This latest issue is only a microcosm," said Sam peacefully, as he began to build up steam. "Same problem that's plagued mankind the last million or so years. Fear!" He pounded the table as he morphed into a preacher. "Fear of the unknown. Fear that if others are allowed to have their own values, their own beliefs, their own religion, it could somehow destroy what you believe in. It permeates not only religion, but all facets of our society, and it knows no geographical boundaries." He paused a moment to capture a breath, perhaps to cleanse the aura of pontification, and then continued, his words taking on a sharper edge as he mocked the nature of mankind, "If it's different, make it conform! If it won't conform, destroy it! Destroy it before it destroys you!" He took a breath, looked at us, his eyes not focusing. "Everyone is so worried that they think false prophets will destroy the *true* religion that they are destroying it themselves with hatred and prejudice and intolerance. We have invoked the name of God to justify our crusades, our inquisitions, our holocausts. Look at Ireland. At the West Bank. Saudi Arabia. Hell, look at our own country! Underlying it is not the love of God, but the fear of life. We live in a world of fear, afraid to ask what if these other beliefs are right. What if my beliefs are wrong? None of us can tolerate that revelation. So, everyone is trying to destroy everyone else's beliefs in order to make theirs stand up. Our self-righteous leaders go to war and claim they have divine inspiration, that they are the willing servants of God's word, that God is on their side. Our overpriced athletes stand up, look into the TV cameras, and declare, 'Ah wanna thank Jesus for this great victory,' as if Jesus had nothing better to do than choose sides, and figure out which quarterback was more religious than the other. Anyone here ever see Jesus in a helmet and shoulder pads? Does he suit up Sundays with the Saints? Think he's swinging the bats for the Angels or Padres?" Another breath, a sigh really, before Sam firmly declared—to us, to the world, maybe more to himself— "These *ganifs* with the *chutzpah* of ignorance aren't attacking us, don't you see? They're after us because we publish the truth, and they can't stand it!" And then Sam stood up, all five-foot-eight of him, shook his mange of salt-and-pepper hair, looked squarely at no one in particular, waited a moment or two, slammed his right fist against the table, and proclaimed, "The environment reeks of decades of abuse. We're killing off our wildlife. There's still too much unemployment and far too many homeless. Only the rich can afford to be healthy, and civil rights still has a hell of a long way to go. But what do we hear? We hear prattling about why we shouldn't publish things!" He paused, looked at each of us, and then commanded, "Don't forget the party at my house!"

8/

Lines of Emptiness

by David Ascher

I looked into her eyes and saw nothing. Not hope. And not despair. Not joy. And not sorrow. Nothing.

She stood in line, one of 15 or 20 people moving slowly on this unusually hot June afternoon, cooled only by an occasional breeze that came and went, bringing with it a calm relief that only served to emphasize the sweating, tiring, exhausting heat of people crowding together in a storefront office much too small and much too weathered to have anything more than the top layer of dust cleaned and swept once a week.

In a few minutes, she would step to a wooden desk, talk to a clerk who is cooled by a portable fan, show government-issued identification, sign a form, pay some money, and be issued a booklet of food stamps worth only a few dollars more than she paid. If she didn't feel lost or humiliated, she soon would.

When you pay for groceries with treasury-issued Federal Reserve notes, the clerk smiles, says "Nice day. How are you today?" When you pay for food with coupons, the clerk doesn't smile. And neither does the person behind you in line. That person had to pay for all of her family's food with her own money.

They look at you, contempt not compassion in their eyes, a silent hatred burning within. Some feel the need to take a public stand. They look at her brass-and-leather peace symbol strung around her neck and challenge her patriotism, screeching, "My husband"—substitute "brother," "father," "uncle," "son," "nephew" as appropriate—"is in a jungle, living in tents, eating K-rations and fighting for democracy while you eat roasts and protest everything this country stands for." They challenge her integrity or her morals.

"Lazy bastard. Oughta get a job," they mutter to each other, knowing she'll overhear them.

"Welfare rip-off," they accuse.

They could be right. There are the professionals who learned the system and made it work for them. There are the deadbeats who resist every effort of help, preferring to be "on the dole," rather than "on the job." There are the upper-class and middle-class college students whose parents are paying $4,000 a year just so their draft-deferred little darlings can attend college and graduate into managerial jobs in a labor market being diluted by cheap college degrees. No one cares that maybe the lady presenting the food stamps once had a job, once paid taxes, that she might again have a job, that maybe she doesn't like what's happened to her any more than anyone else. But, that's the past. Or the future. Not the now. In line, it's the now that matters.

The food stamp worker doesn't know this woman. The unemployment clerk doesn't know this woman. The welfare caseworker doesn't know this woman. She's just a nameless, faceless body the government labels a "client." One of hundreds each would process that week. Week after week after week.

Perhaps at one time they wanted to help, to listen to her problems, help her look for answers, help find her a job, get her off welfare and food stamps. But they don't help. There are just too many, and not enough time to do more than process paperwork and enforce a dehumanizing web of regulations as impersonal as two people on opposite sides of bureaucratic desks, each of them imprisoned by cumbrous loose-leaf notebooks prepared within antiseptic governmental walls by people who never went hungry but who now determine who deserves help and who doesn't. The words outline eligibility and procedures; they don't outline compassion and help. Their clients are case files, hand-written and typed, graphemic shapes on governmental forms; nothing more.

Whatever their concerns, it no longer mattered to this young lady on this hot humid summer afternoon. She took her food stamps and turned around. For a couple of moments she looked into my eyes, was about to say something, and then turned away. Her eyes said nothing, yet they told her story.

9/

Isotopes of Change

"More beer!" came the cries from the living room, drowning out the last notes of P.F. Sloan's "Eve of Destruction." The entire week had been a bitch at *Century*, with Friday, my first day back from a two week promotion tour, proving to be even worse, so Sam Weissmann called a full staff meeting in the morning, and then declared the afternoon to be a holiday. *Go home*, he had told his staff; *cleanse your blood from printer's ink; bring your families and beach blankets to my place Sunday.*

And so it was that on this particular Sunday there were bodies on the beach and bodies in the surf; bodies lying, sitting, standing, leaping, swimming; bodies of every description in every room of the four-bedroom Colonial that Sam and Ruth Weissmann had first begun remodeling more than two decades earlier.

"Beer!" came the call once again while we continued discussing the issues that made the Commonwealth great.

"Perky blonde on the *Atlantic*?"

"No way! Brunette with the boobs."

"Logan's press aide? You sure?"

"As sure as I am that he's a pig."

"May not have been his fault this time—"

"Spare me!"

"I'm serious, Sylvia. It seems that Muffy—"

"*Melissa*, Frank. *Melissa*."

"Yeah. Anyhow, she sees the White House in Merrill Logan's eyes. Figures if he runs, he'd take her along."

"Have we really become that tolerant as an electorate?"

"I don't know, Karlen. Gary Hart didn't think so two years ago."

"You vote for Logan?"

"No way! I always thought a governor should only have one mistress."

"And only one sunlamp."

"Whatever turns him on."

"Sunlamp?"

"You've got to stay in the office more, David. Added another one last month. Had them more than a year now."

"You *sure?*"

"That he's been turned on?"

"That he's got sunlamps."

"How'd you think he got that California surfer tan in the middle of a Massachusetts winter? He's spewing more radiation than Pilgrim ever did."

For years, we believed the only reason the Pilgrim plant on Boston's south shore, only a few miles north of Plymouth Rock, was allowed to exist was because either God owned stock in Boston Edison or else Boston Edison was blackmailing God. There could have been no other reason for what was probably America's worst run nuke. A two-part series in *Century* in late 1985 had detailed safety and health violations, but the plant still sent its radiated energy all over the Northeast corridor.

Nukes had begun to ring New England, their owners telling everyone how cost efficient nuclear power was, while applying for, and receiving, rate increase after rate increase. It was almost surreal how the geniuses at the electric companies were able to convince the speed bumps at the PUC how much money was needed from the users to build a plant that was supposed to be the source of inexpensive electricity and a 12 percent return on investment. But then the Chernobyl meltdown in 1986 shook everyone up. For awhile, no countries were building any reactors. Massive protests led New York state to stop the Shoreham plant from going online after years of deception and lies, combined with blatant management incompetence and greed. But now there was Bellevane. Different place; different company.

"Better track record," Gretchen Peron casually pointed out.

"Just because it's done well with conventional energy doesn't mean it'll do as well with a nuke," coutered Aaron Lyons.

"We need to get away from our fossil fuel dependence," said

Karlen Aroian with a professorial tweak. "Gas is now—what? Buck-fifteen? Buck-twenty? Will go higher. Maybe up to buck-fifty. Probably more."

"Yeah, like Americans will accept two bucks a gallon!"

"Doubt it'd go that high. Americans won't let it."

"Like they had any say when gas broke buck a gallon? Don't you remember the lines a decade ago to get gas? Their protests didn't mean a rat's ass fuck to the oil companies."

"So we drop a chunk of U-238 into every car? Run silent, glow deep?"

"All I'm saying, Sylvia, is that if we keep praying to the gods of oil, we'll have more than just an addiction."

"So we trade oil dependence for uranium dependence? Same problems. Same limited resources. Same corporate bullshit."

Frank Mitchell drew a breath, gave us a moment of anticipation, a look that commanded us not to say anything in the moment before he announced a breakthrough doctrine for saving the world, and then calmly announced in a one syllable clearly resounding canon, "Clean."

"Clean?!" Brandi Domenico sputtered a lexicon of contempt in her one word reply.

"Clean," Frank calmly pronounced. "Oil is dirty. Coal is dirty. Pollution caused by cars and factories is dirty. Nukes are clean."

"Clean isotopes shooting up, and then falling quietly onto pristine beds of lettuce," Brandi sarcastically mocked. "Clean electrons in the water. Clean protons in the air."

"You people amaze me," Frank declared pompously, casting us together into the same super-heated waters. "You Luddites sound like the morons who protested coal as an energy source, then their children and grandchildren who feared oil and then electricity. And now nuclear energy. I don't know how you even put out a magazine since you're afraid of anything more revolutionary than quills and papyrus."

Kathy Steck rose to the challenge. "We're afraid only of the probability there will be mistakes."

"*What?*" said Frank in his phoniest voice of feigned shock. "Editorial is so pure it doesn't make mistakes? Your monthly Corrections column is fiction to keep the masses entertained?"

"Our mistakes," Kathy declared, "don't kill anyone."

"So the pen *isn't* mightier than the sword, and what we all do here is to publish little fuzzy bunny stories that massage rather than stimulate our readers' minds? And for this I have to sign expense checks?"

A half-dozen half-responses were abruptly cut short.

"Bellevane will be stopped," Sylvia said intently, in biting measured words. "Long before the first operator falls asleep in the control room." She was quiet. Determined. And absolutely sure she was right. God's chosen words put into her mouth.

"What you smoking?" Shane Kistler asked. "Weed strangling your brain cells? Of all people, you should know the clam chowderheads of government aren't going to snap closed this one. They gave Seabrook its full power license and it's—what?— a couple of months from going commercial? All those protests— they didn't mean squat. Government will use Frank's *clean* as a base for their support for Bellevane, add in equal parts of economy and jobs, spice it up with something about national security, and then serve it up to a starving nation."

Sylvia Bachman was no wild-eyed innocent, and certainly not one to trust any form of government, benevolent or otherwise. In two decades as a journalist, she had developed more knowledge about nuclear plants and utility companies than anyone in the house or on the beach, more than most journalists. Newspapers and magazines came to her for information about the industry, and she was never one to back down on a controversy. "We couldn't stop Seabrook. We'll stop Bellevane," she said intently.

"A few months, perhaps, but not permanently," I stated, not understanding her logic. "They put TMI back on line after the ass-wipes in the control room came close to blowing Pennsylvania into Mexico. Pilgrim's back on line. Bellevane will be just another moneymaker for the greedy."

"The people will stop it," said a determined Sylvia. "Even if they support nuclear power, they won't tolerate it in their back yards."

"Jobs," said Frank. "Repeat after me. Jobs trumps safety. Pure. Simple. Close the book."

Whether or not the Bellevane Steam Electric Plant, one of corporate America's better euphemisms, would be stopped was something we may have hoped for, but few would have seen as realistic. Now that Iraq was threatening to invade Kuwait, and with what looked like a military build-up in the Persian Gulf, all of a sudden "alternative energy" once again had become the prevalent rallying cry while Americans were forced to defend the Exxonization of the world. All of us were well aware that oil drives the American economy, and even Frank had grudgingly admitted that George Bush and his oil-slimed corporate buddies would eventually put us into a war just to guarantee our daily fix.

Except for Frank, the rest of us weren't convinced that nuclear energy, his "clean" energy, was the fix we needed. Nevertheless, in what we had hoped was the end of the "Me Generation," apathy didn't just run rampant, it had jet packs. And even if a few thousand protestors could convince a few million, it wasn't good enough. Who were they to convince? The Public Utilities Commission? The one headed by Debbie Jean Lynch, former nuclear engineer and vice-president for Pioneer Power & Energy? The protestors—even with truth, justice, and a few good journalists on their side—couldn't match even a fraction of the Pioneer Power publicity mill. And when the battles were over, the Pioneer Power campaign would be a case study in how to manipulate public opinion and the press. Nothing was going to change its destiny; in 20 years the protestors would be cumbersome footnotes. The $4 billion plant, with a 40-year lifespan, was close to going online, and had more approvals than a cheap whore at an Elks convention.

Two mountains of paperwork had gotten Bellevane this far; a few more hills would finish it. The NRC and other regulators would make Pioneer Power jump through a few more hoops and improve its plans for dealing with nuclear waste. But when all the acrobatics were over, there would still be a power plant in southwestern Massachusetts, pouring out turbine-driven millirems all day long, and the nuclear glow would show up in fish miles from the four cooling towers.

"Irradiated tamales from a defective microwave!" shouted Sam, bringing another rack of *noshes* into the living room, trailed by Bernie Abrahams and a case of cold beer. "Rewarmed by a thousand watts of microwave power. Eat one and you'll radiate energy all next week."

"You radiate any good will for *Century* on your tour?" asked Katy Chen, *Century*'s peripatetic promotion director. Surrounded by tamales and knishes, liver pâté and crackers, chips, dips, and barbecued chicken strips, fighting off Frank Mitchell's smoke and Ruth Weissmann's motherly concern for all of us—

"Eat! Eat! It'll make you healthy!"—I tried answering everyone's questions. No, I didn't have that much time to promote *Century*. Yes, I talked about *Century* at every stop. No, I don't know if anyone is going to buy a subscription. A few may even cancel theirs after meeting me. Yeah, I ran into a lot of comment about the June book, but all I could do was be polite and show concern for their half-assed statements. Yes, the *Today* show was fun. Yeah, I, too, wished they had given me more than six minutes.

More! They wanted more! "The seamy life of an author," Shane Kistler begged. With a beer in one hand and a kreplach in the other, I continued recounting some of the more memorable stops on the highway to fame, talking about the reporter who shook my hand and handed me a résumé, about the TV host who asked me three different times who my favorite radical journalist was, and of me changing the answer each time since I figured I didn't get it right the first time, about some broadcast journalists who didn't even read the book, of crowded subways and late planes, about a shower that didn't work and a heater that always did, about time schedules that were as based upon reality as an afternoon soap, about running station to station, newspaper to bookstore to dinner, smiling and pretending to be completely fresh. There was the 30 minutes in Washington in a taxi with a hack who left school in the ninth grade but managed to put his six children through college.

On the book tour were also Herald Square and City Lights Bookstore. In New York City, shortly after a book signing, I tried to talk with a bag lady, but she shooed me away. I tried to give her a few bucks, which she threw back at me. How was I supposed to know she was an undercover anything?! I had been in San Francisco a half dozen times during the 1960s, but only once managed to visit City Lights, home of writers, lost souls, and anyone looking for a group hug, mental stimulation, and a center for social justice. More than two decades later, at a building where North Beach and Chinatown merge, and where the bohemian and beat generations dissolved into the psychedelic hippie generation, I returned. Lawrence Ferlinghetti—former World War II sub-chaser commander who later earned a doctorate from the Sorbonne, and would become one of the most influential publishers and poets in America—co-founded City Lights with Peter D. Martin in 1953. Three years later, now sole owner, he published Allen Ginsberg's *Howl*, and became involved in one of the nation's most important First Amendment cases when authorities declared the book obscene. Ferlinghetti and store manager Shigeyoshi Murao won that case, and precedent was set.

Of course, I also had to talk about Sunday in the park, about a hundred or so booths and thousands of lookers, of non-profit hotdogs and a cheesy rock band, a jingoistic general carved in stone, and a peace-loving free spirit who could be the hook for a profile.

"A real flower child or just another sophomore who's lost her way?" Gretchen Peron playfully asked.

"When you go beyond the headband and funky sneaks, this one's for real."

"When you go beyond the headband and funky sneaks," Frank Mitchell suggested, tapping his no-wind watch to make sure the battery was still active, "you'll probably find a flake. Pot smoking, acid-high flake who paints her face and burns flags on weekends. Like, oh wow, man. Like this here anti-war movement is, like, oh wow, real groooovy." He took a puff on his cigar, almost choking Sylvia who, restraining herself, didn't shove the smuggled Havana up his nostrils, ash end first. "Ship her off to Hah-vahd," Frank mocked. "She'll fit in with all those other pointy-head Commies." A wrapped-in-the-flag conservative on a staff of what he knew were knee-jerk bleeding heart liberals, Frank never forgave Harvard for admitting W.E.B. DuBois— although it was almost 20 years before he became head of the NAACP and a progressive labor leader, and decades before he became an apologist for Stalin and the Soviet Union—and Frank couldn't have been admitted to Harvard even as a specimen. O.K., so Frank and I never got along; you try running an editorial staff when the business manager forces you to get his approval for everything from 3-by-5 cards to computer systems.

Frank was just the enforcer; the restraints were Sam's, a lesson he learned from *Ramparts*, a lesson Sam never wanted repeated at *Century*. For 13 years, beginning in 1962, *Ramparts* leaped from small insignificant counterculture rag to the major voice of the New Left. With advertising and circulation revenue pouring into its San Francisco headquarters, the magazine still spent itself into more than a $6 million deficit. Even with new management, it never recovered from its own excesses, from a few bad editorial decisions, and limped into its last five years, dying with the death of the anti-war protest movement. Sam, who had written for *Ramparts*, and occasionally benefited from some of the outrageous expenses, periodically reminded us of the lessons from *Ramparts*, and why *Century* would always pay well, treat its staff and readers well, but fly us coach not first class. We understood. We didn't blame Sam for our inconvenience; Frank was the easier target.

"Like, Frank," I countered, "she speaks better English than you do, y'know, man."

"Probably figuring out a way to dupe you into joining her cell," Frank mumbled sarcastically. "Suppose she drives a beat-up VW bus with 'Flower Power' painted on the sides."

"'81 Chevette. White."

"Ahhh. White for purity. White for innocence."

With Frank, we never knew how much was real and how much was put-on. But, what we did know was that in a sea of liberals, he kept us from drowning in our smug self-righteous need to save the world.

"What do you make of her?" asked Karlen Aroian, slowly drawing another puff from his Meerschaum pipe filled with whiskey Borkum-Riff, his antidote to cigar smoke. "Another washed-out over-aged starry-eyed hippie unable to adjust to a new world?"

"Could be," I replied. "I peg her as a free spirit. Just wanders in and out whenever it's comfortable. Pops up here. Pops up there. Does what she wants when she wants. Probably an over-age hippie trapped by her dreams."

"Overage like 30? Or overage like 60?" Sylvia wondered.

"Overage like late 30s, maybe early 40s. Hard to tell."

"But she looks 30!" Bernie Abrahams suddenly cut in, drawing amused smiles from the 20 or so people in the living room.

"You *met* her?" Sylvia asked, suddenly turning back to Bernie, her half full Bud Lite gripped firmly in her left hand almost knocking him from his own grip on a munchies platter.

"Nah, David—Hey, watch my tamales! They're the only ones I have!—told me at lunch Friday."

"*David* told you she looked 30?"

"No, that she had a great bod."

"Oh, *David* said she had a great bod," said Sylvia, twisting in my direction, again almost knocking Bernie out cold, focusing her eyes upon my sexist discomfort.

Now, Bernie is the magazine's production director and my best friend—a loud-mouthed manipulative best friend, but a best friend, nevertheless. And Sylvia—well, Sylvia and I go back a long way.

"Tell us about the weekend you spent with her," said Bernie energetically, suddenly causing Sylvia to swing back in his direction, but this time, he had outsmarted her; the munchie platter was in his left hand, his body jealously guarding the booty. It didn't help. Sylvia's left arm accidentally hit his right arm, and Newton's Third Law of Motion put the chips onto the floor. The Amazing Abrahams, so named because he never stopped amazing us with his ability to manipulate the printing and distribution industries, quickly recovered; Sylvia didn't.

"You spent a weekend with her?" asked Sylvia.

"It wasn't a weekend. She drove me to Philly—"

"She *drove* you to Philly?"

"Yeah, Sylvia, she *drove* me to Philly. Turned in the Rental, saved some bucks, paid for her gas, and she drove me south. Showed me around the city."

"That *all* she show you?" Dawn Kavanaugh, a 25-year-old temptress currently in disguise as an advertising account executive, seductively suggested, making sure Sylvia caught every microscopic innuendo. Dawn was barely into elementary school when Sam first created *Century*, and could only gets ads from bands that were in the process of transitioning from the club scene, from lonely souls whose personals dominated the Classifieds, or from strip clubs which lured those lonely souls into a fantasy world they would never enter. Two decades later, full-page color ads from everything from Cleveland Amory's Fund for Animals (which always received substantial off-the-rate card discounts) to perfume manufacturers (as long as they didn't use animals in their testing) shoved the music and personals into smaller, less costly, but more sexy alternatives. Some of us wondered just how much more advertising Sam could have gotten and how much faster *Century* would have developed had Dawn been there at the beginning. But, it was Dawn who was at the center of the staff's probing eyes.

"Dawn have a point?" asked Sylvia. "Something more there than you're telling us?"

"It's just a story," I shrugged, trying to be cool under a mini-spotlight. "Nothing more."

"A throw-away for us, or a major feature?"

"Don't know. May start out as a feature, then—"

"Then a book!" I don't remember who said it, but it was on everyone's mind.

"Maybe. It'd be a good follow-up to *Revolution*."

"Ahh, those TV lights and book signings. Sucks you out of that anonymity of being an editor." That one, I *do* remember who said it.

"No, Frank, it just seems like a good subject that could develop further."

"That's it, just use us and abuse us," Sylvia semi-playfully suggested.

"Not it at all," I semi-defensively responded. May not work out. May not even be worth a short."

"But, it *could* be a book," suggested one of the voices.

"Yeah, could be. Depends on what I find out."

"Why her?" asked Lil Cuellar, one of our freelance photo journalists. "There's still a few free spirits around. Go to Cambridge. Go to Amherst. Go see any of the revivals of *Hair*."

"Anti-war feel-good hippie B.S.!" We ignored Frank's mumbled comment, knowing he often interjected comments he didn't even believe just to stimulate discussion.

"What Lil's asking," Karlen Aroian tried explaining, "is why is she special? Why is she worth the ink?"

"How should I know?"

"Then why waste the time?"

"Because there's something there."

"Because maybe there's nothing there." Sylvia was back on the attack.

"Maybe the story is that she lived through the past couple of decades, saw everything that happened, and while all of us changed, she didn't."

"She doesn't change?" asked Sylvia caustically. "You're going to sell me a half-baked story about a one-dimensional Flower Girl in the eye of a social vortex, and she's unchanged? You have to show change. The lit-crits will burn you if you don't show change."

"The story might be simply that in a world of change, she's seen it all and is the one who didn't change. That could be the most important element."

"You have to show development. Editors like development," said Dahn St. Michaels, half-erudite, half-puckish. "Critics can be harsh if you don't rip open her soul and reveal—"

"Sex!" Dawn Kavanaugh called out. "Every story must have sexual tension. Will she? Won't she? Does she? Who with? How many times? How many ways?"

"Could be asexual," I noted. "You don't need sex to tell a story." Five wadded napkins from different parts of the room came at me. "OK, so maybe *some* sex."

"Lots of sex!" Dawn Kavanaugh shouted. "Readers demand it. Critics love it. Just keep pumping those sexual references over and over and over!"

"And make it visual," added Gretchen Peron. "That'll guarantee a book sale because it'll lead to a movie. Publishers don't want words. They want graphic visuals. You need sex."

"And conflict!" shouted Bernie Abrahams. "Have to show conflict. Coming soon to a theater near you, David Ascher's steamy epic of *The Flower Child Versus the Establishment*. Fully developed for your erotic stimulation."

I flipped off his comment, while trying to dignify my story. "I'll go where the facts lead me."

"A long and winding road," Dawn half-sang.

Karlen Aroian weighed in with professorial logic. "The facts may lead you to the reality that the strongest people are those who are influenced by others, who influence others, but retain their own identify, their own values."

I weighed in with my own observance. "Maybe the story is that it's easy to be liberal and care about social issues when everyone around you is pretending to be liberal, but damn hard to actually *be* liberal when everyone around you wants to return to the glory years of Ike and Studebakers." My staff wasn't about to let me alone.

"Did she do it in a Studebaker?"

"Did she do it with Ike?"

"Did she do it with green eggs and ham?"

"Was Ike in the Studebaker?"

"Did it with Kay Summersby during the war, but that was probably in a Jeep."

"Maybe the story," I noted, uncommonly serious, "is really about someone who in the face of great adversity still retains her passion for life and exploration while we all went establishment."

"Well, not *all* of us," Sylvia sniffed.

"Oh, come on," Frank challenged, brushing cigar ashes from the front of his shirt. "You're drawing a weekly check just like the rest of us. You put down the business operations and ad reps, but you're still Establishment. Managing editor on one of the country's better publications. Not just one of the writers, but an *editor*. You boss people around. You're planning to take over David's job, maybe even Sam's some day if you don't jump back to the *Times*. You live in a Back Bay apartment, drive a cute red Triumph, lust after those $5 million condos on Lewisburg Square, jet off to Club Med and write it off as research. Sounds establishment to me."

"Bullshit!"

"That's it? Big time editor, and all you can say is *bullshit?*"

"Bullshit, *asshole!*" She said it with a half-twisting smile, but if Sam hadn't accidentally sprayed himself with a newly opened beer, much to the applause and laughter of the rest of us, Sylvia might have gone upside Frank's head.

"As you get older, you lose some of that fire and individualism," said Sam, wiping his face with a paper napkin he grabbed from the table. "America exacts a tremendous price because it forces conformity in order to uphold the concept of the classless society." He was serious, and I was gleefully contemplating how Radical Sam in his Hawaiian shirt and chinos, who had a long history of activism, who had been fired from one newspaper and removed as a Guild officer in 1954 for being a socialist, could ever be establishment. "Your story," asked Sam, "it will explain this, maybe? You will show us our own selves, maybe? You will maybe record life and history and social problems?" He paused a moment. "But first we have questions."

Sam and his questions! Socrates never asked as many questions as Sam—and few had as much insight. "We—all of us, I think—we're the editor. We are you. And you"—he said it with a grin even Lewis Carroll could not have plastered onto his Cheshire Cat—"you are the writer. Your story, you are ready to defend it, maybe?" Before me flashed the images of Custer at Little Big Horn. No, I didn't want to be Custer. Chief Joseph surrounded by the army. Right kind of person, wrong kind of result. The Egyptian Air Force in 1967. Get positive. Dunkirk. Not positive enough. David and Goliath? Daniel in the Lion's den, The Lion in Winter, the Winter of Our Discontent . . .

"David! . . . You with us?"

"Could you please rephrase that, Sam?"

"You want another beer, David? You've been sucking air the last couple of minutes."

From throughout the room came a swarm of questions. *Where does she live?* Harrisburg. Maybe somewhere near Harrisburg. *Where?* I don't know. *Didn't she say?* Maybe. I don't remember. *If you don't know where she lives, how you gonna find her?* I'll find her. *Ever used drugs? She use them now? Pot? Acid? Coke? Pepsi?* I don't know. She didn't take any shit while I was around. *One of them McCarthyites?* No, Frank, that was me. She worked for Bobby. *She know Manson? He was a hippie.* Frank, that was two decades ago, and only the establishment media thought he was a hippie. *She in the SLA? Know Patty Hearst? The Weather Underground?* I doubt it, Frank; her world is peace and love, not violence. *What about violence? She ever throw tacks on the streets? Molotov cocktails?* Yeah, Frank; said something about your house late tonight. *She involved in the love-ins? Woodstock?* Don't know, Bernie. Wasn't there. *She believe in free love?* How the hell do I know! *Ever married?* Don't know. Could have been. Maybe didn't believe in marriage. *She believe in children?* Don't know. Said something about a kid. *What?* Just in passing. *What in passing?* Something. Maybe she just said she took care of kids. Wanted to take care of kids. Maybe that's why the school. *What school?* Said she was planning to build a school for peace. *A what?* A school for peace. She's got this idea that people need to learn about peace and— *David, does insanity run in your family?* It's a good idea. We teach war, but we don't teach peace. *Quakers do.* Don't know if they're involved in this or not. Mentions them, but doesn't talk about funding. *Where's she gonna get the bread? Gonna 'loose change' the neighborhood?—Grant from the Defense Department?* She's been saving for it. *Where's this free love school gonna be?* It's not a free love school, Frank. *O.K., so where does she plan to put this Hah-vahd of Tranquility?* On the Susquehanna, up in northeastern Pennsylvania. *She a licensed teacher?* I don't know. *She ever teach?* Don't know that. *Where'd she go to school?* She talked about Berkeley and Penn State. *She graduate?* I don't even know if she enrolled. *War protestor?* Yeah. *Where? When?* She mentioned Chicago. *SDS? Yippie?* I think so. Has the kind of playful mind the Yippies would have loved.

Anything else? Lots of time in California. Frisco. Delano. *Grapes?* Said she took pix for the Farm Workers. *Published?* Said something about the alternative papers. Does a lot of freelance work. *Flack? Hack?* Hardly. *See any of her pix?* No, but she's good. *How do you know she's any good?* Instinct. *Instinct?* Yeah, instinct. She knows photography. I think she was involved in a lot of the shit from the '60s, early '70s. *She know any of the Movement's leaders? Hoffman? Rubin? Krassner? Paley? Could she provide insights into their personalities?* Don't know. I'm not doing a profile of the leaders, even the dead ones. *From the sounds of it, not enough to do a retrospective either. Enough insight to understand her personal development over the years?* Don't know. *What* do *you know?* Enough. *Enough?* Enough to get started. *What the hell did you talk about all weekend?* It wasn't all weekend, it was— *O.K., don't get hostile; so what'd you discuss?* Movies. *Movies? You talked about movies?* That and the environment. She also likes Chinese food. *Just Chinese?* That's what we had Sunday night.

"You spent a weekend with her and you don't know shit!" said Sylvia.

"I *didn't* spend a weekend with her."

"O.K., so you *didn't* spend a weekend with her, and you still don't know shit."

"It's locked up inside of her, but it's all there."

"O.K., David, we believe you," said Sylvia, a trace of smile trying to hide eyes that were drilling into what once was a relationship. "Let's say there's substance there. How do you know she's got anything our readers want?"

"I just have this feeling."

"*Feeling*, David?"

"Yeah, *feeling*. We sent writers out with advances on story ideas that were less than this."

"Sure, David, but you're no I.F. Stone or Truman Capote." Sylvia had, in a few moments, cut the fun and challenge from the roasting; others had squirmed uncomfortably, a few trying to calm her down or turn the questioning into friendly territory, but it was Sam who interrupted.

"You tell her you're doing an article about the hippies?"

"Not yet."

"Why not?"

"I don't want to scare her off; maybe get false readings from her as she adjusts to the spotlight."

"Shouldn't you tell her?"

"Yeah."

"So when?"

"Soon."

"You should tell her."

"I know."

"David," said Sam, "You're in some kind of journalistic fog."

"I'll get it together."

"O.K., all you surfers and hodads, it's party time!" And with that, Sam grabbed Sylvia from the couch, and boogied out to the patio to the incessant pulsating beat of the Surfaris' "Wipe Out!" on the tape deck.

10/

Glazed Eyes Penetrating a Soul

by David Ascher

Her eyes were glassy, her voice slurred. She was strung out on something, but no one knew what. It could have been acid or pot, mescaline or peyote. It didn't really matter; she was on her own trip, wandering aimlessly from table to table in a luncheonette near Golden Gate Park, showing a paperback photo book to freak and tourist, to whomever would interrupt their own trips long enough to listen to whatever she was saying in this Summer of Love.

"I love you," this hippie girl-woman tells everyone as she wanders among the tables. "Peace is love. Love is peace." Most gawk, but what else can you expect in Haight–Ashbury? Sometimes, she spends only a few seconds at a table; sometimes, a couple of minutes. Two men maliciously tease her, making lewd suggestions, which she answers with, "I wish you peace." But others just ignore her, as they swat her off like the pest she is. Just a stoned hippie on a Friday afternoon, and they're important people with important things to do. But first they have to stare, to remember what they have seen, to let others know that they bravely wandered deep into the bowels of another culture, observing but never understanding.

Throughout the Haight–Ashbury section of San Francisco, signs proclaim, "Haight is Love." The hippies believe if they can spread enough love they can change America's direction. For hippies, love and drugs are a liberating force, something they say breaks down barriers to give them new ways to look at life, new colors and new patterns to understand. Their drug philosophy is Biblical, they say, slyly quoting from *Genesis*—"Let the Earth bring forth grass."

Drugs don't come cheap in Haight–Ashbury, but they're all over, and it's almost impossible to go anywhere in "the Haight" without the ubiquitous sweet aromas of the *cannabis* plant permeating your senses. Hashish, better known as hash, is put into foods or smoked like marijuana, which originates from the same plant but is less powerful. A marijuana cigarette—a "toke," a "roach," held together by a roach clip, something similar to a sweater clip—can cost a buck, but most buy a "lid," an ounce of marijuana—weed, pot, maryjane, hemp, boo—for a few dollars and roll their own, just like the cowboys of the Old West. But unlike the cowboys, hippies identify more with the Indians, an oppressed tribal people who lived and shared in communal settings and, against the nation's racist prejudices executed by the U.S. Cavalry, just "wanted to do their own thing."

One of those things was peyote, a cactus-derived mind-altering drug that the cowboys and the Army banned from the reservations, while cowboys and businessmen forced alcohol, a more "civilized" form of waste, upon them. Hippies don't use booze, a depressant, for they believe that drugs should be used to expand one's mind not retard it. For that reason, only about a half-dozen bars survive in the district.

Although there's peyote in the area that journalist Hunter S. Thompson calls "Hashbury," the hippies prefer to complement hash and marijuana with psychotropic drugs packaged in a rainbow of colors, and with LSD—usually known as "acid" or "the mind detergent." Sometimes they use methamphetamine— "speed"—a powerful stimulant that has often led its users into exploring new vistas of hospital emergency rooms. None of the buyers really know what's on the sugar cubes or papers. It could be acid, meth, or even water. Sometimes, it makes little difference—the buyers get high no matter what they inhale or lick. A 250 milligram tab of acid, the usual dose, can cost as much as $5, but these flower children of peace will share what they have, whether it's drugs, food, clothing, or ideas. And, when they mischievously say they will put acid in the city's drinking water reservoirs so they can share the experience of life with the uptight establishment, to help them become free of their inhibitions, the uptight establishment does what the hippies expect— it freaks out, and the media exuberantly spend their headlines on the terror that could take over the city. California is the first state to criminalize possession of LSD, but the hippies don't notice the fine lines of legality

Like many of the hippies on this sunny August afternoon, she was barefoot, wearing clothes of a psychedelic rainbow, a day-glo linen headband of reds, oranges, and yellows which kept her unkempt black hair from falling entirely on her eyes, a pair of faded and torn jeans, an equally well-worn and faded blouse of yellows and greens. She wore no bra, and when the sun came through the naked window and hit her just right, it was possible to see an outline of her breasts. If she was aware of it, it probably meant nothing to her. Many would call her a "loose woman." For some, recreational drugs and recreational sex are just part of a lifestyle of freedom.

A Polaroid Swinger and a brass peace symbol hung from a leather strand around her neck, the camera in flagrant contrast to her clothes, which she could have picked up for free at the Diggers store.

The Diggers—many of them actors, artists, and musicians—are the hippies' social workers, providing free food, clothes, and spiritual help for the several hundred thousand teens and young adults who believe Timothy Leary's gospel of "tune in, turn on, and drop out," joined his recently-formed League for Spiritual Discovery, and ran off, penniless and homeless, to find their own nirvana in San Francisco, home of the notorious Barbary Coast, of the illicit North Beach, and now of psychedelic Haight–Ashbury.

What had become a deteriorating crime-ridden 40 block slum primarily of Victorian-era houses has been transformed by "love power" into a relatively safe haven for hippies and residents. Safe, that is, unless you trip over a dirt-caked hippie wasted by acid, writhing on the street, or you're pushed and shoved by one of the thousands of "rubber-neckers," tourists who come to gawk at the hippies, their cars and Gray Line tour buses now blocking the streets of Haight–Ashbury. In one of the more ironic twists of this movement, it's the gawkers who mostly bring cocaine and heroin into the area. Few have come to San Francisco to hear the poetry of Allen Ginsberg, high priest from the early 1950s; even fewer have come as followers of

Hillel, the first century prophet of modesty and peace. A few parents with pictures of their children desperately walk the streets, asking if anyone has seen their children. But compared to everyone else, they are but a small part of the masses. Most have come to Haight–Ashbury as sightseers. That includes students, business executives, and cops. The area is swarming with every kind of cop from almost every kind of jurisdiction— local cops, Highway Patrol, FBI, IRS, Treasury, and even the Army and CIA. Uniformed and obvious; undercover and not so obvious. All of them are looking for drugs and anti-war activity among a young counterculture that wants freedom and peace, a counterculture that can often spot undercover cops yet treat them as a necessary part of their society.

To those who believe appearance is the equivalent of the soul, innumerable shops will sell $25 sandals made from tires, $5 headbands, $20 wigs or, for $67.50, an economy model hippie costume, consisting of pants, shirt, vest, headband, and trinket-cheap peace symbol—person extra. The prices have become so outrageous that the hippies no longer can afford the clothes, and wear whatever is available at the Goodwill. Most can no longer afford the $3.50 admission to the Avalon Ballroom or Bill Graham's Fillmore, places where high decibel acid-rock from amped-up electric guitars can fry your brain every weekend, places where the yo-yos go because they can afford it—and that's where they think they're supposed to be on a weekend, listening to the the Fugs, the Jefferson Airplane, and the Grateful Dead.

To earn money, the hippies, thousands of whom had come to San Francisco with little cash and no health insurance, work in myriad "non-establishment" jobs—as artists drawing sketches for tourists, as silk screeners making prints for tourists, as poets selling hand-inscribed poems to tourists, and as musicians, whose instrument cases are always open for the loose change from tourists. And, they work in one vast bureaucracy.

The U.S. Post Office may soon find itself taken over by hippies; they score well on civil service exams, and find nothing degrading about sorting or delivering mail. For its own part, some very tolerant post office supervisors say little about the long hair, beards, or even the modified regulation "blues."

"Would you like to see my . . . my . . . *book*," she said, fumbling for just the right word. "It's a book of photographs. It reveals . . . *people*." She showed me the book, a slick softcover photobook, maybe 64 pages, 8-1/2 by 11, opening horizontal. "I took these pictures. They tell a story. Do you want to know a story?" She waited patiently while I reluctantly nodded. "A story. A story about people who are oppressed. It's about people who are—" she shouted out— *"exploited!"* The black-and-white photos were clear—somehow you'd expect psychedelic fog—and told the story of the migrant farm workers of California and of their struggles. "The book is only three ninety-five," she said. "That is not too much to help the people, is it?" she asked. "All the . . . *All* the money . . . Every *nickel* of the money . . . *All* of it goes to the Cause." For a few minutes we talked about the migrant farm workers, of the two days I had spent with them on a march more than a year ago, of the six months she spent living with them, of the two or three or four decades they had spent in substandard housing as they moved from farm to farm, chasing the sun.

It's not common for hippies to become involved in the political struggles against oppression. Most hippies are apolitical, unbothered by the establishment, possessing and passing along "warmth," yet trying to become a "vanguard of a newer way of life," one that allows a world of peace and light and love. In contrast to the Beat Generation's world of black, white, and shades of gray, the hippies believe in a psychedelic rainbow world that is reflected in their clothing, art, and even their living spaces. Hippies often put down the beatniks of the '50s as too negative, while espousing their own philosophy of a positive outlook, one that reduces conflict. In the past couple of months, the world gave the hippies every opportunity to become political, but most just dropped more acid, expanded their minds, and preached love. When Biafra seceded from Nigeria, May 30, a few hippies seemed concerned; most just "floated along." When Israel struck hard at Arab lands, June 5, in what became a "six-day war," the hippies just "floated along." When China exploded its first H-bomb, June 17, the hippies just "floated." A couple of miles from Golden Gate Park, several hundred thousand Americans were "processed" before they were shipped to Vietnam—and the hippies, preaching love and peace, just "float along." Poverty? Unemployment? *Love will conquer*, these hippies say. *Watch us. Emulate us. We will bring you the future*, they say in their drug-induced nirvana.

But in this counterculture of love, with its hard-driving music underscore that allows sitars to harmonize with electric guitars, has been a growing and far more militant concern for the greater social issues. Until love does conquer, the revolution must be fought, many believe. The Vietnam War. Injustice. Poverty. Worker exploitation. Mankind's assault upon the environment. And for civil rights. Some hippies had been in Alabama and Mississippi to help Negroes register, helping them fight for the rights every citizen is assured but not always given. Led by Jack Weinberg, Mario Savio, and dozens of others, they tried to liberate Berkeley during the beginnings of the Free Speech Movement, only to be arrested for exercising their Constitutional rights; freedom of expression is one of the most important freedoms they cherish, a freedom that is slowly being dissolved by an über-patriotism of support for the war in Vietnam, of a nation that has been convinced that if Vietnam falls, the dominoes would fall until Iowa becomes a Communist state. And so the more militant of the hippies march; they protest; they sometimes get in your face. But most of all, they live the life they preach, helping others while, they hope, helping mankind.

"The key to being a good photographer is to have a good eye," she suddenly said, enunciating every syllable as she took the book from my hands, fumbled and dropped it, and then clumsily fell to the floor to pick it up. She probably would have tried to finish the conversation from there had I not helped her up, and put her on a chair. In college, I had helped friends who became drunk from nearly drowning in cheap booze; I didn't enjoy it then, I didn't enjoy it now, but this was a person who found her own drug of choice and in her own way was recording life.

"They wanted to take a picture of me for the back cover," she said, her glazed blue eyes millimeters from my weary hazel ones, "but I said that . . . I said . . . Do you know that you have nice eyes? Eyes are keys to the soul. You have a pretty soul." Before I could answer, she continued. "I like my eyes," she slurred, "Maybe they should have taken a picture of my eyes." Perhaps once she had pretty eyes, perhaps she'll again have pretty eyes. But now her eyes were glazed, a faraway look penetrating her soul.

"I want to be a photographer and I want to take photographs." She thought a moment, her mind clouded by confusion. "No, that is not right. I *am* a photographer. Yes, I *am* a photographer. I talk with the world through my photographs, and I hold up a mirror and see within people, and capture them so others can see the happiness, and the pain . . . and the suffering. All the suffering. All the pain. I want them to see what they have done . . ." Her thoughts wandered off, a tear dropping in mid-sentence.

For three ninety-five I bought a photo book and helped *La Causa*.

"Our spirits shall be as one, and we shall form a bond with the mother of the universe," she said, stuffing the money into her camera bag.

"Perhaps we'll meet again," I said vacuously.

"Groovy!" she said, snapping a picture of me at the table. "I'll keep this picture. You can't buy it." And with that, she left—sort of. "Would you like to take my picture?" she asked a salesman–tourist at a table near the door. When he paid the one dollar "sitting fee," she sat on his lap, gave her Polaroid to his dining companion, another salesman-type, and smiled. *Click*. For another dollar, she traded laps. *Click*.

In restaurants and luncheonettes, in Golden Gate Park, on the streets of San Francisco, hippies are trying to spread their messages of love, while the tourists are taking pictures for scrapbooks.

"May you go in peace," she said, leaving the necktie-stained "glad-to-see-you" salesmen with mementos of a Friday afternoon at the end of another week trying to boost some company's product, while this hippie, this activist in a world being torn apart by hate, greed, and injustice, walked out the door of the luncheonette, and back into Golden Gate Park, into the world's largest picnic, in this, the Summer of Love, a celebration of life.

11/

Patriotic Dreams

She drove into the parking lot of the one-room shack known as a bus station a little after 3 p.m., the afternoon of the Fourth, parked her car, locked her photo equipment in the trunk, waited for me to arrive about a half hour later, greeted me, put my luggage into the trunk, and said she was ready for the parade.

There were, maybe, 15,000 people at the moment, a nice cross-section of America waiting this Wednesday afternoon for a parade. Every year, for the past 70 years, Newburg, Pennsylvania, a rural community of about 13,000 people living in what had become an economically depressed area of the northeastern part of the state, has had a parade. Through wars and peace, depression and prosperity. Every July Fourth. Every year. For 70 years. And always at 4 p.m., a little after the hottest part of the summer's day. The elders of the community say it was because the first parade was on a Sunday, and the organizers wanted to make sure everyone had enough time to go to church, and then dress down for the afternoon parade, picnic, games, and fireworks. Others believe it was to give the cooks enough time to prepare the chicken barbeque. And others say they wanted people to become so hungry in anticipation that they would spend even more for food in the evening. But, everyone believes it's so no one became too tired and went home before spending their money on the food and games, and then stayed late enough to see fireworks. No matter what the reasons, today's parade and carnival were being held on a hot, humid, and most unpleasant muggy day.

Along Market Street, with its eclectic mix of shops, stores,

110

and boutiques fighting extinction from the mall about 15 miles away, were corporate executives who, in the spirit of the revolution, drove their own Buicks and BMWs to the parade; the marginally-employed who were fighting to make monthly payments on their ten-year-old Chevys and Fords; the unemployed who helped maximize profits by becoming suddenly redundant and then obsolete; teachers and plumbers; secretaries, lawyers, and ministers; and all kinds of children who don't know what life is about to do to them.

But for now, they'll watch a parade and then take over the 52 acre town park to continue their celebration at a carnival, dinner, and patriotic foot-tapping, show-stopping music, topped off by a 15-minute fireworks show sponsored by the Newburg Lions Club. They'll all be there. Corporate executives and the unemployed; gold-chained Yuppies and a funky-sneak former flower child. Standing, sitting in foldable lawn chairs or on curbs, cheering, laughing, and enjoying life together this Fourth of July. And once again, the media can report that America, which had long ago forgotten what the revolution was all about, is well and celebrating yet another anniversary.

A few days ago, Apryl had called. "Can a credit union just up and commit suicide?" she asked. I explained there were state and federal regulations that would prevent that. "Then why did they allow mine to do so?" she asked. With a lot of patient questioning—Apryl's mind doesn't always follow a natural or logical progression—I learned that her father had secretly deeded her a 40-acre parcel of timberland along the Susquehanna in northeastern Pennsylvania, made monthly payments, and hoped to give his daughter something she could finally hold onto. It was his intent to pay off the mortgage and then give her the land. But it came with an albatross legally known as a right of reversion. Within five years after he formally gave Apryl possession of the land, she would be required to establish a business. If she couldn't, title would revert to the Susquehanna Valley Workshop, a rehab program of which he was executive director. Things might have worked out as he wished had he not died and left 38 monthly payments instead of clear title. The insurance money went to her stepmother who went to the Bahamas to get over her grief. Innumerable people innumerable times advised Apryl to challenge the will, to modify, annul, or skirt the provisions, but it was her father's wish, and she would carry it out, so now she had to worry about not only paying off the land but also finally creating a school for peace, which she had been thinking about for almost two decades.

The Susquehanna Valley People's Federal Credit Union refinanced the loan, giving her a full five years, not 38 months, to pay it off and meet the now-extended right of reversion clause. Not as concerned with money as she was in bringing happiness to the world, Apryl managed to be late with the payments not just every now and then but just about every month, skipping a month here, a month there. Now and then she received a polite reminder from the credit union; a letter, a phone call. "We understand," they said. "Please try to get us even a partial payment," they suggested, sometimes stronger than at other times. With less than year before it would return to the Workshop, but with a refinanced deed, Apryl was almost five months behind on the monthly payments, with little hope for building her school.

Had not the National Credit Union Administration become involved, Apryl would still be paying off the loan on a "whenever" basis, and getting that five year grace period to build a business. But government has a genetic code to screw up lives, so it looked at the credit union along the Susquehanna, declared that it was getting too large for its members' own best interest, that it had too much of its assets in investments, and in so doing had committed some minor violations of two ambiguous regulations. It said nothing about any problem with outstanding loans, and ordered it to be absorbed by a larger credit union in Philadelphia that was cash-short at the moment. *Poof.* Just like that. No appeal; no recourse.

In less than a month, the Gray Suits in Auditing at Metropolitan Federal Credit Union noticed a record of Apryl's irregular payments. As Gray Suits are wont to do, they considered such a breach of monetary ethics to be of catastrophic proportions. But because they were with a credit union not a bank, they only politely scolded her for her transgressions; still, they made sure she knew she needed to become current in her loan. They even gave her a couple of months to catch up. They suggested she might get a loan—well, *they* couldn't give her any more money for a loan, but *someone* might, maybe a relative or friend, or maybe one of those storefront money stores. Gray Suits, even if they're employed by member-owned credit unions, don't have much sense of reality. So, Apryl made another plea, and the Gray Suits had a final offer—she could sell the land. That one stung most, since those acres of wildlife and timber and a creek that flowed into the Susquehanna were a part of her school, the one where she would teach peace and happiness, the arts and sciences, if only she could save enough money to get it started. So, she made three payments on the land, leaving her savings account with an anemic $195.42.

The rest of the hour on the phone, we chatted about parks and crafts shows, of music and alternative lifestyles—with me making sketchy notes, trying to capture her thoughts and language. When I asked how I could get back in touch with her, to see if I could help her with the new credit union, she just said she'd find me.

On the afternoon of June 29, sometime between when the copy machine broke down and yet another writer called asking for more expense money, Apryl called. I wasn't too surprised to hear from her, always assuming she'd pop up again. *Since you're going to be in Philadelphia anyhow*, she said—I assumed my secretary had said I was going to be out of town on the 3rd—*and since you're going to be in the neighborhood*—Philly was "only" a couple of hours away—*how about getting together awhile— that is, unless you have something else planned.* I hadn't.

Joyce, my ex-, who occasionally felt a need to show up on one or two holidays a year—guilt I assumed, pity she probably felt—was in Seattle with whomever her latest was. Sylvia, who helped me forget Joyce, was in Cleveland. Even mellifluous and sexually-seductive Joanie, she of lithe body and long legs, was with family in Kansas City, a stay-over before touching down in L.A. where, as an account executive for Bernard, Shepherd, and Golden, or some such ad agency, she would be schmoozing Schwab Industries, a Fortune 500 company that got its start selling multi-flavored Pet Choice.

Joyce, Sylvia, and Joanie weren't on my mind when Apryl called. *Come to Newburg and we'll go to a parade*, she suggested. *Come to Boston*, I answered, *and we'll spend the day at the Harbor Fest.* I figured I could meet her in Philadelphia and fly back to Boston. *No*, she said, *how about a celebration outside Boston, somewhere in the rural heart of America where there won't be as many people?* Why not Boston, I suggested. *Harbor cruises; annual turn-around of the U.S.S. Constitution; historic waterfront walking tours; Boston Pops concert on the Esplanade, with one great fireworks show afterwards. The spirit of America, said she, was not just in Boston or Philadelphia but in all the little towns, and that's where she intended to be this July 4th.* I had little desire to return to the land of stoned generals, polka bands, and nonprofit hotdogs, but that's where I was this Fourth of July, with every intent to help Apryl and to pursue my story.

In a tie-dyed day-glo T-shirt, a backdrop for a leather-and-brass peace symbol, faded jeans, lilac-and-white high-top checkered rainbow-laced sneaks, oversized silver and turquoise earrings and psychedelic headband, Apryl caused more than one person to take a second look. That in itself was strange since all around us were strangely-costumed people about to get onto floats or march in the parade—twirlers in gold lamé, and musicians in costumes imitating Spanish conquistadors; Cub Scouts and Boy Scouts, Brownies and Girl Scouts; the 4-H and the FFA; volunteer firemen, clowns, and Shriners who thought they were Arabian genies; fake Indians in Revlon war paint that was melting to reveal pink cheeks on their blond bodies; and imitation cowboys whose closest experience to the Old West was grabbing a cold beer from an old Westinghouse. Hundreds held small American flags; dozens wore blouses, shirts, or headbands of stars and stripes; several had American flag patches on their jeans. Two decades earlier, these flag-wearers would have been called anti-war traitors who showed not one whit of respect for what millions believed was the symbol of America; now, they're patriots. In the crowd were razor-cut lawyers wearing denim blue Osh Kosh bib overalls, a few blue-haired grandmothers, and a plethora of peroxided and mascaraed housewives wearing pedal-pushers. But, it was Apryl who drew stares. That's why I had to do her story. By finding out who she is, to learn about and then report what happened to the hippies' dreams of peace and love, I might be able to help others to better understand their own lives. In a world more than two decades removed from the cultural uprising of the '60s, Apryl seemed to be out of place, an alien caught in a time warp who never adjusted nor seemed to care what others thought, working only to spread her hopes for love and peace.

Sirens crawling at three miles an hour led what was to be a 90 minute parade of innumerable politicians, clowns, and horses;

antique fire trucks and tractors; more than three dozen floats, all of them built on flatbed trucks, decorated and populated by three dozen civic and fraternal organizations; the American Legion drill team, a VFW rifle squad, bayonets flashing in the sun; Miss Lydia's Junior Girls Drill Team, seven rows of 4-, 5-, and 6-year-olds dressed in red, white, and blue sparkle, carrying small wooden white rifles with gold trim; nine marching bands, their banners and bass drums pounding their names into the minds of Independence Day Rural America, most of whom politely clapped their passage, while one overage hippie clapped, laughed, and danced to their music, even dragging me on a two-block journey while she followed a high school band from Bloomsburg. It made no difference whether it was a march, a polka, or "Lady of Spain" rendered unconscious by Johnny Cavaletti's All-American Accordion Band seated in the bed of a pickup truck, Apryl felt the spirit of the music, and was an active participant. But when Cub Scout Pack 32 marched by, singing camp songs, I tried to envision Apryl as a den mother.

"What's so funny, David?"

"Nothing," I lied.

"Why are journalists so secretive?"

"*Me*? Secretive? What about you? How long would you have gone without even telling me you owned land for your school? Or that you were having financial difficulty? Or would even have called me?"

"Maybe never. There was no guarantee we'd see each other again. Besides, the taxes are paid."

"Great," I sighed. "But what does that have to do with why I'm here or with the credit union?"

"Every year I pay the taxes. My father always said that no matter what the deed says, the land belongs to the people, and that taxes are a form of rent to help the people."

"So, what's with the credit union?" I asked, trying to get her to stick with one issue at a time. "They still hassling you?"

"Not any more. Now it's the First Minuteman Boston Bank." She thought a moment, and then corrected herself. "That's not right. It's the First Boston Minuteman Bank and Trust Company. You know them?"

"Just another giant bank with branches all over New England. What'd you do to them?"

"I didn't make enough payments, so they got nasty. I mean,

after all, I did pay my taxes. David! Look! A Brownie troop all dressed up in whiteface! Oh, David, they're the cutest little clowns!"

"What do you mean you didn't make enough payments? You have a loan from them, too?"

"As of two weeks ago. I got a phone call yesterday."

"You borrowed from them to pay the credit union in Philly?"

"No, David! Oh, David, look! Over there!"

"Yes, Apryl, but what about the Minutemen? What'd you do?"

"Nothing. They did it all." With a little more patience, I learned that the Philadelphia credit union had sold her loan, and the Minuteman bank's computerized forms went upside her mortgage when she said she didn't have any money for them. Apparently, this company was determined to collect the back-due payments or own that parcel of timber. "I had a loan with a nice credit union until the government murdered it, and then the other credit union got rid of me. How can they do that?"

"Greater Whatever of Philadelphia probably went through all the loans it inherited, contacted all the problem debtors, kept the ones that looked good, quickly sold off the rest. No more worries or problems. Probably made a few thousand by selling them off at a lower interest rate."

"David"—a tear almost broke her voice—"that land is for the school." O.K., so I'm a sucker for a sob story. I agreed that I'd talk with someone at the bank. Three police units spread across the street marked the end of the parade a few minutes before 5:30 p.m.

From three blocks away, the sounds of a carnival beckoned. Hopping, skipping, jogging, singing, dancing, oblivious to heat and humidity, Apryl quickly arrived at the town park. Huffing, puffing, wheezing, panting, faltering, sweating profusely, I was, as usual, left in her wake.

If they had been staffed by professional carnies, they'd be known as "joints," the customers would be "marks," and there would be incessant "come-ons." They would also make more money since even greenhorn carnies know 200 ways to "work the mark" to get just one more quarter from the sucker's perseverant quest of the perfect plush panda. But, these were booths not joints, and the barkers were volunteers from service organizations. It was also easier to win at the Newburg Park.

Two dollars and four booby prizes later, we left the ring toss game—"It's easy; it's fun! Everyone wins! Toss this *large* red ring over any of the *small* bottles and win a *huge* prize!"—and headed for the milk bottles. "Try it!" I commanded Apryl. And that's how Apryl Greene got three baseballs, threw two of them somewhere east of Pittsburgh and south of Hartford, but with the last one somehow bounced it on the ground, the rebound barely tipping over two of the six leaden milk bottles; for her efforts she was rewarded with a medium-sized green velveteen stuffed snake, a prize that most assuredly didn't go to everyone who knocks over two milk bottles, no matter how feebly. I had spent a buck, knocked over three bottles, and got a ten-cent plastic whistle. Seemed fair enough. After all, she has the nicer eyes.

At Bingo, we lost five games in a row; at a mechanized horse race game—the kind where you keep flipping a rubber ball into a scoring hole—Apryl's horse came in first, mine dead last. Every booth had a line, even the Red Cross tent, whose volunteers, working in heat that had now dropped into the mid-80s, were doing a brisk business in sunstroke and heat exhaustion repairs.

"Frogs!" screamed Apryl, off to the next booth. Just put the stuffed fabric frog on one end of a miniature catapult, take the rubber mallet, hit the other end, and if the frog flies into the aluminum milk can, you win a frog. I didn't. . . . Yeah, she did.

We walked around, looking, playing, losing, winning, piling up trinkets to fill pockets and purses, donating most of it to whatever child was nearby. Skee-ball. Whack-a-mole. Darts. But it was the smell of barbeque chicken, which had been wafting our way since we first got to the park, that now overwhelmed us, enticing even the most hesitant on this sweat-filled day to part with $4.25 for half a barbequed chicken with all the trimmings, cooked upon one of four large grills by members of the town's all-male service clubs, and served by their wives.

"Two dinners," I requested of a Rotarian with the name tag, "Joe."

"One dinner," said Apryl correcting me, "unless it would be possible to buy a dinner with everything but the chicken." Now here was an interesting request, one that the ticket-taker from the Rotary Club undoubtedly never before encountered. "Can I buy everything but the chicken?" she again asked.

"Our dinners are chicken dinners," he said pleasantly. "I'm

sorry, but we don't have beef or ham."

"I don't want beef or ham. I don't want chicken, either."

"Our chickens are the best quality you'll find anywhere," said Rotary Joe.

"I'm sure they were nice chickens at one time," said Apryl, "but I don't want to eat them. David?" I was pretending to be a blade of grass. "I don't want to eat the chicken. But the corn looks so succulent. It'd go nicely with my trail mix. Against murmurs of impatience behind us, I quickly bought two tickets. Behind me, I thought I had heard clapping.

Like all good lines, this one had a beginning and an end. At the beginning, we buy a ticket, pick up paper plates, plastic utensils tied with a rubber band into a napkin, and continue along, being served coleslaw, mashed potatoes, an ear of corn, a cold roll, butter pats, and tea or punch. At the end, Apryl conveniently forgets her chicken. Raisins, unsalted seeds, and nuts trumped barbequed chicken.

Harry Cameron is a farmer, 55, maybe 60 years old, 35 or 40 pounds over what insurance companies believe is "ideal weight," and probably stronger and healthier than all the actuaries. What's left of his hair is in a closely-cropped brown-gray horseshoe ring that does nothing to cover a ruddy red-tan complexion. For more than 30 years, he has farmed a 160-acre plot of land just outside Newburg. But now he sat alone at one end of a six-person picnic table, about to eat a chicken bar-b-que, accepting the reality that his wife was busily selling 'dogs-on-a-stick in the Cabot High PTA booth, and that both of his children preferred to take their dates to the midway for hotdogs, fried mushrooms, cotton candy, and who knows what else. Harry Cameron was about to get another dose of reality.

"Hi! I'm Apryl. This is David. He's editor of *Century* magazine." Apryl said it proudly. "Would you mind if we sit with you?"

"Nah," he said disinterested, hardly looking up, patting his forehead with a napkin; said he didn't mind; said it's a free park. We sat at the table, but gave him space.

"They suffocate baby male chicks because males don't make for good fryers," Apryl said calmly, without bitterness or anger. "As soon as they're born, they throw them into large bags or crush them alive." I thought I heard the farmer choke on a drumstick, but he said nothing, and I had my mouth full of chicken. For a couple of years, a time when I was more idealistic and definitely more militant, I had been a vegetarian. Some become vegetarians because they think it's healthier; others because they believe a vegetarian diet helps them to look all trim and buffed. It was a selfish reason, but a reason, nevertheless. I was once a vegetarian because I despised how the food industry raises, slaughters, prepares, and sells meat. My views didn't change. I just didn't have the resistance to meat, although for more than 30 years I still refuse to eat veal, lamb, venison, or anything killed in a hunt. Apryl, who once ate meat, now is a vegetarian for all the right reasons. "The ones they let live, they crowd into cages too small for them, pump them full of drugs, and then at the right moment *kill them*," Apryl continued. Although sympathetic, I was close to indigestion, while Apryl kept munching away on trail mix, coleslaw, potatoes, and corn. Munching and talking. "We call the Nazis barbarians," she said, "but we call the factory farmers good businessmen." Apryl attacked society, just as pleasant as ever. Harry Cameron put down a thigh and attacked the corn. "It's immoral, you know, to cause the conception and birth of a bull, castrate it, take care of it, only to slaughter it." I agreed, hoping to finish my chicken before I choked. "Don't you think it's immoral to keep calves in closed darkened pens so small they can't lie down? And isn't it immoral to deprive them of iron just so the butchers could sell pale veal for seven ninety-five a pound?" Again I agreed, so Apryl kept talking, about slaughter houses, electric probes, the smell of pain and death that hovers for miles, and the men whose job it is to club animals all day long. "We don't consider if the cattle love or hate or are confused. We care only that it's so many dollars per pound." She may have been talking to me, but the conversation certainly wasn't for me.

Whatever the farmer was thinking, he said little—either his blood pressure was going to bounce off some clouds or he had just taken five pounds of Librium—so Apryl made him participate by asking him if he ever raised cattle or hogs. He mumbled a few words to her first question, grumbled a few more to her next one, and then began speaking in sentences, possibly believing it would shut her up. He said he had nothing against it, even went hunting in his youth, like most youth in the county, but that he just preferred raising crops—sweet corn, barley, oats—did it his entire life, saw no reason not to.

"You put your hands in the soil, and you can feel the vibrations of life, and you know there's a reason for the universe," Apryl said. "There's joy in being able to plant a seed and fertilize it and water it and watch it grow." The farmer looked at her, just looked. "Farming taught me patience," said Apryl, munching on raisins. "More than anything, I learned you can't rush the natural order of life."

Harry Cameron was now interested—and a bit confused. He still wasn't too sure about Apryl Greene. Perhaps he might even have overlooked her clothes and refusal to eat meat. He thought she was a hippie—definitely not one of them Helter-Skelter Charlie Manson types, but certainly one of them anti-country love-and-peace types who burned American flags. He didn't know for sure, not as he knew when Apryl first sat down, but he had to find out. "*You* were a farmer?"

"Along the Russian River in California. There were 30, sometimes 40 of us living there in the late '60s, early '70s. Big house on five acres."

"That's a lot of people for just five acres."

"Not if it's all you had in the world," said Apryl. "We all worked together. Learned a lot about plumbing because the toilets often overflowed. Learned about electricity because we had to maintain our generators."

"How'd you survive?"

"We made a kiln and then made vases, bowls, and mugs. We also made clothes and pictures. We grew crops. Lettuce, turnips, other vegetables. We ate them, sold them, gave them away to the poor. We couldn't give away enough zucchini. It just kept growing and multiplying, even when we didn't do anything for it. We let one grow until it dwarfed the Goodyear blimp."

"Zucchinis are like that. They'll take over everything if you don't harvest them. Eat a lot of zucchini pies?"

"Pies. Cakes. Bread. Fried zucchini. Zucchini casserole. Even zucchini pot pie. It helped us survive."

"That's about all it is anymore. Just surviving. Banks own the land. Big corporations have taken the farms. They have lawyers and businessmen running thousands of acres, and I can barely afford 160. Corporate farms—they get the big discounts on equipment. Pull in millions in federal welfare subsidies. Me, I gotta fight for any kinda discount. Bank's always breathing down your neck. Government doesn't give us a never-mind any more. Never did." He paused just a moment. "Even with all the work and problems, I never wanted to do anything else."

But it was something his children didn't want. His father was a farmer, and his father before him. But, his daughter just finished a degree in architecture at Penn State, and his two sons planned to get their degrees and then go into business in a city far from rural America, make a lot of money, maybe wear designer sneaks to a members-only gym, own a lot of stock, buy a "Beemer," a cabin cruiser, and a house with a spa. It was the American dream.

"Relatives do what they want, not always what's right," said Apryl. "My father always tried to do what was right, and he hardly ever had money. My brother would cheat a nun, and he lives the good life." Apryl's father, I later learned, had escaped to Denmark and England during the Holocaust, and then to America after the war. In Austria, he was a lawyer, but never enrolled in an American law school because, like medical schools and other colleges, liberal and professional, there were quotas on Jews—if they admitted them at all. So he sold vegetables from a cart in Brooklyn until he could complete college, one or two courses at a time, in social work. "I loved my father," Apryl said, although she needn't have said the words for us to know. "He had large sad brown eyes, and in them you could see a world gone mad."

Apryl loved her mother, but never had a chance to watch her grow from a young lady into a grandmother. Apryl's mother, a refugee from Russia, came to America at the age of 14, in time to escape most of the pogroms but not the Depression that defined America during the early 1930s. Two months before she turned 40, she was dead from cervical cancer.

Apryl's younger brother was an insurance agent, working on his third marriage, this one to a cutesy cheerleader no more than three or four years out of college. He had promised Apryl he'd pay for her first five years of insurance if she ever got a business started. It wasn't a fraternal gesture on his part; he knew his sister well and figured if she ever started a business, a highly remote possibility, it'd probably be some kind of a charity, and any donations would be tax-deductible. As much as she had loved her parents, she had stopped liking her brother.

"When I was working with the farm workers," said Apryl,

"he was buying scab wine for his fraternity. When I was in Chicago, he was writing articles for his college newspaper about how the radicals should be arrested for high treason." They barely talked after that, and not at all during the five years that she lived in a residential commune along the Russian River. She stumbled a moment. "He just didn't wish to have any black sheep in his family line," she said softly, not with anger, but with sadness, perhaps the same kind of sadness her father had known.

"That farm of yours, that one in California? Was it one of those communes I read about? With all the sex and drugs?"

"Only if you believe what the media say." She looked at me, smiling; he looked at me, and I thought I saw him smirking.

"You all get along OK?"

"We wasted a lot of time arguing. We voted on just about everything, but the group often couldn't make any decisions so we didn't make many decisions." She paused a moment. "Sometimes it was hard to get things done because we didn't have any rules. All of us were running away from something, and rules were just reminders of what we were running away from, so a lot never got done."

"You need some structure in your lives," Harry Cameron said with more than a hint of fatherly concern. "People need to know there's someone who cares. That's why God gave us the Ten Commandments. To tell us there are rules."

Apryl followed the Ten Commandments, as best as she could, but sometimes, she said, rules destroy what's good. "Even planting corn," said Apryl, "sometimes you have to overlook the rules since corn doesn't always follow directions."

Harry Cameron, a farmer his entire working life, sitting at a picnic table, now illuminated by a string of artificial light, in a park on a Fourth of July, looked at Apryl, and in his own way tried to understand how this early 40ish hippie radical could also have loved the earth so much. But there was a more important question. "If you loved farming so much, why'd you leave?"

Apryl didn't say anything for three, four seconds, so Harry was about to rephrase the question when Apryl spoke softly, reflectively. "Its time was up. Things changed. Views of life changed. One by one they left. Got jobs. Promotions. Got older and moved on. Tried to find the Good Life in other ways. One even went into real estate. Bought and sold land. Rejected everything he once stood for. Soon, there were only a few of us, and we couldn't continue. I guess there was no longer a need." A tearful pause. "Sometimes, it's hard to keep what you value— what you believe—when everyone seems to be rushing to be something else." Another brief but tearful pause. "Dreams die hard, Mr. Cameron."

"Don't let those dreams die, because that's all that's left when they take away everything else," said Harry Cameron. I could have sworn he wiped off a tear, although he disguised it by brushing his arm against his forehead, as if to wipe off sweat.

For awhile they talked about farming, but the conversation always returned to Apryl's grand scheme to build a school for peace. An hour or so earlier, Harry Cameron might have been appalled at the existence of such a school, especially in his own backyard, but now that he knew Apryl, a school for peace didn't sound like such a bad idea after all, even if its director had a lot of strange ideas. "Well, Apryl Greene," he said, "maybe some day I would like to help you build that school." He quickly and almost inconspicuously stopped a tear from choking him, and then brightly told Apryl that if she were ever in the area again, all she had to do was to stop by the Extension Office and they would be more than happy to tell her how to get to his farm. "You're welcome anytime," he said. Quickly remembering his manners, he turned to me. "You, too, Mr. Ascher. You just come visit me and there'll always be a place for you. Just leave your notepad behind."

The Witchita Whipsaw, a beast of a ride developed not in Wichita, Kansas, but by technologically sadistic Germans and licensed to Gerber Amusements, consists of 15 brightly-colored oversize metal and fiber glass brooms, each one encapsulating one semi-frightened human being. When the power is off, the brooms just sit there on a large saucer-like base, looking relatively harmless. The ride jock collects four 25-cent tickets from each of 15 people, gives each one a fiberglass helmet that looks like a crushed witch's cap, straps each one into a vinyl-covered seat between two parallel pieces of metal designed to look like a witch's broom, puts down a roll bar, and then goes into a small booth and pushes a large green button on a control panel. The saucer begins its counterclockwise rotation, tilting one way and then another, while the brooms seem to take on their own lives, spinning wildly, seemingly moving in and out of the patterns of other brooms. Once on the ride, it's impossible to tell the real screams from the pre-recorded witches' howls and bleats heard over the pounding, driving electronic rock music designed to attract riders and raise their blood pressure to the edge of terror. Three minutes later—four minutes if it's a slow day—the riders wobble off the saucer, hold onto reinforced handrails, and step onto the ground where, if they fall over, it's no longer the company's fault. The Witchita Whipsaw was the last ride I wanted to be near; it was the first one Apryl wanted to try after dinner.

Screaming and laughing, Apryl gleefully bounced from ride to ride, as excited by the passive no-terror rides as by the Whipsaw. With hot chicken on a hot day gnarling my insides, I had placed a greater value on holding in my dinner than in experiencing the depths of fright, and challenged only two more rides, one a haunted castle, the other the Ferris wheel.

"I wish I had brought my cameras," Apryl said, somewhere between the house of mirrors and a ride where the bottom drops out. "There are so many pictures here. So much happiness. A lot of good feeling."

"Maybe you should have," I agreed.

"Should have what?"

"Should have brought your camera to all this." She thought a moment, and then contradicted herself.

"That wouldn't be right. This is a celebration. It's meant to be remembered, not photographed. Photographs reduce it and freeze it and make it sterile. All the photographs and all the stories can't tell the story of what the revolution meant." An odd statement, I thought, but a lot of what Apryl says seems to be, well, odd. "Fireworks! We're going to miss the fireworks!"

"Yeah, Apryl, got to see those Elks light up the sky."

"Lions, David. For the third time, it's the Lions Club not the Elks that sponsors the fireworks show."

"Lions. Elks. Moose. They're all the same. I suppose out here a Kiwanis is an animal?"

"Lives in the suburbs and eats in tacky restaurants once a week."

"I wonder what the animals would think about men trying to imitate them. If I were an elk or moose, I'd file a libel suit."

"Case of Bullwinkle J. Moose versus the Loyal Order of Moose. Claimed they discriminated against him. Wouldn't let him become a member because he had antlers."

"So what happened?"

"Got thrown out of the Supreme Court. They said it was a squirrelly case."

"Let's watch the squirrels light up the sky."

"And let the revolution continue!"

12/

100 Injured in Chicago Riot; Humphrey Blasts Police Tactics

by David Ascher
Special Correspondent

CHICAGO, Thursday, Aug. 29, 1968—More than 100 persons, including 25 policemen, were injured yesterday evening during an anti-war protest in front of the Chicago Conrad Hilton Hotel, housing site of the 35th Democratic National Convention. The convention itself, which last night nominated Vice-President Hubert H. Humphrey, is at the nearby International Amphitheater.

Sens. Eugene McCarthy and George McGovern also received delegate votes. Many of their supporters had backed Sen. Robert Kennedy. However, his assassination, June 6, combined with the continuing war and the strength of the McCarthy campaign, guaranteed a heavy youth presence in Chicago. Their anti-war campaigns, combined with their hope for a stronger national commitment to the impoverished and under-represented, had helped energize the youth movement.

During three days of violent confrontation, more than 500 persons, including many bystanders, were injured. More than 100 persons were hospitalized. There were more than 700 arrests. Among those injured were several persons who were across the street behind police barriers.

Using clubs, rifle butts, Mace, and tear gas, helmeted Chicago police, assisted by Cook County Sheriff's deputies, the Illinois National Guard, and private security forces, waded into the crowd, estimated by police at 2,000–3,000, in what some observers call a "police riot," but which police claim was started by the violence within the anti-war movement. Chanting "The Whole World Is Watching" and "Give Peace a Chance," the protestors went limp when confronted by police violence. A police department official says that Chicago police reacted only after sustaining several injuries from the crowd and "only after 50 or so hardcore leaders" led a charge into police lines north of the Hilton.

In actions yet unexplained, two lines of police trapped a large group of onlookers between the Hilton and police barricades, and then forced them against a large plate glass window of a restaurant in the hotel building, causing several to fall into the glass. Witnesses say that police officers followed bystanders through the broken glass into the restaurant, continued to club them, and then arrested several on charges of disorderly conduct.

Witnesses say they saw Deputy Police Supt. James Rochford and several senior police officials trying to pull police officers from individuals, but direct orders to cease and withdraw, they say, were met by jeers and hostility by the police officers, many yelling "Kill! Kill! Kill!"

As they had done the previous two nights, some of the police removed their badges and identification nameplates before moving against the crowd. Police Supt. James B. Conlisk earlier in the week had announced he would personally suspend any officer who removed a badge or ID. There have been no suspensions so far.

Wednesday, Conlisk assigned several senior officers to give personal protection to the press, which had been targets of police brutality. Even with police protection, more than 30 journalists have been injured in the past three days. Several have been treated at local hospitals for injuries ranging from severe bruises and lacerations to broken hands, internal injuries, and concussions. Among those clubbed by Chicago police were Hugh Hefner, *Playboy* editor–publisher; Winston S. Churchill, *London Evening News* reporter and grandson of the former British prime minister; Hal Bruno of *Newsweek*; and Samuel A. Weissmann, former national correspondent for the now-defunct *New York Herald Tribune* and currently editor-in-chief of *Century*, a small liberal magazine published in Boston.

In critical condition in a Cook County hospital jail ward is Rachel Greenberg, a young photojournalist on assignment to several West Coast counterculture publications, including *The Realist* and *Ramparts*. The hospital will not release the extent of the injuries. She is charged by police with inciting to riot, assault and battery, resisting arrest, and disorderly conduct. Ironically, witnesses say several protestors had earlier tried to take away her camera, shoving her, and calling her a "nark." Undercover police photographers often blend into the crowd.

Miss Greenberg apparently had been part of the protest at Grant Park, but was behind police lines later in the evening photographing events at the Hilton when two police officers, swinging batons, broke through the crowd and rushed to her.

Joseph Schwartz, 61, Skokie, Ill., reports that one of the police officers grabbed her camera and shoved it against her shoulder before smashing it against the ground. Three other police officers, says Diane Roberts, 14, Madison, Wisc., repeatedly hit Miss Greenberg in the stomach, chest, back, arms, and face with their batons. She said when police tried to rip off a peace symbol on a leather band around her neck "she began kicking and clawing. I think that's when they dropped her to the ground." Roberts was vacationing in Chicago with her parents.

Although a target of anti-war protests, Humphrey—one of the nation's most liberal statesmen and one of the strongest advocates of civil rights legislation—has repeatedly spoken out against police violence. Insiders to his campaign said he was furious that Mayor Richard J. Daley had ordered microphones in the hall silenced when delegates earlier in the week tried to speak out against Chicago's tactics. Last night, Daley said that the Chicago police "are all good and decent men and they don't respond with undue violence." However, sources say Daley is the person who allowed and may even have encouraged the police beatings.

The police, National Guard, and Army troops had begun systematic patrols of the downtown shortly after 9 p.m., Wednesday, with several arrests made as far as two miles from the convention site. By 12:30 this morning, an uneasy calm had been restored to the area.

Shortly before dawn, police raided Sen. McCarthy's 15th floor convention headquarters, shouted obscenities and attacked staff they accused of throwing beer cans and other debris at them during the night. McCarthy, whose "Clean for Gene" volunteers had cut their hair and shaved their beards, are mostly pacifists. It is believed this is the only incident in American history of police forces raiding the rooms of a U.S. senator.

McCarthy's hotel room served as a temporary first aid station. Police threatened to arrest members of McCarthy's staff for destruction of property after they tore bed sheets to make bandages for the injured.

Violence was not always a part of the anti-war movement. Until New York City police violently broke up a peaceful demonstration, March 20, several anti-war factions had been arguing among themselves about the strategy for peace. The hippies called for a "peace and love" platform; the politically-radical Yippies called for confrontation.

Yippie leader Abbie Hoffman later said the actions of the New York City police in dealing with what had been a largely peaceful demonstration "knocked out the hippie image of a [peaceful] Chicago, and let the world know there would be blood on the streets." The murders of John F. Kennedy by a man whose motives may never be known, of the Rev. Martin Luther King Jr. by a White supremacist, and of Sen. Kennedy by an anti-Zionist Arab militant, further led to the belief that violence must be met by violence. But it is Sen. Kennedy's last words, "Is everybody O.K.?" before lapsing into unconsciousness that still resonate in the souls of his followers.

Perhaps the most powerful protest, however, was not from violence but from a banner. Yesterday, in Chicago—a little more than a week after the world watched in horror as 200,000 Warsaw Pact troops invaded Czechoslovakia to crush the spirit of freedom that had developed the past few months—American anti-war demonstrators marched behind a banner: "We mourn the suppression of human rights in Vietnam, Czechoslovakia, and Chicago." In less than a couple of days, the American government had crushed American decency.

"There comes a time when the operation of the machine becomes so odious, makes you so sick at heart, that you can't take part, you can't even passively take part. And you've got to put your bodies on the gears, and upon the wheels, upon the levers, upon all the apparatus. And you've got to make it stop." —*Mario Savio, Free Speech Movement rally, University of California at Berkeley; Dec. 2, 1964*

13/

Full Frontal Assault

"War!"

Sam Weissmann was mad. Not the kind of mad you get when the department store loses your order or the network cancels your favorite SitCom. Not the kind of mad that causes you to swear at your car, your mechanic, and all of Detroit when a grinding sound and a puff of smoke greet you early in the morning. Not even the mad you get at imperious petty administrators whose sole mission is to justify their existence by repeatedly stamping "NOT ACCEPTABLE" upon your soul.

No, this was *mad*. Violent, wrathful, savage mad. The kind of mad that unleashes the furies. In this case, evil took the form of the First Boston Minuteman Bank and Trust Co. and the IRS, both of them formidable opponents.

"War!" declared Sam once again, slamming the phone against the desk. "Get Rabinowitz on the phone! Get me Stacy Lyman! Get me Fred Goldberg's private number!" Helen Grishka, whose title was executive secretary, but whose primary mission was to keep Sam and *Century* organized, would have no trouble finding Sam's accountant and lawyer; it would be a little more difficult to get the private phone number of the IRS commissioner.

"War!" Sam repeated, growling and snapping, rushing past Helen into the hallway, sweeping everything in his path. "David! Get in here, please. MITCHELL! Get your *tuchis* up here!"

It was 8:10 a.m., Friday, July 6th. After a non-stop whirl in Philadelphia, Marshfield, and Luzerne counties in Pennsylvania, and now Boston, I was mentally and physically exhausted, but still had work to do at *Century*. Sam had offered his staff a half-and-half—pick out four vacation days between July Second and Ninth; he thought it was fair—four days for the workers, four days for the magazine. Sam, who planned to be in the office most of the days, today decided to spend an hour, two at the most, and then go shopping with Ruth in Cambridge; I planned to meet Apryl at First Boston Minutemen and plead her case for leniency on a loan. No one wanted any problems. Not me, and certainly not Sam, but Sam had problems, and that meant I also had problems.

An officious assistant vice-president of something-or-the-other at First Boston Minutemen, working well before the bank opened to the public, had just called, polite but formal. *There are two IRS agents in my office, said he; they have orders to seize $223,418.87 from your accounts; no, there's nothing I can do; no, they have their orders; no, they said there wouldn't be any point talking with you right now; yes, we know you've had problems with them before; yes, we're sure it's all some bureaucratic mix-up; no, sir, we can't garrote them for you; yes, sir, Mr. Weissmann; yes, sir; yes, we too are upset about this; thank you for understanding; have a nice day, sir.*

"A hitman!" Sam the pacifist screamed at me. "Get me a hitman. The kind with a broken nose who wears a yellow tie against a black shirt. Pay him whatever he demands. Have him kill the IRS! *All* of them! Start with Boston Minutemen, but wipe out the IRS!"

Sam's war had begun about two years earlier when the First Boston Minutemen Bank and Trust Co. had somehow managed to send the Century America Corp. and the IRS different statements for interest earned on certificates of deposit. It wasn't just a little different, but $10,000 different. On a routine check, IRS computers had no trouble spotting the discrepancy. From out of the Boston district with a hearty "Hi Ho Tax Cheat!" came a junior auditor to scoop up the red flag and drive home the IRS Code's Sword of Righteousness. It only took three months before the IRS finally agreed with *Century's* auditors. No one at the bank knew how it happened. Something about a computer glitch—or an accidental digit creep—or maybe a clerk did something and another clerk tried to fix it and then in trying to reconcile the balances . . . *So sorry*, they said. *It was a freak accident*, they noted. *It won't happen again*, they resolutely declared. *We have all kinds of checks and balances*, they pointed out. *We'll do better*, they whined.

Sam would not have declared war had that been the end of it, but the IRS doesn't like to admit defeat. *As long as we have your file opened*, they politely suggested, *why don't we just go ahead with a field audit; just routine; at your convenience.* Back issues of *Century* are not taxable inventory but are file copies with minimal income potential, the corporation accountants pleaded. *Disallowed!* Depreciation on a computer system that was replaced after only three years rather than the seven-year IRS guidelines should be allowed since the effective life was four years less than guidelines. *Disallowed!* Deductions should be allowed for . . . *Disallowed!* Six months after the routine audit began, the corporation paid $21,265.42 in back taxes, plus 25 percent penalty, plus eight percent interest. Sam and his scowl dominated the magazine that week.

Had *that* been the end of it, Sam would still not have declared war, for he knew that part of the price of staying in business was having to deal with innumerable layers of tax-imposing bureaucracies. Almost a year ago, a computerized bill came from the IRS for $2,882.62. No one at *Century* knew why; even the IRS was a little puzzled, but promised to look into it. Three clerks and two auditors later, no one still knew why, but the bill was now up to $3,346.52. By the time the bill made it past $5,000, the accountants and the IRS had finally figured out that it was for the non-existent $10,000 interest income that the bank had over reported to the IRS. *No problem*, the IRS declared, *we'll just wipe it off the books.*

Now, had *that* been the end of it, Sam could worry about his high blood pressure being caused by the quarterly increase in paper prices, two hallelujah-evangelists who were suing us for libel, and the League of American Freedom which declared *Century* was un-American. But, such was not to be, for there was soon another bill and another, and more were coming in daily, more than all the Ed McMahon "win-a-million" letters, more than all the department store flyers and time-share condo brochures, sometimes two or three letters a day, each one demanding more money than before, each one more threatening than the other. On two occasions, letters stated that the problem had been resolved.

Four or five weeks ago, Sam had received such a letter in the morning mail. In the afternoon mail came a certified letter threatening extinction. With the bill quickly approaching the national debt, Sam became furious. What once was the office joke now became a battle of wills. And so it was that the IRS had willed that Century America Corp. pay $223,418.87 within ten days or face the wrath of Marshal Dillon, Boss Hogg, or whomever it was that would be assigned to carry out the orders of the tax court. Two days later, *Century*'s accountant and general counsel were able to get a lukewarm apology from the IRS. "I thought we took care of that," said one official. "Those things happen," said another. "Tell your client he can rest easy," said a third. And for eight more days, Sam rested. Until 8:06 a.m., Friday, July 6th, when an assistant vice-president at First Boston Minutemen Bank and Trust Co. called Sam to tell him that two IRS agents were there.

"Get me a vise!" Sam bellowed to Helen. "I'm gonna put their nuts in it and squeeze until their faces turn blue!" The fury that Sam Weissmann was about to unleash not only kept me awake after only four hours of sleep, it would have made Armageddon a Sunday afternoon picnic. He began by shaking up a GS-5 in the IRS office in Andover, Massachusetts, who had the temerity to suggest he write a letter explaining the problem. "May an elephant live in your dining room," Sam wished upon the clerk. From the 5, he proceeded to decimate a GS-9 who said, after a few taps on his keyboard, and without much inquiry into the authenticity of his caller, that it appeared that the Century America Corp. did, in fact, owe the money, and that the seizure was proper and authorized. Benign, benevolent Sam was neither kind nor charitable. "May all your teeth fall out, except for one," Sam cursed, "and may that one be left in your miserable head so you have a toothache!" Having taken care of preliminaries, Sam went into overdrive. Fred Goldberg wasn't in his office; no, no one in Washington knew where he was—or even if he was available. *No problem*, said Sam, *there are others who wouldn't mind answering questions about governmental incompetence and harassment.* "I'm sorry," said an assistant press secretary, who had just come into work for a couple of hours, "but I can't help you." Slamming his phone against the desk, Sam left only an amplified dial tone on the speaker until he shoved the receiver back onto the cradle.

"Who the hell needs him anyway!" said Sam to no one in particular, although by now an accountant, a business manager, a secretary, and I were in his office. It didn't matter that the IRS commissioner was unavailable, Charlotte Friedman was.

"How the hell do you get into all these problems, Sam?"

"Me!? *I* get into these problems? Char—"

"Stop your *kvetching* and calm down or else Ruth'll be treating you for a stroke."

"Calm down!? I've got 119 bogus letters from the IRS, my bank accounts have just been seized, accountants and lawyers are on overtime, and you want *me* to calm down!" He paused for a breath. "I don't care how you do it, but I want this *mishigas* off my back!"

"Sam, first of all, it's not even 9 a.m., so not a lot of people are around. Next, Goldberg's a down-to-earth kinda guy. Sharp. Runs a tight operation at IRS. No scandals. His rep is he'll make things happen."

"Makes shit happen." She let Sam's comment fall quietly.

"Second, IRS may be under Treasury, but you know we give them a wide berth."

"Should have given them an abortion, the mother-fuckers! Would have been a *mitzvah* to every American."

"O.K., Sam, for old time sake, I'll make a couple of calls; find out what the hell's going on."

"You're just absolutely wonderful."

"You're just an absolute bullshitter."

"When the Democrats get back into power I'll be the first one to frame a dollar bill with your signature. Put it right over my desk."

"I won't hold my breath."

"Thanks, Gorgeous."

"Tell Ruth I send my love."

Maybe there'd be help, maybe not. Even Treasury officials with Charlotte's title of Assistant Secretary don't mess with the IRS. Either way, Sam wasn't about to take the chance.

"Where's Kennedy?" Sam asked. We didn't know. He could have asked us the same question any day of the week, and we still wouldn't know the Senator's schedule. It didn't matter. "Helen! Please dig into the black Rolodex and go down the list until you locate him. No aides; no family; just him. Interrupt whatever he's doing." Just in case any of us weren't as worried as he thought we should be, he casually mentioned that he sure hoped we had cashed our payroll checks. "Anyone know if the 101st Airborne takes private assignments?" he mused, while waiting for a return call. He didn't have to wait long. A few minutes later came an incoming call by marine telephone from somewhere off the coast of Cape Cod. A few minutes after that, Sam had another assurance that there would be inquiries made within the next couple of hours.

"I'll call Bush if I have to! This is war!" Now, Sam barely knew the President, and what he did know he seldom agreed with. But Sam also had worked with a dozen or so senior presidential aides and advisors; most of them, like their boss, were likable enough. Several were still in Washington rather than with the President during the past week as he jetted from Kennebunkport, Maine, to London. On this Friday morning, he was somewhere between the NATO summit in London and the upcoming world economics summit in Houston. Sam dug into the Rolodex and came up with one of the unlisted direct numbers of Jack Stander, special assistant to the President, and one of only a dozen or so aides who had complete, unlimited access to the President—anytime, anywhere, for any reason.

"Morning, Jack," said Sam. "How's it going?"

"Not bad," said a sighing Jack Stander who knew Sam didn't call just to check whether the President enjoyed Trafalgar Square. "How's things in Boston?"

"Can't complain," said Sam. "Well, maybe not so good. I've got this one little tiny complaint." For five minutes, an unvented Sam blew steam, drawing quick breaths now and then, sighed, and just stopped.

"Gee, Sam, I'd like to help," said Jack, "but the IRS runs—"

"Yeah, yeah. Runs its own show. Doesn't take kindly to interference."

"That and the reality presidents don't want to be involved in politicking the IRS."

"Must have just been one humongous coincidence when the IRS ran back-to-back field audits on my personal accounts in '71 and '72. Remember them, Jack? First audit occurred not long after I made Nixon's hit list."

"Different president."

"Same government."

"Maybe then, but no one believes there's a correlation now. This President doesn't do that shit."

"Play the tune, Jack, and see who catches the refrain. This time IRS seizes the bank accounts of a magazine that once ran a two-part series on IRS civil rights violations, and whose editor once personally faced the IRS wrath. Add to that the fact that the editor has hit this administration a little hard now and then, and you have more scandal than on the daytime soaps."

"It won't wash, Sam. You and I both know it."

"What I know, Jack, is that soiled linen never comes clean, and whoever has to wear it still wears dirt. That applies to agents, advisors, and *presidents*!"

"I'll think about it."

"*Bupkes!*" declared Sam defiantly. "How can you insult me with your thinking?"

"You want I should do something?"

"No, Jack, I want you should bake a lemon meringue pie. Of course I want you should do something!"

"Sam, I can't just barge into this."

"While you're deep in your river of snakes, think about this. What about the poor common laborer who doesn't have the ability or connections just to phone up some big presidential muck-a-muck to defend his case? Did the IRS clean up its act once, but is now once again running amuck, seizing bank accounts of struggling farmers and unemployed auto workers and steel-workers instead of crooked lawyers, stockbrokers, and politicians? I'll bet you a government pension that my case is only one of thousands. Probably make one heck of a great article. Article, hell! It'd be a great series!" Sam paused a moment, punctuating the silence for effect. "Oh, yeah, Jack, *we already did that!*"

Five minutes later, Sam had a promise that Jack Stander would discreetly find out the extent of the problem and see if it affects more than just one person. *No assurances*, said he; *understood*, said Sam.

"Executive. Legislative. Two down, one to go!"

"You're going to buy a judge!?" It was an astonishing statement of incredulous naiveté, but business managers are usually focused only upon business and ways to manipulate data to a company's best advantage. They are often lost in worlds not run by cost-efficiency models. Sam looked at Frank Mitchell, a look proclaiming "You stupid shit."

"Helen," demanded Sam, "Where the hell's Stacy Lyman?"

"Right where you want her. Got her mojo working down at District Court. Said she'd get back to you in a couple of hours."

"Tell her for two hundred an hour, she better be working better magic than pulling coins from behind ears."

"Sam, it takes time," said Helen Grishka, trying to soothe Sam's temper. He wasn't about to be soothed.

"Bunch of legal mumbo jumbo. No one but lawyers and the demented understand it. Anyhow. It's all *meshugge*."

In four decades as a journalist, slightly more than two of those decades as editor-in-chief of one the nation's most influential liberal magazines, Sam had developed an incredible file of contacts, acquaintances, and friends. He had the artillery to fight a full-frontal assault against any of America's sacred institutions—educational, business, financial, medical, and governmental. He used the ammunition well, but never for personal gain, and when the balance of payments would come due, it would be recorded that Samuel Abraham Weissmann had done for the people more than all the leaders ever did for him. He would survive this case of bureaucratic incompetence, not because he was right, not because he cared about people, but because he was an influential person who knew how to use the people who created the system.

It would not be so easy for Apryl Greene.

14/

Voices of America

by David Ascher
Special Correspondent

KENT, Ohio, May 4, 1970—The spirit of last August's Woodstock Nation was murdered early this afternoon in the northern Ohio city of Kent when Ohio National Guard troops opened fire at Kent State University, killing four persons and wounding at least 12 others, including a photojournalist who arrived only minutes before the shooting began. It is unknown whether the four dead, believed to have been students at Kent State, were part of a thousand student demonstration against the war in Vietnam or whether they were spectators. Dead are Allison Krause, 19, Pittsburgh, Pa.; Jeffrey Glenn Miller, 20, Plainview, N.Y.; Sandra Lee Scheuer, 20, Youngstown, Ohio; and William K. Schroeder, 19, Loraine, Ohio. . . .

"They got their own nation—the Pig Nation. We got ours— the Woodstock Nation. It's where we liberated our minds from the American bullshit, and just grooved on the beautiful vibes. It was our own celebration of life. But the pigs wouldn't let it be. John Sinclair is looking at ten years for giving two joints to a nark. I don't fuckin' care what their fuckin' law is, they went after him. They went after him 'cause he was leading the Revolution. And they got Abbie [Hoffman] and Jerry [Rubin]. Abbie got up on stage and tried to tell everyone all about Sinclair. . . . Everyone says that Peter Townshend [of The Who] threw him off the fuckin' stage. That Townshend grabbed the

microphone and smashed Abbie with a guitar. Ain't happen that way. I was there, man. I was there! Abbie gets up on stage. Grabs the mic. Gives his little speech. Townsend was tuning up, or somethin' like that. Bumped into Abbie. Don't think he meant it, but bumped him. I saw it. Didn't smash no guitar. . . . May not have liked what Abbie did, but he didn't do that shit that everyone's talkin' about. Never happened."

"I was 20 years old. Same age as them. I didn't get to go to college. Parents couldn't afford it, and I don't get no breaks. I'm working at an auto parts store right now. Makin' extra bucks on weekends servin' my country. I put most my Guard pay into a separate account. I want to move to Colorado, find a job there. But them hippies! They don't know how good they got it. Mommy and Daddy payin' all the bills. Parties all week. They get those high-pay jobs when they graduate. This is the best god-damned place they'll ever live in. Ain't no better place anywhere on earth, and they want to tear it down."

"We want to build. Build a new society. One that cares about people. One where people help one another. Where we don't have to kill anyone. That was the soul of Woodstock."

"They got some good ideas, but we don't agree on much. One thing we agree upon is that government shouldn't be in our faces. Telling us what to do all the time. I was artillery in World War II. Got recalled in Korea. I love my country. I'd have died for it. But, I don't like them telling me how to live my life. Pretty soon, they'll be telling me what to eat or not eat. How much exercise I'm supposed to get every day. Heard that the government even plans to ban cigarette ads on TV. Let them just try taking away my smokes."

"Lot of us figured these hicks were going to bust our butts. Protest the music. Complain about the weed and the noise. Call us Commies and disgraces. Say we were unpatriotic. Get in our face. Wasn't like that at all. Surprised me. Shit, man, it was freaking scary!"

"None of us wanted to hurt no one. But we were juiced. They make trouble, then we have to give it right back at them. We took an oath to protect America, and we have to do that. We have to protect the people and their property. That's all we were trying to do. But they kept coming at us. They just kept coming."

"When I heard that the Festival was being moved [from Walkill to Bethel, N.Y.] I was going to pack it up and take a week's vacation. Just leave. I'd heard about those long-haired hippies and what they do to property. 'Bout that dirty language and the nudity and that thing they call group grope. Read some- where that the hippies think when they shed their clothes they also shed their inhibitions. Poppycock. Just pure poppycock! Also, read about how they wanted to destroy our country. Tear down everything that the good God-fearing people built up over the years. But my wife and I, we just couldn't afford to take a vacation, so we stayed. Y'know, it wasn't all that bad. Oh, there were a few that thought they were the Hell's Angels, but most were decent and respectable. A lot of us in town made sand- wiches and gave them water. Didn't charge them nothing either. Not like them stores that charged a buck or two for a 29-cent loaf of bread. Things like that. But most just gave them the food. You treat them well, they treat you well. No need to hate. Them and us, we don't agree on politics. But, now that we seen all what's happening over there [in Vietnam] maybe they were right all along. I mean, when Walter Cronkite says the U.S. can't win the war, and that the generals and the president himself were all wrong—well, that's pretty powerful stuff. Maybe the hippies were just tryin' to tell us something, and we weren't listening."

"Figured the SDS [Students for a Democratic Society] was behind all this. Stirring trouble, y'know. That Tom Hayden fella, real bad news. He was one of them Chicago 7, y'know. The ones causing all the problems at Chicago. Him and that Jerry Rubin and Abbie Hoffman. That's the jerk who threw money onto the stock exchange and caused a panic. Don't have no respect for this country and what makes it the best place on God's green earth. Don't know why they had to cause the trou- ble. There's already enough trouble in the world, and they're in your face giving even more trouble. They turned that trial into a circus. A circus I tell you! No respect for authority. Least they got what they deserved."

"Right after the Port Huron Statement [in 1962], I joined the

SDS at the University of Michigan. Our government was being run by the elite, and we wanted to give our nation back its soul, to develop a government of participatory democracy, to empower all people. To bring social justice to America. To make sure that Blacks weren't excluded from any part of society, that the poor and the disenfranchised had a voice. To give people OK wages, and to have a voice in their own lives. Chicago was where it all made sense. The war is tearing this nation apart. It's an unjust war. An unfair war. And we send out our young and our poor and the minorities to fight it because of the will of the politicians, not that of the people. . . . Month ago, Neil Armstrong landed on the moon. Brought all of us together. Made us all proud. He and Alan Shepard and John Glenn and the other astronauts could see all of the earth and, man, is that beautiful or what! . . . but they didn't see the poor, the homeless, the people who couldn't afford to see a doctor. The money the government has spent on space, well maybe some of it could be spent on taking care of the poor. Woodstock was what it's about. People coming together. Doing for each other. No gang bosses. No politicians. Just people."

"They called us on a Saturday afternoon [May 1]. I don't think it began as a war protest. I think they [the students] were drunk and looking for more excitement when the bars closed. They sure as hell made a mess out of that town! Broke damn near every window; set fires in the streets. Don't know why they sent us in. Students do it every spring. The civil authorities should have handled it, but that wasn't my decision. I'm just supposed to follow orders. Did my job. I don't hate them. Not any more at least. Not after what I seen [in Vietnam.] I had a job to do. I had to do it. Anyhow, next day [May 2], Nixon says he was sending troops into Cambodia, and that really lit their fuse. Worse than anything Johnson ever did. They couldn't get to Nixon, so they used us."

"I worked in Operations [at the Festival] and I'll tell you this. I didn't hardly crap for a week, it was that bad. I signed up [with Woodstock Ventures] last May [1969] so I was in on some of the early stuff. Mainlined coffee and coke. Worked 80, 90, a hundred hours a week going into the weekend [August 15-17], and just about around the clock that whole weekend. Man, were there

problems! Every kind you could think of. We had a whole fuckin'
city to worry about. Medical. Sewage. Food. Recreation. Hundred
departments all working together. Well, mostly working together.
John and Joe [John Roberts and Joe Rosenman, festival direc-
tors, with Michael Lang and Artie Kornfeld] got soaked on this
one. It was really too bad because they cared, and all they got for
it was shit. Do you know that on Friday [the first day] there were
roving bands trying to 'liberate' the Festival by breaking down
the fences? Yippies wanted the festival to be free. They could
have easily reinforced the fences, but Roberts decided to take
them down and make it a free festival. He was afraid people
would get hurt. Now, I'll tell you what others would have done.
They would have reinforced the fences and said, 'Screw you!' But
these two birds [Roberts and Rosenman], they still manipulated
and wheeled and dealed and tried to make it cool. They cared,
and they ate shit."

"We weren't too organized at first. Best I could recall, none
of us knew what was going to happen. All we knew was we were
supposed to protect life and property. Most of us weren't long
out of Basic, but we all worked together, kinda looked after each
other. Somehow, we got it set up and organized."

"Security? Yeah, there was security. Well, Woodstock way.
Wavy [Wavy Gravy, originally named Hugh Romney] and the
Hog Farm set up the Please Force. The Please Force, 'cause they
were polite. Said, 'Please do this,' and 'Please don't do that.' And
. . . oh, wait, here's something real cool, when the reporters asked
them how they planned to keep order, Wavy just laughed at them
and said he was going to use seltzer water and cream pies."

"Guns? You crazy? Hell, yeah, we had guns. Them college
assholes were likely to kill us. You don't threaten the United
States government and get away with it."

"Hog Farm set up these food tents. Ran 'em just like a busi-
ness. Most efficient operation I ever saw. They were the most
unselfish people you'd ever meet. Hardly none of us had much
cash. We just kinda drifted out when we heard what was going
down. The Hog Farm people, they were there cooking and dish-
ing out food. And when we'd trip bad, they'd bring us down."

"Bunch of selfish pricks! All they cared about was themselves. Didn't care about no one else. I think 'bout it all the time. Maybe they thought it was cool, maybe groovy to shout 'Pigs!' and 'Fuck the establishment!' and go destroying other people's property. They was screamin' and yellin' and actin' just like a bunch of foul-mouthed assholes. Burned the ROTC building, then cut the fire hoses. We got hit by rocks and molotov cocktails. Can you fuckin' believe it! They was yellin' for peace, and they was a-throwin' molotov cocktails! I wanted to take one of their cocktails and give them a fuckin' enema!"

"You get half a million people in 35 acres of open field, and I don't care how good you plan, how many johnnies you set up, it's still going to smell like shit. It was hot and muggy, and that made it even worse. They kept digging ditches, but the odor was still there. Not even all the hash and weed in the world could kill it. I never smelled anything that bad."

"With all that yellin' and screamin', and them sayin' how the country sucks, they were still singin' 'This Land is Your Land.' Ain't that a riot? They were singin' patriotic songs and torchin' the flag. Not some Commie flag, but *our* flag. The stars and stripes! Old Glory! Some of the chicks tried to stuff flowers into our muzzles, and get us to sing with them."

"That music was something else, man! Like—you know, like up there in one place was the best there ever was. [Among them were The Who; Credence Clearwater Revival; Blood, Sweat, and Tears; Jefferson Airplane.] And there was Joplin and Guthrie and Hendrix and Johnny Winter and Joe Cocker and Santana and about 30 bitchin' groups, man. And they was shakin' that stage, and you could feel the vibes all 'cross the land, and they got into your soul, man—know what I mean?—they got into your soul—and they stayed there. We were singin' stuff from 'Alice's Restaurant,' and 'Sgt. Pepper.' We were singin' stuff like 'Hey, Jude.' You know, the part that goes, 'Take a sad song and make it better'? And when we got tired of that, we took off on 'Day Dream Believer.' Just over and over. Mostly just the chorus. But it sounded right. Like it belonged."

"Assholes! They don't belong anywhere. Maybe 'cept on a college campus protected from reality. Anyhow, they was selfish. Didn't give a dang about nobody. Not their country. Not themselves. No one. A year from now, ten years from now, I'll remember what happened. It probably won't be any easier in ten years, but it hurts. It hurts real bad, and I get these dreams right now and I can't make them go away."

"I was at the Be-in [Human Be-in in January 1967 in San Francisco's Golden Gate Park.] That's where it all began. Gathering of the tribes, man. We came together. Moved to our own beat. You know how important that was? Do you? Do you really know how much that meant?! We planned the Revolution there, man. The whole fuckin' revolution. Music and newspapers and what the Man said was the counterculture. It emerged there! It came together there! Damn straight it did. . . . Then there was Monterey [Pop Festival; June 16–18, 1967]. Just me and a couple of hundred thousand others. Paid a buck to get in, and all the artists, the best there were, all of them, they didn't charge nothing. Nothing! The Movement was free of commercialism and shall always be free. Now and forever. Music by the people and for the people. Paul McCartney said he wanted Hendrix there, so Jimi shows up in front of more people than he ever knew existed, and just blew all of us away. Did licks like no one else ever. Just angry raw power. The Byrds. Jefferson Airplane. . . . Can't remember. . . . So long ago. Oh, yeah, the Who. Mamas and the Papas. The Dead, of course. . . . Can't remember. Maybe it was the acid. You know the Diggers laced the turkey sandwiches. . . . No, wait, that was at the Be-In. . . . Maybe not. Just can't remem— . . . Oh, yeah, there was Otis Redding. Booker T. No one cared what color anyone was. Joplin. Lots of us didn't know who she was, but she sure belted out what we were feelin'. Three days of music. There was a shitload [of people] at Woodstock, but the Be-In and Monterey, that's where it all began. It's why there was Woodstock."

"These freaks have no idea of history. About all the wars we fought over two centuries just to preserve the American way of life. They say to make love not war, but most of them are so wasted I don't figure they could do either."

"They had this amateur stage away from everything else,

and anyone could perform. Bands and poets and jugglers and people who just wanted to have their say. Well, Joan Baez—can you believe it, man, Joan Baez!—well, she sees that there are people kinda just hangin', so she does an hour! A whole freakin' hour on an amateur stage! Know what else? She didn't just go up on that stage. She waited her turn. Must have waited an hour, two hours. No one knew she was waiting, I guess, but she waited her turn, just like everyone else. Was almost late for the main stage. You know what? Best of them all, the very best, that was Country Joe [McDonald]. Now, that's one heavy dude, and that ain't no shit. Y'know, man, like on Friday, they was havin' trouble getting their shit together. Afraid there might be dead air on stage. But they find out Country Joe was there, and they asked him to do a set. Now, he ain't on their program, and he was just hangin'. But, y'know Country, he just played just about every gig anyone asked him for. Lot of them were for nothing, just to help the Cause. Even wrote some good shit, too. Powerful political shit. That 'Fixin' to Die Rag' gave America a conscience. At least some of America. Last couple of years, hardly anyone seen him. He'd been lying low, and he didn't want to do this gig. Well, they told him they needed him. I mean they really needed him. So he gets out there and follows Richie Havens. Can you believe that?! Anyhow, there's a whole mess of us out there. More'n Country's seen in his whole freakin' life! And he's scared shitless. And we don't know 'bout Country, him bein' out of circulation so long. But he gave us the Fish Cheer, and everyone went wild, just a-yellin' and a-hollerin'. And Country, he was just a whoppin' up there, doin' his thing. I mean, like he couldn't do no wrong. He made it happen, man. But, wait, that's not all of it! When the big rains came [Sunday], and there were electrical lines all over the place, and all of us were scared shitless 'cause we thought we might fry 'cause we didn't think they'd ever turn off all that electricity fast enough, Country [and the Fish] gets up on the stage and they sang to us. Got our minds off things. None of us could hear him. But he was singing for all he was worth! Calmed us down. Sucker sure do know his shit!"

"My unit had been called up for the race riots in Cleveland [1966] and Akron [1968]. But I'll tell you this, I was more scared at Kent. They was gonna kill us, like thinking that wiping us out would end the war. We was scared shitless, but we was there 'cause we had to be. They should have let us be. They shouldn't have messed with us. We were dressed in full combat gear. Flak jackets. Helmets. Bayonets. Hell, we never even used bayonets exceptin' for Basic. And them hippies, them godless unpatriotic traitors, these stoners, they thought they'd take us on. . . . I . . . there's . . . I just . . . can't forget what happened that day. Mom's been tellin' me just put it all behind me. Get on with my life. But, I can't do that. I can't can't fuckin' do that!"

"When some people think about Woodstock all they think about is the drugs and nudity. Lotta chicks were laid low by the acid. Bands just threw out acid to the crowds. Media focused on that. Sure, we were stoned. 'Least I think we was stoned. But we weren't hurting no one. 'Long as you don't hurt no one, government shouldn't be telling us what to do or how to live. Yeah, I went swimming nude. Lot of us did. Some walked around nude. It was fuckin' hot, for Chrissakes! Hot and muggy, and we sure as hell didn't have showers like the vacationers at Howard Johnson's got. It wasn't no giant sex and drug orgy like the papers tried to make it out to be. It was bitchin', man. People getting tuned up, groovin' to the music and free of the Man."

"They just shoulda let us be. You can't commit violence without getting some of it back. I didn't like what happened, but it had to happen. They made it happen. We had to fire! We didn't have no other choice. If we didn't fire, we would have sustained casualties. We told them to disperse. We warned them! We told them what would happen but they kept coming at us. Tried to surround us. We warned them! We told them to back off! None of us wanted to have trouble. We was real scared. I couldn't see the Looie [lieutenant], and Sarge was in the line somewhere, and none of us knew what the hell was going down, but we had our orders. They told us to return all fire. Then I heard a shot. Then a lot more. I was sure there was a sniper. I'd swear to it."

"They hired hundreds of rent-a-cops, told them to protect life and property, but don't hassle us. Kinda just blend in. Help out and be cool. Even the cops from the local towns, they were cool, rappin' with us. It upset the locals, though, 'cause there's these laws about drugs, and on the grounds the cops were lookin' the other way except for the big dealers, and you step off the grounds

one foot and they'd bust you. Locals thought they shoulda been bustin' us no matter where we were, but there weren't enough of them, and they knew we weren't gonna cause trouble."

"They had to be on drugs. All of them. Drugs make you crazy. They was crazy. Destroying everything. Messin' with armed troops at bayonet-ready. No doubt about it, they were stoned, otherwise why'd they destroy everything. Why'd they try to attack [combat-ready] soldiers? Don't make no sense."

"I was working Big Pink. That and the White Tent were for the medical problems. The yellow tent was for other stuff. Any time you get half a million people together, you'll have problems. We had to watch for hep [hepatitis] because the sewage facilities weren't much better than open ditches, and the stench—man, the stench was unbearable at times, especially after the rains. All the chemicals in the world didn't get rid of that smell. They don't teach you about this in Med school. It's a whole different kind of medicine. Almost no injuries caused by fights. But drugs were all over. Mostly acid, hash, pot. Problem was that a lot of the junk was bad. We put out the word that the blue acid was bad, but they took it anyhow. They didn't know. A lot of them didn't get too much sleep, not much food. That made it even worse. There were always people waiting for treatment for bad trips or cut feet. But didn't get hardly anyone from fights. Five hundred thousand people and almost no one was fighting. . . . Humidity was high. Damned near impossible to work. It was like a combat zone. And the casualties were coming in all the time. They had to airlift in supplies, it was that bad."

"We didn't have enough [ammunition and supplies] if they went all-crazy on us, but we did have more than enough to scare the holy be-jeezus out of them. Some of us were scared that they might have guns, might launch an assault. Just up and shoot us. Not all of them. Just a couple. That's all it would have taken for us to level that freakin' college.

"I came with 20 rolls of Tri-X and a dozen of Kodachrome. With all the humidity and heat, I was worried about what I was shooting; if any of it was going to be any good. I had ice at the tent, and kept the film there, but you never know. I wish some-

one could figure out a way to create a camera that doesn't need film. It'd sure cut down on problems. I was scared I wouldn't have what the LNS [Liberation News Service] wanted. If I just get them a few pictures, they'd be OK, I figured. But, I really hoped that I got enough. LNS took just about everything I could send them. A couple of music mags and some other alternatives took what the LNS didn't. Maybe I can get a picture book out of this. That's why I brought color. . . . Got called a nark a lot. Bunch of cops out there with cameras, pretending to be a with-it bunch. But everyone knew what they were. Some kids shoved me around a bit. No big deal. They were just as scared as everyone else. . . . It's harder now than ever to trust people. You just don't know. We need to see what this is all about. Not from the eyes of the establishment, but from the people. Maybe some day the people will all have cameras. Then, we'll see what's really happening, not just what the police say is happening."

"No, there was no official order to fire. The situation didn't allow it. A Guardsman always has the right to fire if his life is threatened. I didn't shoot. My weapon still had its issue [bullets]. Didn't fire nothin' at no one! You gotta believe me! I didn't shoot no one! God no! Didn't fire my weapon. Most of us didn't fire. No matter what the press said, most of us didn't fire. It wasn't good what happened, but violence isn't the answer. I . . . I don't regret what we had to do. I was just doing my job. You do what you're told. You can't think about the consequences . . . There was a burst of fire, then it was over. Captain called for a cease-fire almost immediately, but there was still some shooting. Then it was over. 'Ceptin' it's never been over, and there ain't enough booze to make it all go away."

"Don't remember much 'bout it. It was kinda blur. 'Bout only thing I remember, yeah, the one thing I remember was that traffic. Backed up for miles. Cars and vans everywhere, and no one was moving. So we held our own little festival on the roads. But when we got to [the site] we . . . I don't know. I know there was good music and some real fine shit, but I can't remember much there. Two years later, and I try, but I just can't remember."

"Been a year now. Everything seemed so focused back then. I mean, we were scared, but we knew what was what. We had orders. We had our plans. . . . But, now, I don't know. Just don't know. Just wish I could forget. Just wish I could forget."

"Woodstock was a burst of our energy; our music; our spirit. Phil Ochs said it for all of us. He wrote a lot of powerful words. But I cried when I first heard 'I Ain't Marchin' Anymore.' I just sat there and cried. I couldn't take it, it was so powerful, and all I could do was cry. I guess, maybe, that was what Woodstock was all about. It told the world that you could live in peace and harmony and celebrate life and not have to march. And not have to kill. And it's your decision."

"I didn't like what we had to do. There's gotta be something real horrible wrong when we kill our own. . . . I mean, there we was. Them and us. 'Bout the same age. Next day, it hit me. I just sat down and cried and cried. I couldn't help it. None of us could."

. . . A candlelight service for the four dead students is planned for tonight.

15/

Waiting for a Bus
on Morrissey Boulevard

"That a peace symbol?"

Swilling and spilling a bottle of whiskey, he did what most people do when someone doesn't answer—he repeated the question even louder. "Peace symbol?! That a fuckin' peace symbol you're wearing?!" He was talking to Apryl, but glanced at me.

It was dark, I was exhausted, and he was drunk, but I moved closer to him, hoping I wouldn't have to defend anyone's honor or reputation, especially mine. Remembering lines from innumerable short stories *Century* had rejected over the past couple of decades, but which get lengthened and published as mass market paperbacks, I growled right back. "Yeah. What's it to you?"

It was a foolish move on my part. I had no idea if he was a panhandling drunk, an escaped psycho, or a mugger who thought a Timex was worth the risk of a stick-up. I hadn't seen a Boston cop for almost an hour, didn't even know if any were working Friday evening. Although the drunken psycho mugger, Apryl, and I were the only ones near the bus stop on Morrissey Boulevard, not far from the *Boston Globe*, I reasoned there were still enough people wandering around for him not to do anything stupid. That also wasn't smart, since muggers, psychos, and drunks don't have the best common sense, and passersby do nothing to interrupt their desire to pass by.

"Lady deaf?" he barked, glaring at each of us. "You her protector, pussy-face?" Maybe *he* had read too many lines from rejected short stories.

151

"It's a peace symbol," said Apryl quietly.

"Lady speaks!" said the drunk; cowboy boots, silver belt buckle, faded and torn 501s, T-shirt and Army summer camouflage jacket proclaiming his masculinity, a large mass of dirty-brown hair spilling from beneath a blue-knit ski cap on an early-50s body barely hiding a brain saturated by years of alcohol abuse. In his left hand was the whiskey bottle; his right hand held a walnut. Sometimes tightly, sometimes loosely. I had no idea why he had a walnut. No idea if he was going to eat it or use it to crack open a skull. But there was no doubt the walnut was his, and his alone. With a loud belch, he burped out a challenge. "See, fag-boy, you don't need to defend her honor."

No doubt about it; he was drunk *and* reads rejected short stories. Suddenly, he turned to Apryl, almost losing his balance, but pirouetted into a remarkable recovery. "Gimme a piece, lady!" he said menacingly. "That peace symbol, it says you want peace. Well, *I* wanna piece."

It was the kind of day you wished existed only in books, not in real life. It had begun in my apartment at 6:30 a.m., less than five hours after I had managed to get Apryl to shut up so I could get some sleep. With most of the journey on I-84, it should have taken no more than seven hours, plus rest stops, to go from her apartment in Pennsylvania to mine in Boston. But, Apryl thought on this day after July Fourth, we should explore side roads and villages. About 13 hours after we began, we arrived at my apartment; I was tired; she wasn't. It was only part of my penance for having become involved with my subject. All I had wanted was a story about what happened to the hippies, to look at how society had managed to crush the ideals and activism of the '60s and replace it with the self-centered greed of a new era. But there I was, chasing parades and picnics, struggling through equal doses of Apryl and work the past three days, getting almost no sleep, and agreeing to sweet-talk a $13.5 billion bank so Apryl could possibly save her land upon which she thought she was going to build a school for peace. A place where everyone from Pennsylvania Quakers to war-weary and retired Army generals could send their children to learn love, not war.

I had reached over to shut off the alarm and brushed a lamp onto the floor, stumbled through morning necessities, tripped over a hassock, stained a newly-purchased shirt when I unsuccessfully tried to keep the coffee from hitting the carpet, stepped into a mud hole just outside the apartment, missed one train by seconds, waited 12 minutes for the next one, got into South Station and, having forgotten subway tokens, had to wait in the world's slowest line while the cashier used his fingers to count out change. At the office, I ran into a cleaning crew which was shampooing and waxing eloquently, and the IRS which was cleaning out Sam and *Century*. And it wasn't even 8:30. Two hours, and several cups of coffee later, I met Apryl. We would spend the rest of the day fighting other battles.

On Federal Street, not far from Faneuil Hall, site of innumerable meetings of colonial revolutionaries, is the headquarters of the First Boston Minuteman Bank and Trust Co., the same one that had led the Century America Corp. into the Valley of the IRS. At the same time Sam, his accountants and legal team were fighting their battles with First Boston, I was about to fight another. Other than an occasional slogan—"A Revolution in Banking"—First Boston knew little about revolution, a fact that became apparent when the first person we talked with suggested that Apryl would be better able to get her life in order and make regular payments if she got a job teaching in the public schools instead of trying to build her own school. She was friendly enough, but couldn't help; she had a small desk and a small chair, so we moved to the office of someone with a larger desk, a larger chair, and a brass lamp.

Wilson K. Thurman moved around some papers on his desk, punched a few keys on a desktop computer, leaned forward in his chair, looked up, and frowned, a deep concerned frown. "Ah yes. However—" No matter what Apryl said, he'd "Ah yes," and then throw in his damned *howevers*. *However*, we just received this loan as part of a fairly large purchase in the past few weeks. *However*, it is now three months overdue. *However*, it is not practical for us to carry a loan that far overdue. However *this* and however *that*.

The nice thing about banks is that a gaggle of gray-suits will interrupt anything they're doing just to tell you that you're still late with your payment. The bank was willing to withdraw its foreclosure actions if Apryl would bring the account up to date within a week. "Perhaps you can find other funds. Perhaps some of your friends could help you out."

"How *dare* you suggest I burden my friends with a problem of money! I'd sooner beg from strangers!" He didn't know what hit him. Had he been at the diner outside New Haven, about two-thirds of the way between Fishers Ferry, Pennsylvania, and Boston, he could have heard the same speech, though with even more fury when I had made the same suggestions. The banker had only one other suggestion—perhaps Apryl could find a full-time job somewhere; possibly as a clerk in some department store; perhaps as a receptionist; maybe since she wanted to be a teacher, she could even work as a teacher's aide.

I had a better idea. We excused ourselves for a moment while I took Apryl to the lobby to cool her down, and to explain a proposal. *Century* would contract with her for freelance work— *no, it's not charity; no, you don't have to come into the office every day; 50 percent kill fee if it doesn't work out.*

"What do you mean if it doesn't work out!" she snapped. "You think I can't do the job? You think I'm an amateur who can't even screw on a lens? Who the hell do you think you are to tell *me* 'maybe it won't work out'? I do my job and I don't take charity! Got it?!" Not only did I get it, half the bank got it, including a loan officer who just sat there pretending to be a wax figure. My mind said, "Fuck it! Who needs this crap!" But what I said was a very irritated, "You want the job or not?"

So I wrote out a check and the loan officer excused himself while he and the check went to a teller's window. Ten minutes later, he and the check returned. Now, under similar circumstances, others might have become upset at what he had said, might have screamed and raged, but not me. Not David M. Ascher, executive editor of *Century* magazine. No, indeed. I was remarkably calm.

"What the *hell* do you mean you can't take my check! I know damn well there's money in that account to cover it! Are *all* of you robotrons, or just the ones who deal with people?!"

"Yes, sir, there is. I mean—"

"You don't like the design on my checks? You'd prefer that I choose Scenic America instead of Wildlife?"

"Sir, I mean you'd have enough in your checking if your payroll deposit had cleared." Every Thursday night, the Century America Corp., Inc., direct deposits my payroll check, less $150 for savings, into my checking account. This Friday, precisely at 8:03 a.m., the IRS computers whirred equally effortlessly, and the payroll deposit was retracted and returned to a Century America account where it became part of the seizure. "I assure you, it has nothing to do with you," said Wilson K. Thurman. What I wanted to say to him probably shouldn't be printed. In my fury, I had still another idea.

"Transfer two thousand from savings, and I'll write a check from the transfer." I figured it would easily cover the back payments, plus give me some spending money until Sam had finished tap dancing on the government's forehead.

"Sir, I can do that, but we would still be unable to accept your check for the payments." I sat there a moment trying to find just the right string of expletives. It was in that moment between silence and Armageddon that Wilson K. Thurman carefully explained that it wasn't the balance in the account or the design of the checks, but a block on Apryl's account, the kind that humans program into computers. In this case, he couldn't enter any data into the account, and could get from the screen only certain basic information. I asked a few questions, and he could only plead ignorance. At the moment, he seemed about as worthless as the long-retired and much-maligned Susan B. Anthony dollar.

So, Apryl tried a few questions, but Wilson K. Thurman still didn't have the answers. If anyone ever wished to have answers, it was Wilson K. Thurman, if only so Apryl wouldn't ask any more questions. He again excused himself; when he returned had more bad news. The bank didn't own Apryl's mortgage, but was merely a fiduciary for a party that did. He couldn't tell us who—owner-privacy laws, he pleaded. He agreed it didn't make sense that a client would keep its identity from a mortgage holder; nevertheless, the bank would honor the client's request.

In measured tones, I suggested that it might be expeditious if the bank called the Client-Who-Prefers-Anonymity and advise the client that a payment was about to be made on the account and that it would be appreciated if the block could be lifted. The trickle of bad news wasn't yet over. The bank not only couldn't reveal the name of the owner of the mortgage, it had specific orders not to accept any further payments and to continue with foreclosure action—"You must have received all kinds of letters about this; the federal and state governments are quite specific on procedures." Apryl may have received the letters, but may have disregarded them; she didn't remember. Clearly, it was time to ask questions of someone with a big desk.

Big Desk had a meeting in five minutes, and didn't want to talk with us, but Apryl was not to be denied. Under a brief but intense cross-examination, Big Desk kept reaffirming the bank's position—"Didn't Mr. Thurman explain it to you? We have no choice"—that the client left specific orders not to accept any further payments and to continue with foreclosure actions. A couple of more minutes of useless cross-examination, and Big Desk had to go down the hall to his other meeting, possibly with his boss, Big Conference Table.

From a public phone a half block from First Boston Minutemen, I called the Philadelphia credit union that had brief custody of Apryl's loan before it sold it to the Client-Who-Prefers-Anonymity. I figured there would be no privacy violation, if ever there had been, since the bank no longer owned the mortgage. I figured wrong. Three transfers and several quarters later, an assistant bank controller suggested that Apryl put her request in writing, but that it probably wouldn't be granted since Metropolitan was no longer involved with the account, and "it would only be proper" for Boston Minuteman to release the information. Desperate problems need desperate solutions.

Back at First Boston Minutemen, Garrison F. Matthews, executive vice-president of operations, had just finished talking with two IRS agents who had returned to the bank, apologized profusely to bank officials for their inconvenience, returned the money they had seized from the Century accounts, and released all holds. Matthews hadn't even planned to be at work today but had come in for just a few minutes, and then got buried under a bureaucratic deluge. At the moment, he was confused, pleased that the IRS could be humbled but wondering what kind of connections *Century* had to have.

Somewhere in his confusion, Apryl and I barged in demanding answers. In my fury, I told him not only was I tired of being fucked with, not only was Sam and *Century* tired of being fucked with, but we were not at all fuckin' pleased with anyone at the god-damned fuckin' moment! It was a rare moment when I swore or even shouted. In surprising contrast, Apryl Greene was relatively calm; Garrison F. Matthews was relatively calm; I was a stroke candidate. "I don't know what I can do to help you," he said, maybe with more concern than Big Desk. "What would you suggest?" he asked. "Tell me what the hell's going on," I demanded. "Sorry," he said. "Perhaps if you gave me a check for the late payments," he said, "something might work out in a couple of days."

So, I did the only thing I could—I gave him the check, reminding him that there should be funds in the account, and asked him to apply it to the mortgage as soon as I had the block lifted. He again looked at Apryl, at her peace symbol necklace and her tie-dyed headband; like others, he may have thought she was strange, although she was wearing brown sandals instead of high-top checkered lilac-and-white rainbow-laced funky sneaks, a skirt instead of faded jeans, a blouse instead of a psychedelic T-shirt. Small Desk, Medium-sized Desk, and Big Desk had all stared at her peace symbol and headband, all in their own ways extending varying levels of prejudice to her; it was something Apryl had accepted; it was something corporate society still had not.

The executive vice-president for operations looked away, coughed, then again said he was truly and genuinely sorry that he could do nothing to violate a client's trust, stood up and again apologized for *Century's* troubles. Turning to Apryl, he casually mentioned that once, many years ago, long before he had earned an MBA and became a banker, in a time he could hardly remember, he had worn a necklace not too unlike hers; he asked if she ever shopped at Deerfield & Plymouth, and suggested there were many outstanding bargains in July. We thanked him and left, ready to do battle with a clothing store.

Four subway stops south, on Boylston Street near Copley Plaza, is Deerfield & Plymouth. As expected, we got friendly receptions but no information. Not from a department manager, not from a customer service manager, not even from the store manager. No one knew anything. They were either very accomplished liars or they truly didn't know anything. Either way, it was 3 p.m. and coffee and diet sodas were keeping us awake. Next stop, Stratford Electronics, mini-conglomerate parent of Deerfield & Plymouth. There was no reason to suspect anyone there knew anything—more than once we had thought that the bank had set us up to chase our tails while it contacted the true mortgage holder—but it was the only other lead we had. This time the chase led us by taxi, racing against the working day.

There was no sense dealing with small or medium-sized

desks. We were there to find out one fact—does Stratford or any of its divisions hold Apryl's mortgage? We were there to get one result—release the block. I was righteously indignant about how any corporation could do this to any human being, the liberal crusading journalist waving the banner of the oppressed, riding hard against the forces of computer-chip evil.

Evil came in the form of a shy, disarmingly pleasant 50-year-old president with a medium-size desk. Dr. Leon Salikoff had founded Stratford Electronics one month after earning a Ph.D. in electrical engineering from M.I.T. He was 22 at the time. From a one-person company that designed in-house video facilities, Stratford and Salikoff rode both the growth of television and the personalization of computers until it had carved out its chunk of Route 128, and was knocking at the gates of the Fortune 500. With his secretarial buffer unable to protect him from intrusion by a pissed-off journalist and an incensed future peace school principal, he was suddenly transformed from evil genius bent on destroying Apryl's dream for a school into just another interesting character who Apryl had picked up on her long journey through life.

"A school for peace? How very nice. Please have more tea, Ms. Greene."

"Why, thank you, Dr. Salikoff, you're such a kind and generous man."

O.K., so that probably wasn't the exact conversation, but it sure seemed like it. While he and Apryl continued the love-fest, I remained aloof. After all, if he was able to compromise Apryl, I would have to be the one to drive the lance of righteousness through his evil heart.

"The mortgage, Dr. Salikoff," I finally reminded him. "We need to know if your corporation owns Ms. Greene's mortgage." He smiled—I saw it was a wicked smile, Apryl later recalled it as pleasant—and excused himself. "If you want more tea," he politely suggested, "just pick up my phone and push number 3." An obviously talented phone, I thought. I wondered if it also poured the tea or if it was in a union of telephone tea workers.

When Dr. Salikoff returned, he told us his corporation did have the mortgage, that it was recently purchased as part of an investment portfolio and assigned to the Deerfield & Plymouth division, and that he saw absolutely no reason why both the block and foreclosure actions shouldn't be lifted as soon as payments were made. He even suggested there wouldn't be any problem if Apryl needed two or three weeks to pay even half the back payments. I told him that such generous terms wouldn't be necessary, that back payments will be recorded hopefully by the end of Monday. In a corporate world run by MBAs and lawyers, it was refreshing to see someone from production, an apparently intelligent and perhaps creative person, running his own show. But, I was not to be swayed by appearances.

Outside Stratford Electronics, I rushed Apryl to a bus stop.
"David, slow down! Why the hurry?"
"We have another stop. This one's important."
"We just got what we wanted. What else is there?" She thought a moment. "Dinner! Yes, dinner in Boston. How wonderful! You're the most wonderful, considerate man I ever met!"
"Later. We have work to do."
"What more is there?"
"The *Globe*. Hurry up, we need to catch a bus."
"What's at the *Globe*?"
"Information."
"But why? We got everything we needed."
"We got nothing. I don't trust that man."
"This is stupid. He was a nice man. He cared about my school." In the short time I had known her, I realized that Apryl somehow has an innate ability to correctly evaluate people. But this time I was sure that her love-and-peace aura had been duped by what was probably a manipulative genius.
"It doesn't smell right."
"Don't be so suspicious. And slow down. There'll be another bus if we miss this one."
"It came too easy. Why would a corporation that puts the strictest security on an account, that orders a veil of anonymity, that demands foreclosure—tell me why would it suddenly not only reveal itself, but also lift the foreclosure, and then give you extra time to pay for it? Answer me that."
"David, you *are* suspicious, but you're wrong. Dr. Salikoff is a nice man. I could see that in his eyes. He enjoys his work, and he has the sad brown eyes of someone who cares."
"Apryl, your problem is that you trust everyone. Well, *I* don't trust him. There's something evil there." She looked at me, her eyes imploring me not to be so harsh on people. "Maybe

I should have . . ." She let her voice trail off.

"Should have what?"

"Should—nothing."

"It's something. What should you have done?"

"Not that I would have, you understand."

"Would have what?"

"Would have sold."

"Sold what?"

"The land."

"*Your* land? Where the school is to be?"

There was a moment's pause. "I didn't intend to do it, you understand, but it wasn't a bad offer. It's $500 an acre more than I was ever offered."

"You had other offers?" I asked surprised.

"Almost every month I get a letter, or someone finds me and tries to get me to sell." They all had stories. Even the musician with two broken fingers who came by three times. "I knew he was faking," she said, "it was just not bandaged right, but I sure liked his smooth delivery." She looked at me, a mischievous twinkle in her blue eyes. "As long as I kept saying no, they kept coming back and buying me dinners, and raising the price." We continued walking to the bus stop less than a block away.

"These other offers—any idea why they wanted the land?"

"I figured they were after it to build a mall or housing developments. They all said they or their clients were interested in building a cabin to get away on weekends and vacations from the rat race." She laughed at mankind's greed, mocking their piteous insincerity: "They just wanted to relax by the bubbling blue waters and stretch out beneath God's clear blue sky." Alas, Apryl couldn't provide many clues as to why she was being inundated with offers to sell. Mineral rights? No, a geological survey several years earlier revealed nothing of any great value beneath the top soil, fertile as it was, unless you wanted to spend five dollars for every dollar's worth of anthracite coal, three dollars for a dollar's worth of granite, or unless you had a grand scheme to mine worms and sell them to fishermen. On all sides, her neighbors had sold their land, even got small profits from the sales, but Apryl's land was for a school—in that spot and nowhere else. On the neighbors' land arose no housing developments, malls, or agribusinesses. Maybe it was just some speculative land development. Maybe. But right now, we had a bus to catch, a corporation to research and, most important, a school to save.

Shirley Dent, the *Globe*'s librarian, extended a rare professional courtesy and gave us access to the newspaper's morgue, the repository of all now-dead newspaper stories. An hour of screen reading revealed the most damaging evidence against Leon Salikoff was encapsulated in a three paragraph story from 1979—he spent a night in jail during a civil rights protest. It had been his third arrest in about a decade for his work in civil rights marches. Hardly the bombshell that would trigger the juices of a crusading liberal investigative reporter. I had unraveled not corruption but a candidate for sainthood. I didn't even have to announce the canonization since Apryl's shit-eating grin would have humbled the Cheshire Cat. Nevertheless, it was enough to push me into an even more rigorous pursuit of truth. The *Globe*'s online clip file only dated to 1977; before that, it was in file folders and cartons, the world in yellowing newsprint. But the yellowing newsprint only revealed odds and ends. Nexis, a database retrieval system that many newspapers and magazines had begun to use, gave us more information about Stratford Electronics, but nothing that could explain why it grabbed the mortgage, invoked a cloak of secrecy, revealed itself, and then was willing to drop the foreclosure. I was determined. If enough information was put together in the right order, truth would slice the air, and my journalistic instincts would have been vindicated.

But such was not to be, for everything still led to the inevitable conclusion that Dr. Leon Salikoff was the leading candidate for "Person of the Millennia"—here an award, there an award, everywhere an award award; patent here, charity there, here a patent, there a charity, *e-i-e-i-o*.

"Admit defeat," said Apryl. "You're tired, and I'm hungry."

"There's more."

"Only if you want there to be."

Fifteen minutes after we suspended our search to grab a non-descript vending machine dinner, we were back in the morgue to look through 8K and 10K SEC reports, and Moody's, Dun & Bradstreet, and Barron's directories. Another hour of searching, a hidden adrenaline supply blocking sleep patterns that were trying to emerge, and I was finally ready to give up.

A full-out search would have taken us to innumerable public offices, and there was no guarantee that hours of searching would have turned up anything damaging. Yet, there was a pattern; there had to be a pattern. The answers were there. We didn't see them, but they were there.

"The peace symbol," growled Wasted Walnut, sucking the last drops from his bottle. "I want that fuckin' peace symbol." He swatted the air, trying to grab it, the bottle still in his left hand, the walnut in his right. He wouldn't give either up.

"No," said Apryl, not bitter, not upset. Just "No." Just as sure as walnuts fall from trees in winter, Apryl was sure no one was going to take that piece of jewelry.

Once again I put myself between Apryl and the ex-soldier. I didn't want to hurt him, but I also didn't want him to hurt either of us.

"Yeah, lady. I have a knife and a bottle, and I know how to use 'em," he said. I saw the bottle. I saw the walnut. I didn't see the knife.

"No," said Apryl. "Money you can have; peace you can't."

"Bull ... *shit!*" He said it burping, cutting the air with his walnut, a movement as menacing as if it were a machete wielded by a Montagnard.

"You have much inner conflict," said Apryl.

"I don't have no fuckin' inner anything," he growled. "You're the ones who's all messed up." He turned back to her, the bottle still in his left hand, the walnut-knife in his right hand.

"Put the walnut away," I said in measured tones, doing a half-assed job of masking my laughter from the absurdity when I quickly realized what I had said. The bottle which could have been a weapon wasn't; the walnut, which no one thought was a weapon, could have been.

"Shut up, asshole! This is between me and the lady." He turned again to Apryl, but his voice was now less threatening as he began a rambling, slush-voiced monologue. "We were in that fuckin' jungle while you were home safe," he said. "Scared all the time. Not never knowing when we'd buy it. Couldn't figure out what was going on. Nobody'd tell you nothing. Pot and booze were the only things we could trust. You ever in a hole not knowing which way was up? Confused by things you don't understand? By events that don't make sense? . . . Fighting humidity and the gooks. Couldn't tell friendly gooks from VC gooks. They all gooks. 'Hey, Joe!' they'd call after you, begging for money. Ten-year-old boys. 'Shoeshine, Joe?' they'd ask. Could blow you up any fuckin' time they wanted. Old women. Girls. Whores who screwed you to take info back to the VC. They were all going to kill us." He paused a moment, stood as straight as he could, and looked at Apryl. "*You're* the enemy!" he growled, stabbing and slicing the air. "We *died* because of you!"

"You died because of politicians and businessmen."

"Screw 'em. Screw hippie bastards!"

"No," said Apryl, still calm, "you can't screw the hippie bastards." The ex-soldier should have been moments from passing out, and we should have been moments from getting our bus, but neither was about to happen. He babbled on about college students with deferments who marched not so much against the war but because they might have to be soldiers and give up their protected good life, of civilians safely at home learning new jobs and getting promotions, while he made E-4 and came home with all the skills of a fire-team leader, of employer apathy and VA incompetence. He was right. Many employers wouldn't hire veterans because they thought the grunts of Vietnam, unlike those from World War II, were too messed up to be good, obedient, employees. And the soldiers couldn't count on the people who sent them into war to help. The government and its VA found it financially beneficial to deny benefits to soldiers whose symptoms, whether physical or psychological, didn't show up until years later, often triggered by a memory or maybe by something more current, such as the military build-up for what looked like an invasion of Kuwait. We didn't know what happened to this man; we just knew he had problems.

"You didn't care about us. More of us that died, the better your cause. You didn't—"

"We cared," said Apryl with an edge of irritation. "We cared why there was so much dying. We cared—"

"If you cared, why didn't anyone help us when we complained that we were poisoned by Agent Orange? When we saw our brothers dying from that shit. Months . . . years after they left the DMZ, they getting every joint pain there is. Go snap, crackle, *pop!* Government don't say what it is. VA hospitals all a bunch of shit. Don't give a crap about you."

"Don't count on government to do what's right. They'll do

what's political. And they won't pay for something they caused."

"Damn fuckin' right! . . . Government. Defense Department. Bush and all of them sons of bitches! Just like the people."

"The people?"

"The *people*! Wasn't no one there when we came home. Tell me why no one cared, huh? Why wasn't anyone here to welcome us home? All that happy horseshit about patriotism and loyalty and fighting for rights and all that stuff. Why didn't nobody welcome us home?"

"Maybe some day we will again welcome home our troops," said Apryl. "And, maybe, some day there will come a time when there will no longer be a need to go to war."

"Shoulda thanked us. We was there for them. They wasn't nowhere for us. Least they coulda done was say 'Thanks, Buddy.' Give us a warm meal. People who stayed home got their warm meals. They got jobs and houses. They blamed us for My Lai. Blamed every last one of us." He looked into Apryl's eyes. "Lady, I wasn't even nowhere near that fuckup! I didn't want to kill anyone. Viet Cong all had their reasons for what they were doin'. Didn't care what they looked like or what they believed. I didn't want to kill them. But we got guns and they got guns and that's just the way it is. Generals and politicians told us we needed to kill them to show that we was winning the war. But we knew better, and no one gives a fuckin' god-damn. Came home and people sat around their warm little homes, with nice little jobs, and called me a baby killer." Had it been daylight, we might have seen tears form. We might have seen a man reaching for help. "Why didn't they have to suffer just like we did? Why didn't anyone understand? Answer me that."

"That was not right, but the war was not right, and we had no right being there."

"I was in Quang Tri province. Where were you? *Hanoi?*"

"It was a civil war to reunify the country."

"Don't talk that trash with me!" His voice was sharp and bitter. "You gave aid and comfort to the enemy!"

"They weren't my enemy."

"TRAITORS!" Had he been sober, the thrust of his right hand would have connected with some part of my chest. But because liquor diminished his strength and blurred his vision, all that happened was that I got a sudden frightening whoosh of cold air while Wasted Walnut stumbled and got an up-close and personal look at the ground. He was shaken but not hurt. In panic, he fumbled around, looking, reaching, grabbing, trying to find his walnut, the one he thought was a knife, or whatever he thought it was. Apryl found it, and gently handed it to him. For a moment, only a moment, they just looked into each other. She gave him her business card, and said if he just needed to talk to someone to give her a call. I took the bottle from his other hand, put it into a trash can."We lost the war," he said morosely, and then passed out.

Perhaps we should have hailed a cab, given the driver ten bucks, and sent him to the Salvation Army or a homeless shelter. Perhaps we should have tried to find a police officer to put him into a holding tank until he sobered up. Perhaps, we might even have taken him home, sobered him up, and given him a few hours of compassion. We all need people—even drunken psycho muggers need to be loved. But we did as thousands of others have done to him. We did nothing, except to place a $10 bill in his shirt pocket and put him on a bench near the street lamp with the blown-out bulb.

Our bus came, we left, and Wasted Walnut was asleep on a the bench. We left upset at what we should have done but didn't. It was another annoyance at the end of a long day's journey into futility.

16/

The Company Spirit

by David Ascher

Shortly before Labor Day, Rachel Greenberg—with $27.50 in her bank account, and a car payment due in a week—bought every daily newspaper within 30 miles. She was going to find a job, a 40-hour-a-week job with benefits, and she was going to have that job by the end of the week. Now and then she had a part-time job; now and then a full-time temporary job. Occasionally a full-time job. But for more than a decade, even when she got odd jobs and was living wherever she could, she was a freelance photographer, chasing stories and dreams. Now was the time to settle down, and she was looking forward to it. If she could combine her love of photography with her love of music, that would be ideal. But, nothing in the creative arts is permanent. So, she looked in the want-ads of the local newspapers.

Baby-sitter. No, the couple wanted a teenage girl for that. Besides, what kind of job is that for a 32-year-old who's looking for permanence? *Machinist*. All-thumbs. *Sales Representative*. "We'll get back to you. Sometime." *Secretary*. It wouldn't have been a bad job, except that the boss wanted someone who could use all ten fingers to type. *Service Station Manager*. She could pump gas, change tires, and keep records as well as anyone, but the owner told her she didn't have the right qualifications—she wasn't a man. *Social Worker*. Now, *that* looked promising. She had worked with labor unions and social service agencies, often as a volunteer or for little money; she liked helping people. Yes, social worker for the county would be just the right kind of job for her. Alas, she quickly learned that most of her job would be to take applications for welfare aid. Besides, to fill out forms she needed a college degree.

She kept looking. *Stock clerk . . . Taxi Driver . . . Welder . . . Administrative Assistant . . .* That last one looked interesting. A day later, she abruptly learned that she looked too interesting to her prospective employer. She left the interview quickly, and didn't even say "Good-bye."

Customer Service Trainee . . . Executive Trainee . . . Management Trainee . . . Retail Sales Trainee . . . Sales Assistant Trainee . . . She applied for several jobs, but never received a job offer. "Is it me?" she thought. "What have I done wrong?" she wondered.

Assembler . . . Bartender . . . Bookkeeper . . . Counter Girl . . . Custodian . . . Engineer . . . Nurse's Aide . . . Technical Photographer . . . She was a good photographer. Her photos were published in newspapers, magazines, and in the monthly publications of labor unions. Several were collected into a paperback collection documenting the plight of migrant workers. So she went to the executive offices of Wolfe–Woodward, waited, and learned that the job was really two jobs. Most of the time, she would be in a laboratory, taking X-Rays of pipes and structures to determine stress levels. Not terribly creative but a job, nevertheless. However, one or two days a week she would be responsible for taking photos for the company's publications and news releases. Two jobs; two bosses; one weekly paycheck. Although, the initial salary would be low—$125 a week, only $33 more than minimum wage—she'd be able to get regular raises and have all the benefits of steady employment—decent medical and dental benefits; ten days of sick leave; seven paid holidays; a two-week vacation every year. And, she'd have enough time on weekends and evenings to still photograph America's struggles.

She was reading a magazine and filling out employment forms at the same time when the assistant vice-president for technical operations, walking and reading at the same time, not looking where he was going, tripped over her. He was impressed not so much by her bubbling enthusiasm for life or her desire to work long and hard, but by her being able to do two things at once. She might be just what the company needed, even if she didn't have a college degree. What she did have, however, was a résumé and clips, unlike some of the applicants who merely talked a good résumé. He liked what he saw, and he especially liked that he could ask her questions about her photography, and in the same sentence she could discuss both the technical and the artistic details with barely a pause.

And so the assistant vice-president for technical operations took her through the plant, something he seldom did with a job applicant, especially since most areas were restricted. And everywhere he went, he talked with stock clerks and pattern makers and drill press operators and technical writers and engineers. And everyone knew him, and all gave him warm greetings, and then went about their business.

Then he took her into the public relations office, and introduced her to the supervisor for communications who showed her the company scrapbooks—all of them bound in imitation leather, resting on imitation wood grain end tables. There were pictures of the company's many bowling teams—"One of our teams won the Pennsylvania Industrial League championship three years ago"; people receiving suggestion awards—"We pay between twenty-five and a hundred dollars; with your sparkle and ability, I'll just bet you'll be receiving a lot of extra money this year"; and construction of the new plant—"We began it three years ago, and it took less than a year to complete. We're very proud of that." And there were the scrapbooks filled with life-cycle pictures—everything from the pictures of babies born to company employees to retirement dinners. "We celebrate every birthday," said the supervisor for communications.

Then he showed her an expensive glass case that displayed service pins—a different one for every five years; the suggestion awards—from a 5-1/2 x 8 inch certificate to an engraved plaque; the company's bowling teams' shirt patches; and other items, all meant to boost employee morale.

The enthusiasm of both the assistant vice-president and the supervisor never waned as they explained how important a photographer is to the company, and how the previous photographer took an early retirement and was now happily living with her brother's family somewhere in central Florida.

And so, Rachel Greenberg, having passed a urine test and a security check, took the job and wore high-neck blouses that covered her brass peace symbol on a leather strap. Two weeks after being hired, she left for a month to attend a special class combining physics and stress radiography at the University of Massachusetts. In her three-month and six-month evaluations, she never received a mark lower than a "9." She was happy with the company; the company was happy with her. After her first year, she received a 5.5 percent raise. "This is better than a party," she repeatedly thought. For almost three years, four days a week she checked for stress in pipes; one day a week she took almost everyone's picture—for bulletin boards, for presentations, for the company's monthly newsletter, for external distribution to newspapers. Every week, for almost three years. And every year she received a raise.

Then, one day, while taking pictures of the almost-retired, she met an employee with the same enthusiasm for life as she once had. "I just love it here," he said. "I don't want to leave, but at 65 it's time to retire. I'm an assembler. Been one all my life. It's the only thing I know. I don't know what I'll do next month. Maybe fish. Maybe my wife and I will travel. See the kids and grandkids. We didn't have much time for it up to now. I'll miss this place. Everyone has been so nice to me. They made me feel comfortable. I began working here when I was 17. I was just out of high school. Of course, we weren't into electronics then, but we still had a number of good defense contracts. I came to work every morning at 7:30, except for the few times when I was ill. But, ya know what, Missy, when I had my hernia operation, and that time I had to have my gall bladder removed, the company paid for everything Blue Cross didn't. They didn't have to do it, but they did. And even in the bad times, we still got a turkey for Thanksgiving and a ham for Christmas. We may not get the best pay here, and sometimes the supervisors don't seem to have all their doughnuts in one box, but every year we always got a raise. I don't think it's ever been less than two percent. With some good planning, and not wanting a whole lot of those luxuries we never needed, I always made my paycheck last. They've treated me right well. Been here 48 years."

That evening at home, Rachel Greenberg looked at her 20-page policy manual, again reflected upon the rah-rah spirit of "one-ness," the job she was doing, the frustration and problems she occasionally faced, the windowless office she was in, the growing number of defense contracts the company had, and especially about the life of the assembler—how he came to work at the same time every morning, did the same work, took the same coffee breaks and lunch times, celebrated everyone's birthdays, weddings, baby births, and bowling team victories, and went home at the same time—almost every work day for 48 years. It was almost the same story she heard from dozens of retirees she wrote about and photographed.

Rachel Greenberg looked again at her newspaper, past the news about guerilla wars in Nicaragua and the Middle East, and again focused upon the four-column story on page 3 that said Wolfe–Woodward just received a $265 million government contract to create, manufacture, and assemble a new missile guidance system, and another $175 million to manufacture tubing for the nuclear Navy. And she looked again at a short article in the business section, which showed that the stockholders for the last quarter of the year had the largest return on their investment in three years, and how they never had a dividend less than eight percent. She looked at it, thought about it, and spent the rest of her evening crying. She didn't know how much longer she would be at her company, but she knew that she couldn't be there much longer.

She walked to a "swingles" bar a couple of blocks away, and got drunk. The party was over.

17/

Snarls of Determination

In Boston, the story is told about the John Hancock Building. Over a period of time, windows in the 60-story office building began falling out, smashing against the concrete of Clarendon, Stuart, St. James, and Trinity streets. So, John Hancock sued the contractor who, in turn, sued the glass manufacturer who was insured by—yep—John Hancock Insurance. I felt no different from John Hancock. Everything was going around in circles and there was no solution. I had known Apryl about six months, had stacks of notes, but no story. I was confused by what was happening to her land; I was confused by her life and how to turn it into a story. She, of course, was probably finished with her fairy tale about knights and princesses.

Writers have dozens of ways to avoid writing, but eventually we have to write. So, I sat at my desk, staring at a cursor flashing four times a second, again trying to make thoughts appear as graphemic shapes of amber against a green-black background. A decade earlier, before PCs had begun to replace typewriters, I would have ripped paper from the carriage, wadded up page after page, and fired them somewhere in the office. It didn't matter where—a wall, a window, whatever was handy. It would clear my rage of failure. But, now, to throw a screen would lead to financial insolvency. And so there I sat, writing and deleting, staring at the screen, trying to record Apryl's life, hoping to bring understanding about the Movement to a world that cared more about designer jeans than clothing for the homeless. I knew I'd finish my story; I knew I had no choice; I just didn't know when or at what cost. What I *did* know was in a literary world progressively more concerned with corporate profits than social issues journalism, a book about a woman and her place in a social movement would always be trumped by ghosted celebrity tell-alls and books of lurid and fast-paced plots written by hacks who tripped over their own two theme sentences. It was reality, just as Apryl and her life was reality. Complicating all this, of course, was my involvement with my story, for Apryl was in trouble, and I was suddenly lost at what was happening to her and, more importantly, why.

Although frustration comes easily for journalists, we don't take it so easily. Under great stress, we're expected to be able to go into unfamiliar settings, look around, ask the right questions, get the right answers, analyze the data, and then write it up in the clearest, most logical presentation possible—hopefully without error. In J-school, we were relentlessly hammered into semi-perfection by professors who threw story after story to us to write, edit, and design. Want to know why the public has a right to know, or why the First Amendment protects the pretentious *New York Times*, the sleazy *Hustler*, tabloids, alternative weeklies, movies, and billboards equally, we'll cite a plethora of Supreme Court case studies, and throw in the words of the Founding Fathers as evidence. If the public wants to sue, censor, or string us up by our thumbs until we reveal our sources, we're ready for them since we studied media law. If they want to talk about pornography, ethics, monopolies, media credibility, or violence in the media, we can debate from both sides of our mouths since we took courses in social issues in the media. Want us to sound erudite? We'll talk about electronic gatekeepers, diffusion theory, and narcotizing dysfunction as easily as we talk about the weather. Plato and Milton? We have them aced. Try ancient Chinese block printing and Gutenberg, Hearst, Greeley, and Pulitzer, Sarnoff, Paley, and Murrow. Yep, they're in our back pockets, their lives a guide for understanding contemporary issues. We can even read type upside down and backwards—well, some of us anyhow, since the art of typesetting is being replaced by computers, desktop publishing, and the business of high-speed duplication disguised as printing. But, most of all, we're zealous in our pursuit of truth, justice, and the American way. After all, Superman was a journalist, and that's more than just coincidence.

Right now, I didn't feel like Superman. Heck, I didn't even

feel like Jimmy Olson! Bernie Abrahams and I had spent several hours over the past few months just talking about all this,
and although he gave me new insights into tracking Apryl's
story, the best suggestion he had, one that I knew was right but
my gut wouldn't accept, was that I could either do a story or
become involved with my subject, but I couldn't do both. Thanks
to my desire to pursue a story and Apryl's desire to pursue a
dream for a School for Peace, I had become a repository of doubt
who not only still didn't know much about the subject of my
article, but now was lost in a sea of bureaucracy and confusion.
It was this confusion that gave me the strength and unbridled
determination to gallop into action and pursue absolute truth—
about Apryl, about what was being done to her.

What was being done to her at the moment was eviction.
State-certified, fully-stamped and processed eviction. Thanks to
the efficiency of the U.S. Postal Service, Apryl had just received,
bright and early Monday morning, a certified letter, return
receipt requested, from the Pennsylvania Department of Transportation. Normally, PennDOT sends letters to residents to
request money for car registrations and driver's licenses—and
they aren't sent certified. This one politely requested her land.

Empowered by a snarl of laws, ordinances, and regulations,
all of them related to the doctrine of eminent domain, the right
to seize land for the public good, the Commonwealth said it
needed her 40 acres—the mule she could keep—for roads. What
the Commonwealth needed, said Apryl to a PennDOT supervisor, was a lobotomy with a dull chisel and without anesthesia.

The Commonwealth haughtily declared it had the authority
to take her land, hopefully with her cooperation at a mutually
agreed upon fair price. As far as Apryl was concerned there
would never be a mutually agreed upon fair price. The Commonwealth gave her two choices—deal with it, get a fair price, and
sell the land; or not deal, in which case it was going to take the
land anyhow and send her a check for whatever it thought was
fair. She could even take five years to appeal the purchase
price, but the Commonwealth would still have the land. Apryl
had no money for a lawyer—the public defender takes only
criminal cases—and she had too much financial solvency for
Legal Aid. But she did have something else—the private line to
the executive editor of *Century*.

When she called, moments after throwing her telephone at

the disembodied voices of bureaucracy, she was furious. Not upset. Not mad. Furious! The kind that curls the hair of a Longshoreman. Even her now-damaged telephone was afraid to scream out in static. *Reason* she wasn't going to listen to. *Logic* she couldn't care a whit about. According to Apryl, the Commonwealth of Pennsylvania, founded by Quakers but now run by Cossacks, had mugged her and stolen her land. Into the telephone she hysterically screamed that it was *A-Day*. *A* for the assholes who were stealing her land; *A* for the annihilation this pacifist intended to leave in her wake. Damn the torpedoes! Screw the establishment! Launch all missiles, and bring on Armageddon!

"You've got to come to Harrisburg!" she pleaded.

"I've got work in Boston," I answered. "I'll make phone calls, get a few answers. I'll see what can be done."

"But the story's *here!*"

Apryl was right, damn her! The answers now had to lie somewhere in Pennsylvania. Because of Apryl, and my pursuit of what I thought was a good story, I already owed most of the staff favors, and almost all them were in the pool as to whether I'd ever finish, all of them amused by the dozens of ways writers have for not having to write. Some were even betting that I'd soon be coming to work in a headband and funky sneaks. As for Sam, he put up with it, chuckling every now and then at my Hercule Poirot tenacity. Unfortunately, at the moment, I felt more like Inspector Clouseau.

So, I worked until 10 p.m., took Amtrak's Walt Whitman into Philadelphia, changed trains and met Apryl in Harrisburg about 8 a.m., Tuesday, not much more rested than the night before. Or the night before that. Or the . . . Oh, hell, journalists simultaneously working stories and putting out magazines don't need much sleep.

There are no secrets. Information available to anyone in libraries and governmental offices are all the data that's necessary to track down anyone or anything. There may be infinite ways to hide or disguise the facts, but there are also infinite ways to get that information. It's just a matter of patience, determination, and knowing what and where to look. Hopefully, the records we were after would be sufficient to find the truth behind why Apryl's land became so important. I was now sniffing out a story, not about Apryl and her hippies, but about corruption, greed, and avaricious exploitation. I didn't know what I'd find, I didn't know where I'd find it, but I knew it was there, and it was a hell of a story—if only I could get a handle on it.

We drove over to the *Patriot–News*, and camped out in its morgue. Apryl had wanted to assault PennDOT headquarters, march into the office of the Head Idiot—she didn't know the title, but Head Idiot would do—and crush that poor fool's head like stones in a quarry. With a little patience, I managed to convince her that truth often emerges from the shadows of library stacks and governmental vaults.

An hour of searching revealed only shreds. A dozen articles gave us information about the Metropolitan Federal Credit Union, the one that had swallowed the Susquehanna Valley People's Federal Credit Union, and which had sold some of its loans to Stratford Electronics which had placed them with the First Boston Minutemen Bank & Trust. However, the dozen articles the newspaper had were routine—an employee-of-the-year award for someone who had grown up in Mechanicsburg, a business brief on the merger, a one paragraph summary on an annual report—that sort of thing. We checked the Susquehanna Valley credit union, the one that had held Apryl's original mortgage; nothing. Even Dr. Leon Salikoff came up squeaky clean. Again. What little ink there was, was of little significance—a speech at Penn State's capital campus, a successful bid on a contract that included a Harrisburg-area subcontractor, the promotion of a local resident to a vice-presidency at Stratford. Not even a parking ticket. We kept recording facts, hoping that truth would emerge.

"David! I found my father!" In the morgue were four articles about Charles Greene, founding president of the Susquehanna Valley Workshop. One was a four-column Sunday feature from 1981 about the workshop itself; one was a two-paragraph brief about Apryl's father being named Outstanding Businessperson by the Pennsylvania Association of Business Executives; one was an agate-type obit; one was a three-paragraph story from less than two years before about the Workshop being merged into Pittsfield Industries of Hershey.

"How come you never told me your Dad's company was absorbed?" I asked.

"I didn't think it was important. He was dead by then."

"Did you know about it when it happened?"

"Oh, sure. Everyone knew my Dad. They told me they had a very good offer from Pittsfield. Said they'd be able to keep the same philosophy of helping others; even keep the same staff. Only difference would be that they'd get more financial assistance and professional help."

"What'd Pittsfield get in return?"

"Tax write-off. They'd be able to say they were helping the community by investing in training for the handicapped, and they'd show a business loss to the IRS."

"Were they in tax trouble?"

"Not that I know of. Just probably a business decision, nothing more." I read the articles again, looking for any clue. Maybe it was only coincidence that the larger credit union swallowed up the Susquehanna credit union and the larger corporation swallowed up the smaller Susquehanna Workshop. Maybe it was just the balance of nature. Whatever it was, neither Apryl nor I could find any link.

"*Now*," said Apryl, standing up, irritated that we still hadn't found truth, "we're going to PennDOT!" A short argument later, during which Apryl grudgingly yielded to my logic that answers could better be found outside sanitized corporate offices, we headed not to PennDOT headquarters but to Shottensburg, the district office where the Declaration to seize Apryl's land had originated. An hour of driving, and we were at a one-story building in a pleasant rural community.

For 32 years, Hersh Walters had worked for PennDOT, the last eight as director of its nine-county Shottensburg district. He sat at his desk, paperwork piled two inches high, calmly solving one problem after another. He may have believed he had run into every kind of problem imaginable, that there wasn't anything he couldn't handle. He hadn't yet met Apryl Greene.

"What do you mean no one knows anything about it!" Apryl thundered, eyes flashing invective. "Your agency sent the notice!"

"Yes, but—"

"—but you don't know anything about it!"

"We have the information recorded on our computer," said Hersh Walters, "but right now, no one I've contacted knows why the Declaration of Taking was issued."

"Then *find* someone!"

"If you'll just calm down, I'll—"

"You'll *what?!* You'll tell me this is all one big misunderstanding? That the computer made a teensy little error? That you'll quash the notice and everything will be just hunky-dory?!"

"I wish I could help, but I don't have the authority to quash this Declaration."

"Then who does!?"

"Ma'am—" said Hersh Walters who didn't get another word out.

"Don't call me ma'am!" said Apryl, her patience tested. My name is Apryl Greene. Perhaps you missed that in our introductions. You can call me Apryl or you can call me Ms. Greene, but you don't call me a ma'am."

"Yes, ma'—Ms. Greene."

"There. That's better," said Apryl, a pleasantness abruptly returning to her voice.

"Now, Ms. Greene—"

"Why don't you just call me Apryl. It seems so much friendlier." Hersh Walters looked at me; I merely shrugged.

"O.K. Apryl. As I was trying to explain, all requests for rights-of-way originate in the district office—"

"So you *do* know about it. It's in your district. You're the district director. You know about it."

"What I mean is that this particular Declaration wasn't requested by our district. We issued it, but it was requested by Harrisburg."

"We're going back to Harrisburg," Apryl declared, standing up, slinging her cloth handbag over her left shoulder. "I told you we needed to atomize the Head Idiot." Hersh Walters smiled.

"We're not ready to talk with the Head Idiot yet," I said to Apryl who flashed the briefest of smiles, and sat down again. With a little questioning, we learned that not only had the plans originated in Harrisburg, they had come to Shottensburg only two weeks ago, complete with the Governor's authorization for the purchase; the district merely recorded it and filed it in Newburg. It was unusual, but not unknown. Hersh Walters suggested that perhaps two or three districts were involved, and that Harrisburg was merely taking control in order to assure coordination—although he did admit that the Harrisburg headquarters itself was seldom coordinated.

"The Department does several Declarations every month," said Hersh Walters, somewhat mater-of-factly. "Rights-of-way are a major part of our work."

"And I assume you spend most of your time trying to explain why the state is stealing land."

"Most are routine, and there are few problems. In fact, most of the land owners are so happy that *someone* will buy the land that some even try to take our staff out to dinner."

"Do I look happy, Hershell?"

"No, ma'—Apryl."

"Do you believe *I'm* planning to take you out for dinner!" At that moment, Hersh Walters had every reason to believe that he was going to be dinner. He looked at her, a compassion for her plight. He didn't get much farther than trying to explain that the seizure of land was done not in maliciousness but for the public interest before Apryl pelted him with a fusillade of contempt.

"You're really a bunch of bastards, aren't you? The government stole the land from the Indians, and now it's cannibalizing its own people." Hersh Walters had to be on a double-dose of something. No one could have maintained that much calm in the face of that much anger. Maybe PennDOT requires its employees to be riot-trained. Maybe his pipe, which he had laid aside when we entered his office, had more than just tobacco in it. Whatever it was, he was one of the calmest public officials I had ever met.

"The Declaration of Taking was issued on September 17," Hersh Walters politely tried explaining. "It was received September 20, an offer was made and accepted on September 22—" Hersh Walters never had a chance to finish.

"I didn't accept any offer!"

"It's right here on the computer," he said, turning the screen so both he and Apryl could see it. "On September 22, Ralph M. Taylor, representing Deerfield & Plymouth of Boston—"

"Who?"

"Ralph M. Taylor of—"

"Bastards!"

"Apryl—" I said, hoping to break her string of expletives undeleted.

"I *trusted* that bastard! That god-damned—"

"Apryl!"

"Don't you *Apryl* me! That bastard knew all along. That's *my* land he gave away. I own that land. He has no legal right to sell *anything!*" We didn't know who Ralph M. Taylor was, but we did know Dr. Leon Salikoff, president of Stratford Electronics, parent company of Deerfield & Plymouth. Apryl was betrayed, and I couldn't even feel good about being right.

"According to our records," said Hersh Walters, attempting to calm Apryl—try calming the Tasmanian Devil—"Deerfield & Plymouth doesn't have title to the land. It owns only the mortgage, but was empowered by the owner to negotiate."

"*I'm* the owner!" Apryl again shouted, standing and putting herself inches from Hersh Walters' face. "*Me!* Apryl Greene!" Apryl wasn't a possessor, not of people, and certainly not of land. Like the Native Americans, she believed that land is temporarily given by a universal spirit and that we are merely the caretakers. But she had a mission to create her School for Peace, and no one was going to take that away from her.

"The records show that Floral Industries is the legal owner," said Hersh Walters.

"Who the heck is Floral Industries?!" I demanded, startling both Apryl and Hersh Walters.

"Some company," said Apryl, brushing off my question.

"What do you *mean* 'some company'? PennDOT thinks it owns the land that you think you—"

"OWN!" said Apryl, turning to me, her eyes determined to make sure I knew who owned what land. "*I* own that land on behalf of the children of peace, for—"

"Apryl! Who's Floral Industries? I thought some construction company had absorbed your Dad's workshop."

"It did," she said impatiently, sitting down. "I don't know what this has to do with the School for Peace."

"When did Floral buy out Pittsfield?"

"They didn't buy Pittsfield," she said. Something smelled, and it wasn't flowers.

"You just said—"

"I *said* it *bought* the Workshop. Pittsfield absorbed the Workshop, then sold it to Floral. Probably for a tax write-off. Don't you know *anything?*"

This was rapidly turning into a chapter of *The Young and the Restless*. However, while soaps and their problems meander through infinite plot twists, continuing indefinitely, Apryl's problems had a built-in termination, courtesy of governments and corporations. With careful questioning, while Hersh Walters sat back and watched, somewhat amusedly I suspected, I was again told—she may have mentioned it once before, but I didn't remember—that the deed to the land had contained a right of reversion; if Apryl failed to make three consecutive payments or if she failed to maintain the property, the deed would revert to the Susquehanna Valley Workshop—or whoever bought the rights. More important, if Apryl failed to build her school and maintain it, or any business—it mattered little what it was—within five years of receiving the unencumbered deed, even with the refinancing and loan extensions, the property would be returned to the Workshop. At the time he made it, Apryl's father believed it was in Apryl's best interest by forcing her to make a commitment instead of chasing a dream. Until the Declaration of Taking was issued, nullifying Apryl's ownership, she had until mid-March to finish her school.

"I don't have until March," she quietly said, again confusing me, something as common as potholes on I-80.

"You *don't* have until March?"

"Contract says that, but with the weather the way it is out here, I have to get it built before the first snow. I figure after that, the ground will be too frozen." But, the weather was also an ally, for PennDOT also knew it also had to begin its work by the first snow, or else face the possibility of delaying the building of a series of major roads until spring when manpower and equipment would no longer be needed for snow removal and maintenance. Apryl was fighting to retain ownership to finish her school; PennDOT was fighting to begin construction.

"Who ordered the Declaration of Taking?" I asked.

"I honestly don't know. That's not in my file."

"Which file is it in?"

"I don't have rights of access to that."

"*Rights?!*" Apparently, Apryl wasn't through ranting and raving. "*Rights!* What about *my* rights! I'm going to build a school. That land is being held by me in trust for our children, not for some conglomerate in another state that's planning to nuke all life forms!"

"Who has rights of access?" I calmly asked.

"It shouldn't be any great problem to get the information," said Hersh Walters.

"By the end of the day, I want answers," Apryl ordered.

Hersh Walters smiled. So much tenacity he had seldom seen in one person. He was impressed, but he was also frustrated that he couldn't get the information quickly, that something was happening in his district and he didn't have control. "I know you're very upset, and if I could do anything to help you I would. All I can do is to try to find answers to why these roads are to be built. That's all the information I have. I wish I could help you further, but—"

"But you're just a lackey doing what you're told and you don't have the right to quash anything!" In that briefest of moments, in what could have been a cataclysmic calm, Apryl had shed a tear, and apologized not once but several times for her rudeness. "It's for the children," she emphasized, trying to explain why the land was so important to her, and why the public might be better served by schools than asphalt. Before Hersh Walters could respond, Apryl stood, thanked him, again apologized, and sadly, quietly, almost unaware that anyone was near, again said, quietly and reflectively, "It's for the children."

"God's speed, Apryl Greene. God's speed."

We had threads of evidence, but no tangible shreds of truth. We knew the players. We didn't know *why*. The road to discovery led along Route 11–15 into Newburg, county seat of Marshfield County. Apryl was sure that a thousand workers and their monster machines were on her land at that very moment decimating the wildlife and trees, and grading land for God-knows-what, although Hersh Walters had calmly assured her the reason the plans weren't readily available was because one of his crews was verifying land surveys. Apryl wanted to visit her land immediately, although by law it was no longer hers. However, I needed more facts, and the facts were located in county records.

From the office of the county assessor, we looked at tract maps and index cards, and learned that within the past two years almost 500 irregularly-shaped acres of land surrounding Apryl's 40 acres on the river had been sold. Some of the sales were of homes and small businesses, but most were cuttings from farms and unprotected virgin timberland. The names of the buyers were a mixed lot—individuals, realty companies, and small businesses. Still nothing suspicious. Maybe some smooth-talking salesmen had hit the area, talked owners into selling and naive investors into buying. Maybe there were plans to develop the area. Housing tracts? Shopping mall? Maybe it was just another routine chapter in the asphalting of America. Yet, that much activity in that short of a time sent up a flag that pointed to the office of the Register of Deeds.

"No." It was deliberate; emphatic. Apryl wasn't budging.

"What do you mean, 'No'?"

"That's what I said."

"We have work to do. The answer could lie in the office of the Register."

"They're going to bulldoze my school under an asphalt sea, and we're taking notes? For what? Because you had a *hunch*? So far your hunch has cost us a day."

"So far," I said testily, "we learned that almost all the land around you, a large number of houses, farms, and small businesses, have been sold within the past two years. It may not be much, but it's all part of the mystery."

"*Okay*, David," she said, shutting me off, "so we learned something. Once again, *you're* right and *I'm* wrong." And, once again, she had managed to fuse pouting, anger, accusation, and cynical contempt into one sentence that was meant to imprison me with her will. "We have a handful of facts, but there's no truth. So what does it mean!?"

"I don't know," I said, weary from eyestrain and lack of sleep, "but we have to have facts before we—"

"Before we *what*, David? Before I lose everything I've been working for? Or do I first have to lose everything and start all over?" These were not the words from someone who would accept anyone's explanations, whether from the government or from a friend.

The land was Apryl's, given to her by her father, paid for by him until he died, and then by Apryl, more or less, every month after that. She would take no offers for it; she would accept no governmental seizure. It was the land where her school was going to be built. No exceptions. She looked at me, gave me a peck on the cheek and told me that I might have been right; we needed more facts.

The facts, which had begun in drips, would soon become a torrent. For two hours, we dug through deeds, and talked with county employees. We took down names, dates, locations—but almost no connections. Even Pioneer Power & Energy, which was planning to build a low-level nuclear waste facility in the area, had purchased only nine acres. We were overwhelmed by facts, washing over us much as Apryl's overflowing toilet at her Russian River commune. The facts were there. The numbers were there. They just didn't add up.

"*Damn!*" Revelation! This wasn't just an animated light bulb flashing above my head, but a whole arc spotlight. I hit the table. "How could I be so stupid!"

"Advanced education?" Apryl suggested.

"We're going to the Clerk of Courts."

"Brilliant," said Apryl sarcastically. "You're going to sue the state."

"If this is what I think it is, we may get a chance to screw the state." That, obviously, pleased her. Apryl still didn't see what any of our rescarch was doing to help her reclaim her land. But now she was about to see results—if I was right. I was.

"Look at this!" I said to Apryl, drawing her attention to one of the PennDOT plans we had spread out on a table in the vault room of the clerk of courts. "What do you see?"

"Roads."

"All over the place. They're cutting through the whole area."

"So?"

"So, where do they go?"

"Over the river and through the woods?"

"*Nowhere*, Apryl! Look at this one! Not some secondary asphalt road. Not some fceder road, but a four-lane concrete highway almost as big as I 80. It curves around for a mile or so, and then stops." I dragged up another set of plans. "Look! No connection. It stops."

"Sounds like a typical government project to me," said Apryl sarcastically.

"Why would a road be designed to go nowhere!"

"Graft? Corruption? Maybe it's a way for the state to keep workers employed."

"It's a way for the state to keep industry. They're building roads for something big!"

"Industrial park, maybe?"

"My guess is something nuclear."

"David," said Apryl, with a slightly disgusted tinge, digging into what she believed was naive futility. "I already know they're building something. It's a low-level waste plant. We've known that for months! We started the protest when we first heard. But, it's still a small blemish not a melanoma upon the earth."

"It may be a small plant," I said, "but there's too much activity. Something doesn't feel right." I pulled out another set of plans from the pile. Until 5 p.m., when one of the clerks politely, almost apologetically, asked us to leave since the office was closed, we looked at plans, took copious notes, made guesses and assumptions.

"*Now* can we see what's out there!?" Apryl demanded.

It was easy to determine the extent of the project since surveyor flags were thicker than black flies along the Susquehanna. We had expected to see flags. What we didn't expect to see was trucks. Not just PennDOT equipment, but pickups from four different construction companies, including Hess & Newhart Construction, one of the nation's prime contractors of nuclear plants. Not waste disposal plants, but nuclear plants. This wasn't just a small low-level nuclear waste facility Pioneer Power was planning to build. The nine acres under Pioneer Power's name were probably just for the main buildings, maybe a parking lot; we had figured that Pioneer Power had put the nine acres under its own name so when the protestors showed up—and they did—Pioneer Power could honestly point out that it would be impossible to build anything large on only nine acres. *No big deal. Nothing to worry about. Everything is safe. Secure. No chance of leaking radiation. Trust us!* However, if I was right, Pioneer Power was behind all the purchases for at least 640 acres, from the river into the mountains—four times the size of Disneyland, and 40 times the size of the waste disposal plant at Barnwell, South Carolina, one of only three low-level waste facilities in the country.

If I was also right, the reason Hersh Walters didn't have all the information was that at least another PennDOT district was involved; there would probably be other plans in other counties. Fronts, dummy corporations, naive stooges—all were part of the Pioneer Power plan of acquiring land. That's why the state needed all 40 of Apryl's acres. Not just a right-of-way, but the whole 40 acres! Forty acres near the Susquehanna, the major water source for a nuclear reactor. Not just a small waste plant. Not just a basic electricity-generating nuke, but a nuclear-driven facility to handle waste from Bellevane and at least two dozen other east coast nuclear plants, as well as from college labs, hospitals, and industry. It would be a facility that would probably bring an economic boon to the region before the plant reached its capacity in 30 or 40 years before being sealed and left to decay.

When Pioneer Power's dummies couldn't get Apryl's land, it had to have made some kind of a deal in Harrisburg to confiscate her land. In months, a couple of years at the most, Apryl's land, the one her father had deeded to her, the one she had been making semi-regular payments upon, would be just another land mass to bury—or perhaps to recycle—nuclear waste. As for Stratford Electronics? It seemed logical that it had bought an investment package of loans, turned them over to First Boston for management, and then forgot about them. It seemed innocent enough. Apryl wasn't into innocence at that moment.

"So, Mister Big-Shot Know-it-All," said Apryl, "why'd they block my bank account? You don't do that when you have nothing to hide." I took a moment to respond; it wasn't long enough. "Answer me that, David. Why was there a block if Dr. Salikoff didn't know anything about it? He lied to me, David! I believed him and he lied to me! He's probably an investor in Pioneer Power. He knew all along!"

To Apryl, it was now obvious that the government and private enterprise working together were determined to take her land; she was just as determined to keep them from doing so. Between tears and outrage, she planned to stop construction. She didn't know how—after all, the protestors couldn't stop even the small nuclear waste plant when it was a small nuclear waste plant—but she had every intention to keep the first ounce of concrete from ever being poured.

"Make love to me." She said it without emotion, almost making it a command. "Just hold me and make love to me," she again said, kicking off her shoes and unbuttoning her blouse. We had just spent more than an hour in the dark at the site of the waste plant—if that's truly what it was to become—a rushed dinner at some greasy spoon on Route 11, and more than an hour returning to Apryl's apartment in Fisher's Ferry.

"We have work to do tomorrow," I said cavalierly. It wasn't

that I didn't want to have sex with Apryl, even if she had just made the offer more physical than emotional. It wasn't that for the first time in my professional career I had become involved with my subject, a distinctly dark-gray ethics issue. It wasn't even because I hadn't brought along any condoms. I just was exhausted. I hadn't gotten to sleep—such as it can be in an Amtrak coach seat—until slightly past midnight that morning, after being up more than 18 hours, and since 8 a.m. had been try-ing to solve mysteries. It was now a little past 10 p.m., and Apryl was unhooking her bra. O.K., so what's a few more minutes?

18/

The Monday Night Football Game

by David Ascher

The minuscule cocktail tables, red cloths draping their round tops, threaten to tip when pushed; nevertheless, they serve their dual functions as repositories for drinks and cigarettes, and as excuses to cluster chairs.

The semi-stuffed chairs that surround the tables, however, are sturdy, made with a wood-like veneer for the back and base, and covered with a synthetic something-or-the-other that is supposed to look like leather. At the beginning of every afternoon, four chairs surround each table, making for intimate experiences; but the chairs roll, and during the evening will roll back and forth from table to table.

Along one wall, with its fake fireplace motif, are recently-manufactured Victorian-style couches and high-backed chairs. On the walls are photomurals—one of deer grazing in the field, the other of geese in flight. Near the geese are pressed-board bookshelves supporting *Reader's Digest* condensed books that were never read and plants that will never die.

A 60-foot U-shaped bar edged in Naugahyde softness, and guarded by 25 oak bar stools, is on the opposite side. Against another wall, not far from wood-paneled restrooms, three mics and four speakers frame a Lilliputian bandstand that supports a set of drums and an electronic organ programmed so that almost anyone who can count to 4 can play it. On Thursdays, Fridays, and Saturdays, three singer-musicians will have their sounds amplified to the threshold of wilting the plastic flowers.

Wood beams and amber chandeliers above, red and black

patterned carpeting below. The lights are forever dim. Dim for effect; dim for illusion.

It's now 6 p.m., Monday. There are a few people here, most in their 20s and 30s. At the bar sits a lady in her mid-20s, maybe more, flanked by two men. The lady could be a secretary or junior executive. Her golden highlighted hair is jelled, curling-ironed permed and blow-dried to give her a perfectly natural look. She wears makeup and lipstick; Max Factor on her face, Revlon on her lips. Her fashionably low-heeled pumps add an inch to her height. Her pink silk blouse and tan wool skirt could not have been bought more than a month ago. The two men, also in their mid- or late-20s, could be lawyers or junior executives or ad salesmen. Suits of blues, ties of reds. Modishly-long razor-cut blown-dry hair covers half their ears. A slight fashion statement but nothing too extreme. Clean-shaven with a gentle splash of Bijan. Expensive-looking watches and 10-karat gold college rings.

First one, then the other, talks to the lady. Then both talk to her. For part of the evening, she'll delight in being in the middle. They'll talk to her and with her; maybe later, about her. But right now, they're both talking with her. About nothing really. They had earlier identified themselves by their occupations; she had identified herself by her astrological sign. Of course, this had meant that the two men had to identify their own signs. Compatibility is important in a place like this.

A man sits nearby, a touch of talcum and after-shave hinting the air, a V-neck casual synthetic drip-dry shirt hugging what probably was once a washboard abdomen, drip-dry 501s hugging his waist and thighs, leather shoes caressing feet that undoubtedly have been adequately powdered. A few moments later, another man, almost a copy, but with a golden chain dangling in his "V"—few men will be bare-necked—sits down. There's now one immaculate lady surrounded by four *Esquire*-approved men. To others, it appears they're close friends—buddies—pals. Singularly, they talk with her. About cars. About careers. They talk about this. And they talk about that. About promotions and job security, racquetball, jogging, or time-sharing. About something each of them had read in the *National Enquirer* or *Penthouse*, but which they remember as having read in the *Wall Street Journal, Esquire,* or *Business Week*. The high cost of apartments and condos is a major problem. Finding a good stereo system or car phone for the BMW or RX-7 is a major problem. Every now and then, there might be a brief and superficial discussion about the apartheid government of South Africa, of the long-ago attempted murder of Larry Flynt by someone who objected not to pictures of nude women but to a multi-racial photo spread in *Hustler*, and how the Blacks seem to be taking over American suburbia. They complain about how Mumia Abu-Jamal keeps clogging up the court system with continual appeals of what he claims are racist court procedures and judicial biases that led to his conviction and sentence to die for the murder of a Philadelphia police officer, and how pleased they are that Native American activist Leonard Peltier, serving life sentences for the murder of two FBI agents, is right where he should be, and all the protests about judicial racism and trial discrepancies is pure crap. Earth Day, they believe, is just a lot of tree-huggers trying to stop progress, the last gasps of a dying hippie culture. They talk of the effects of Nixon establishing relations with China, and Carter recognizing China not Taiwan as the true representative of the Chinese people; about the Middle East and the Camp David Accords, of the hostage crisis in Iran, about the Soviet Union's invasion of Afghanistan and President Carter's demand that American athletes boycott the Moscow Olympics, their mouths parroting *Time* and *Newsweek*, their concern as deep as cocktail glasses, as lasting as cocktail napkins.

Cocktail waitresses—costumed in black high heels, black-net hose, black mini-skirts, push-up bras disguised beneath titillating-cut blouses—hustle the drinks while the customers hustle each other. No glass will be allowed to be empty more than moments. There's always another drink to be served, another tip to be earned.

At a table, a young man orders a Vodka-7; at another table, a young lady orders a Vodka-7. They have something in common. They glance at each other, and away from each other. She gets up, goes to the *hors d'oeuvre* table, and delicately places small carrot sticks, dip, and shrimp puffs on a small paper plate. It's just enough, but not too much. Must watch that waist. She turns, and almost falls over the gentleman who exchanged glances with her. She apologizes. He apologizes. They apologize. They giggle over their embarrassment of almost falling into each other, begin some small talk, and then wander to a table at a neutral site. It's all so superficial, but no one cares. They need to be with someone. So they'll keep searching . . . reflecting . . . being conversationally attractive.

A pair of "barely-21s," a few months into the work force, enter and sit at a table. She's carded, her ID discretely checked by a waitress. This is too lucrative a business to be jeopardized by a Liquor Board violation. Her companion, blowing smoke rings from a Marlboro positioned beneath an anemic brown-blonde mustache, is accepted without ID. They order piña coladas and think they're in love.

Two 30ish ladies sit near one of the bookshelves. They talk "girl talk." Two 30ish guys sit near another bookshelf, talking "man talk." It isn't long before there are four people at one of the tables and no one at the other, and God-only-knows what they have to talk about.

The regulars greet each other; the infrequents settle in—watching—waiting. Four more razor-cut, blown-dry junior somethings enter, survey the swingles scene, find everyone attached to someone else, order Heinekins and Millers, talk, joke, make polite noises, and imagine they're successfully cool.

Near one of the photomurals sits a lady with medium-length black hair, light makeup, and a peace symbol on a leather strap around her neck. It seems so out of place here. There's a vacant sadness in her eyes as she sits alone, reflecting—thinking—maybe waiting. For a friend? Lover? It's hard to tell her age. Late 20s? Maybe even late 30s? Nevertheless, she's attractive and probably won't be alone long. Someone will claim to have just the same values she has—and wouldn't she like to go somewhere else?

It's now 8:30. More than a hundred people are here. Talking. Chatting. Discussing. Talking about jobs and vacations, cars and condos. Every day it's the same. Every day the people are the same. And they all talk about never—*ever*—planning to get into a rut like Jim or Karen or Matt or Maureen. They all reaffirm that although they love their jobs and are more than amply rewarded, soon they'll be promoted or move to something better. There's always something better, whether people or jobs. And they're so busy hearing themselves that they don't know that no one's listening, but they'll be sure to "thank you for sharing that," or letting us know that they "can relate to that."

For the last time this evening, the *hors d'oeuvre* table is replenished, and the price of drinks goes up another 50 cents; Cokes and beer are now a buck-fifty, mixed drinks as much as three-fifty. The sandwich-and-salad special is $7.95—chips and pickle slices included.

Nine O'Clock. The bartender finally pushes buttons on a remote control, and from a large-screen television, Rams and Eagles appear. There's noise from the television and noise from the lounge. People are chatting and watching, hustling, munching, and drinking. In their confusion of who they are, and what they want, they'll settle for instant friendships made in front of a cathode ray tube that changes pictures 30 times a second. The Monday Night Football Game is about to begin.

19/

Questions Without Answers

The search for facts resumed 8:30 Wednesday morning when we showed up at the Department of Energy's front lobby. We had already decided that PennDOT's Harrisburg office would provide little more than we already knew, and what we didn't know was probably in Energy's files.

If you're an average tax-paying citizen dealing with corporations and the government, you get the run-around from receptionists to mid-level managers. If you're a journalist, you get the run-around from a press secretary.

"Who ordered the evictions?" I asked. "PennDOT? Energy?"

"I don't know, but I'll get right back to you on that."

"Are the new roads going to cross the land for this nuclear facility?"

"I don't know, but I'll get back to you on that."

"Did Energy order PennDOT to negotiate the land and to issue Declarations of Taking?"

"I don't know, but I'll find out and—"

"What *do* you know?"

"Not much, but if you'll wait right here, I'll see what I can find out and get right back to you. Want some coffee while we wait?" Yep, he was a PR-person all right. In many cases, "right back to you" means an hour or so after deadline, if at all. In Lance Carpenter's case, it meant 15 minutes. Fifteen minutes to find nothing was certainly no national record; in terms of the universe, it's not even a nanosecond, but to Apryl, who had believed 15 minutes was a minor eternity, the news that there wasn't news was enough to bring her out of her chair, stand

192

straight up, and declare in a voice firm with conviction, "Then it's on to Dr. Simpkins."

Lance Carpenter saw his career flash before him. Part of his job was to keep the media informed; part of the job was to make sure that no negative information was leaked to the media; and much of his job was to keep the media away from the director unless she specifically wished to speak to the media—and, even then, only with coaching from the public affairs office. Jeanette Simpkins, like all cabinet officers, was a political employee who would probably still be content to be an associate professor of chemistry at Temple had she not been thrust into appointive office. The fact she had gone to college with one of the governor's senior advisors didn't hurt her political advancement, but what helped guarantee her an appointment was neither her friendship nor her knowledge of chemistry, but that she, her father, and an uncle had made large contributions to the governor's campaign war chest.

"I'm afraid," said Lance Carpenter, "that Dr. Simpkins isn't available right now, but—well, let me check another area, and get right back to you."

This time, it was only 10 minutes. We were running out of coffee, and the doughnut holes weren't surviving well either. "I'm sorry, but I couldn't find out anything from Legal. They have quite a lot of—" he laughed an awkward smile— "shall we say legal information—but it's mostly routine. Applications. Amendments. Filings. Just what you'd expect."

"Is it too much to expect the truth?" Apryl asked sweetly.

"I've already tried Administration and Legal. They don't know anything about any evictions. Have you tried PennDOT?" For an unstable element, Apryl was remarkably calm.

"Perhaps," I suggested, reiterating an earlier set of queries, "you could dig a little deeper and—"

"Dig!" shouted Apryl, even more enthusiastic than usual.

"Dig?" replied a baffled PR man.

"Dig! Before you steal my land, you have to do an archeological dig to evaluate for cultural resources." She looked at me. "That's the law. They have to do an environmental impact statement. The Native Americans were here 10,000 years before we stole their land and massacred them. There's sites all the way from Harrisburg north." Apryl was pleased with that revelation.

"I'll check with Operations." This time, he left—we never

figured out why he kept leaving when he had a computer and a telephone—and returned about five minutes later. The coffee was gone. The doughnut holes were gone. Most of all, our patience was gone.

"The good news," he announced, after apologizing for the delay and asking if we wished any more coffee—"Doughnuts? I can get you more doughnuts. Coffee cake? It's no bother. Really."

"Is it a bother—*really*—to get us information?" asked Apryl.

"First of all, it seems there was an impact statement."

"There was?"

"Actually, the law doesn't require an actual archeological dig, it just requires an evaluation," said the bearer of bad tidings. "Got it right here," he said showing us a one page report." The report, signed by a state employee with a dual title—road engineer/archeologist—essentially said there *might* be arrowheads, there *might* be some broken but useless artifacts, but there was nothing of value."

"Nothing of value!?" Apryl was furious. "If there's *nothing of value*, why are you all so determined to continue stealing land?"

"We do have some good news," brightly said our Little Mr. Sunshine. We have quite a lot of information about a plant that is scheduled to be built in Districts 4 and 5."

"And?"

"And the bad news is that I'm afraid that I don't have full rights of access to that file."

"Rights? You don't have rights?! What rights do you think *I* have? Don't *I* have the right to information? Don't you think *my* children and *your* children and *our* children for generations have *rights*? Don't you think that schools for peace are more important than weapons for destruction?"

"Ma'am, I was only—" Poor Lance. He didn't get much more out when he learned all about monickers. When Apryl was finished, he tried to cook up an apology. "I understand where you're coming from," he said, awkwardly remembering a line from a badly-scripted course in interpersonal communication he once took in college. If he said anything more, he was likely to be fricasseed, so I quickly interrupted.

"What *can* you tell us?"

"I can tell you that the Department has approved applications for a low-level nuclear waste disposal facility that will border both Marshfield and Coal counties." We, and almost every one of the state's 11.9 million residents had already known this. He then detoured around the forthcoming questions by giving us even more information we already knew and had little use for at that time. "Do you know," he said excitedly, "that Iraq and Kuwait each control about 10 percent of the world's oil reserves? If we can't control Saddam in Iraq, we may need far more nuclear power than ever. Nuclear power plants need places to safely put their waste, and—"

"And!" Seldom in mankind's history had a one-syllable word, spoken with so much depth and unharnessed power, cut anyone as efficiently as that one word uttered by Apryl Greene did to bring Lance Carpenter back from the Arabian desert and into Marshfield County.

"And that surveying began June 5, after a series of public meetings."

"And?"

"And that construction is scheduled to continue for a period of three years."

"And?" For the next few minutes, Lance Carpenter dribbled trinkets of information, and then paused; Apryl supplied the conjunctions, and he would then give out more information. Finally, he ended his report, and clumsily apologized for not being able to tell us more. Apryl wasn't clumsy in her next question.

"And just *who* could tell us more? Or do we march right past you and and see Dr. Simpkins? Dr. Simpkins *does* know something, doesn't she?" Lance Carpenter promised that as soon as the cabinet secretary of the Department of Energy had a few spare moments he would—yep—check with her and get right back to us.

Periodically, we would check up on Energy; periodically they would "get right back" to us. But for now, we merely exchanged pleasantries and left the building.

"Asshole!"

"PR person," I said.

"They're redundant."

"Many are quite competent. Usually far more than their bosses."

"Bullshit! Their words are no more honest than the promises the government gave to the Native Americans."

"Some publicists are actually very bright and do everything they can to tell the truth."

"You're doing her, aren't you?!" spurted Apryl, mixing jealousy, fascination, and glee in just five words. "Jillian! You're doing the publicist who had me shoot you in the park. How wonderful! You and she—"

"She and me nothing."

"Hey, it's OK with me what you do."

"I'm *not* doing her!"

"She's really pretty intelligent for being an Ivy League grad. Got three assignments from her, and no problems." Apryl was teasing. Apryl was playful. Apryl, alas, was right.

"One date," I said. "That's it. She isn't as naive as I thought."

"You're dating a PR person," she mocked. "You and a PR person. Aren't you risking your membership in the Reporters of America Fraternity if they find out?"

"One date. Museum opening and dinner reception."

"Save money at the children's table?"

"One date," I firmly stated. "It's not what you and I have."

"We don't *have*—" She abruptly cut herself off, retreated and ran an alibi past me. "What you do and who you do it to is your own business. We have our own thing. It's cool."

"I'm not doing *anything*!" I protested, uncomfortable with Apryl's sudden revelation. Of course, I didn't mention I planned to see PR Jillian again next weekend.

"It'd be a nice family," Apryl said, teasing joy quickly returning to her eyes "You, me, my dog, and the child. How old is she? Eighteen? Twenty?" And just as quickly as she mocked me, Apryl remembered her philosophy of life, and made sure I didn't attack her for it. "Makes no difference. Some of us are older than we are. Some younger. Age is but a reflection of a need to quantify life to understand it. Like sports scores and body counts. But, we're all people."

"Twenty-four," I mumbled.

"Now I remember. We were all born into the '60s. You and me were born again. She was just getting her first Pampers."

I didn't want to do the Dozens with Apryl. Heck, I didn't even want to do six with her right now. "Are you done?"

"For now."

"For now we need to talk to some people." As quickly as her eyes had reflected a playful delight, they were now the gauge of struggle. Of determination.

We went into the office of the Secretary of State having been able to deduce that this project was no ordinary $400 million waste disposal plant, give or take a few million, but possibly a major plant, possibly the largest in the country, covering more than 600 acres including buffer zones, that it was probably designed to run on nuclear energy, and that it might even be designed as an experimental plant that might be able to recycle nuclear waste, including spent nuclear rods. Hiding it in the middle of rural America, buffered by the Poconos, would have lessened the protest from urban America as well as the activists who congregate in the nation's population centers. Even if they were able to get to the site, the bus, train, and plane schedules would have worn them out long before they could find the place.

Missing from our investigation were still the questions of the ties to Apryl's land. If we could get that, we could possibly begin a process that could unravel some mysteries and restore her land—although I repeatedly warned her that even if she did get her land back, she could very well have cooling towers not a forest for her neighbor.

For more than two centuries, American reporters had to spend endless days looking at governmental records, *if* they were available and *if* the public officials believed in the aphoristic "public's right to know" in order to find out even the most insignificant facts. Even then, the most efficient reporter missed most of what happened, and public officials, no matter how well intentioned, could continue doing whatever it was that they did. Now, with computers, it's relatively painless to buy tapes of governmental records, run them through a mainframe, compare data, and find evidence. Want to know how many physicians had their driver's licenses revoked for drunk driving? No problem. Just buy a tape from the Bureau of Motor Vehicles, compare it with a tape from the Board of Medical Quality Assurance, say a few magic computerized words and up pops answers. Interested in finding out how politicians will probably vote on a controversial issue? Never *ever* listen to their public pronouncements. Just get computerized governmental records and check out the contributors and contributions. You can even come up with interesting statistics, like—11.3 percent of all individual contributors to Sen. Sludgepump's recent campaign contributed 85.6 percent of the campaign funds, of which 63.2 percent of the funds were contributed by members of the

American Association for the Preservation of Artichokes. Yes, indeed, Boolean logic and computerized government records have been a god-send to the journalist—*if* the county and state had computerized its records and *if* we had a ready mainframe. They hadn't and we didn't.

If we had a computer, we wouldn't have had to ferret hard copy documents. We would have seen comparisons and could analyze data. More important, we would have seen that the name Ralph M. Taylor was like shit in a barnyard. As a former city councilman for a small town outside Harrisburg. As a real estate broker. As owner or partial owner of land in Dauphin, Columbia, Luzerne, and Marshfield counties. As an officer or member of the board of directors of six companies. As a major contributor to the re-election campaigns of two state senators, five state representatives, and one auditor general. We would have typed a few codes, computer tapes would have whirled, and we would have seen that Ralph M. Taylor, vice-president of finance for Stratford Electronics, had his fingers into the Susquehanna Valley Workshop pie, the Pittsfield Industries pie, and the Floral Industries pie, and had been the agent who sweetened the deal for the Metropolitan Federal Credit Union to sell a mortgage to Deerfield & Plymouth, to front for Pioneer Power to assure land purchases for what was likely to become the largest nuclear waste disposal plant in America. With a little tough analysis and data comparison, not necessarily of official documents, we might have seen that Ralph M. Taylor was not only a boyhood chum of the governor's but also of Dr. Debbie Jean Lynch, chair of the Massachusetts Public Utilities Commission, and a former senior nuclear engineer for Pioneer Power & Energy. More important, we would have quickly learned that Dr. Jeanette Simpkins and her husband owned land in Marshfield County, filed under her maiden name, and that there were sweetheart deals cut between various Commonwealth agencies and the NRC to grease Pioneer Power's applications—all of it, naturally, for the betterment of mankind.

But we didn't have the tapes or the computers, and so knowledge would come in spurts and dribbles, eating up time and energy. It would take another month, and a detailed tip from a bitter former state representative who didn't get much of Ralph M. Taylor's "milk of politics" donations that had kept us anywhere near the path to knowledge. For now, we had a lot of facts, myriad leads, and a faint suspicion that Taylor was the nuclear industry's designated lackey. It wasn't everything we needed, but enough for Apryl to begin researching laws and statutes, to use the government to regain her land and— maybe—block development of the nuclear facility.

That evening, we ate a leisurely Chinese dinner on Front Street, and then retreated to Apryl's apartment, where we watched a VHS of *The Rose*, made a brownie sundae, and then made love.

"David?"

"Yes, Apryl."

"She was damned good."

"The best."

"All of that talent. The fame. The struggle. . . . Those demons. They overcame her. They destroyed her."

"People overcome their demons. Joplin just didn't."

"What destroyed her was what made her a success."

"We all have our own demons."

"Bette was the only one who could capture it. The fame. The tragedy."

"The only one."

"David, please stay with me."

"I have to return to Boston."

"I'll go with you."

"You have work to do here. At least a week of research, then you have to check with the NRC, go back to the county building, verify information with the county, retrace steps to the secretary of state, call a few people—"

"David! I'm not the Flying Karamazov Brothers. I can't juggle everything!"

"You don't have a choice, Apryl."

A tear welled within her. When it fell, it would fall upon one of several dozen law books and journal articles as Apryl began preparing for her rendezvous with bureaucracy.

20/

Sounds of the Concrete City

by David Ascher

On Fifth Avenue near Rockefeller Center in the Concrete City is a flutist, her long black hair tied into a ponytail by a blue and green silk scarf; a peace symbol, conspicuous by its presence in a city that shows little tranquility, caresses her bosom. She sits on the sidewalk, her back against a 21-story spire of steel, concrete, and glass that blocks out the sun, places a black ebony flute to her lips, and blends haunting Mozartian melodies into an upbeat jazz tempo.

"That's very pretty," I said as she gently let a coda float off. She looked up, and her eyes smiled, telling me, "Thank you." She continued playing.

"What's your name?" I asked, thinking perhaps there was a story here. She looked at me. Tried to figure me out.

"Just call me—" she said, stopping suddenly, then starting over again, a refreshing brightness in her voice—"Just call me *Rachel!*"

"O.K., Rachel, I'm David. Have you been here long?"

"Since the White Rabbit died." A strange answer in a strange town. She looked up. "Am I interesting?"

"Maybe it's the music."

"Maybe it's because you're a reporter." Before I could ask how she knew, she answered, "Your eyes are beautiful, but they're always searching."

"Since you know, would you answer a few questions?"

"No," she said equally polite, "but I'll play you some songs."

"Songs are nice," I countered, "but I write about people."

"Doing a story on the street musicians?" she asked, knowing the answer.

"Maybe. Can I interview you?"

"You don't need to ask questions. Let the music guide you."

"Where's your home?"

"Wherever."

"Can you at least tell me where you were born? Why you're here in New York? Are you hoping to be a music teacher, or become a member of an orchestra? Is it just a way for you to make loose change?"

She smiled, a clever impish smile. "Does it matter?"

Again she placed the flute to her lips, closed her eyes, and squeezed every emotion from "Where Have All the Flowers Gone?" A couple of tourists stopped to listen, dropped spare change into her case, then walked on. She looked up. I was still there. Perhaps that surprised her. "Why do you want to write about us?"

"It might be a good story." She looked at me, searching for her own answers. "I'm an editor," I explained. "I don't write much anymore." She was searching. "I liked the music," I hastily added. There's something more than the music."

"There is nothing more than the music. Listen. Just listen."

"Where were you born? Where do you live? How much can you earn in a day? Do you mind people running past you? Do many stop? Do the police hassle you? You're a little older than most of the other street musicians. What did you do before this?" She answered with "The Sounds of Silence."

In an open flute case on the ground was ten, maybe fifteen dollars, mostly in change. On a good day, street musicians can make more than a hundred dollars, but this lady probably won't make half of that today.

Congress delivered a $250 million loan guarantee to bail out Lockheed in 1971; then, eight years later, it delivered $1.5 billion to bail out Chrysler. Our government, appropriating our money, will continue its practice of corporate welfare. Perhaps airlines next. Maybe banks. The politicians have already determined that Big Business, which "donates" to political campaigns, has more value to America than do artists, musicians, actors, sculptors, dancers, photographers, and writers, many of whom struggle to survive in a society that neglects the creative arts unless something offends their establishment values.

202 / WALTER M. BRASCH

Some of the street musicians, in an industry once vital but now encumbered by a bottom-line profit mentality, once had recording contracts, but are now selling what's left of their 8-tracks; a few more have put their own music onto a cassette tape, and then duplicated them one-by-one to have something to sell. Whenever they can get it, they play the small clubs, making a few more bucks. But to survive, to continue to be a part of America and the arts community, they take in loose change in exchange for giving the people a brief moment of enjoyment and mental stimulation.

Pleased to receive random applause and the change dropped into their open instrument cases, these musicians blend their melodies into the noise of the city. Maybe a club owner one day will hear them, and sign them to a six night a week contract. Maybe one day they'll play in Lincoln Center or Carnegie Hall. Maybe a big shot music producer will stop, offer them words of encouragement, or even a recording contract. Maybe, they'll get a *Billboard* chart-topping hit, like Bette Midler's "The Rose," or Frank Sinatra's "New York, New York," or even Gloria Gaynor's disco anthem, "I Will Survive." Maybe they won't have to work evenings and weekends as waiters and waitresses, as clerks and custodians, and will be able to leave their crowded East Side or Queens tenement apartments or row house existence and move into one of the outrageous rents of "oh so tony" Tribeca or the rarified atmosphere of the Upper West Side. Maybe . . . There are so many maybes and so few choices.

Nearby, each with a predefined space against the walls of commerce this warm spring day, were a brass quartet, a saxophonist, and a couple of guitar players forced to abandon their amps and to endure an acoustic lifestyle to avoid getting disturbing the peace citations. A few yards away, in counterpoint to the flute, a trio of steel drummers beat out a Jamaican tune. This is the real Jamaica, not the one on Long Island. The three Jamaicans, in New York because of the "opportunity" they heard exists, have been here at the same spot for almost a year. They arrive every day at mid-morning; they leave every day in the late afternoon, seldom staying until 5 p.m. Very few people stop at 5 p.m.; they have subways and trains to catch, and there's nothing more important than making your connections and leaving the City.

All around is the reality of the city, of people waking early, grabbing trains and subways, people rushing to work, expediting the day, mastering gamesmanship, worrying about performance ratings and promotions, lost sales and the stock market, mergers, acquisitions, and even bankruptcies, fortified by a lunch of Maalox and martinis. Perhaps one day, before their first heart attack, they may be able to afford one of those overpriced half-million-dollar mid-town condos where they can plant a potted tree on the veranda or move to a home in the suburbs where there are lawns. Perhaps one day they, too, will stop and listen to the sounds of silence.

21/

Revelations and Curiosities

On Barron Point, a half-mile stretch of sandy non-developed beach on Cape Cod that not many people visit, even in summer, is a fisherman, his eight-foot fishing pole held by a metal tube stuck deep into the sand, the nylon line stretching beyond the surf. The fisherman, sitting peacefully in a foldable short-legged green and white beach chair, quietly looking at the ocean, has probably been here since before sunrise. He's too far away for me to see if he's caught anything. It's the seeds of a good story—lone fisherman early in the morning, looking out into the ocean, waiting for the right fish. I wondered if he came here every day, what he was looking for, how long he fished, what he caught, what he did when he wasn't fishing. Perhaps I could tie this one fisherman into some greater scheme of life and—

"Must you always be thinking about your work?!" It was Apryl, and we had just begun walking in front of the vegetation edge of a series of dunes. "You're always thinking of writing. Everyone and everything is a story. It consumes you."

"It's just random thoughts," I said trying not to make much of it. "There might be nothing there. There might be something. If we don't ask, how will we know? Even Oscar Wilde agrees."

"Oscar Wilde?" she challenged.

"In *The Canterville Ghost*, he said the reason he didn't like the U.S. was because we had no antiquities and no curiosities."

"He might have been referring to oddities not inquisitive-ness," she suggested.

"Whatever. All I know is that curiosity is the foundation of good journalism."

"Perhaps your curiosity is no more important than that fisher-

204

man's right just to sit by the ocean and fish."

"Journalists are curious."

"Journalists spend their time invading other people's lives."

"It's just an idea. Don't make a big deal of it," I snapped. She let it pass.

"It's just part of your nature. Pisces are creative people. Always thinking. Always doing."

"I have to keep busy."

"Like fish." It was a soft, contemplative voice. "I think you're a fish. Always swimming. Always doing things. And you have to forever swim. Sometimes you swim with the current. Sometimes against it. But you're always swimming."

"Swimming is just part of life," I said cavalierly, but Apryl in her own logic was trying to make a point, and it would take a train to do it.

"When was the last time you rode a train?" she asked.

"A train?"

"Too difficult? I can start easier and build up to the tough ones." Her mind was alert; her eyes bright. "Want an easier question? It won't be as many points but you might feel better about yourself."

"No," I smiled, "that'll be fine. Now, what was that question again?"

"The train," she said patiently. "When was the last time you rode a train?"

"Awhile back, I guess."

"Think!" she commanded.

"A week ago. Amtrak to New Haven."

"Good," she said, a devious calculating smile overtaking her face. At least that's what I thought it was. "David, when you're on a train, looking out the window, what do you see?"

"I don't know. Things."

"*Things?*" she said incredulously. "You're a big-time editor and you see *things*?"

"What am I supposed to see?"

"You're not supposed to see *things*!" she said, now mocking me. "'I'm a big-time editor and I see *things*. Lots of things. Big things and small things. Blue things and short things and all kinds of *things*.' With ability like that, you'd be one great administrator somewhere."

"Give me a chance to think," I pleaded to her twinkling eyes.

"Think."

"Roads. I see roads."

"Good. But that's the wrong answer. Try trees."

"Trees?"

"Trees. Big giant things with leaves. You see trees."

"O.K., so I see trees."

"When the train is going fast, the trees beside you are just whizzing by; you can't even count them. They just blend into each other. One tree after another. You don't really see them. You can't even remember them. But the trees that are farther away, they're not a blur. They're distinct. You can see them because they seem to go even slower. And the farther the trees are, the better you can see them. You can see forests and birds." She paused a moment, and then turned to the ocean. To collect thoughts? To get her breath? For effect? "David," she said, turning back, her eyes staring into mine, "when we ride trains, you and me, you see the trees up close, always rushing past, everything a blur, quickly, one tree becoming yet another tree, all of them looking alike, but none of them different, one tree after another, and you don't remember any of them. Me, I look beyond the tracks. I see each tree."

"O.K., you see trees, and I see blurs."

"I didn't say you didn't see trees. With your incisive mind, you'd probably stop the train, get out, inspect one of the trees, cut it down, count its rings to see how old it was, and then get back on the train and write a story. A week later, you'd have no idea what you did, or even if you ever met the tree. But you'd have informed the world about that tree."

She was wrong. Everything she said was wrong. But I wasn't going to argue.

"You've never gone fishing, either, have you?"

"Am I supposed to go fishing in the trees?"

"Something like that," she said, playfully suggesting that I didn't have the patience to just sit there, relaxed, waiting for something to happen, that I was always rushing through life and never stopping.

"I'm a Pisces," I reminded her. "Fishing would be cannibalistic." O.K., so in the grand scheme of things, fish eat fish. *You* try arguing with her.

"What about hunting? You ever hunt anything?" Not another damned metaphor. This was supposed to be a fun morning, and

I wasn't about to let trees and trains ruin it.

"Once."

"Once what?" she said surprised.

"Went hunting once."

"What'd you kill? No! I don't want to know." A moment of silence was too long for her. "Tell me! I've got to know." She was rethinking our universe and our relationships within it.

"One day, I spent an hour following a set of tracks. Through mud and dirt I followed them."

"What'd you kill?" she screeched. If Apryl wasn't a pacifist, she might have shot me for the sins of all the hunters. But since she, like me, was curious, I was sure I'd be spared.

"I followed these tracks almost forever."

"You killed it! You killed something! How could you!" Another quick moment of reflection. "What was it? No! Don't tell me. No, tell me! You killed a little animal, didn't you?"

"Actually, it was rather large."

"Oh my God, that's just as bad!" She spun around, almost grasping my chest hairs through a sweatshirt that was barely protecting me against the cold. "Tell me!"

"I saw it out there just zipping along so I raised my rifle, took careful aim, and . . ." I paused; the literary world would call it a dramatic pause; I called it taking a breath.

"And? And *what!*"

"And I shot a silver-skinned Amtrak. Got that sucker right between the horns." It was barely moments before she recovered her heartbeat, and began to throw sand on me. "I felt so remorseful about shooting that Amtrak that I joined the Save the Vinyl Foundation. All those hunters are out there shooting little motherless vinyls and selling their skins to furniture manufacturers."

"Anything else you want to tell me? Pepperonis, perhaps?"

"I *never* shot a pepperoni. Never!"

"And a good thing, too. They have a right to life, to go to school, grow up, marry a pizza, or join the military and die for some politician's worthless cause. Race you to the surf!"

"Bullshit. It's at least 50 yards away."

"I'm supposed to run along the surf, and you're supposed to chase me. You know, in slow motion like in the movies." In the movies, we would be running towards each other, not chasing each other. But, Apryl had creative control. Before she was even finished talking, she had stripped off her shorts and sweatshirt, and in a two-piece purple swim suit, her black hair trailing in the breeze—yeah, just like in the movies—was now skipping, jumping, jogging, running in her quest for salt water. There was definitely a lyric poetry about it. And it was definitely not in slo-mo. In less than a minute, she was in the surf, splashing and playing in the 55-degree ocean. As for me? I was huffing and puffing, running and jogging. It had been three years since I had been on a tennis court. In my piteous condition, I was seeing my life flash before me, while Apryl was full of life. No one in her early 40s should be in that great of a condition.

A few yards away, the fisherman looked over, probably wondering about these two strange people so early in the morning who were not only disturbing his rest but, for all he knew, all the fish in the sea. "David! Hurry!" Splash, Apryl. You're splashing and I could use a resuscitator. "Come into the water!"

"It's freezing!"

"It's warm! Like a sauna!"

"I don't believe you."

"Jump in! Be daring!" I had no desire to be daring and every desire not to freeze my ass off. I know oceans. I also know cold. Unfortunately, I also know Apryl, and she wouldn't have any peace in her butt until I tested what she claimed were warm waters of the Atlantic, so I took my sweatshirt off, prepared to swim out to at least where she was bobbing and splashing in child-like wonderment—and damned near froze my ass and every other body part. I don't know why I listened to her. In the few months since I first met her, I was chasing down corporations, facing psycho muggers, and trying my damnest not to fall in love. Maybe it was her devious look of naive innocence, that impish face that appeared it could never lie, yet concealed a volcanic rage that erupted without notice. Maybe it was because she's so excited by life, or because she so manipulates life. Whatever the reasons, I had run into a wind-chilled ocean, and was now standing back at the surf, wet and cold, almost out of breath, a perfect candidate for cryogenics.

"The seaweed," she said, picking up a strand from the water and draping it around her neck. "The future of the world. From seaweed, we will feed a world left starving by drought and greed." In 1983, *Century* had run a story about food products from seaweed. It was the first time the issue had hit the mass public. I wasn't aware that Apryl had read it; she hadn't. "My friend Mark," she said, "is a marine biologist." Bubbling with enlightenment, seized by enthusiasm, she told me seaweed would be even better than soybeans to feed the people, and another five minutes telling me about all the kinds of food that seaweed could become.

"Mark told you all this?" I asked.

"The ocean told me all this," she replied. "You learned about seaweed from one of your writers," she said smugly. "I learned about it from the ocean and from a marine biologist!" She bent down, scooped up a handful of ocean, and looked at her wet hands. "An entire universe," she said. "In just one drop of ocean water, you can learn the secrets of an entire universe." She scooped another handful, then another and another, splashing and talking. "It's not always so wonderful," she said reflectively. Typical Apryl. Go in one direction, warp to another. "Agnes wasn't wonderful." Agnes? "1972. I was in Wilkes–Barre when Agnes hit. Susquehanna rose to the bridges. Left a couple of billion dollars damage. What mattered was the lives that were damaged, not the houses. People saved their whole lives for their houses and in a few hours it was all gone, and nothing anyone could do would bring back their faith in nature." She thought a moment. Reflective? Contemplative? "It's all part of some master plan for us but I don't know what it is." I was about to inject a piece of layman theology when Apryl spouted forth again. "It doesn't matter. Maybe it's just important that we try to live with our environment, to try to understand the forces of nature and not the *why* of nature." This time I didn't even get a chance to think of amateur theology before Apryl warped again. Even the fledging human genome project would have trouble mapping the causes of Apryl's moods.

"You remember Ronnie Soifer don't you?" I didn't. "You met him in the park," she said annoyed at my memory blackout. "I introduced you, David. He's a wonderful woodcarver." My mind was still fuzzy. "He's a wood carver," she said deliberately punctuating each word, as if her irritation would stimulate my memory. "The stone mason, David. Does things like fireplaces and—" *Now* I remember. "I ran into him last night. He's up here for a few days helping a friend finish off a motel. Another contractor did most the work around May, but it was never right, so Ronnie and his crew came up to do some repairs and finish it."

"You seeing him?" I asked, not knowing at the time that it had a tinge of jealousy.

"He's just a friend," she said annoyed.

"Close friend?"

"A friend," she said impatiently. "We talk."

"Hey, it's OK with me."

"Damn straight it is!" Yeah. Right. Ronnie. Woodcarver. Stone mason. Whatever. "Why are Pisces so inquisitive, yet so secretive?" she asked as we walked along the surf, sweatshirts protecting our bodies from the cold and wind. "You're always trying to soul-search everyone else, but you never reveal anything about yourself. Maybe the sign of the journalist is to be merely the observer, never revealing who he is."

"In my writings is who I am," I replied, "but you have to read them carefully. It's all there."

"Like your Ph.D.? Think you could hide that as well?"

"I don't hide it," I protested, "I just—"

"Don't publicize it?"

"How'd you know I have a Ph.D.?"

"You ashamed of it? If I had one, I'd have it tattooed on my forehead!"

"A doctorate isn't who I am," I responded, an egotistical humbleness coexisting in my mind.

"You live an illusion," she said. "*Education* is who you are. *Knowledge* is who you are. You teach a course every semester at UMass. You think the school hides the identities of its faculty? You're a journalist, for god-sake. Not only that, you're a Jewish journalist so you're doubly cursed with having to know *and* tell!"

"I'm not secretive," I said.

"Now you're secretive and pouting," she said slyly.

"I'm doing neither!"

"Then tell me about your new book. How's it going?"

"OK."

"Just OK?

"Too many things are happening. I still have to promote the first one. Still have to edit a magazine. Still write occasional articles." OK, it stretched the truth a bit. But, I wasn't about to tell her that although I had piles of notes, I hadn't yet had insight. Apryl knew I had been working on a retrospective of the Movement and the death of the Spirit of the '60s. I hadn't told her all the details—like the fact that she would be the subject, or that some of the disjointed information she readily dropped as casual conversation were parts of a puzzle I was trying to fit together.

"You're worried if you have enough information. If the characters have a life. If they're two-dimensional. Whether there's too much narrative. Or not enough. How the dialogue sounds. If you need more or less. Whether your agent will take it. If a publisher will want it. If critics will like it."

"I don't worry about critics. James Michener said if they could write, they wouldn't be critics."

"I hope you won't put *that* into your book."

"Don't know why not. In the past year, I've already alienated publicists, book agents, and editors who think they know more about writing than writers, and corporations which have layers of executives who have never had a creative thought, yet make decisions about those who do. Critics need a jab now and then. Keeps them honest."

"Then you're not worried about them?"

"Nope."

"Not in the slightest?"

"Not a bit." OK, so maybe a little bit. No one likes to receive bad reviews. Even worse, no reviews at all.

"Then what worries you?"

"That I don't have enough time."

"Time can be both your enemy and your ally. The story will write itself when it's ready."

"The story—" I sputtered, then dropped the thought.

"What about the story?"

"Just a random thought. Nothing more."

"If you couldn't be a journalist what would you do?"

I once wanted to be a doctor. Not just any doctor, but a general practitioner who makes house calls and takes care of the whole family. Just like Dr. Adams or Dr. Carlson, my role mentors when I was much younger. I'd be good at both diagnosing and treating. But, in a world of specialization, horse-and-buggy doctors were disowned by the medical establishment. It really didn't make much difference. By the end of my sophomore year at UC Santa Barbara, with science grades that were passable but not distinguished, I realized that the sciences weren't as much fun as writing and becoming involved with all kinds of causes. "The world didn't need more mediocre doctors," I said, "and it did need better journalists."

"Tell me about Joyce," she said suddenly, her words bisecting my thoughts about stone masons and fishermen, knowledge and secrets, doctors and journalists. I didn't know how she found out about Joyce, my ex-; maybe I once mentioned something; maybe not. Either way, it wasn't worth finding out how she knew.

"There's not much to tell. She and I once had something, then we didn't." O.K., so it was more than just something, but why rehash faded loves; better just to leave them faded.

"Why won't you open up, say something. It was seven years of your life!"

Had I told her seven years? How'd she know seven years? "I just don't remember much about it."

"You can't be married seven years and not remember anything." Apryl had guessed we were both journalists. I sketched in a few details, telling her that in a moment when both of us were in the same spot at the same time, bags unpacked from recent assignments, we got married; it was that or a movie. We had lived intensely at times, separated by our upwardly mobile jobs much of the time.

"Tell me about the divorce," she asked." I wished I knew about the divorce—at least before it happened.

"Short version, I got defaulted."

"Like a fault in tennis?"

"More like San Andreas. She said we could split the fees for a lawyer and he'd represent both of us."

"And you fell for this?"

"Seemed reasonable at the time. We sat down, divided what we wanted. When the time came for the preliminary hearing, I was on assignment but figured there'd be no problem. After all, we worked everything out. So, she took the stand, said a few words, and claimed most of the property."

"Didn't you protest?"

"I got back in time for the final decree; sat in the back of the courtroom and tried to object. Judge said I had no standing in court. Before I knew what happened, I was defaulted. It was a true 50–50 split. She got most of the property and $550 a month for a year. I got the debts."

"You didn't get *anything*?"

"Personal possessions—typewriter, clothes, books; a car and a little bit of furniture. I kept the apartment. She went back to L.A. Couple of weeks later, some of my friends came over and threw me a Recycled Bachelor Party. It was BYOC—Bring Your Own Chair." She managed to stop giggling long enough to ask a serious question.

"You talk with her?"

"Shows up every now and then. We talk. Sometimes we go places. Just two people with a past."

"The past is what helps us understand tomorrow."

"Ever tell you why she did what she did?"

"Few months after the decree, I ran into her at a convention and asked what happened to our agreement. I wasn't even mad anymore. Just wanted to know what happened. She said the lawyer told her to do it that way. I told her she didn't have to listen to the lawyer. She should have done what's right."

"What'd she say to that?"

"Said 'That's why we pay lawyers.'"

"The law is a funny beast," Apryl said. "It seems so complex, so intimidating, but if you understand it, if you understand the people who wrote it, you can use it to your advantage."

For more than a month, Apryl had been researching municipal, state, and federal laws, looking for direction in her quest to bring about the reversal of the Declaration of Taking that had led to the seizure of her land by eminent domain rules, and was part of a master scheme to nuke northeast Pennsylvania. I had offered to help her find an attorney—I even begged her to get legal assistance—but she said that for this battle she wouldn't use professionals, for the law must work for all people not just those able to afford an attorney. This would be her battle, she said; if she could win it, then it would be a victory for the people. Even if she were to get her land, she had to worry about the right of reversion clause in her mortgage. No matter who owned the mortgage, she still had to get her school built. Although she had until March, the snows would come by the first of the year, the ground would freeze, and construction would be stopped. Without question, losing the land, again, meant access roads would eventually be built to the waste disposal plant that absorbed Pioneer Power's leftovers. In the face of a nuclear holocaust of her spirit, she was calm, infinitely more so than when we first began searching for information. She wasn't worried, she said. Things always work out, she believed. Before the first snow, the school would be built, she declared. I didn't know how; what I did know was that she probably should have taken the state's money and found another parcel of land. I had no doubt that she had been possessed of the land and her idea for a school. Was it self-destructive? Probably. Could she have even a minimal chance of getting her land back? Probably not. Was she going to mount an all-out campaign? Without question.

We had come to this stretch of Cape Cod for a couple of hours after spending the night at my apartment. Apryl would return to Pennsylvania the next day to complete her preparations for the Thursday morning meeting with the county commissioners. Sam Weissmann and I planned to join her at that meeting.

"David! Look! I found an army helmet with a tail." What Apryl found was the shell of a horseshoe crab, a life form that had changed very little in millions of years. "No wonder you love the ocean. You're a Pisces."

"I doubt being a Pisces has anything to do with it."

"It has *everything* to do with it. Pisces love the ocean. And you know a lot about horseshoe crabs. I'll take it home!"

"It smells."

"We'll give it a bath."

And that's why, on a chilly November morning, between dips into a cold ocean and worrying about county commissioners, Apryl and I were digging a hole with our hands, burying an army helmet with tail, and covering it with seaweed to hide it from interlopers, not that many would have had plans to take a horseshoe crab home—"Oh, look, Denise, there's a horseshoe crab; let's steal it and take it home and put it on the fireplace mantle, along with darling Aunt Gertrude's picture."

In moments, Apryl was again skipping along to the ocean, challenging me to catch her in the cool waves, and I was having a bad case of *deja vu*, although by now I was again wearing my sweatshirt, and Apryl recovered her shorts and sweatshirt. We splashed some more, walked some more, stopping every few steps to dig into the surf or look at the seagulls or imagine what was in the ocean.

"My princess is real," she said, from out of nowhere. I didn't have the slightest clue what she was talking about. I knew her extemporaneous lifestyle, with its abrupt diversions, was just a part of her mystique, something to be appreciated although not necessarily understood. "My *princess*. My princess is real. But I don't know if I should make her a symbol of oppression or just a symbol of confusion." I had no idea where this was leading. She did. "Even children's books have to be real. Just because a book is for children doesn't mean it has to be a fairytale. It should talk about reality." I agreed, if only to give her time to warp into another subject. "The *Twilight Zone* was real," she said. "In fiction, Rod Serling spoke the truth of human life. The truth always over-rides the facts." We talked about *Fail-Safe, On the Beach, Dr. Strangelove,* and *Star Trek,* science-fiction popular in the '60s that were masks for the reality of the present. "You need to write fiction," she said, determined.

"I don't do fiction," I again reminded her. "I also don't do lunch, windows, whitewater rafting, or lead commando raids into Central America."

"You should."

"Lead commando raids?"

"Do fiction." It was the second time she had brought it up.

"I do what I do best. Gynecologists don't do brain surgery." O.K., so it wasn't much of an argument, but here I was on this beach, watching my ethnic light brown skin turn blue, burying army helmets, and figuring out plans of how to capture three county commissioners in a county I never even heard of until last spring.

"Faulkner was a journalist," she said. "Bet you already knew that." I did. Most great novelists had their base as journalists.

"I don't do fiction," I again stated, a bit more irritated.

"By the end of World War II, all of Faulkner's books were almost out of print. Commercial failures. And then an editor named Malcolm Cowley interpreted Faulkner's greatest works for the common person." I also knew that. But I didn't know if Apryl had a reason, a thought, or was just throwing unrelated facts at me. So much of Apryl seemed unrelated. "After Cowley's introduction to Faulkner's stories was published, Faulkner won the Nobel, and his books haven't been out of print since. Maybe you'd write a novel with hidden meanings, intertwining stories, and unusual characters, but need someone to interpret it."

"I'm a journalist!" I huffed. "I write rather clearly."

"Maybe *I* could interpret your book" she said excitedly. Now, *that* would be interesting. A book about Apryl, interpreted by Apryl—who didn't know she was the subject.

"You'd probably do a better job interpreting it than I could do writing it," I replied, again emphasizing that I was a journalist not a novelist.

"The best journalists try to explain the fabric of society, but truth is in fiction," Apryl said, picking up a shell. "David, do you know what's common to almost all of the shells?"

"They keep the souvenir business from collapsing?"

"Look at them, David," she said reflectively. "The beach is filled with broken shells. As many broken shells as there are human lives." Sitting there, the waves sneaking to her feet, Apryl looked at the ocean. "I was married once, too" she said quietly. I said nothing, but my eyes must have said something. "Isn't that the kind of information you were looking for?" she asked. "I found out you were married. Didn't you want to know how I knew, or if I was married?" I did, but for months I had tried to be subtle in my questioning, allowing her to fill me in on her life story in her own way. "You want to know about me," she said, her eyes playfully tweaking my self-imposed discomfort, "so you need to know about Thomas." The longer I knew her, the more I learned—and the more bogged down I had become in her story. "One day," she explained, "before he was shipped overseas, we went to Monterey, stood at the edge of the ocean, exchanged peace symbols, and recited our vows. A few friends were there. It wasn't recorded in the county's books because we didn't have a judge or clergyman, but we knew and God knew and that's all that counts, isn't it?" Thomas had been a frycook who was taking two or three courses every semester at Hayward State, hoping one day to become a social worker. I also learned he was Black.

In the 1960s, it was fashionable for White chicks to glue themselves to Black dudes to show their defiance of parental and societal norms, and to prove how liberal they were, how *with it* and *together* they were. Perhaps Apryl read something in my eyes, but before I could say anything, she fired at me.

"It wasn't like that!" she said firmly. "We were just two people who loved each other." "You don't approve?" she asked, challenging.

"It's not that," I quickly answered. "I just figured—"

"—Wrong. You figured wrong." She paused a moment while

I mumbled some liberal apology. She apologized for unsheathing her claws. "You're OK about that, but many weren't."

"Friends?"

"Friends. Parents. His; mine. My stepmom, actually, since my Mom—" She choked back a tear. "Since my Mom died when I was only seven. I guess we caused a few heads to turn, and most turned away from us. Like they were embarrassed for us. Or maybe even disgusted with us. I remember the stares. Without one word being spoken, there was so much being said."

"So what happened? Divorce?"

"Vietnam," she said quietly. Thomas Jefferson Brown, with no semi-rich parents and unable to support himself as a full-time student, couldn't get the prized II-S deferment; for not having what the government claimed to be a "legal" marriage with a child, he couldn't get a III-A deferment. He didn't choose to defect to Canada, declare himself a CO, pretend he was gay, claim to be a farmer or minister or sole surviving son, take pills to artificially inflate some blood chemistry reading—or, as some did, chop off a finger—and be declared 4-F. What he was was 1-A, fit for service. A friendly, neighborhood Army recruiter promised him a stateside assignment and time to take college classes if he enlisted for four years instead of waiting to be drafted for two, and so he enlisted. He completed Basic at Fort Leonard Wood, Advanced Infantry Training at Fort Benning, and then was shipped to Oakland, and then to Vietnam. They returned him to Oakland in a government-issue gray box in May 1966. A tear slid slowly down Apryl's cheek, but she wasn't crying. "His legs were gone. His uniform just hung on him. And on the uniform, they put his medals. I guess they didn't usually do that, but they pinned his medals on him." She looked at me, just looked, almost without emotion. "David, they gave him five medals, and he gave them his life." Three of those medals were given to just about everyone who served during the war; two weren't—the Purple Heart and the Bronze Star with a "V" for valor. "The Memorial!" Apryl said sharply. "Etched onto a wall, they put the names. One after another after another. . . . So many names. So many lives! And that wall, you've seen the wall, David; you know what I'm talking about. That wall is just far enough from the White House that no President ever has to look at it except when he goes there on Memorial Day to get his picture taken and pretend he cares."

"Doesn't have to. He has underlings, advisors, and speech writers who make it seem he cares the rest of the year."

"Damned politicians should have spent the money to find a cure for MS or cancer, not to create a war that killed our children!" For a minute, maybe more, probably not less, she ranted, her fury building, while I remained silent. Nothing I could say would calm her fury, nothing would ease her pain, even two decades later. "There should be memorials for America's callousness. For America's neglect. For the homeless. The impoverished. For those who died because they couldn't afford adequate health. For those who died from AIDS. They can't make *those* memorials because they'd have to be so huge they would overwhelm every monument and building in Washington. It'd have not thousands but millions of names. Michael. Merritt. Alvin . . . Keith Haring. . . . So young. So talented."

"The artist?"

Tears welled within her, but never fell. I asked no further questions, she volunteered no further information. Some other place. Some other time. Some other book.

We walked some more, neither of us touching, both of us eerily silent. At the northeastern point, where the sand becomes a path to a wall of rock, where fishermen sometimes sit and cast their lines, we climbed to the farthest point of the jetty and sat there, quietly looking at the ocean, each of us thinking a million things, each of us thinking nothing.

"I felt guilty," she said peacefully.

"You couldn't have known."

"I didn't feel guilty about Thomas dying. I felt guilty about not wanting the child." *Child?!* "When you first learn you're pregnant, you want to run around and tell the whole world about it, about how happy you are. But when I found out, I didn't feel happy. I was angry. I was stuck here and Thomas had just gone into the Army, and I was protesting the war and I was alone and I didn't want to be pregnant. There were a thousand people around me, but I was lonelier than all of them." Before I could ask her anything stupid, like if she ever heard of birth control, she gave me the details. A couple of days after a radiologist shot tracing dye into her body, her physician had told her that because she had damage to her tubes, not only couldn't she get pregnant, but a hysterectomy was necessary. Two months later—after she refused to get the hysterectomy because she thought the physician was scalpel-happy—she was pregnant. The only explanation anyone could give was that the dye must have cleaned out the tubes. "Then one day," said Apryl, "I could feel her kick, and then everything was all right. I didn't care what society thought, or what anyone thought because I realized that I had something alive within me, and I wanted to protect her and do things for her and make the world right for her." She choked back a tear, but it escaped anyhow, and was soon joined by others. "Thomas didn't know my anger. He only saw my happiness. And he was happy. And we cried and we hugged and we loved that baby. . . . But he never saw her." She cried, shivering with the wounds of love for a man and the anger for a government. I held her. Moments? Minutes? I don't remember. She wiped away the tears but not the memory. "I didn't want society to get my child," she said. "I didn't want anyone to harm her. After Thomas died, I knew I had to make everything right for our child. I wanted to be the best mother possible, just like mine was." A tear slid slowly down her cheek, again wiped by the back of her hand. "And my father so loved her, his only grandchild, and he—he—" I held her, to comfort her while she shivered the tears of remembrance. "I wanted to do everything right. I went to child-care meetings and read every magazine article I could about child development." She paused a moment, remembering a time shortly after Rebecca was born, when she was living in State College, and trying to raise an infant daughter, while Thomas was overseas. "One day, a lady from the neighborhood invited me to a luncheon with some other neighbors. And here were these neighbors, and they weren't like me but that didn't matter because they seemed to want to be my friends. They talked about their children and their husbands' jobs, and their vacations, and the clothing they bought, and the clubs they were in. Do you know, David, that in America anyone can belong to a club? In clubs, everyone can be someone. But if everyone is someone, then everyone is also no one." It was an interesting piece of logic, but before I could say much, even to mention the clubs I had once been a member of—and the ones that I never thought about joining because they would never have accepted me—Apryl was onto her next thought. "In these clubs, they talk about each other. Only, at this luncheon club, they talked about the people who weren't there. And when one person left, they talked about her. And when another one left, they talked about her. Then it was my turn to leave, and I didn't want to leave. I was sweaty, and I could feel their knives, and I wanted to stay there forever and ever." She sobbed a deep breath. "And then I left. And when Rebecca and I got home, I just cried and cried. I tried to fit in, but it didn't work. Pretty soon, I didn't even care about all those pompous biddies who'd greet you and say, 'Hello dear,' and then talk behind your back and say how horrible it is to have a Black baby and not to be married. I was going to be the best mother possible, no matter what anyone thought! I was going to be happy and I was going to make my child happy."

But such was not to be, for Rebecca, daughter of Apryl and Thomas, would die at 21 months from a fast moving cancer that had begun in the eye and spread quickly into the brain. The pathologist identified it as retinoblastoma. Like Sam and Ruth, who lost their only daughter to leukemia, Apryl would curse God for allowing such suffering.

Apryl Greene climbed down from the jetty, stopped at the surf, picked up some seaweed and shells, and then put them back into the ocean. The waves came onto the shore, and the tide slowly receded. As it has for millennia. For eons.

On the way back to our car we dug up the horseshoe crab, and then looked back to the ocean. The fisherman was still there.

22/

The Cost of an Education

by David Ascher

One Monday morning, three months after graduation, Rachel Greenberg called the Registrar's office to find out what happened to her diploma.

"Where do you live?" an assistant registrar asked.

"Fishers Ferry," she answered.

"Well, *that's* your problem."

"Because I live in Fishers Ferry?"

"Because you live within 50 miles of the college."

"Because I live within 50 miles of the college, I can't get a diploma?"

"You can get a diploma, but you must pick it up in person."

"But why can't you mail it out?"

"Because you live within 50 miles of the college."

"If I lived *51* miles from the college, could I get my diploma by mail?"

"If that were the case, we'd mail out your diploma, but you live in Fishers Ferry and that's—"

"—within 50 miles of the college."

The assistant registrar politely explained that it wasn't cost-effective for the college to mail diplomas to graduates who live within 50 miles of the college—there's all those costs associated with buying, stuffing, and addressing the mailers, paying for the postage and, for all anyone knew, the time involved in putting the mailers into a mailbox. Graduates living within 50 miles of the college could just stop by the office, between 9 a.m. and noon, and 1 p.m. and 4:30 p.m., Mondays through Fridays.

But, Rachel Greenberg worked from 8:30 a.m. to 5 p.m. every day, a temporary job, but a job nevertheless, so she offered another plan. She'd send a check for $5 to cover the cost of mailers, addressing, stuffing, and postage. That's when she learned another truth.

"I'm sorry, but we wouldn't be able to do that. We don't have any accounts established that we could put that check into."

Another plan! She'd have a friend stop by and pick up her diploma. "We'd really like to help," said the assistant registrar, "but you need to sign for it in person."

"I'll send a notarized statement authorizing him to sign for me."

"I wish that were possible," said the assistant registrar, "but we have a book with your name, major, and graduation date printed in it, and you have to sign in that book."

Rachel Greenberg, with a B.A. in fine arts but no diploma, had completed college by testing out of almost a year's worth of courses, and by mixing courses from previous colleges, correspondence courses, and courses while in attendance, all while working a dozen assorted jobs, most part-time or temporary. She was almost 40, and had no reason to do the academic shuffle any longer. So, she talked with the registrar himself, and then talked with a dean and a vice-president. She would have talked with the president if she hadn't been out of town on some fund-raising mission. They all sympathized, but rules are rules.

So, one fine autumn morning, Rachel Greenberg took off a half day without pay—employers who hire temporaries don't throw in vacations, sick time, and benefits—went to the college where she picked up a diploma which had already cost her more than $12,000 in tuition and fees, and then returned to her car, determined never to send the college any money ever again.

On the windshield was a college-issued parking ticket.

23/

Interlude in A Flat

Twelve hour work days aren't unusual, especially since I had been mainlining caffeine the past three days. But I wondered how much of Apryl I could balance in my life. By late evening, I had been dragging, and Apryl, who had been in overdrive for days, was now brooding. A reflective brooding, probably brought about by the body's need to balance its manic state. But brooding, nevertheless.

"David, I'm worried."

"Don't."

"Don't what?"

"Don't worry."

"It won't happen."

"It will if it's meant to."

"We worked a long time for this, didn't we?"

"A long time."

"David?"

"Yes, Apryl."

"They can cut me off before I even utter a word."

"You're on the agenda. You'll get at least three minutes."

"Yeah. Three whole minutes. They'll nod their heads and move on to other business."

"They can also flap their arms and run around like chickens, but they won't."

"Won't flap?"

"Won't cause a flap. You have experts. You have media. No one likes to look dumb on TV."

"It'll be a show, David. Nothing more, and nothing will be accomplished."

"You're prepared, Apryl. Look around!"

"There's dirty clothes on the floor."

"Not the bedroom! The kitchen. The table is creaking so bad it'll need a chiropractor." That brought back a smile that broke some of her depression.

In neat piles on the kitchen table were books, magazines, files, and random acts of papers in all sizes. All numbered. All in order. Finally.

It had been a long day, begun at 4:30 a.m. when I awakened to get a cab to the airport, a flight to Harrisburg, and a rent-a-car ride to Apryl's apartment in Fisher's Ferry. Greeting me was an accumulation of three months of research. On chairs. On tables. On the floor. Displacing Apryl, displacing Kashonna, her Shepherd mix now happily curled in a corner of the bedroom where once there were magazines, her ears relaxed but her bright brown eyes still alert, still seeming to understand not only everything that was happening, but also able to penetrate even the most closed souls as well. Several hours earlier, with five of Apryl's friends, we had begun the final process of discussing, sorting, filing, and cataloguing the Fisher's Ferry annex of the Recycling Garage. But, it was really the plans for an invasion of Marshfield County's history, its values, and possibly its hopes for an economic recovery. The friends were gone now, and late into the evening we were alone in her bedroom.

Apryl sat up in the queen-sized bed, took a slow drag on a joint, and let out a deep sigh. Apryl isn't a pothead, for she believes that life, not drugs, gives her a natural high. But, now and then, mostly to help her relax, to reduce her anxiety, sometimes to bring her out of a funk, which psychologists might call an acute depressive realism, she smoked. Not tobacco, just weed. And in open defiance of laws in every state, which condemn the non-addictive marijuana while promoting the government-subsidized tobacco crop. The marijuana may not have been what brought Apryl out of her funk, but it apparently didn't hurt.

"Do you really think we have a chance?"

"We won't if you don't get some sleep."

"I'm not sleepy. I'm worried, but I'm not sleepy."

"Count sheep."

"I like sheep. Sheep are nice animals. They're very smart. They don't deserve the reputation people give them. You know what I mean—meek as a sheep; always following; never questioning. Sheep have courage."

"Yes. Sheep have courage."

"Do you know there were battles between shepherds and cattlemen in the Old West?"

"Yeah."

"Cattlemen didn't like people who owned sheep. Shepherds didn't like the cattlemen. Something about fences and grazing land. Maybe even lifestyle differences."

"Yeah. Something like that."

"And a hundred years ago the ranchers killed wild horses and burros because they didn't want anything taking up the land they thought should belong only to cattle?"

"Something about food supply," I said, deliberately keeping my response short. I knew more about the problem—how the ranchers poisoned their water supply, ran them over cliffs, or shot them. But desperately seeking sleep, I wasn't about to contribute much more to this conversation. Apryl was.

"Yes!" shouted Apryl almost in my face. "Cattle were an edible commodity. Horses weren't, so they just killed them. Killed them because they said horses were eating the food supply that cattle should have gotten."

"No different today," I said, trying to keep my part of the conversation from deteriorating into a snore.

"Damn right it is! Government herds up the horses, sterilizes the mares, sells off the foals, and all because the cattlemen's lobby is so powerful, and because Americans want beef on their tables. And they say the same thing—that horses and burros take up too much space—that they eat too much of the land." She again turned right into my face. "David! Do you know how much space the cattle take up on public land compared to the wild horses and burros?"

"Like about a hundred times more?"

"Right! And ranchers pay almost nothing to the Bureau of Land Management to graze cattle on public land. And they have the nerve to say that mustangs and burros are starving because of a lack of food supply, so it's humane—*humane*, David, they say it's *humane*—to cull the herds so they don't get too big and starve. David, they'll be saying this crap for the next two, three decades until every mustang and burro is killed." Apryl knew I agreed with her that the government was little more than a tool to be used by the cattlemen's associations, but she was doing a good job of trying to keep up both ends of our conversation.

"It's all about land. Do you know that people once found their own piece of land, and they developed it and farmed it, and they never paid for it? They were called squatters."

"Uh-huh."

"And do you know that the government used to throw the people off their land because they said it was the government's land, but that the government eventually gave up?"

"Uh-huh."

"Do you know why the government gave up?" I didn't, but knew I wouldn't have to wait for an explanation. "It gave up because there wasn't one politician in America who wanted to be known as someone who was responsible for throwing people out of their houses and off their land. Especially since they improved it, and made it habitable . . . David?"

"I'm listening."

"That's how it's been in America. There's always been wars. If we couldn't find someone else to fight, we'd have a civil war, or a cattlemen's war; maybe it was just the government against the people." I wanted just a tiny bit of peace, but Apryl was at war, and I knew I was not only a recruit but about to be indoctrinated—again. "Our politicians know that as much as we hate war, we'll thrust out our chests, go gladly into battle and raise those politician's popularity scores until we realize that the product of wars is body bags. Saddam invaded Kuwait, so we'll retaliate and march into Kuwait and maybe Iraq, and there will be death and destruction one more time. But, we'll control the oil fields, and that's why we'll go to war. Not to protect anyone, not because it's right, but because we want to get the oil. Our nation's history, David, is a history of war. War over land. War over resources. War over political beliefs. War because of our racism. That's why we lost in Vietnam. Our soldiers were trained to fight for land, and theirs were struggling for the people's loyalties. The government doesn't own the land. The people don't own the land. Do you know who owns the land?"

"Banks?" I suggested half-conscious.

"Banks!" she shouted, assuring medical science that comas can easily be broken. "Banks and corporations! They stole the land from the people, and they don't have anyone they have to answer to. They don't have to worry about being re-elected. They don't have to have a moral conscience. They hold deeds.

And it doesn't matter to them who lives on their land, as long as the payment is on time. And even when it's not on time, it doesn't matter since the bank can just come in, take the land, and then sell it again. And corporations tear down and build and tear down without even thinking about the people and the animals. That's not right."

"Not right."

"David?"

"Huh?"

"We'll be successful tomorrow."

"It's almost midnight. We haven't slept. I'm tired. You're tired—"

"—No I'm not."

"O.K., *I'm* tired. I've got to get some sleep."

"You'll be with me tomorrow. You didn't change your mind, did you?"

"No, I need sleep."

"There'll be a confrontation."

"Maybe," I mumbled. "Probably."

"But they'll be reasonable."

"Perhaps."

"Everyone can be reasonable. God endowed mankind with reason. I'm counting on that."

"Mankind is a reasonable creature, created in God's image," I said, somewhat mimicking Milton, Mill, Locke, and the reasonable philosophers who came before us.

"David?"

"Yes Apryl."

"We make good music together, don't we?"

"Yes, we do."

"David?"

"Yes Apryl."

"Thank you."

"Apryl?"

"Yes David."

"Go to sleep."

24/

The Soul of a Fisherman

by David Ascher

Greg Diamond, 18 years old and only two months out of high school, sat on the banks of the Susquehanna in northeastern Pennsylvania, patiently waiting for a large mouth bass, and with absolutely no idea of what he wanted to do with the rest of his life.

He felt alone, worried there was no place for him in Young America's salacious rush toward remunerative careers and avaricious lifestyles. He just wanted to be with nature, to live in peace, maybe find a cause to support. But for right now it was him and the fish.

For awhile, he had flirted with the idea of becoming a professional bass fisherman. Not the kind who go out on boats, catch a load, and then sell it to wholesalers for distribution to the local grocery store. He didn't believe in killing fish, only in the sport of catching them, looking at them, chatting with them a few moments, making sure the lure didn't hurt their mouths, and then releasing them back into their streams and lakes. No, Greg Diamond wanted to be a *competitive* bass fisherman, the kind who enter contests, practice "catch-and-release" on ten-pound big-mouthed beauties, and win money. Lots of money. A few competitors can make five-figure incomes; a handful have even gone into six-figures. He didn't know if he could even get a three-figure income from tournament fishing, but he knew he was a fisherman, and he knew how to tie wooly worms, Bitch Creek buggers, and jig minnows onto a 12-pound test line and place them exactly where he wanted better than an Eagle Scout knew how to follow tracks and stars to get home.

For several years, in mornings and evenings, and even when he was supposed to be in class, he enjoyed the companionship of nature and fish, quietly looking and respecting all God's creations. Fishing—and earning money for it—could be the best of all worlds. But, he had doubts. He didn't know if he wanted to take something he enjoyed and commercialize it into a *job*! Perhaps, he thought, the fish would hate him if he used them to make money, rather than just be their friend. Somehow it just didn't seem right. Not to him. And certainly not to the fish.

He was confused. He didn't know what he wanted to do; he knew what he didn't want to do. The one thing Greg Diamond never planned to do was to go to college—unless it was one that offered a B.S. in bass science. His high school grades weren't even good enough to be mediocre; his SATs were even lower. Had he thought about attending class or doing homework, he might have had respectable scores, but he didn't care much for history, political science, economics, and geography. The Civil Rights struggle occurred long ago and somewhere else. The withdrawal of the Soviet Union from Afghanistan, after more than a decade of occupation, wasn't in his consciousness during his junior year; he didn't know where Afghanistan was, and he certainly couldn't spell it. The day he graduated from high school was the first year anniversary of the Tiananmen Square Protest; several hundred had been killed by the Chinese government; about 10,000 were injured. None of the speakers at his graduation even mentioned it; like most of his fellow students, Greg had no idea what the protest was all about.

And then Iraq invaded Kuwait. A decade earlier, when Iraq invaded Iran, the United States gave military and financial assistance to Saddam Hussein, knowing there was a rich oil supply to be protected, upset about the fundamentalism of the ruling Iranian ayatollahs, the ones who the previous year had condoned the invasion of the American embassy, and the taking of 53 hostages for more than a year, releasing them only when Ronald Reagan took the presidency from Jimmy Carter. But in the fog of world diplomacy and self-interest, now built upon a blatant disregard for the fundamental values of decency that formed America, it was under the Reagan–Bush Administration that the United States secretly sold weapons to Iranian terrorists. The logic, at least what passes as logic in government, was that by law the U.S. couldn't fund the Nicaraguan Contras, who were trying to overthrow the democratically-elected but social-ist Sandinista government, so it "made sense" to use deception, and then to cover it up under a web of lies and deceit, wrapped within the cloak of "national security."

For eight years, with Greg Diamond and most of his friends not knowing or caring what was happening half a world away, Iraq and Iran were at war. But this time, two years after the cease-fire, it was different. Iraq, which still had American-built weapons, took a few thousand Kuwaiti hostages, which they called "guests," and made some blustering noises. The noises led American oil conglomerates to raise prices, claiming the invasion could threaten God, mother, apple pie, and the right to obscene oil profits. Vacationing in Kennebunkport, Maine, President George Bush analyzed the situation, put all front-line military forces on alert, ordered several thousand troops to Saudi Arabia, called up the Reserves—and asked his caddie to give him a 5-iron.

This country, Greg Diamond's country, was calling him to take up arms or to declare his patriotism by supporting the war.

On a Sunday morning in late August, Greg Diamond, a kind soul who floated through life, but who was suddenly learning more history, political science, economics, and geography from CNN than he ever did in his classes, who believed in the American Dream, who worried that Iraq would invade all the Persian gulf and threaten American security, who continuously thought about Americans defending, but perhaps dying for their country, who never *ever* could kill anything, neither fish nor man, who never had a plan for his life other than to sit on a riverbank and enjoy nature, knew what he had to do.

On a Monday morning, he showered, put together his best appearance, summoned all his courage, bid his parents and friends a tearful farewell, traveled 30 miles—and enrolled in a community college for the fall semester, where he would major in general studies and, hopefully, have a II-S student deferment should the President restore the draft.

25/

'A Spark of Heavenly Fire'

For 95 years, the Marshfield County Courthouse, headquarters for most of the county offices, sat in the middle of Town Square, surrounded by trees, shrubs, and in later years an asphalt moat upon which cars could either park at a diagonal to the sidewalk or circle endlessly looking for either a parking space or an exit which would have allowed them to leave the square undamaged.

The three-story brick courthouse wasn't much of an architectural triumph when it was designed by the brother-in-law of one of the county commissioners. By the time it was built, brick by ugly brick by the construction company owned by another of the commissioners, it was truly a first-rate blemish upon the quiet rural county. Many residents called it gaudy; others weren't as kind. A superficial investigation initiated by a reporter at the local newspaper turned up no irregularities in the awarding of the contracts.

During the next few decades, people became more tolerant of their courthouse as it weathered snowstorm after snowstorm, standing as a fortress in the slowly changing downtown of Newburg. Eventually, it even took on an aura of being "quaint" or "rustic." In 1976, the state declared it to be an historic site, duly protected by the Historic Preservation Act. Because it was the country's sesquicentennial, Marshfield County made the courthouse the center of a week long celebration, to which local and state dignitaries were invited to try to say something nice about the building. Knowing that others thought so much of the county's history, the people soon began admiring the courthouse's "quite sturdy construction" and its "bold primitive neo-gothic architectural lines."

The presence of 13 steps leading to the first floor, and the absence of elevators leading to the other floors, had been forbidding problems to the handicapped and the elderly. The lack of space was a problem for the 15 county agencies and one court which were continually fighting for space, each one trying to squeeze the other out of the building designed for less than half the current personnel and paperwork.

It had long been obvious that the county needed a new building. But it had also long been obvious that because of the way tax laws were written, the county commissioners—unlike Pennsylvania school boards which have almost unlimited and unchecked power to raise taxes, increase budgets, and build schools whenever they feel like it—couldn't raise enough money to build a new building. Even if they could, the county commissioners, no matter who they were, no matter what their political party, were as frugal as their constituents, and were unwilling to risk their limited political futures by raising taxes. So, for 95 years, things existed in the building and in the county as they had always existed. Somehow or the other, the county always paid its bills and its anemic salaries, and also maintained what little services it had, surviving one crisis after another through a combination of fierce determination not to allow big government to dominate the lives of people—and through lethargy that allows problems to dissolve by their own weight.

But now the commissioners were about to face a problem that wouldn't dissolve, and they were going to have to make a decision. It was five years since the Bellevane plant in Massachusetts was proposed, three years since it was begun, and less than a year since it announced it and three other corporations were building a low-level nuclear waste site in the uninhabited woods of a rural county in northeastern Pennsylvania, far from what it considered civilization. The formal announcement also mentioned that this would be the fourth major plant in the country, and would accept waste from throughout a ten state New England and mid-Atlantic region as well as from Ohio and four other Midwestern states. The nuclear power companies, as well as numerous hospitals, schools, and private companies would save millions by not having to truck their waste to Barnwell, South Carolina. Of course, the spent uranium fuel rods would still have to be sealed and buried on-site in Massachusetts, but since every nuke had to do that, and the NRC had more watchdogs than a chain of junkyards, it was no big deal. With three minority co-owners, and with several mountains of permits and approvals, Pioneer Power was about to build another nuclear plant. It had even gotten approval from the state and the Board of Commissioners of Marshfield County who held out tax credits, abatements, and even subsidies to attract the plant to the county. It was, so said Pioneer Power's public relations machine, a "secure" group of concrete-and-steel buildings and caves built into a "secure" site with constant "security" to assure a "safe" operation. It was a "benefit" to the tax base, a "benefit" to the unemployed, and a "good corporate neighbor." What Pioneer Power told the public was factually accurate; what it didn't tell the public was the truth.

During the past couple of weeks, Apryl seemed distant, the fire gone from her soul. Even Thanksgiving couldn't light that spark of heavenly fire. Every year, she holds a community feast for friends, the unemployed, the impoverished, and those with nowhere else to go. Amid games and discussions about myriad issues, the guests feast on a surprisingly delectable giant turkey she fashions from tofu, chopped and grated vegetables, and herbs; on kugel and kasha, which she makes better than anyone I know, except for my grandmother; and on whatever any of the guests choose to bring. This was the first time I had been to her feast. At first, I just assumed her lethargy was from all of the preparation. As usual, I assumed wrong. She had tried her best to be cheerful, sprightly moving from here to there to yonder, but her friends noticed; it was an exhaustion caused not by physical fatigue but by a weariness in her soul.

Late that night, after all the guests had gone home, Apryl was more reflective than usual. "What if it doesn't work?" she again asked. And, again, as I had several times before, I tried to explain that even if the plan failed—and there was every indication that it might—there are many places to build a school. And once again Apryl tried to explain the "oneness" of that land and how the already-standing-but-much-in-need-of-repair stone mill would be the perfect site for her school and weekend crafts fair. Sleep came with a brooding silence.

But the night before we were to begin the battle with the

Board of Commissioners of Marshfield County, she was energized, ready for an assault. This morning, she shampooed and
combed her black hair, swept it into a modified bun, put on her
dress of imitation doeskin, tied a hemp-rope belt around her
waist, put on a pair of fake-leather knee-high boots, and added
a mist of makeup. Around her neck she carefully placed her
leather-and-brass peace symbol, and then brightly commanded,
"O.K., Writer, grab your quill. It's time to slay dragons."

At the 10 a.m. Thursday meeting of the Board of Commissioners, Apryl Greene had every intention to end Pioneer Power's
grand scheme to build not just a low-level waste disposal plant,
but a nuclear-driven plant that could handle more than half of
the nuclear industry's 2,000 tons of waste a year, as well as its
spent control rods. But, as of now, the only thing the commissioners knew was that one of its property owners who had been
ordered from her land by eminent domain eviction was planning to protest that eviction. And the only thing the media
knew was that the president of one of the nation's larger electronics corporations and the editor of *Century* magazine were
going to be in the audience.

Most commissioners' meetings draw a reporter and, maybe,
a half dozen residents at most. This one was different. Seated
in the audience were a half-dozen reporters and a two-person
TV camera crew. Also in the audience, which was now standing-
room-only and spilling into the hallway, were two dozen or so of
Apryl's friends and several dozen more county residents. But,
within the audience were dozens of vociferous residents who
wanted to see that plant built, to give a boost to the languid
economy if only for a few years.

At the Commissioners table, amiably chatting with county
employees, the media, and local residents, sat county clerk Ray
Reichley; Commissioners Frederick Reinholdt, Harry Cameron,
and Ted Schumacher; to the far right was county attorney Bolton
Drake. Harry Cameron, the newest member, was appointed by
the president judge of the Court of Common Pleas two months
earlier when Scotty Savidge resigned after taking a job in Allentown, and each of the two remaining commissioners wanted to
become chair, so they effectively blocked each other's nomina-
tions. Harry Cameron was a compromise, a life-long resident
and hard-working farmer only mildly active in politics, someone

whom the other two commissioners figured would just fill space until the May election almost two years away. However, because Harry Cameron never wished to be chairman, and had never given much thought about the compromises and shadings of truth necessary to be elected and re-elected, he could speak his own mind, and do what he thought was important without the burden of worrying whether he'd lose a vote or a contribution to a campaign war chest.

At 10 a.m., on schedule as it has been every other week for who-knows-how-long, the county clerk led the audience in the pledge of allegiance and a silent prayer. This battle was about to begin. In less than 15 minutes, Harry Cameron, wielding a homemade gavel of oak with machine gun efficiency, moved through a dozen routine items. And then came Apryl Greene.

"We have a request here," said the chair, "from a taxpaying resident of Marshfield County, Miss Apryl Greene, who wishes to appeal the state's actions that led to condemnation and eventual seizure of her land for the public good. The Commonwealth has already determined a fair price for that land, and officially took possession about a month ago. Miss Greene did not accept the state's check. I have carefully explained to her that this public body doesn't have the authority to overrule a state condemnation. She still wishes to address the board." He looked up from his notes, hesitated a moment, and added that the state had begun grading for a series of roads in the area, and that both Pennsylvania and the federal government approved construction of a low-level nuclear waste disposal plant that will bring jobs to the people of this region. He paused, ever so slightly. "We all know there have been protests. We all know a lot of people don't want that plant here," said Harry Cameron, yielding to a growing concern among his county's residents and the opposition of the state's anti-nuclear activists. "But," and he made this point sharply, "most of the people want this to happen. They want the jobs. Not just any job, but the high-paying jobs this industry will bring to our area. Not just at the plant but in the supporting industries as well. We believe it will raise our tax base and help our schools. They want this clean energy source, so we aren't dependent upon oil. We are responsible to all of our people, not just the special interests." There was clapping and whooping from some of the audience; there was selective silence from the rest. And then there was Apryl.

In wide-eyed innocence, Apryl talked about the beauty of northeastern Pennsylvania, of rolling hills that turn green in summer and assorted colors in Fall; of rivers where people of all ages could swim and fish; of relatively clean air and of people who said "Hi," even to strangers, and of how neither hitchhiker nor driver needs to fear the other. But most of all, she talked about her School for Peace and of the land she had hoped to build it upon. For their part, the Commissioners were tolerant—after all, everyone likes to be praised. After four or five minutes, Ted Schumacher politely interrupted her, explaining that although he appreciated her love of the area, the Board long ago had established a three minute time limit on any one speaker. "We must follow these rules," said Ted Schumacher, addressing both Apryl and the chairman, to which Apryl also politely suggested that although she wasn't finished, she understood that rules, like ordinances, must be followed. "But," she pleaded, "maybe just a few minutes more? I promise you won't be bored."

No one else understood why Harry Cameron made an exception, especially since dozens of others were frothing to speak. Harry Cameron may not have known why he made an exception, but he knew that Apryl Greene would eventually get around to her reasons, no matter how many ages of mankind it would take. Apryl didn't disappoint him.

She quickly recounted how she acquired the land, the financing, problems with credit unions and banks, how Deerfield & Plymouth, a subsidiary of Stratford Electronics, came to own the mortgage, how it sold it back to the investment group that was going to own the waste disposal plant as well as the nuclear energy plant, and how the state finally seized the land under the eminent domain statutes.

"This still has no relevance to how the county can get your land back," Frederick Reinholdt declared.

"Mr. Chairman," said Apryl confidently, addressing Harry Cameron and disregarding Frederick Reinholdt, "upon the land that I or my father had leased from nature, the land upon which I wish to build a School for Peace, the state has claimed it."

"To build roads and highways for the people," said Frederick Reinholdt politely interrupting.

"To build access roads to a nuclear waste disposal operation," said Apryl sharply. Frederick Reinholdt wasn't about to be out-debated, especially by what he knew was a Commie and her radical God-destroying un-American comrades.

"The plant," said Frederick Reinholdt, a bit testy, "although scheduled to be built in this county, is in Madison Township. That's to the south of your land that was taken." And, as if he had to re-emphasize it, added, "purchased at a fair price."

"The money is unimportant," said Apryl. "What is important is the use of the land. The land that was taken in Madison Township was, indeed, for a nuclear waste disposal plant. It's a terrible thing to do with land. Do you believe the thousands of Iroquois Federation Native Americans would have approved of this? Do you think the fish in the river and birds who live in the trees and the deer and bear and all the animals who graze upon that land would approve?"

"It's not their approval that's necessary," smirked Frederick Reinholdt, a professional trapper when he wasn't playing commissioner. And since he had gotten just a faint laugh from some of the audience, playfully added, "besides, since they don't vote or pay taxes, I doubt we care what they think."

Apryl was about to respond when Harry Cameron brought the discussion back to the business of government, asking her to "please just stick with the facts." She smiled, readily accepting the request. But she would respond in her own fashion anyway.

"My land in Jefferson Township was taken so the nuclear industry could not only have access to the river, but also to build the access roads it needed." Looking directly at the commissioners, she argued that radioactive waste would be traveling over roads the state built on land that was supposed to be used to help people learn about peace.

"Your school isn't even built. It's still a far-fetched dream," sniffed Frederick Reinholdt, sputtering mental farts beneath a surly belligerence.

"It *will* be built."

From the audience came a mixture of applause, jeers, and boos. From the commissioners table came Frederick Reinholdt's retort, "Only if you build it somewhere else." Once again, there came applause, jeers, and boos. To Frederick Reinholdt, those who jeered and booed this time didn't matter since they didn't vote in Marshfield County. The ones who did matter were the ones he knew to be loyal patriots of Pennsylvania and Marshfield County who came to the meeting to oppose the transgression of radical Commie hippies or, if they couldn't be at the meeting, were at their jobs—if they had one.

Quietly, almost softly, Ted Schumacher raised another issue, one the commissioners undoubtedly discussed among themselves several times, although not in public. "The improvements to the land," he said, "will significantly add to our tax base. It will help all of our residents to keep our property taxes low. The state's actions—our actions—are for the public good." He looked at Apryl, not harshly, not in condemnation. "The land will benefit all the people, not just a few," he explained.

"My school," replied Apryl, just as calmly, "is for the many—for the children."

"Just as impassioned as you are about your school," said Ted Schumacher "so are the state and a lot of business people impassioned about what they think is right. Nuclear energy is clean energy. No one disputes that." Except for solar energy, which not one megacorporation planned to develop, nukes were relatively clean—when they didn't leak. But, nuclear waste wasn't clean radiation. It was dirty, so dirty that there were hundreds of rules and regulations directing how to prepare everything from contaminated clothes to X-Rays for transportation to a waste site to make sure it didn't bring a pandemic episode of cancer. Ironically, neither the U.S. Department of Transportation nor the Nuclear Regulatory Agency required trucking companies to have any special licenses to transport the waste. Maybe in the future, there would be regulations, but for now transportation of waste products was regulated only by free enterprise capitalism. I was sure Apryl would viciously object to being told about nuclear cleanliness which she knew was certainly not next to godliness, but she said nothing. Ted Schumacher again raised the dominating issue, that the waste plant would again stimulate the county's languid economy.

"I doubt more than a handful of residents of this county will be working at that plant," said Apryl. "The contractor said that building a nuclear waste plant requires many skills that don't exist in Marshfield County, and it will have no other choice but to bring in crews from its other jobs." She paused for just a moment, and then emphatically added, "It'll be even worse after the plant goes on line. Do *you* want to try to operate a control board?" That brought a glimmer of laughter from many in the audience, and Ted Schumacher who conceded that even if only

a few dozen jobs went to county residents, the imported workers would become county residents, patronize local businesses,
and pay taxes that would improve the county's schools and
infrastructure. The support industries alone, he said, would
magnify the tax base. "That isn't wrong."

"What is wrong," said Apryl, "is destroying God's land."

"No one is destroying anyone's land!" said an intemperate
Frederick Reinholdt, to which Harry Cameron again interrupted
to plead with Apryl to stick with the facts in explaining why she
thought a county Board of Commissioners could revoke state
and federal actions that in themselves carried mountains of
permits. At no time did Apryl let anyone know that she knew
the nuclear plant wasn't just the small waste disposal plant
they had been led to believe. If she was to get her land back, she
would do it on principle, not on size—although she did hold size
in reserve, just in case it was needed.

"Two states away," said Apryl, operating in her own time
frame, "a conglomerate is finishing a nuclear plant. Because of
it, there are jobs and a stronger tax base for its county. Therefore,
they believe, minor problems are to be tolerated. One of those
minor problems is a vibration." During the past two weeks, we
had all heard about a mysterious vibration in the turbine in
Bellevane No. 1. It showed up on monitors one Sunday morning
and hadn't yet left. Naturally, the newspapers, quoting Pioneer
Power public relations people, said it wasn't serious and was
currently under investigation. But during the two week investigation, Pioneer Power engineers ruled out everything from a
monitor error to an impending Armageddon. Since they ran all
the tests and couldn't find the cause, they said it must be a nor-
mal function for a steam turbine generator. That's it. Problem
diagnosed. Solution presented. "Maybe, Pioneer Power," said
Apryl sweetly, "could solve its problem by taking that vibrator
and shove it up its cooling tower."

Shock, laughter, and clapping greeted her statement, but
before Harry Cameron could restore order, Apryl continued. "I
doubt nuclear energy will help the people, unless you get turned
on by nuclear vibrators." Even Frederick Reinholdt smiled,
although he tried his Puritanical best to disguise it. Apryl continued, "Nevertheless, at least the people in Bellevane's evacuation zone will have to learn to live with steam clouds in their
backyards. But, what do *we* get? We get the waste from that

plant and several others from throughout the country. Here, in our county, there's even more of a chance for disaster."

"Objection!" declared Frederick Reinholdt.

"Overruled!" responded Apryl Greene.

"Miss Greene," said Harry Cameron patiently, "this isn't a court of law, and even if it was, you wouldn't be allowed to overrule an objection raised by one of the commissioners." She apologized, and again asked for more indulgence. Frederick Reinholdt demanded an executive session. When Harry Cameron said he saw no reason for it, Frederick Reinholdt threatened to walk out. "Oh sit back down," the chairman commanded, as if scolding an errant child. "If you walk out, Ted will be the only one who might call for a quorum, and since two commissioners is a quorum, the meeting would continue anyhow." He chuckled, and then explained to Frederick Reinholdt that although the meeting was taking much longer than anyone figured, if it were to end early, the commissioners wouldn't be able to get to the last item to open the bids for the new tool barn, something that Frederick Reinholdt had a keen interest in since his son-in-law was one of three who had submitted sealed bids.

"Move to table the nuclear discussion," Frederick Reinholdt blurted.

"Out of order," ruled Harry Cameron.

"Is not!"

"I said it is, and it is." He slammed his gavel on the block. "Now, Miss Greene, please continue with your story."

"In western Massachusetts, the nuclear plant with the vibrations is almost completed. The nuclear industry is telling the people that nuclear energy is safe in spite of what happened at Rocky Flats, Chernobyl, and TMI. They're telling us that even if there would be a situation—aren't PR people wonderful with euphemisms?—even if there's a *situation*, it wouldn't affect our food crops or our animals . . . or us. We only have the assurances of a multi-billion dollar conglomerate that their workers are well-trained to run a nuclear plant, that the 2,000 operating errors a year documented by the NRC at all the nuclear plants, including the ones in our backyards, won't be repeated at that plant."

With biting commentary and a modicum of humor, Apryl outlined a litany of nuclear industry problems, focusing upon workers who cheated on tests, slept on the job, or made mistakes in judgment. She detailed an instance where the management of a plant bought radiation monitors that weren't as sensitive to radiation levels as previous monitors that showed the workers getting too high a dose. She pointed to several cases where radioactive waste overflowed into rivers or became mixed with the drinking water supply. She ripped into the Diablo Canyon plant in central California that was built three miles from an earthquake fault, and with the wrong set of plans; other plants, she emphasized, were not only built near faults but met seismic qualifications requirements by what she called "creative manipulation." Roaring past any attempt to stop her, Apryl talked about doctored figures from the TMI meltdown a decade earlier, of correlations between infant deaths related to thyroid problems and the release of iodine-121 from the meltdown. "In the grounds of central and northeastern Pennsylvania," Apryl thundered, "are excessive levels of strontium-90 released during the TMI meltdown. Even if there were no leaks, the grounds and rivers are still polluted with strontium-90, cesium-137, and iodine-121. The strontium gets into the ground. Animals eat the grass. We eat animals. We get strontium. We die from bone marrow disease. We decay in the ground and the strontium continues infesting future generations because its half-life is 28 years, and doesn't become stable for ten half-lives! To keep the waste tanks from overflowing with radioactive waste—the kind that would normally be taken to the dump site in this county—TMI dumped several thousand gallons of radioactive waste into the Susquehanna. And not one community downstream was ever notified. People boat upon that river, water ski upon it, and even catch the fish that swim in that waste. That's not all! People around TMI began complaining that their water tasted like iron or metal. It was the same taste that people at Rocky Flats complained about when that plant almost melted down." And then Apryl drew a breath. Finally. There was applause and encouragement from her friends in the audience; from others came sighs, gasps, and even a couple of challenges. Apryl continued, stopping only the briefest of moments to take on a few more particles of air, pleading her case by pleading humanity's case. "An abnormal number of farm animals were born with genetic defects around Harrisburg," said Apryl. "More than can be explained away by the state. Too many still births. There are almost no snakes left in the area. Deer are disappearing. Small game are gone. It's as if they knew! If rabbits and squirrels know about the environment, why can't humans!" What Frederick Reinholdt was thinking at that moment might have been if there weren't as many rabbits, squirrels, groundhogs, and those other *pests*, he wouldn't be able to bag as much income. But, he said nothing, probably thinking of ways nuclear energy could be used to modify the gestation period of animals to increase birth rates that would yield even more joy from trapping. Moving back and forth before the commissioners' table, stopping momentarily to look each one in the eye, to gesture, to emphasize, Apryl lectured about Church Rock, New Mexico, where 90 million gallons of radioactive waste were dumped into the Rio Puerco, flooding towns 30 miles downstream. She told of radioactive fires in Rocky Flats and Windscale where use of water led to even greater dissemination of radioactive air and water. "And what happens?" she concluded, giving no one any opportunity to reply. "What happens is that the NRC slaps everyone's hands. The corporations apologize and promise never ever to do it again. Newspapers run editorials saying that this was a horrendous problem but that since everyone apologized, everything is now just peachy-keen."

And then Apryl Greene took a deep breath to gather energy, and quietly explained a reality. "Beyond the posssibility that earthquakes, sabotage, poor construction, and human error may cause pollution of our waters and the air, beyond the health problems that will most certainly affect us and the animals that live upon this earth," she explained, is that most evacuation plans are useless. May they never have to be tested, but if they are, local emergency management agencies and the nuclear plants are not prepared for a full-scale evacuation."

"I demand you rule her out of order," Frederick Reinholdt sputtered. "We're almost at war in Kuwait, and we can't depend upon Arab oil. We need nuclear energy. It's clean. It can run cities. We need it. This county needs it. And this nation needs it!"

"Oh, cap it!" snapped Harry Cameron who ignored the advice of the county counsel and asked Apryl to continue. She took another giant breath and continued, much to our amusement and Frederick Reinholt's displeasure.

"Did you know that Marie Curie and her daughter died from radiation poisoning?" Apryl asked. "And did you know it wasn't until the 1940s that Industry finally told its workers that radiation could be dangerous. In the '20s and '30s, radium dials on watches were the big thing. Still were until a decade or so ago. Anyhow, these radium dials glowed in the dark. Now, if you're the boss of a radium-dial manufacturing company, you're not going to say that radium could be unsafe. So, the bosses said not only was radium a boon to night vision, but that it could make people healthier and increase their sexuality. Honest! They said that radium had all these great side effects, so the workers who used brushes to paint the dials and the watch hands would put the brushes into their mouths to make finer points and, I suppose, add to their sexuality." Turning to economics, Apryl tore through argument after argument, reasoning that if people weren't moved by issues of health and safety, she'd just use good old-fashioned capitalism. "The nuclear industry tells its investors that nuclear energy is cost-efficient," said Apryl, who explained that the proposed plant, like every other one in this country, including the one at Bell Bend, which most observers, even the harshest critics, agree is fairly well run, has only a 35 to 40 year life expectancy, and it costs about $6 billion, about $150 million a year. "After 40 years," said Apryl solemnly dangling reality before her target audience, "it becomes so radioactive hot that no one can safely work in it, so the utility spends a few hundred million more, seals it up and then abandons it. They'll be nothing more than radioactive blights upon the land. But is it safe?" Apryl quickly answered her own question with a thunderous "NO!" explaining that no matter how well the plant was sealed, radiation would leak, and that the walls would be so loaded with radioactivity that "anyone walking through the plant a thousand years from now would receive a lethal dose."

"No one would be stupid enough to walk through a moth-balled nuclear plant," challenged Frederick Reinholdt.

"No one has to," she replied. "The concrete used to build the walls will crumble and turn to dust, and this will occur thousands of years before the radioactive elements that man created become stable. At a certain point, our ground will receive at least one-fourth of all the radioactivity of the walls."

"What does Pioneer Power say about all this?" asked Ted Schumacher. "Certainly they have more evidence than you do."

"A scientist-type with a title says that by the time the plant is too old and must be retired, modern technology will have the solution."

"That's their answer?!" asked Ted Schumacher. "They're asking us to trust them?" He paused a moment, and then asked point-blank, dead-on-target, if Apryl was telling the truth.

"Dang right she is!" came a voice from the audience.

"More honest than the press and the government!" came another voice, this one from an elderly woman who 15 minutes earlier sneered at Apryl.

Harry Cameron just smiled, a benign smile of tolerance.

Apryl looked at the Board of Commissioners, her eyes sadly giving them their answer. Quietly she told of plutonium that was "lost" by the nuclear industry. "If just 16 ounces of plutonium were to be divided and ingested equally among the five billion people of this world," said Apryl, "within only one generation, we wouldn't have anyone left on earth."

Frederick Reinholdt shifted uneasily, and again wanted to know what all that had to do with her eviction, and lectured her that a county commissioners meeting wasn't the appropriate place to object to the problems of the nuclear industry. He kept raising the issues that some wished they had raised. However, Apryl asked for indulgence, and continued, much to Harry Cameron's amusement and Frederick Reinholdt's annoyance. "That plant you're talking about, the big one, not the small waste plant in our county but the big one," Frederick Reinholdt spurted out, "isn't even in our county. Not even in Pennsylvania. It's in—" he spit it out, emphasizing each liberal syllable—"Ma-ssa-*chu*-setts."

"Chernobyl was half a world away," said Apryl, "but the radiation cloud eventually floated over the United States. Four years later, we're still getting some of the effects." Having cut him off, Apryl continued weaving a series of knots that she hoped would not only tie up her request to set aside her eviction, but also would close down a nuclear power genrating plant in one state and a nuclear waste site in another.

Again asking the Board's indulgence, Apryl and two of her small contingent of friends efficiently set up an audiovisual presentation, part of my contribution to today's show. Years ago, I had produced multi-media multi-screen shows, using as many as 32 slide projectors, three film cameras, and innumerable special effects, all of them programmed into a precursor to the PC. This time, Apryl required just two slide projectors, an Overhead, and a portable screen. She would dazzle the audience and elected officials not by the presentation itself, but by the content. Two large portfolio cases—no one else knew where they had come from—were now at her side, their contents to be released soon. In the now-darkened room, Apryl Greene showed photographic slides of the intricate lacework of pipes within a nuclear core. "These pipes," said Apryl, "are critical to the operation of a nuclear reactor." She left the last slide on the screen, and then projected onto the cream-colored wall behind the commissioners a full-color transparency diagramming the interrelationships of the components of a nuclear power plant. A masterful teacher, Apryl reduced nuclear power to its basics, carefully and quickly explaining a power plant's operation to a classroom of students who still had no idea how it would lead to recovering her land. But Harry Cameron reminded everyone, there wasn't much else happening, so why not just sit back and listen awhile. Now and then Frederick Reinholdt threw out a sigh of disgust but didn't say anything, resigned to letting Apryl babble on.

"The key to a safe, efficient operation," said Apryl, "is to be able to cool down this tremendous heat that's the result of the reaction. To do so, many techniques are used. But at the Bellevane plant, light water . . . the kind we swim in, or drink, or water our gardens with . . . is used. The water comes from the river, and it returns to the river. The only difference is that this is a pure water. Most of the foreign matter is removed after it's taken in. That's the only difference. If the cooling level becomes too low, there is a danger of a meltdown, like at TMI. But we're assured there are so many back-up systems designed into this plant that the odds of that happening are about as remote as the farmers of this county *not* getting screwed by the government and big business." Even Frederick Reinholdt chuckled.

Reaching into one of the art portfolios, Apryl pulled out six large negatives, placed them on a table, and reminded the commissioners of the pipes. Remember," she said, "water is taken from the river, purified, then used to pass over the core, and also into a condenser to drive the turbine to create steam which, as I pointed out, produces this clean and cheap electricity that the nuclear industry has been telling us about the past few years." Giggles and shouts of support from the audience punctuated her discussion. "This is an efficient and safe way to get electricity, so we've been led to believe. Remember those pipes? The key to safety is in those pipes. As long as those pipes are safe, then there is less of a chance for meltdown, or radiation and other pollutants seeping back into the rivers and affecting our food chains." She paused and looked at Harry Cameron, and somberly informed him that something was wrong with those pipes. "And that something," said Apryl, can affect the health of every person not only in western Massachusetts but in this county as well." She took a deep breath, waited a moment or two, and exploded another of her carefully planted mines. She revealed that off and on, over a period of years, she worked for a large company as a photographic specialist in stress radiography. "What I did was to direct radiographic photographs of industrial pipes under construction, and from those plates I had to determine levels of stress, and if there were any structural defects," she explained.

"I assume you're not here to ask for a job," Ted Schumacher said, a pleasant laugh underlying his question.

"I'm here to try to help all of us from being killed by incompetents," said Apryl, quickly glancing at Frederick Reinholdt. She placed one of the photographic negatives on the overhead, and matter-of-factly announced, "This is a radiograph of one of the pipes at the Bellevane plant. In very simple language, in order to measure stress, you expose the pipes to radiation and photograph those pipes. Structural weaknesses and bad welds appear on the film. This film indicates there is a defect in the pipe." She pulled out another piece of film, explaining that it was a radiograph of a pipe already installed at the Bellevane plant, and said it didn't appear to have any defects. On the Overhead, she put another film; that film, she said, was a close-up, magnified seven times, of the previous film. "Notice the approximate center of this film," she directed the commissioners, "there is a shadow, barely visible. I have 32 radiographs of sections of pipe near the reactor core. These radiographs not only show structural weaknesses and improper welding procedures, but also that at least one person used a lead pencil to touch up the radiographs to make them appear there was no longer any problem, that the welds had been made."

"Say that again, Miss!" shouted the Channel 24 reporter, caught with her lights off. "Did you say the X-rays were touched up?" Questions from the reporters came quickly.

"Are you sure it was Bellevane?"

"Are your facts conclusive?"

"How do we know you're telling the truth?"

"How long have you known this?"

"Have you told anyone else?"

"What relevance is it to Marshfield County?"

"What makes you an expert?

"Order!" commanded Harry Cameron, only to be drowned out by a swarm of reporters' questions. "ORDER!" he again shouted, gaveling the wooden block in front of him. He must have hit that block three or four times, sighed, and sat back, resigned to waiting until the reporters got through with their questions. Questions were all they had.

"Do you have copies of this?"

"Are you sure they've been doctored?"

"Is there other evidence?"

"Who doctored this? Who's guilty?"

"Is this just some trick designed so you won't be evicted?"

"Are you sure?"

"Can you say that again, Miss?"

"ORDER!" snapped Harry Cameron, sharply rapping the block. To his surprise, that's exactly what happened. With a sigh, he told the audience it was evident that Apryl wasn't going to answer any questions, at least at that point. He and Apryl exchanged smiles. "This is the meeting room of the Board of Commissioners of Marshfield County, Pennsylvania," Harry Cameron scolded, "and I will have order. If that is not understood, I will throw all of you out of here."

"The public has a right to know," said a reporter who couldn't have been more than a year out of Journalism School. Probably even got an "A" in his media law class. "You *can't* throw us out!"

"Young man," said Harry Cameron with fatherly concern, looking at the reporter, eager to carry the First Amendment sword of righteousness against the evils of the bureaucracy—and a front-page byline wouldn't be all that bad—"the news media have no more rights than anyone else. And we have the right to conduct the people's business without having the press make a mockery of the process."

"The public has a—"

Harry Cameron finished the sentence. "—right to know." He stared at the reporter, and then lectured him. "Young man, I doubt there's anyone in the room who believes that more than I do, and I count every reporter in this room. If your newspaper cared a dang about the people's right to know, it would be more accurate in its reporting. It would increase its coverage of education and government, and would report with the vigilance and intelligence that the forefathers demanded." Other politicians might have thought it, even said it among friends, but never in public, afraid to rattle the media cages that could be beneficial to their next campaign. Harry Cameron didn't worry about his next campaign but about what he was appointed to do. "I'm sure Miss Greene will eventually explain how all this ties together," he quietly said. The reporter objected, mouthing some platitude about the press being the only savior of mankind. "Young man," said Harry Cameron, again politely trying to explain the facts of life to one of his children, "when I was younger than you are, my pappy told me it never pays to get into a pissing contest with a skunk. Now, son, I don't know whether you think I'm a skunk or not, but I can assure you that it really doesn't matter because as sure as squirrels hide nuts in the Fall, I'm going to prevail. Now, please, just sit down and take notes." The reporter was about to say something when Harry Cameron looked right into his eyes; the reporter sat down. I made a note to talk with this reporter. While other reporters took notes and regurgitated whatever was told them, at least he was willing to speak out, to challenge authority, something that is slowly dying within our profession. The chairman turned to Apryl. "You have raised serious questions. I don't know if you're qualified to judge nuclear pipes, or whether this is just a cheap trick to arouse the media into giving you sympathy for the land that the state seized—legally I might add." He paused briefly. "I'm still not sure how any of this is relevant, but I assume you're not wasting our time with something 300 miles away."

Apryl looked at him, somewhat wounded, and handed him a letter, saying that it would help establish her qualifications. He unfolded it, and noted for the record. "It's from the personnel department of Wolfe–Woodward, dated November first of this year, and is a verification of employment for a Miss Rachel Greenberg. Who is this Rachel Greenberg?"

"I am. I mean I am sometimes. I've had other names, but right now I feel like an Apryl." Her eyes mischievously teased the commissioners. "You should have seen my boyfriend's expression when he found out my born-name wasn't Apryl. It almost blew him away!" She was right about that. For months I had been chasing facts about an apparition named Apryl Greene.

"Well, Miss Greenberg," said an amused Harry Cameron, "It *is* Greenberg, isn't it?"

"Oh, yes sir," said Apryl in all innocence, who produced both a copy of her birth certificate and the decree that allowed her to change her name, and now prepared to enmesh everyone in her own form of rambling logic. "You see, I was born Rachel Greene. My father, however, wasn't born with the name Greene. He was Gruenberg"—She spelled the name slowly for the Commissioners—"but Immigration changed his name to Greene when he came to this country from Austria because they thought he should have an American name, so that's why my father's last name and mine are Greene. That's Greene with an 'e' at the end. But when I was young I took my family's real name. That's because I never knew my grandfather, but thought we should preserve his name, but I dropped an 'e' where the 'u' used to be. It seemed to combine the languages of his two countries. I used it while I was searching for who I was, because I needed to assert my heritage, then I liked the name Apryl, but Apryl just didn't seem to fit with Greenberg so well, so I changed it back to Greene and became Apryl Greene. Then, shortly before I graduated from college, I officially changed it to Rachel Greenberg because I wanted something that was more formal to honor my family, but informally I'm Apryl Greene. Don't you think that's a nice name, too?" She did that entire monologue without seeming to take one breath, and as masterful as the best quick-change con artist.

"Well, Miss Greenberg, or whatever you call yourself," said a chuckling Harry Cameron to a chorus of laughter for what could easily have been mistaken for a stand-up comedy routine, "this letter indicates that you worked as a radiographic stress technologist for Wolfe–Woodward full-time for about three years and as a part-time temp on-and-off after that. Are you sure you are who this letter says you are?"

"Pretty sure," said Apryl/Rachel.

"I guess that means you know what you're talking about."

"Just because she says she knows what she's talking about doesn't mean she's telling us the truth." The statement could only have come from Frederick Reinholdt.

"I agree," said Apryl, whom the Board now knew as Rachel Greenberg . . . or maybe Rachel Greene . . . or, maybe . . . "So, I brought along an architect."

At first, Harry Cameron didn't hear the new voice addressing the commissioners, so she quickly repeated it. "Mr. Chairman, may I have a few moments of your time?"

"Kerry?" said the chairman softly, but not as surprised as the other members of the board, "I assume you have something to tell us." In quiet, measured tones, Kerry Cameron, B.Arch., AIA, talked about the core structure of Bellevane, supporting the statements that Apryl had earlier made.

"Kerry," said her father, just as gently, "I love you dearly"— he needn't have said that since everyone in the room knew that—"but you design offices not nuclear plants."

"I can read blueprints." It was short. It was sharp. And there was no doubt about her knowledge.

Two weeks earlier, Kerry Cameron had called Apryl and volunteered to help. It was just an instinct. A feeling. Nothing more. "She thought it was a trap at first," said Kerry, drawing a near-quiet laughter from Apryl and her friends, and sighs of acceptance from just about everyone else. None of us knew she and Apryl had even talked. For one full day, the two of them looked at blueprints and structural X-Rays, and on this beautiful Thursday morning in November, Kerry Cameron put her license and reputation before the commissioners of a small rural county. She wasn't the only one.

"I support Miss Greene's analysis." There was no question that the CEO of one of the nation's leading electronics corporations was there not only to support this activist, but also to challenge the shell that the commissioners and their county had built around themselves.

Less than a month earlier, Apryl was convinced that all the evidence pointed to Dr. Leon Salikoff as the mastermind of an elaborate plot that got his corporation a turbine load of money in exchange for fronting for the nuclear industry. She had trusted him. She had believed in him. And he had betrayed her. Not just her, but all humanity! "Leech!" she had called him. "Parasite!" she had screeched, but only northeastern Pennsylvania had heard her. Her hatred worked on her, poisoning everything that was so wonderful about her, bleeding her energy to conduct the research she needed to do to present her evidence to the Board of Commissioners. But, there was just an ion of doubt. She had to find out. So one day three weeks earlier, after making sure that Dr. Salikoff was in town, Apryl flew into Boston, grabbed a taxi to Stratford Electronics, stormed past receptionists, secretaries, and security guards, into the office of Dr. Leon Salikoff and demanded to know why. Nothing more. She just wanted to know why he had lied to her, betrayed her, sold his self-respect and friendship. But Dr. Leon Salikoff had neither lied nor betrayed her, nor had he sold any part of his soul. It took several hours to sift through the facts and the dirt that covered up the facts, but by the end of the day Dr. Salikoff had been vindicated, Apryl appeased, and Ralph M. Taylor— known by various aliases in northeastern and central Pennsylvania, and in Massachusetts as the vice-president of finance for Stratford Electronics—fired. No recourse. No appeal. He left the building shortly past twilight, accompanied by two security officers, swearing revenge and declaring the Labor Relations Board would restore his job, an irony in itself since he despised unions and all they stood for. Within the next week, Dr. Salikoff fired seven more Stratford employees for being part of Taylor's scheme, although he gave them generous severance allowances for their silence.

But now, in Newburg, Marshfield County, Pennsylvania, Dr. Leon Salikoff would help Apryl once again, and in doing so possibly help a county avoid a problem without end. He stood, identified himself—a murmur rumbled through the reporters, stifled quickly by a sharp glance from Harry Cameron—and said only that he had looked over the photos, that he believed what Apryl had told the commissioners was accurate, and there could be a serious problem with the Bellevane plant.

"How do we know you're telling the truth?" demanded Frederick Reinholdt.

"How do I know," said Dr. Leon Salikoff softly, "that you're not as dumb as you sound."

"I demand that this man be thrown out of these chambers!" howled the commissioner on the right.

"He didn't mean anything by it," said Ted Schumacher.

"He insulted me! He insulted this board. He—"

"He's just defending his reputation. Maybe we can learn what the heck is happening to us." Frederick Reinholdt was about to raise another objection when Ted Schumacher interrupted. "Where are those pipes located?" he calmly asked, hoping to defuse his colleague.

"Near the reactor core," said Dr. Salikoff quietly, to which Harry Cameron glared at the press corps, silencing them with only a scowl.

"What could happen if these pipes were left the way they are?" Harry Cameron asked.

"Maybe it'll be caught. Maybe not. Maybe a meltdown." The TV lights came back on, and even the reporters who believed if it didn't happen locally it wasn't worth reporting began writing furiously. Dr. Salikoff continued, "The ECCS— that's the emergency core cooling system—should prevent that. What is more likely to happen is that the water taken in from the river, then purified, will pick up some contaminants, perhaps from the time the reactor is put into operation, and will probably forever be a conduit of radioactivity. In time, should a rupture occur because of the position of the tubes that have the defects, the water will back up and flow not in one of the two major loops in the design but back into the river. It will be carrying superheated water and abnormally higher concentrations of radioactivity, primarily uranium, plutonium, iodine, and radium. The superheated water would probably kill much of the water life in the river. The radioactive materials would probably get into the food chain. That's why there's extensive testing of these tubes."

"Are you absolutely certain these photographs are from the nuclear plant?" Ted Schumacher asked, the commissioners having long ago given up on the relevancy issue. Apryl produced another letter. Again, Harry Cameron paraphrased it for the audience, noting it was a notarized statement from a nuclear engineer working for Hess & Newhart, the plant's construction company, that the X-Rays were from the Bellevane plant, that a decision was made by the construction company, with the concurrence of Pioneer Power & Energy, that in order to meet certain deadlines H&N had to move onto other areas of the project. Going back and placing new pipe or welding existing pipe could cause a delay of as much as three weeks, forcing temporary layoffs in other areas, so H&N planned to fix the situation later. *When*, no one knew. Harry Cameron looked up. The only thing missing from that letter, he said, was the engineer's name which had been blacked out at his request.

"How do we know he isn't just some disgruntled employee?" Frederick Reinholt asked.

"We don't," said Dr. Salikoff, "just as we don't know why you continually object to allowing the people of this county to know the truth."

Frederick Reinholt bolted straight up, and thundered that he lived in Marshfield County, worked in Marshfield County, and would not tolerate some outsider challenging his integrity. Harry Cameron agreed, cautioned Dr. Salikoff to stick with the facts, and asked him if the pipes could have been fixed later.

"It's not logical to leave pipes with structural damage and then come back at some later time to repair them," said Dr. Salikoff, who pointed out,"There would be additional tubes in place. The cost at that point would be unreasonable and possibly prohibitive."

"You're absolutely sure of this?" asked Ted Schumacher.

There was a moment's silence, followed by a one-word reply. "Yes."

A dozen questions shot out from the reporters and citizens, followed by an equal number of raps of the gavel, none of which had much effect. So, Harry Cameron stood up, excused himself for a moment, walked to the back of the room, unplugged a cord leading to the portable TV lights, announced that the lights and the noise were giving him a headache and the reporters could either have noise or lights. After the briefest of moments to think about it, the print reporters, their only technological worry being pens that ran out of ink, continued their questions, while the TV crew whined for quiet. Returning to the commissioners table, Harry Cameron again raised the basic issue, arguing that even if all the evidence were true, the county had absolutely no authority to shut down a nuclear reactor two states away, especially one which held a dumpster's worth of federal permits issued after years of review and a handful of public meetings.

"I'm not asking you to close that nuclear plant," said Apryl in sweet innocence. Did you ever come to a dead stop from warp speed? Kinda twists your head into knots, changes body chemistry, reverses time. If their bodies would have done what their minds were doing, the observers of this tragi-comedy would have been writhing on the floor in convulsions. It was time for Apryl to jerk them into reality. "There are others who are working to do that at this very moment," said Apryl.

"If you don't wish us to close the nuclear plant, which we certainly have no authority to do, what is it that you wish?" asked a very exasperated Ted Schumacher, voicing everyone's sentiments.

"I direct you to a series of state ordinances that may help in this situation," said Apryl. While one of her friends gave the five men at the table and the audience copies of the ordinances, Apryl began reading. "Section 691.1 of Chapter 5, Volume 35," said Apryl, "defines pollution as the 'contamination of any waters of the Commonwealth such as will create or is likely to create . . .' Please note that phrase, 'or is likely to create'— 'a nuisance or to render such waters harmful, detrimental or injurious to public health, safety or welfare, or to domestic, municipal, commercial, industrial, agricultural, recreational, or other legitimate beneficial uses, or to livestock, wild animals, birds, fish or other aquatic life, including but not limited to such contamination by alteration of the physical, chemical or biological properties of such waters, or change in temperature, taste, color or odor thereof, or the discharge of any liquid, gaseous, radioactive, solid or other substances into such waters . . .'"

"Are you suggesting that the problems at Bellevane could pollute the Susquehanna and other waters of this county?" asked Ted Schumacher, trying to be helpful.

"Not at all," said Apryl, explaining that because all waters eventually merge, she and a small team of geographers tried to find ways to connect the Connecticut to the Susquehanna, but logically could show only indirect hazard should radioactive pollution be accidentally released into the Connecticut. She also explained that because the Bellevane plant was north and east of Marshfield County, and because of prevailing wind direction, any radioactive clouds would have to travel almost an entire world before they reached Marshfield County. "But, we are all tied together, no matter how distant, by our mother planet," she said. "Eventually nuclear pollution into the waters and into the air will reach this county."

"So you *do* want us to tell another county in another state how to handle its own affairs," said Frederick Reinholdt triumphantly emerging from his self-imposed silence.

"I mean what I say," said Apryl, again rebutting him. "I said it'd be nice if you could do that, but there are others who will."

She turned to the reporter from Channel 24, who was patting down her hair, and suggested that now would be an appropriate time to turn the lights back on. With a few more years of experience, the TV reporter, destined to be a local news anchor, might be allowed in the same county as Walter Cronkite. "What I am asking," said Apryl, "is that the people of this county use all legal means to stop the construction of the nuclear waste disposal plant, and force this Board to accept the people's voice."

"Revolutionaries!" stammered Frederick Reinholdt, his face red, his fury unleashed. "Who gave you the authority? Just who made you God of the county?!"

"The people gave me the authority," said Apryl still as sweet as ever. "In accordance with County Ordinance of 1851, as a free White property owner of this county, I petition this Board to place on the May ballot a proposition asking the people of Marshfield County if they want a nuclear waste disposal plant in our backyard. We must be the ones to decide our own fate, not six-figure businessmen or bureaucrats in Harrisburg and Washington." This time, applause came even from the county residents who had been willing to give up their doubts about nuclear waste in their back yards in order to get economic security. The reporters again attacked their note pads, while the Channel 24 reporter quickly checked her lipstick.

"I'm not sure we can do that," said Harry Cameron, turning to Bolton Drake who said he needed time to research the ordinance, so Harry Cameron called for a recess to allow the commissioners and the attorney to meet in conference.

From the younger of the reporters came the media law question. "Isn't that a violation of the Sunshine Law?"

"Could be," said the Board's chairman. "Why don't we all take a recess. We'll look up some law. You look up some law. We'll be back in a few minutes." And with that, he pounded his gavel. When he next pounded his gavel, it was to announce a decision.

"Mr. Drake informs me," declared Harry Cameron, "that by the 1851 ordinance, property owners may orally petition the Board to consider placing a proposition on the next ballot, if the general welfare of the people is at stake. The Board may agree with or reject such a request. However, as best as we can determine, Miss Greene is not now a property owner, her land having been legally purchased by the Commonwealth. At this time, we believe that it is inadvisable to place such a proposal on the

ballot." Harry Cameron turned to Apryl Greene, and with compassion, an understanding that no one else in the room knew,
simply said, "If I could have changed anything to help you, I
would have." He closed his eyes for the briefest of moments.
"Now, the final item on today's agenda—"

"Mr. Chairman!" Apryl was again standing.

"I just knew this wasn't over," sighed Harry Cameron, intel-
lectually tired but delightfully curious about what the next
battle tactic would be. Apryl directed the commissioners to
another set of state statutes. "This is Section 691.601, paragraph 'a'," read Apryl. "It clearly points out that 'Any activity or
condition declared by this act to be a nuisance . . . shall be abat-
able in the manner provided by law or equity or the abatement
of public nuisances.'"

"What does she mean?" asked Harry Cameron.

"It means," said Bolton Drake, "this county might have to
consider this problem a nuisance that needs to be addressed by
this board."

"*She's* is a nuisance!" came a voice from the audience.

Even Apryl agreed, but continued anyway. "I direct the
Board's attention to Section 691.501, as amended," said Apryl.
"'In addition to the powers and authority hereinbefore granted,
power and authority is hereby conferred upon the department,
after due notice and public hearing, to make, adopt, promul-
gate, and enforce reasonable orders and regulations for the protection of any source of water for present or future supply to the
public, and prohibiting pollution of any such source of water
rendering the same inimical or injurious to the public health or
objectionable for public water supply purposes.'"

"That's well and good," said Frederick Reinholdt, thinking
he was about to finally end all this radical babble with one per-
ceptive observation, "but those are state statutes, and we are a
county. You should petition the state Department of Health if
you think that the nuclear waste disposal plant is unsafe." He
looked directly at Apryl, and enunciated almost every word, just
so she understood, "But you better be prepared to tell the people of this county why there will continue to be unemployment,
why the economy won't be making a recovery, and what happens when we can't get oil from the Mideast. And all because
you are worried that decades from now there *may* be a problem." Frederick Reinholdt lightened up a smidgen, and to no

one in particular said, "Besides, that's not our concern. The nuclear waste plant has all the required permits." He took a breath and concluded, "Please just sit down and let us continue with the business of the county."

"The business of the county," Apryl said firmly, "is to improve and protect the lives of its residents." She disregarded advice to sit down, and corrected a misconception. The Home Rule Charter, Apryl explained, emphasizing almost each word, "specifically gives this county all the powers and rights of the Commonwealth to deal with matters within this county. It also specifies that unless an exception is made, by petition and vote of the Board of Commissioners, that all state statutes, rules, regulations, and interpretations of the Commonwealth's codes are considered to be county domain, to be enforced by the county unless it specifically asks for Commonwealth intervention. That would include a Department of Public Health."

"The county doesn't have a Department of Public Health," said Frederick Reinholdt brightly, again believing he was going to get points for out-thinking that overaged radical liberal hippie chick who stood before him so god-damned self-righteous, mocking him and the entire free capitalistic world. "So it's still a state matter. Besides, whatever Bellevane does two states away isn't our problem." A broken record on an abandoned turntable would have played that song fewer times than Frederick Reinholdt had played it.

This time, Bolton Drake interceded. Most attorneys in rural Pennsylvania are generalists, handling everything from wills and real estate transactions to the occasional criminal trial, begging and hoping that the part-time DAs would plea-bargain their cases so none of them would have to go into court for anything more serious than routine DUIs with no injuries, of which the county had more than its share. But, Bolton Drake had two virtues the county needed right now—he had no political alliances and he did have an inquisitive mind that loved challenges. The Home Rule Charter, said the part-time county attorney as carefully and in as measured tones as Apryl first outlined the law, "directly invests in the Board of Commissioners with all duties and responsibilities on a local level of all state agencies should there not be a similar agency at the county level. Therefore, because we don't have a Department of Public Health, it is the responsibility of this Board to act in that capacity. Secondly, what I think this lady is saying is that because the treatment plant is to be built by the same company that is building the Bellevane plant, and because the ownership of both Bellevane and this plant is the same, there should be serious concern about safety for the people of this county."

Apryl thanked Bolton Drake. "Almost every day," she said, "several companies truck radioactive materials through Marshfield County on their way to Barnwell. The local plant, of course, won't be ready for another two or three years, assuming this Board allows its construction." Apryl was determined and in control, explaining that Pioneer Power would soon bring Unit 1 to three percent of authorized strength, and would soon be shipping its waste to Barnwell until the Marshfield County waste plant could be completed. She then recited a litany of facts—the pipes at Bellevane were weaker than they should be, there was sloppy construction practices, there is potential for pollution of both air and waterways, and that a nuclear waste plant that could handle just about every kind of nuclear waste possible from throughout the country was about to be built in Marshfield County. She next directed the commissioners to section 691.402(a), which stated that "Whenever the Department finds that any activity, not otherwise requiring a permit under this act, including, but not limited to the impounding, handling, storage, transportation, processing, or disposing of materials or substances, creates a danger of pollution of the waters of the Commonwealth—" She stopped for emphasis. "Let me read that again," she stated, "'a *danger* of pollution'. . . not that *is* causing pollution, or that it *has* caused pollution, but that it *'creates a danger* of pollution'. . . or 'that regulation of the activity is necessary to avoid such pollution, the department . . .' That's you, gentlemen . . . 'the department may, by rule or regulation, require that such activity be conducted only pursuit to a permit issued by the department . . .'" Tightening the noose, Apryl read from paragraph 'b' of Section 691.601 that directed, "In cases where the circumstances require it or the public health is endangered, a mandatory preliminary injunction or special injunction must be issued." She took a dramatic pause. "Nuclear waste will travel on I-80 through this county. Today, it will just pass through from the western part of the state en route to Barnwell. But, it will eventually stop here. The end point from New England and the West Coast, from the South, Southwest, and the Plains states. From every state in the nation." She had said it earlier. She re-emphasized it now. "And, it *will* be deposited in a facility primarily owned by the utility that has covered up structural defects in a nearly-completed plant in Massachusetts. There is no guarantee *this* plant about to be built won't have the same problems during construction. There is no guarantee it won't have similar problems in the storage of nuclear waste not just from Pioneer Power but from thousands of other sites, from routine medical waste to spent control rods." Apryl took a measured breath, and then calmly, with not a trace of tension in her voice, told the commissioners their option. "This Board that represents the people has every right to stop the movement of nuclear waste through the county. It has every right to stop construction of a waste disposal plant that could threaten the health and safety of its residents." The ordinances, said Apryl, steaming ahead, "dictate that you have the right and responsibility to protect the public health and welfare. You have the authority to block the transportation on any road, private or otherwise within this county, of radioactive waste from Bellevane and every other nuclear facility to the nuclear waste disposal plant."

"Are you saying that we have authority to issue injunctions and to require permits, even on state highways?" asked Harry Cameron.

"That's what it seems," replied Bolton Drake.

"We can't afford for the work at the waste treatment plant to stop," said Ted Schumacher, "but, we can't afford to imperil the health of our residents either." Ted Schumacher and everyone in the room, pro-nuke and anti-nuke, understood the need for jobs in a culture that was infested by unemployment and poverty. But the residents also knew, even if they never openly acknowledged it, that the history of the county was one where industries came, boosted the economy for a few years, stripped the resources, and then left, leaving the land and its people worse than before. Ted Schumacher, more than most, loved the county, understood its history—and was now struggling to do what was right, not for now but for future generations. "Until we know there won't be a hazard to the people of this county," he concluded, "we should exercise all our legal powers to prevent transportation and construction." He paused a moment. "Failure to do so might open us up to litigation."

"This is going to cost us a lot of money," said Frederick Reinholdt.

"It will cost even more if we're accused of negligence," Bolton Drake responded, but cautioned the commissioners that such action would delay construction and cause myriad legal problems. He again explained that hordes of corporate and government lawyers would descend upon the county with sheaves of paper that would gag the courts.

"Our residents have rights!" Frederick Reinholdt declared. "They have a right to be heard! They have a right to present their side. All we've heard is one side. We must be fair." It may have been one of the few times that the commissioner on the extreme right actually believed in fairness.

"This isn't a court of law," said Harry Cameron. "We have enough evidence to make initial decisions about the health and welfare for our constituents."

"We *don't* have enough information," Frederick Reinholdt declared. "All we have is a series of statements, none of which has been verified. All of which are suspect until we evaluate them." He was right. Apryl, as naive as I often wished she had been, was experienced at manipulating public opinion. This presentation was nothing less than a well-designed plan to manipulate public opinion and put it against the commissioners who, Apryl believed, would do the right thing. Frederick Reinholdt, in his mind and his heart, knew he was doing what he thought right. He had no choice but to push his views.

"Even if you could stop the trucks," he said, "you won't stop the trains. They'll bring far more radioactive waste than all the truck fleets combined." By his very statement, he defeated his own views, but he didn't realize the impact of what he had just said.

Apryl was quiet. Deliberate. Controlled. "We'll stop them" was all she said.

"Executive session!" bleated Frederick Reinholdt. This time, Harry Cameron announced that the Board wished to discuss a personnel matter, effectively blocking reporters' objections that the county again violated the state's sunshine laws. It was doubtful they were discussing personnel matters; maybe they just needed lunch. Nevertheless, a half hour later, four hours after the meeting began, more than three hours after it should have concluded, by a 2–1 vote the Board of Commissioners, trapped by an intricate web woven by Apryl Greene, announced that the county would not allow any individual or company to use any roads, highways, or rails that bisected the county to transport radioactive materials, except to directly meet the needs of the health professions, for teaching and research, and some limited uses in Industry. Unlike larger bureaucracies which would have established sub-committees and unleashed a pack of lawyers and technicians to draft several dozen pages of a proposed set of rules that would be revised several times by different layers of management, and modified by a horde of paid lobbyists, the commissioners merely put their concern into two sentences. If the lawyers wanted to nit-pick, that was their right, but the ban would remain until there was assurance that Bellevane had complied with all legal and—Harry Cameron emphasized—ethical concerns regarding construction and safety for nuclear plants.

"Miss Greene," said Harry Cameron, "you have caused us a lot of problems, have shaken some of our values and beliefs, and may have cost this county much-needed jobs and a stronger tax base, but you have shown us that there is something more important than our selfish interests." He now spoke softly, almost regrettably. "But, you still don't own your land. And, maybe that's as it should be. We all have given up something."

Apryl thanked Harry Cameron, again apologized for causing such inconvenience, and now meticulously laid out the final argument in her deconstruction of a nuclear waste plant. "We are only stewards of the land," said Apryl, who was about to reclaim her stewardship. By an ordinance of 1935, resulting from a Commonwealth court case two years before, she told the Commissioners, the county has the authority to set aside a writ of eminent domain issued by any governmental agency if in its opinion seizure of the land would result in that land being used for purposes which would endanger the general health and welfare of the people.

"Bolton?" asked Harry Cameron. A few minutes later, Bolton Drake emerged from a set of Pennsylvania law books and gave a more formal explanation of what Apryl had said. By another 2–1 vote, the Board of Commissioners ordered the state's writ revoked, and the land restored to its former owner. A roar of approval from the audience, including many of those who had come solely to support the new industry, made it useless for

Harry Cameron to try to restore order. And so all he did was just sit back and grin.

Not grinning was the nuclear industry. As expected, a gaggle of Pioneer Power lawyers, three-piece suits on their bodies, leather attaché cases molded to their hands, descended upon a half dozen state and federal agencies, two municipal courts, a Common Pleas Court, a Commonwealth court, and a federal district court. The paperwork used for injunctions, temporary restraining orders, interrogatories, show-causes, cross complaints, answers, exceptions, and decisions, combined with a heavy armor fusillade from Pioneer Power's slick public relations division, would have denuded a small forest. The three county commissioners, none of whom had been in anything more controversial than if the county should buy the Kesler Building for additional offices, were now escorted through their lives by lawyers and reporters.

For its part, the Press, seldom an institution at the cutting edge of social change, sent wave after wave of reporters into the battle to capture charges and counter charges, man-on-the-street opinions and "expert" opinions, all to be smeared across the front pages and on the 6 o'clock news. First they quoted one side, and then they quoted the other side. And when the media finished being clerks whose primary mission was to take everyone's statements and put them into print or on the air, only then were they able to fulfill some inner need to call themselves totally, completely, one hundred percent genuinely objective. But they had also missed not only the truth behind the facts but much of the story as well. A few newspapers—and the "Our Views" page of the February issue of *Century* magazine—called for the full and complete investigation at Bellevane. But the *Newburg Press–Chronicle*, the county seat daily, in its editorial pages called Apryl Greene a "misinformed aging radical who thinks she could halt progress with spurious charges and elementary school tactics." It demanded the resignations of Bolton Drake, Harry Cameron, and Ted Schumacher, but spared Frederick Reinholdt, whom it dubbed "the only voice of reason in the county government."

"Communist-inspired radicals bent on causing chaos to our democratic system" is what the mayor of Hollysburg wrote in a letter to the editor.

"Carpetbaggers!" wrote another county resident.

"The ACLU is behind all this," wrote a third, with absolutely no evidence.

Dozens of residents wrote about how clean and safe nuclear energy was, and how many jobs would come to the county. Their arguments, like Frederick Reinholdt's, was as sensible as the Reagan Administration's claims that ketchup was a vegetable so it didn't have to increase the budget for the school lunch program.

But, dozens of residents also pointed out that although they didn't agree with what Apryl did, they also distrusted Big Business and Big Government, and recognized that what she and the commissioners had to do was done for the people not just for a few years but for a few generations.

Spread among the resident staccato was wave after wave of heat generated by politicians in almost every state and federal agency, most of them threatening Harry Cameron's political future. But Harry Cameron, a 60-year-old conservative farmer and part-time chairman of the Board of Commissioners, knew no one could intimidate him or destroy his political future since he never wanted a political future. More important, he would never allow anyone to bribe him, not those who said they could grease his political future or help him with his farm operation, nor those who threatened to block his credit and supply lines if he didn't change his vote. Like the nation's forefathers, all he wanted was to be a citizen and, when needed, serve the people. And so he stood firm, arguing that the safety of the people came before their economic welfare, a position not popular in a county that had been in double-digit unemployment figures for almost two decades. Harry Cameron took all the heat the nuclear industry could generate, and he kept a promise to Apryl Greene to use his power as chair to keep anything off the agenda that could lead to further discussion and a possible reversal of the commissioners' earlier votes.

For his part, State Rep. Clarkson Leonard felt the waters, decided there wasn't an overwhelming consensus on either side, and went on vacation to Myrtle Beach. When he returned a week later, trees were still giving their lives to the lawyers and PR people who were grinding out interminable mountains of paper. Upon their efforts rode the fate of what was now exposed as one of the largest nuclear waste treatment plants in the world, a $4 billion project that would handle the spent nuclear rods of numerous plants and all major military waste, to be housed in rural northeastern Pennsylvania. Everyone knew that the longer it took the less chance of success there would be since the access roads had to be built before winter's fury or be delayed until the spring thaw. A month after Apryl Greene fired her verbal canons, and with almost no possibility for a road ever being built onto her property, Pioneer Power raised a soiled white flag, and announced a conditional surrender.

In exchange for the county agreeing to enact special ordinances to temporarily protect the waste disposal plant and to reroute roads around Apryl's land, Pioneer Power would halt all "nonessential" work in Massachusetts until an independent inspection of all tubing and an audit of construction records— the NRC was already swarming all over the plant—indicated that Unit 1 did indeed meet all safety standards. Pioneer Power further agreed to pay the county for all costs incurred during the battle, put aside $1 million in an interest-bearing trust fund to cover any potential claims of radiologic illness, and to donate $45,000 to the county's recreational program—a "bribe" Apryl called it, a "gift" the utility said. That "donation," combined with a $100,000 fine imposed by the NRC, was about 0.00362 percent of the plant's total construction budget.

However, as Pioneer Power's PR push emphasized, the forced compromises delayed putting Bellevane online at least three months, causing layoffs not only in Massachusetts but also in Marshfield County, which its executives kept calling a "severely-depressed economic market." The loss of revenue because of governmental actions, the corporation explained, also compelled it to file for yet another rate hike. When the audit was finished, claimed Pioneer Power, the only problem uncovered would be why residents had to wait several more months to benefit from all the "inexpensive electricity" the plant would produce. It was a lie when the plant was first proposed; it was still a lie.

Soon, the lawyers retreated to their plush-carpeted offices, leaving only the PR people to mop up, trying to convince everyone that it was the government in its folly not the purer-than-driven-snow utility that surrendered, and which cost the people jobs. The school would eventually be built; the waste treatment plant wouldn't.

26/

Land of the Preferred Address

by David Ascher

It's called Meadowbrook, but the meadow is being bulldozed to make way for 42 houses the developers are promoting as "a preferred address," and the closest brook is about a mile away. In less than three months, about 35 acres of farm and forest land will have been leveled so that families able to purchase the $40,000 half-acre lots can spend another $150,000–$300,000 to hire private companies to build their dream houses which will surround another $50,000 or so of furnishings.

Where once scarlet, red, white, and black oaks stood, there will be asphalt roads ending in cul-de-sacs. Where once there were sugar and red maples, there will be concrete foundations supporting overpriced shells of brick and wood. Where once there were a few dozen black bear, hundreds of deer, thousands of birds, mice, chipmunks, squirrels, and groundhogs, and millions of insects and flowers, there will now be the sounds of only a few dozen children who will learn about botany and zoology, about soil and the hole in the ozone layer, in freshly-scrubbed whitewashed plaster classrooms in million dollar brick buildings.

More than three centuries ago, the virgin forests were first cut back so that families from England could begin farms. From one generation to another, the farmland produced corn, beans, and just about any kind of vegetable that would grow in the fertile land of northeastern Pennsylvania. But the past few years haven't been good to the farmers. Throughout the nation, farmers have had to abandon their crops, and marginal farmland has been growing back into forests or being sold to corporate agribusinesses or subdividers who strip the land in order to plant malls and developments.

On the land of the "preferred address," without the trees, brush, and wild flowers to filter impurities of air and water before they enter the water table, will be more pollution. On that same land, because of the lack of plant life, there will be a greater risk of soil erosion, sedimentation, and flooding, even though local requirements require developers to have an anti-soil erosion plan. Keeping many of the trees while building houses to conform to the land so that all life could live in harmony with each other might have been a good idea if the people with bad judgment didn't think that to build houses you had to first strip the land of its life. Perhaps the developers believed that brick or stone houses would filter rain and pollution, chain link fences would stop erosion, and road signs would provide shade. And, perhaps they really didn't care that asphalt would be the grave marker for the nests and dens of wildlife.

Thirty-five acres that are being converted from farm and forest land to housing may not be much. But, since the end of World War II, an estimated 70 to 100 million acres of farmland have been converted to commercial or residential use or to certain public works programs; in the past two decades alone, while America celebrates yet another Earth Day, more than 20 million acres of forest land have been lost. In the nation, about 2.5 million acres of fertile farmland a year are lost to sprawling developments, and there are 1.2 million fewer farmers than a decade ago.

Perhaps on the 35 acres of the land now called Meadowbrook, some families will hire gardeners to plant lawns and to carefully sculpt bushes; perhaps they will hire masons to build walkways, patios, and fountains to add to what they believe is a "natural" atmosphere; perhaps they will direct their hired help to buy saplings from a local nursery to plant in the backyards. And, perhaps, in a century those saplings will grow to the size of the oaks and maples that once were destroyed so that houses could be built in a "preferred address."

27/

The Amazing Stone Mill

Morrison Grove rests in the elbow of Laurel Creek as it turns southeast slightly north of where it intersects with the Susquehanna River. It wasn't known as Morrison Grove until 1890 when Izzy Morrison cleared away some of the underbrush and a few trees and built a stone mill to grind flour. Since he didn't need all the land he bought, he added picnic tables and a shelter, opening the land to anyone who wanted to enjoy it. From the creek, he carved out a lake nice enough that lovers, young or elderly, could rent rowboats and find their own corner of solitude. Three years later, he built a dance hall, and brought in some of the better fiddlers and bands. To this, he eventually added a carousel with hand-carved wooden animals, other rides and attractions, and two food stands.

By 1905, his 40-acre grove was one of the largest amusement parks in the entire country, hosting more than 10,000 guests a week, most of whom rode the steam train from their villages and from the larger cities of Harrisburg, Scranton, and Wilkes-Barre. Seven times a day during the week, and nine times on weekends, trains stopped and took on water and coal, for Morrison Grove was in the heart of the nation's anthracite coal region.

For 49 years, as long as there was coal to be mined and converted into energy, as long as there were forests to be cut into timber, as long as there were trains to move people, and employment for just about anyone who wanted a job, Morrison Grove was a prosperous host. And then the coal barons decided it was no longer economical to mine the coal, closed the mines, and left the southern half of the county scarred by pockmarks upon the ground, slagheaps upon its horizon; a barren land of dirt and waste.

A few years after the mines closed, the lumbering companies in the north decided there were no longer enough trees to cut down, so they too left, leaving in their wakes unemployment and villages that would soon wither.

Morrison Grove lowered all of its prices and barely survived the Depression, but by the end of the war, with trolleys and the railroad no longer a part of the county, and gas rationed because of the war effort, the third generation Morrison family was unable to keep the park viable during its shortened season that began with Memorial Day and ended after Labor Day. For less than $1,000 in delinquent taxes, the county took possession of the land.

The trees, brush, and animals have now reclaimed their rightful places in nature. The carousel is now in an amusement park somewhere in southern New Jersey. For a few years, the 17 rides were attractions at other parks, and then were probably salvaged for parts. No one knows what happened to the band shell, the roller skating rink, and the dance hall. Where once there were food stands, the county maintained salt licks for the deer. But even the county, which never had the financial resources to develop the Grove, couldn't figure out what to do with the land and the abandoned stone mill; decades after it claimed the land, the County sold it to the Susquehanna Valley Workshop which had planned to develop the area as a retreat for its clients and employees, but never did. Eventually, the Workshop sold the land and stone mill to Charles Greene, its executive director, who deeded it to his daughter, a photographer–musician named Rachel Greene who planned to build a school for peace.

By Christmas in northeastern Pennsylvania, mid-day temperatures are often in the 20s and 30s, and snow is usually on the ground. But this was a surprisingly mild winter. No snow had fallen, and the temperatures, while not torrid, were in the 40s and low 50s, with little wind, something that let the construction season roll on to the end of the year.

The Madison Township board of supervisors, even after the county commissioners had given their approval, could have blocked Apryl's building permits. By a 3–2 vote at a special emergency meeting, it didn't. The Commonwealth could have denied access to the land while it was fighting to keep possession; it didn't. Pennsylvania Electric Energy could have filed objections in court and harassed Apryl by refusing to string electrical lines to the stone building; it didn't. Even most of the legislators, whose campaigns were energized by contributions from power corporations, were reluctant to do much more than languid sabre-rattling during the Christmas season. It was as if the same albatross that had been lifted from Apryl had also been lifted from the agencies that were enmeshed in the building of the waste disposal plant. It was finally time to build a school.

Apryl was taking a chance building the school. If the courts ruled that Pioneer Power, or any of a half-dozen other contenders, had rightful possession of the land, then all of her work would have been little more than a case of gullible thrusting at windmills. And, there was every indication that appeals would probably reach to the Supreme Court. But, if the work wasn't completed by March, the land would default to Pioneer Power anyhow, something Apryl's father could never have foreseen. On a Thursday night, beneath a new moon, Apryl Greene, wrapped in heavy blankets, sat against a wall of an old stone mill, and just looked at the sky, black and twinkling.

Shortly after sunrise, Hersh Walters showed up in boots, dirty jeans, and a red-and-black flannel shirt. "How you going to get your trucks in here?" he calmly asked, drawing out the question, a little like a bad impression of Jimmy Stewart.

"Thought we'd just drive them from SR2460 onto SR518, then onto the dirt roads."

"Could do that," he said, matter-of-factly, drawing a puff from his pipe. "Probably not the best idea, but you could do that."

"Got a better idea?"

"Yeah." No emotion. Just "yeah." He unholstered his radio-transceiver from his belt, extended its 18 inch antenna, calmly said, "Let's move," and then waited. We asked what he was doing, but he said we'd see it soon enough. I had wondered if he was our last obstacle. We didn't wait long. Apryl's dog, which had been sniffing the new arrivals, playing with all of them, was now on alert, her ears focused, her eyes telling us that she knew something unusual was about to happen. You've got a state road on your property," said Hersh Walters, finishing a cup of coffee. "Runs right past that old stone mill. My records say it's been more than five years since we did anything to it. We're supposed to work it twice a year, oil it once. Just can't seem to find anything that says it's been abandoned. I think it's time to bring it within specs."

Within minutes came a terrible rumbling nearly enclosed by several clouds of dust. A small army of earth moving machines— a roller and tractor-rake followed single-file behind a grader— had reached the stone mill. Apryl was leaping and bouncing, laughing and crying. I wasn't much better off. Kashonna, barking and wagging her tail, took her cues from us and was bounding around, celebrating with us.

"Pulled 'em off a job a mile upstream," said Hersh Walters, with just the slightest mischievousness in his eyes. "Didn't see any reason why they were needed on that one since it doesn't look like the gentlemen at Pioneer Power are going to get their act together for an awfully long time." Hersh Walters, a district engineer with 32 years with PennDOT, the one person in charge of a nine county district, was probably going to get a reprimand for this; he didn't care. He was tired of Harrisburg's political machinations that left large chunks of the state's roads permanently potholed. Besides, he figured he was a darn good civil engineer; he'd take his state retirement and find something else. Hersh Walters was only the first to help; there would be others, most of them carrying union cards.

In high school, in the early '60s when Uncle Ho was beginning to replace Ike as America's father figure for thousands of alienated youth, Apryl had tried to get her senior class to produce a revival of *Pins and Needles*, a 1930s Broadway musical about the garment industry. She figured there might be a few problems with the school administration, but didn't expect the student body executive board, none of whom had ever read the play but were planning to grow up and become America's morality patrol, to have unanimously ruled it not fit for a senior production, declaring that if Apryl had studied her civics lessons better she wouldn't even have suggested staging such a piece of socialist propaganda. These were the same kind of people who would later decide that "Puff the Magic Dragon" and "Rocky Mountain High" were drug songs that should be banned

from radio, that "Eve of Destruction" not only glamorized suicide but also was an anti-war song, and that anything by Pete
Seeger or Bob Dylan was subversive. But, for now, the students
at Apryl's school were just concerned about *Pins and Needles;* it
was Apryl's first taste with fascism. She would overthrow it
with her deeds, and her target would be injustice wherever it
appeared.

For more than two decades, Apryl had worked with fledging
unions, everyone from farm workers to atomic workers, often
just for expenses. When they marched for better working conditions, she was there. When they needed housing and meals, she
provided shelter and food; when they needed publicity for their
plight, she provided the photographs and words that recorded
their struggle. And when a Local was finally established, or a
strike won, she'd move on, helping other workers to gain recognition. Now it was the workers' turn to repay her.

From Allentown and Philadelphia, Newark and New York,
they came, their pick-ups and 4-wheelers throwing up clouds of
dust as they drove from concrete four-lane highways onto oil-
covered two-lane roads, and then onto abandoned dirt roads
and into a School for Peace. Some may have disagreed with
Apryl's political views, but they were there, some to work a few
hours and then leave, some to stay a week or more. As long as
there was hot coffee and cold beer, they worked without pay and
little concern about the cold. Nine union roofers brought with
them leftover plywood and tiles from other jobs; it made little
difference if the new roof was a quilt of shingles, as long as it
held back the rain and snow. Five journeymen electricians didn't
have to bring supplies since Leon Salikoff brought two portable
generators and a van's worth of electrical supplies. Several union
painters brought power sanders, sprayers, brushes, and paints
of every kind. About two dozen union carpenters, with Sam and
Ruth Weissmann as honorary members, came to the school to
lay new flooring, build cabinets, and repair interior walls. Union
masons came to help after Ronnie Soifer, the stone mason Apryl
had met in Victory Park more than six months earlier, had put
out the call. Ronnie would stay almost the entire time, repairing
the exterior walls, finishing with a 20-foot by 30-foot stone slab
patio. All of the 100,000 members of the United Farm Workers,
who Apryl more or less adopted and was, in turn, adopted by
them during their struggle for recognition, would have helped if

they were anywhere in the area. As it was, about two dozen migrant workers put on heavy coats and came by for a long weekend to help cut underbrush and do whatever else was necessary. If he wasn't in Haiti to monitor the nation's first democratic election, Jimmy Carter, who had worked with Apryl and thousands of others on Habitat for Humanity projects, might have quietly stopped by to do some carpentry work.

The utility infielder for the project, able to do virtually any job imaginable, and maybe even brain surgery on a slow morning, was Tony Sedaris, a 10-year ACLU chapter president and the best tool and die maker in all of the Mid-Atlantic states and maybe New England as well, at least if you believed him. And who wouldn't? A gruff, imposing 6-foot-6 300 pound hulk of a man who looked as if he should have been a pro football player or a building belied the soul of a pacifist, Tony was an evangelist for social justice. Not many were willing to challenge his fiery condemnation of racism and sexism. And when Tony draped his tree-limb white arms around a frightened or infuriated Black's shoulders, lily-white unions became integrated.

And then there were the amateurs from *Century*. We didn't even need Sam's bribe to help Apryl. Sam has a standing offer that most of the staff takes up every year; it's a small part of his charge to *tikkun olam*, a belief that Jews must help heal the world. He adds one extra day of vacation time, to a maximum of two extra weeks, for every day we work helping some charitable cause. Many non-profit organizations in the Boston area were the beneficiaries of our staff's generosity and Sam's willingness to overlook bottom-line economics. Sam had grown up believing that the donation of money is a distant second to the donation of one's time and energies. He believes anyone can write a check and ship it off to some charity, salving their own consciences while getting tax write-offs at the same time. Although Sam and Ruth are generous with their bank accounts, they also give their time, and encourage others to also donate time. I was here because I cared about Apryl, and there was a story. Others came because they just cared to help someone accomplish something. Some of us had just learned the difference between a screwdriver and a screw, some of us were excellent trades people—and others put our skills together as best we could.

Mixed in with everyone else were a couple of dozen of Apryl's friends, many of whom I had met only in the month before our meeting at the Courthouse, some of whom I saw for the first time at the Courthouse.

"Gravel! Get your red hot gravel here! Drop it onto paths! Drop it onto roads! But whatever you do, don't drop it on your gonads!" From the cab of a 24 ton dumpster—we didn't know how he got it, we didn't ask questions—the Amazing Abrahams had brought in a load of No. 2RC gravel. "Gather round children, and gather your tools," Amazing sang out, "'cuz this load's being dropped by nobody's fool!"

Some people look like they've been working hard their whole lives; you can see the sweat and hear their moans, although they burned little more than 10 calories energy. Others seem to be more goldbrick than gold, yet their production is greater than all of us put together. Bernie Abrahams was like that. We never truly saw him working, but we always saw results. When one of our printer's platemakers broke down, putting the magazine into jeopardy of being a day late to the distributors, Bernie made a few phone calls and got a new platemaker out in three hours, a feat almost no printer—or manufacturer—could figure out. When every other publisher was sweating price increases for paper, we got a deal better than a Vegas shuffle. When two of our best designers, within a week of each other, gave us a month's notice—one for motherhood, the other to join the Peace Corps—Bernie cut a deal for them to provide "just a teensy bit of work," even from Chad. Within days, he brought out of retirement a designer from *The National Geographic* who reluctantly agreed to do "just a few pages a month," and then became our principal designer. None of us could figure it out. Sam Weissmann had given up long ago; he no longer cared how Bernie got the magazine through production, only that it made the deadlines and didn't embarrass the company—at least too often.

Amazing and the dump truck returned an hour later. This time, however, he had learned a little about how to drop a load in the same county where it was destined. Even with dozens of us on the job, supported by dime-store wheelbarrows, rakes, and shovels—which Amazing had thoughtfully provided for us to spread around his generous endowment to the school—we still would need almost two weeks to level the land. For two long weekends, Amazing was on site, coordinating and manipulating, bringing in a cement truck and its booty of finishing cement one time, a few pipes the next. From Apryl, he had her $7,452 personal fund for building the school, but whether by donation or by appropriation, by the time construction was over, more than six times that amount was put into the school.

Amazing's first job, however, had occurred long before any of us got to the site. Apryl had arranged for three space heaters and a Port-a-Johnny to be delivered. By Thursday morning, through nothing she or I had done, there were three 75,000 BTU portable kerosene heaters and seven Port-a-Johnnys. Not just any Port-a-Johnnys, but the executive deluxe models, the ones that exceeded all outhouse specifications and weren't all that far from appearing they could have been closeted into some modular home. It wasn't any great secret how they got there— a hand-painted marker stuck into the ground pointed the way to The Amazing Shithouse.

The Port-a-Johnnys would do during the construction, but a School for Peace would need something more permanent. Sam was reluctant to contact Phil Haskin, a member of *Century*'s board of directors, and CEO of Haskin & Dworin Plumbing and Heating; Amazing wasn't. A little persuasion—we never asked— and Phil, his wife, both of their sons, and three journeymen union plumbers, who Phil paid as if they were working full eight hour days, showed up for two three-day weekends.

By the end of the first weekend, all the old plumbing and the now-rusted heating system had been torn out, replaced by two multi-station bathrooms and a heating system in the mill. By the time they left after the second long weekend, the three deep wells on the property had been inspected, pumps added, and pipes connected; there would be water for both heating and plumbing. If all went well, two 5,000 gallon septic tanks would be in place within a month.

"Tote that barge! Lift that bale!" It was The Amazing Abrahams, his arms full of timber, zigzagging his way across a field, hopefully to the stone mill. "Build that school! Break that back!" Behind him, picking up logs as they fell, were assistant editors Allison and Fite. "Logs for cabin syrup! Get your logs here! Free log to whomever wins the wet T-shirt contest! See me for qualifications!" It was barely 6:30 a.m. "Logs!" the Amazing Abrahams triumphantly announced, dropping what was left of his load onto the large barn door entrance to the stone mill. "Yeah. Logs," came the tired echo from Allison and Fite who dropped their loads not far from Amazing's feet. But by 7 a.m., Amazing, assisted by Allison and Fite, themselves assisted by Sam and Ruth, Apryl and me, and a few other volunteers, had finished pouring and flipping the first batch of iron-skillet flapjacks. By 8 a.m., we were back at work. About noon, we got another shot of love and vitamins.

"Got room for a farmer? Can't build a school without food." After attending mid-morning services, Harry Cameron drove a truckload of fruits and vegetables onto the site, said that his farm was overproducing and that he had to get rid of a lot of crops or else they'd spoil. Now, since almost nothing grows in northeastern Pennsylvania in December, I figured that Harry Cameron didn't grow the crops but had to have bought them either from the local supermarket or from some wholesaler. I had no intention of challenging his story; his reasons were his reasons.

Monday morning, only a few of us were left. Sam had returned to Boston with one of the vans, but he was planning to fly back later in the week. Tuesday morning, I Amtraked it back to Boston, returning two days later. My muscles were tired; my energy level, once sufficient to work around the clock, was gasping. After years as an executive, it felt good once again to be a worker. I just hoped this feeling wouldn't last too long.

By the second weekend, more *Century* staff had arrived— Kathy Steck, Megan Prescott, and Dawn Kavanaugh, who caused wolf whistles and then embarrassed silence from the workers; Karlen Aroian, who could wield a router better than any of us; Helen Grishka, who couldn't; Dahn St. Michaels who surprised us with his ability with a bandsaw; and Shane Kistler who seemed to be able to do anything anyone wanted, and worked harder than any two people I ever saw. Even "Doc" was there. Dr. Elliot T. Boone, who led the league in hacking coughs, was working as hard as anyone. Two months earlier, our in-house statistician and all-around semi-scientist had given me advice on data retrieval that had helped make Apryl's case at the Marshfield County commissioners' meeting. Now, 300 miles from his computers and charts, he wanted to see the results of his research. Also wanting to see what was happening 300 miles from his home was Frank Mitchell, who spent four days helping, sweating, and laughing with us. He would soon set up the School of Peace as a 501(c) corporate charity, and become Apryl's volunteer business consultant and accountant. When Sam tried to give Frank extra vacation time for his help, the only thing Frank quietly said was that no one should profit from charity.

Not able to help at the work site was Gretchen Peron, our circulation director, who had planned to come out the second weekend, and had even slipped Apryl a $100 bill to buy "something nice" for herself, but who stayed behind to help take care of her six-year-old son who had just gotten the mumps—and, maybe, her husband who never had mumps. And then there was Sylvia. She and Apryl talked by phone a few times, mostly exchanging information about nuclear reactors and the anti-nuke movement, but neither told me any specifics. All I knew was that some of the information Sylvia told Apryl made its way into the meeting of Marshfield County commissioners. I had hoped Sylvia would be in one of the two vans that brought the staff, but—well—as she stated, she had "other things" she had to do.

By noon, everyone was working—except for The Amazing Abrahams, of course, who had come back late Friday night, and deserted shortly after dawn, Saturday. When he returned, a couple of hours later, he was toting the one thing we needed the most—a 400 gallon water buffalo, hooked onto an Army deuce-and-a-half.

"Je-ZUZ, Bernie, we're going to fry for this one!"

"It's a fuckin' federal offense!"

"How the hell did ya grab that!"

"Allenwood! They're gonna send us to Allenwood!"

"Forget Allenwood. This is a Leavenworth crime."

"Relax," said Amazing, amazingly calm. "The lieutenant knows it's missing."

"The lieutenant? Some shavetail just said, 'Excuse me, Mr. Abrahams, since you seem like such a clean-cut fine gentleman, would you like to steal our water buffalo?'"

"First lieutenant," corrected Bernie. "Shavetail is a second lieutenant. This was a first lieutenant. Silver bar. Higher rank."

"Whatever."

"Important to know these things."

"So this *first* lieutenant said it was acceptable to allow a civilian to steal a military truck?"

"Something like that."

"How much like that?"

"Sort of like that. Even threw in this fine young PFC." From out of nowhere emerged a fine young PFC.

"Ho-lee SHIT! You kidnapped a fuckin' soldier."

"Didn't kidnap anyone. He came voluntarily."

"Double shit! You got yourself a deserter!"

"He ain't no deserter. Trust me!" Right there, we knew we were in trouble. "It'll be ours until the Army needs it again. We use what we can, fill all our containers, then return it." We needed a water supply since we had used most of the store-bought water, the deep wells weren't yet working, and the creek wasn't yet deep enough. After almost two weeks, all of us were tired from toting water a couple of hundred yards from the Susquehanna, boiling water from the Susquehanna, and pouring water from the Susquehanna into containers to be cooled. We wanted to cheer Bernie's assistance, but we didn't believe his story that the Army "donated" all this help, especially after the PFC said something like he didn't know what was going on, only that he was told to take Bernie Abrahams to a nearby parcel of land. And who told the PFC to take Amazing to the site of the stone mill? Why Bernie Abrahams did, of course. Had even told the PFC to look up on the pathetic little hill where the lieutenant was waving his approval. Working up sweat in a winter's dryness we didn't ask many questions, gave the 19-year-old freshly-scrubbed PFC a cold beer, hid the buffalo in the largest clump of trees we could find, and prepared stories we could try to slide past a federal magistrate. But for most of a long weekend, we had fresh water, and a large supply to take us into the third and, hopefully, last week.

And then it happened. As we knew it would.

"It's the whole freaking army!" Usually cool MaryBeth Martinez was hysterical. Her left ear was beet red. "We're gonna fry! They're gonna bomb the mill and take the survivors out in leg irons!"

From behind a slight ridge less than a football field away was an entire platoon of soldiers—and one fuckin' furious first lieutenant. Although we outnumbered the army, not even our Vietnam veterans had any desire to tangle with what lie ahead, and so we sent Bernie out while we retreated to shelter, hoping that weekend warriors don't shoot weekend idiots. Not even Apryl, who could calm Tasmanian Devils with her innocence, was going to attempt this trick. Amazing had no such qualms.

"No problem," said The Amazing Abrahams. "Easier than selling Vegomatics at a fair."

"Damn. Now we'll have to figure out how to drag his body back to Boston."

"Throw him into a hole here. No sense struggling with the body."

"At least we have enough to sit *shiva* with him."

But up on the ridge, just before sunset, Bernie was flapping his lips.

"Lieutenant! Hi! How are you!" This was one fool journalist. Bernie's my best friend and the rest of us had gotten used to him, admiring his cunning brilliance. We didn't want to see him become cannon fodder. But, then again—

We waited, cowards in the face of battle, pathetically praying they wouldn't slice, dice, and pulverize our Amazing gift.

From 30 yards, we heard thunder. This was one mad dude— and he had four squads of support. "He's dead," moaned Brandi Domenico. But instead of being dead, Bernie was very much alive. Fifteen minutes later, Bernie was escorted back to base camp by four infantrymen toting M-16s. He stopped at the mill, cheerfully thanked the soldiers for their help and waved them into the direction of the buffalo.

"Nice bunch of fellas," said Amazing. "Had a nice campout this weekend. A little thirsty, though." A few minutes later, four soldiers and a PFC had mounted that buffalo and were herding it back to the ridge.

"What the hell happened?" we asked, incredibly perplexed.

"In due time," Bernie said nonchalantly.

"NOW!" we demanded, knowing we were going to be in for a story of a lifetime. We weren't disappointed.

In admiration and curiosity, we listened to Bernie's tale of intrigue and manipulation, embellished as only The Amazing Abrahams could. Cheering him on were the veterans who had put up with military discipline and nonsense for their two or four year hitches. As best as we could figure out, for with production directors there are usually shreds of truth in their methods, Bernie had wandered into their camp about 7 a.m.,

Saturday, saw the water tanker and decided we needed it. To get it, however, since the Army doesn't usually loan camouflaged trucks to civilians, Bernie went up to the highest-ranking soldier he could find—in this case a silver-barred lieutenant who was either too stupid, too green, or too egotistical to wear the more appropriate non-reflective burnt bar on his camouflage uniform—announced he was lost and wanted to know which way to SR518. The lieutenant pulled a map from a khaki case, unfolded it, surveyed the terrain, and then waved Bernie into a southeasterly direction near Bungy Falls, which happened to be where the water buffalo was grazing. So, Bernie went about a hundred yards to the PFC, exchanged greetings and said that the lieutenant wanted the water buffalo—and the deuce-and-a-half to pull it—moved onto a parcel of land about a mile away, stated that it was to be a secret operation and that the PFC was to stay with the equipment until relieved. "Something like a search-and-find mission," said Bernie.

"You sure?" the quizzical PFC had asked.

"Look over there," said Bernie. And sure enough when they looked up, Bernie shrugged his arms as if he were confused about something, the helpful lieutenant waved in the direction of SR518, and the PFC assumed that Bernie had permission to "capture" the water supply and take it into hiding. When the rest of the platoon left, so did the buffalo, truck, and PFC—along with one amazing dude who was thinking about maybe going after Army Quonset huts next.

Everyone had questions, but the one we all had was how Bernie escaped shackles and a diet of bread and water. More important, we wondered why none of us were facing federal warrants as accomplices.

"Piece of cake." In another five minutes, Bernie explained his half-baked logic. He said he had told the lieutenant the truth. We didn't believe him. "Swear on my sainted mother's grave." Maybe his mother had bought a plot somewhere, but I knew she was definitely alive and living in a Detroit suburb; besides, the possibility of his Jewish mother becoming a saint was remote.

"The truth, Bernie."

"Told him that I had—well—sorta shaded the truth at first, but that we needed the water, that we'd been using river water for almost two weeks. Told him we had to drag all that water to base camp then boil it or drop our pellets into it so we could use it, and that we were real tired of all that lugging and boiling."

"And that fool bought it?"

"I said I understood and was sorry for violating a dozen laws by bringing his pretty green and brown truck all the way over here, and then hiding it in the trees. Apologized like heck. It caught him completely off-guard."

"So why aren't you making big rocks into smaller ones?" Shane Kistler asked. What Bernie did was what any good soldier does when backed into a corner when there's no hope—he takes the offensive, and makes the enemy believe that being pushed against a wall is just what the plan called for.

"I just told him that he could tell his captain the truth. That a sweet-talking unarmed civilian showed up one morning, stole about $50,000 worth of equipment from under his nose, and that four squads of military spent most of the next two days trying to find it when it was less than two miles away."

"I'll see you hang for this!" the lieutenant had screamed.

"That may be true," said Bernie, "but you're going to be busted to second lieutenant where you'll be the rest of your life, and maybe in any afterlife. By the way, did you ever see all the paperwork you're going to have to fill out on this? Why, I heard that some lieutenant in Delta Company is on his second box of typewriter ribbons from the time he lost a canteen." According to Bernie, what the lieutenant said next wasn't worth repeating. "Here's how you avoid becoming a 40-year-old lieutenant," said Bernie, recounting the battle. "I just told him that if anyone asks—and 32 soldiers were already waiting for the lieutenant's explanation—that he was to say that as a training exercise in cold weather he sent the driver and truck off into hiding to simulate what would happen if the enemy destroyed the water supply. His maniacal attempts to send the troops off in search of it was just—uh—yeah—that's it—a "training exercise" to live off the land. It made as much sense as the Pentagon sending an Army Reserve unit, all of them disguised by green jungle combat fatigues to conduct winter maneuvers in 50 degree weather, apparently to prepare for the impending war in the Arabian Desert half a world away. The lieutenant could teach his soldiers how to get water from the land and how to find the river, said a loquacious Amazing Abrahams.

"That's a damned lie!" the lieutenant roared.

"Got any other explanation how you lost a tanker?" Bernie deviously asked. The lieutenant didn't, so he just mumbled a few almost unheard obscenities, ordered his men to retrieve the equipment they had lost, and for which they would be busted to buck privates if they said anything about this special top-secret mission, and then called retreat.

"One question," calmly asked the Amazing Abrahams of the lieutenant. "With all that activity going on in our camp, why didn't anyone figure out to contact us earlier? That confuses me." Bernie? Confused? It didn't make sense. But neither did the lieutenant's answer.

"Orders said we were to make no contact with civilians."

"But you eventually did contact us."

"Sometimes, orders have to be disregarded," said the young lieutenant.

"That's when I knew," said Bernie, "that maybe there was hope if he ever got to the Persian Gulf that he might not become cannon fodder."

Late Sunday evening, around battery-powered space heaters in the mill, we ate barbequed steak—Apryl had provided enough money for veggie burgers with all the trimmings. With the help of two locals of the United Food and Commercial Workers, Amazing had turned a paltry veggie burger menu into steaks and side dishes fit for well-pampered CEOs. Vegetarians and carnivores, in a peaceful coexistence, reflected upon world events and why the Patriots were again in last place in the conference, and why the Eagles couldn't win playoff games. We moaned, bitched, and complained about our aging muscles, and slathered Ben-Gay on tired bodies before we dropped into sleeping bags on the mill floor. We were no longer rednecks and radicals, laborers and professionals, but a family, most of whom were planning to miss yet another Monday at our regular jobs.

Around a campfire, we told and retold stories of battles against decaying wood, rusted pipes, wires that led nowhere, and the Army. We sang songs from the Beatles, Beach Boys, and Chuck Berry. Folk. Rock. Ballads. Classic Country and Children's songs. And, we also sang the music and history of the labor and peace movements, stimulated by activist folksingers/ songwriters Joe Glazer and Anne Feeney, who had rolled into the fledging School for Peace a few hours earlier, bringing inspiration and a renewal of energy as they wandered throughout the camp, singing, motivating, and doing innumerable odd jobs. Joe, in his early 70s, almost as agile as any union carpenter, every day proves he has the stamina to match any activist. Anne, three decades younger, may be his successor. Name an organizing rally or a social movement, and Joe, Anne, or Apryl, with the spirit of Woody Guthrie, Cisco Houston, and Pete Seeger burning within them, was probably there, often at their own expense, sometimes to crowds that numbered in the thousands, mostly just to a few in a work camp or meeting hall.

Long after everyone was asleep, Apryl was still bounding around, fixing up this, fixing up that, getting ready for the next day's work.

By Christmas eve, most of the *Century* staff and union tradesmen who had stayed had also left, leaving a few of us— Ronnie Soifer to do some more work on the walls; Kathy Steck because she had suddenly felt a "oneness" with nature, and had convinced Sam to give her just another week to regain her "sense of life"; two of the journeymen carpenters whose families were states away and who said that work was slow anyhow, and they'd prefer doing it for something that mattered than for a contractor who didn't; Apryl, Ruth, and myself. Roads were cleared, a decaying stone mill was rehabilitated, and not one tree was cut down.

We had done more than we ever believed possible. SR2460 and two gravel paths had been completed; the roof was finished; the exterior walls were repaired—rebuilt, actually; two bathrooms had been nearly finished; most interior walls were ready for painting or wallpaper; the wooden floor was almost ready to accept the feet of dozens of students; and the electrical connections, had been installed. A ten-foot by four-foot wooden sign, supported by two logs stuck into the ground, declared the site to be the School for Peace. At its base, one of the workers had carefully placed a single walnut.

It took more than $4 billion, four years, and 5,000 workers to build a nuclear power generating plant in western Massachusetts; it took less than $50,000, three weeks, and about a hundred people to build a school.

28/

The Azalea Bush

by David Ascher

It was only an azalea bush. A four-foot tall, 15-foot around azalea bush. A dead brown azalea bush. No flowers and no leaves. Not even the microscopic appearance that there would ever again be a leaf. By the middle of April in northeastern Pennsylvania the other azalea bushes had begun to sprout leaves; many had even begun flowering. But not this one. It was an unsightly bunch of dried hard-brown spindly sticks jutting hodgepodge from the ground, every stick dead. Not just cryogenic dead from its winter hibernation, but cease-to-exist dead. As in never again.

In the back yard, the other bushes were coming to life, and this one was just taking up space. And so Carol Patton, a young housewife who had moved into the house in a rural northeastern Pennsylvania community the previous fall, decided it was time to get rid of the dead bush, clear the ground, plant something else. A hatchet would do the job just nicely, she thought. The kind that Boy Scouts use to chop firewood.

Whack. She wasn't as strong as she thought. *Whack.* The branch had fallen off. *Whack, Whack.* A few more chops, a small drizzle of sweat, and she had a half-dozen dried branches lying on the ground.

Maybe I'll just chop the trunk, she thought, figuring that by devoting all her energy into wiping out the base of her problem she would get it over faster, and then let her husband dig up the roots. She took a deep breath, reared back, prepared to put all her strength into a half-dozen well-placed chops, get rid of this relic, and move on to other parts of her garden. She didn't get another chance.

"Oh, Sweetheart, sweetheart, don't do that! Please, don't do that!" came the frantic cry of her 77-year-old neighbor who rushed out his house, across the back yard and to her side. "I know this is your house," he said, "and you can do to your yard anything you want, but please don't kill that bush."

The neighbors sure are strange here, she thought, but she listened to him. After all, he was a friendly chap, always put out water and bread crumbs for the birds, always had a kind word to say to everyone.

"Oh, please, please don't kill that bush," he begged. Yes, thought the new home owner, this was truly an odd neighbor, one who apparently liked dead bushes. Maybe his memory was more alive than this eyesore he was so fervently pleading for. Elderly people sometimes remember how things were, not how they are.

"Well, it's dead," she said, wiping her brow with the back of her hand.

"No it's not!" the neighbor said emphatically. "Yours is the most beautiful bush in the block." A dead plant is beautiful? she thought, but she listened. "This plant," he explained, pleading for its life, "always blooms later than any other around here." He didn't know why. It just did. "I know you can kill it if you want to because it's your yard, but please wait," he begged. "You'll see. Soon, it will come to life and it will be the most beautiful plant in the whole block."

The homeowner didn't buy that. Maybe once it had come to life; maybe once it had bloomed. Maybe it had never come to life, a still birth planted in hope by a former house owner. Whatever. But now it was dead. Dry wood dead. Stoke the fireplace with its branches dead. And, it was taking up space that another plant could use. But the man was persistent, a tear coming to his eye. So she put aside the hatchet, and agreed to let the dead plant take up space. For awhile at least. More to appease him than true belief.

As carpets of white, purple, and orange petals bloomed, fell off, and covered the freshly trimmed lawns of her neighbors, Carol Patton looked at her own pathetic bundle of sticks, wondering why she hadn't just dug it out and planted something that would have caused her to worry about aphids, not termites.

Then one day she noticed a small, almost insignificant green bud. Illusion? Imagination? Soon there was another. Then another. And another. Not long after, there were leaves. Within a month, the bush was covered by deep pink flowers, on top of each other, beside each other, beneath each other, overtaking the brown sticks and green leaves. A blanket of color had buried what once was a dead brown bush that seemed to have outlived its usefulness. For three weeks, it bloomed, then the lush green of life re-emerged, staying until the first frosts.

Two years later, her neighbor became a widower; almost eight years later, he suffered a hip fracture and had to go to a nursing home; a few months after that, William Young, known as Bungy by his friends, was dead. But the plant he had saved still blooms. And like he had said, it is truly the most beautiful plant in the neighborhood.

29/

Hidden Truths

For more than four months, the nation's media had been reporting the largest troop build-up since Vietnam—and how well the commander-in-chief could pilot a cigarette boat on the Maine coastline. The concern and fear were measured not by polls, but by a rapid increase of Americans subscribing to cable so they could watch CNN, flipping off network commercials to see was happening in the world.

Unlike the Vietnam War and the wars in Central America where Americans were entrenched in jungles of political decisions that would tear the soul from its own people, this "deterrent" force in the arid Arabian Desert was America's front line of a "popular war," one where American strength would stop the maniacal aggression of a nation that threatened to destroy America's dependence upon fossil fuel. With the media channeling whatever the Bush Administration was spinning, the United States would go to the Gulf, kick a dictator's ass, preserve the right to drive 14-mile-a-gallon cars, and then come home, never more to worry about a foreign war. President Bush would be triumphant, and could easily coast into a second term.

At home, families tearfully told their frightened children in uniform that they hoped the crisis would end quickly, but that—perhaps more to reassure themselves than their children—they supported the commander-in-chief, that America was doing what was right, and that their sons and daughters were the best-trained, best-prepared military in the world. And then, having seen their children leave on ships and planes, they cried the tears of loss. For their children. For themselves. For America.

And so America mounted up not to go into the jungles of

Southeast Asia a half-world away but into the desert of Middle East Asia, a half-world away.

But there was another war, one fought by those who refused to take up arms. A war fought by those who didn't want America to have to build another war memorial like the one honoring the 58,193 American soldiers who died in the Vietnam War. Like the symbolism of this memorial, they didn't want to walk deeper and deeper into the ground until all they could see were the names of those who sacrificed their lives for a war this nation couldn't win.

Carrying home-made signs and chanting "No blood for oil!" hundreds of thousands marched into the streets. In protest were youth who had never been to war, and their parents and grandparents who had; teachers, factory workers, and the clergy, a cross-section of America, a minority of Americans. Speaking against this war were Protestant minister William Sloane Coffin, and Catholic priests Daniel and Philip Berrigan, activists during the Vietnam and civil rights eras who were cursed and arrested, but who hadn't lost their enthusiasm to fight against the uncivil wrongs perpetuated against the people. Condemned by the majority of Americans as "unChristian" were the Religious Society of Friends, which sponsored candlelight vigils, and the Amish, Mennonite, and Church of the Brethren, which also opposed war. Of course, there were also the Jews who are seen by the jingoistic American people as not only heathen but also unpatriotic Communistic heathen at that, even if some were conservative Republican businessmen who had been combat Marines.

With all of them, liberal, moderate, or conservative, Christian, Jew, Muslim, Buddhist, or atheist, was the "pediatrician to the world," Dr. Benjamin Spock, now 87 years old. One of the leaders of the anti-war movement during the 1960s and 1970s, and like the Rev. Mr. Coffin arrested for counseling young men in how to protest and resist the draft, Dr. Spock spoke out against the impending Gulf War, charging that President Bush, a young Navy fighter pilot in World War II, may have wanted to go to war because he is "a macho person, trying to deny the accusation that he is a wimp." When challenged how he could have become so political, Dr. Spock said he said he didn't turn away from children to take up politics, but turned to politics because he cared about the children.

But it was neither the students nor the religious leaders whose protest brought the TV networks to give a few seconds of network coverage, a contrast to the hours it gave to the Administration's drumbeating. On the front lines were Ed Asner, Mike Farrell, and Martin Sheen, Barbra Streisand, Noam Chomsky, Tim Robbins, Susan Sarandon, and thousands of others in the creative arts. And, because good TV is also good conflict, the networks duly recorded the counter-protestors who absolutely positively *knew* that these protestors were un-American unpatriotic cowards.

More than a half-million American soldiers and allies were now in the Persian Gulf desert, the largest military arsenal assembled since D-Day; oldies "Okie From Muskogee" and "God Bless the U.S.A." dominated the radio; CNN constantly interrupted its own news to update the world on what was happening in the Middle East.

A world away, Apryl and I spent New Year's Eve together in a former stone mill on 40 acres of forest, streams, and among all kinds of wildlife on land in northeastern Pennsylvania. Apryl was tired. You could see it in her eyes, you could hear it in her voice. For more than three weeks she had been a sprite, bounding from here to there, painting a board here, slopping plaster there, but always providing for the food and refreshments, for like me she had grown up hearing "Ess, ess, mein kind"—"Eat, eat, my child." No one would go hungry trying to help her. But now, she needed nutrition, and it couldn't come from food.

"David," she half-questioned, "it seemed too easy. Like a novel where the good guys always overcome ridiculous odds, and ride home into the sunset."

"The hard part was the mental gymnastics to set up the victory," I reassured her. I had always told myself, any writers or reporters I came in contact with, and Apryl several times that if something was set up right, it would be executed right.

"Good people will eventually do the right thing," said Apryl. "I guess that's why it seemed to be so easy. Inside of people is the will to do good."

"You showed them truth," I said, reaffirming her own world of illusion, "and they did what's right."

"It shouldn't have been so easy," she lamented. "The commissioners should have stopped me. They should have made me keep coming back. It should not have taken a day, but weeks."

"Maybe," I suggested, "they knew more about the people and the land than we gave them credit for. But, it matters only that your school will now become a reality."

"We'll open a school," she argued, still not satisfied with her victory, "but at what cost?"

"This can never be measured," I said somewhat reassuringly. We didn't say anything for awhile.

"Its cost may have been too great. We had to hurt people. Some very nice people."

"Did you see all those you are going to help?" I asked. "The ones who donated a few cents or a few dollars? The ones who busted their butts to put this school together. The ones who believed in you!"

"I'm sure I hurt Mr. Cameron," she said. "And Mr. Walters is going to be reprimanded. I just know it." She rubbed the back of her hand against her eyes. "He tried to help us, and he risked his job."

"He works for the state," I said. "He has protections. He knows the system. Besides, I suspect he's planning to retire. Probably has a dozen consulting jobs lined up."

"Private Turner," she said. "He's in a lot of trouble."

"I doubt Private Turner has any great desire to make the military his life. He's in it for college tuition." As an afterthought, I added, "Besides, Bernie probably had that idiot lieutenant believing that Turner was some senator's only child."

"What about that nice Dr. Salikoff? I said some very nasty things about him."

"We learn from our mistakes."

"How many other mistakes are there? In my selfishness, how many other people were hurt? How many jobs were lost? How much hatred will there be just because I wanted something? Are we any better than Pioneer Power?"

"A school is more important than something that will create excess corporate profits."

"Don't you understand? We hurt people by building this school. We hurt the people of this county by taking away the taxes and consumer spending that could have improved the life for all of us. And because we incorporated as a non-profit, the county won't even get taxes from the school."

"We gave the people a conscience."

"We didn't give them anything they didn't already have. We just helped them realize some truths. But, we cost them jobs. No matter what I said at the Commissioners' meeting, some jobs were going to go to people who needed them. Even if only a few dozen residents were to be employed, that's still a few dozen. Unemployed and impoverished people can't wait."

"The unemployed and the impoverished have always waited," I said with tears in my heart but not wanting to push Apryl any further into a reflective depression. "The politicians know that and they count on that because they don't contribute to political campaigns. The politicians don't care about the people, and anything you or I do won't change that!"

"There will be hope some day," said Apryl, a tear mingling with a twinkle. "There will come someone, sometime, who will restore our hope and give us back our country from the dumpster Reagan and Bush put us in."

"Flash-and-grin politicians preaching a new beginning are as common as the dirt pellets on your roads."

"Sometimes you just need hope," she said. "If there's hope, there's a future." She thought a moment. "There will be a school, but it won't bring money to the businesses and it'll only help a few people." It had almost become a mantra.

"That's nonsense, Apryl. There'll be classes for all people. It'll teach about peace and labor and our environment. The weekend bazaar where creative people can get together is a great idea! You're even planning on a natural foods store!"

"They're your ideas, David."

"My ideas? You're the one who wanted the school. You said you wanted all that stuff. You even raised all of those ideas yourself."

"But in *my* fashion. In *my* way. You took it and ran with it."

"You're the one who told me about the school. You're the one who called me about your credit union being dissolved. You're the one who called when the Declaration of Taking was issued. You—"

"Yes, *me*! I wanted support, but you took over. Even all this around me. It's your friends and your ideas and—"

"*My* friends? Most were here because of you not me."

"And I appreciate that. But I wanted to do it on my own. In my own way."

"And the school probably wouldn't have been built!" I regretted it as soon as I said it. But instead of attacking me, Apryl just looked at me. I couldn't figure out what she was going to say, what hurt she felt.

"Hold me and tell me everything will be all right."

"What could be wrong?" I answered, my feelings hurt. But before she could say anything, I quickly added, as bright and pleasant as I could, hoping my enthusiasm would infect her. "You're about to be the first director of the first School for Peace. Now *that's* something to be proud of—and you, not me, are going to do that!" She smiled, her blue eyes moist.

"I love you, David," she said. "Please remember that."

"I will," I said, my mind thinking of many things, yet thinking of nothing.

"David, do you remember the day we spent at Hershey Park? Like when we first got there? You wanted to walk around looking at everything. I wanted to ride everything, and you wanted to observe."

"I wanted to get the lay of the land," I said. "Make it more systematic. I told you that when you complained the first time. That wasn't wrong."

"It isn't a matter of wrong, it's just that we see life differently. I want to ride everything; you want to observe everything."

"Am I supposed to say something?"

"That's how it usually works. I talk, then you talk. It makes for a better conversation that way. But the problem is that you talk but never listen."

"What do you mean?" I asked irritated. "That's my job. I listen. I write!"

"You don't listen!" she said again. "You pretend to listen, but you're always playing at listening so you can record. But you only record what interests you, and even then you only observe."

"That's a lie," I said, again offended, quickly reminding her of my years as an activist, but she said only that I was a damned fine journalist, probably better than anyone else she knew, but that to understand life I had to stop recording it. She looked at me. Curiously. Questioning. Then she asked another question. Was she playing Socrates? Or was she just playing with my feelings?

"David?" she asked, "you like old newspapers, don't you?" I agreed. "And you enjoy reading old newspapers because they provide clues not only how to better understand journalism but also society as well." I had no idea where this was leading. Apparently, Apryl did. Then again maybe she didn't. With Apryl, who's to know anyhow? She had created her own world, and was happily living in it. "Let's say you find an old newspaper. A real old one. All brown and fragile. Maybe an early issue of Horace Greeley's *New York Tribune*." She knows both Sam and I admire Greeley. "There's a lot to read in that newspaper," said Apryl, "and you're curious. So, you read the front page, maybe carefully turn it over to read the back page, and you become even more curious. So you open it up because you must explore every line of it, because you're a journalist and can't bear to know that some things are best left as they were found. So, you open it up and *poof*, just like that, it just falls apart in front of you, and you have but a glimpse of what was inside and have lost everything else." Not bad as far as home-spun philosophy goes, but Apryl was still going her own direction, and I had no idea where it was leading. As deftly as the Starship Enterprise, she warped to another example.

"Just like that one small flower in a vase on a restaurant table. *David*, are you listening to me?—You look at it—the flower. You don't know if it's real or artificial, but you're curious. Maybe it's plastic. Maybe fake wood. Maybe it's real. You can smell it, but maybe it's some cheap scented perfume a manufacturer put onto the petals to simulate reality. You've been thinking about it awhile and it's driving you nuts. Is it real? Is it artificial? So you look around, seeing if anyone is looking. You sneak another look at the flower, turn away, then look again. You reach up and touch it, and learn that the flower is real. You know its color and its smell and how large it is and maybe a few other things, but that's all you know about it. Soon a petal falls, then another but you don't notice because you learned what you wanted to know. No matter how hard you try, you won't learn much more. Other petals will soon fall, but you won't notice them because you will have finished your tunafish sandwich, chips, and diet soda, chatted briefly with the waitress, paid the bill, and left a tip. You'd leave a large tip because you're a very generous person, but you wouldn't remember what the waitress looked like because there'd be another waitress and another and still another, and only now and then would they make any kind of a lasting impression. You write far too many stories, and remember none of them. And so you come, you look, maybe you record, and then you leave. And all that's left is a dying flower. And the only thing you and it had in common was that you were curious."

I was about to tell her she didn't have any fuckin' idea what the fuck she was fucking talking about, but what I said was nothing. I couldn't get control over my words or emotions to defend or challenge. We sat in silence, both of us looking at the woods and in it ourselves. "Do you remember the horseshoe crab we brought home?" Apryl quietly asked. Her eyes were again moist. "That horseshoe crab, it's never changed in all those millions of years. You told me that. It reached what it wanted to be and didn't try to become anything else. It's content just the way it is and nobody can make it change."

"So?"

"So, maybe we try too hard to take what we love and change them, to make them what we are."

"I didn't try to change you," I said defensively apologetic.

"Nor did I try to change you but we did, and each of us changed as we thought the other wanted us to. Maybe we tried too hard."

"Maybe." There was a painful silence. While looking at Apryl, I was really looking at myself.

"David?"

"Yes."

"Your story? The one about the Movement?" I silently nodded. "You have everything you need. I said nothing, not knowing what she had meant. "Look within you, within what you've done the past 25 years, within what you have written. It's there. It's all there."

We hugged beneath the new moon, each of us feeling a pain neither of us could describe. She told me that except for her parents, Thomas, and their daughter, she loved me more than anyone she ever knew. That hit me in the gut again, especially since I still didn't know all my feelings; she said she'd always have room in her life for me, that some day, maybe after our stories were published, maybe in a less intense time, we might again have something special between us, untainted by governments and the search for stories.

"David, please know this. No matter what happens. No matter how far away we are, or what we are doing, we are one." I said nothing. There were tears in our heart.

I gave her a single red rose. She gave me a faded snapshot. I was younger, maybe 20, maybe 25. I had longer hair. I was definitely slimmer. But I had no idea where I was at the time. Frisco? San Diego? Chicago? Baffled, I asked the usual journalistic questions—when? where? how'd she find it? All she did was to gently put a finger over my lips, told me to reflect and think of a white rabbit. I asked nothing more.

When I finally left shortly before noon on New Year's Day, Rachel Greenberg, sometimes known as Rachel Greene, sometimes as Apryl Greene, was sitting on the ground, her back against the east wall of the mill, playing haunting melodies on her flute. The School for Peace was about to be born.

Epilogue

With flags flying, Buck Rogers technology, and an allied army of 500,000 from a loose and temporary coalition of more than two dozen countries, led by a charismatic teddy bear general, we sounded forth the trumpets, declared we believed in democracy, and systematically decimated Iraqi forces in a one-month air and artillery barrage, and then Hail Mary-ed them in a four day ground assault. When it was over, and more than 20,000 people lay dead, at least 2,500 of them civilian, almost 200 of them Americans, and another 150,000–200,000 injured, the Bush Administration proudly declared we defeated not only the "Butcher of Baghdad," but dictatorships and territorial aggression as well. A Memorandum of Understanding between Iraq and the UN ended the war.

The first snow had come January 11, five days before Operation Desert Storm, but dropped less than three inches; ten days later, a weaker storm front passed through Marshfield County, dropping only two inches. There would be five more snowfalls after that; none dropped more than four inches, enough to cover the ground, only to melt within a week. With temperatures dropping into the teens and 20s at night, rising into the 30s and 40s during the daytime, it was enough to keep the ground frozen much of the winter, restricting significant construction yet warm enough not to disrupt business—and education.

For reasons best known to theological meteorologists, God had given the people of northeastern Pennsylvania one of the mildest winters they ever had. Mild enough for flowers to again sprout. Mild enough for a School for Peace to open. It would stay open throughout the year, in harmony with the beauty and fury of nature, to provide the home for a philosophy of the understanding and preservation of life. Apryl Greene, always short of money but never enthusiasm or friends to help, would be the beacon who would give a hope that although peace was harder to maintain than war, it was everlasting.

Ronnie Soifer never did become a full-time woodcarver. He's still putting mortar and brick together to help build America.

Hersh Walters retired from the state not long after he left a string of expletives for the speed-bump minds in Harrisburg. He's now doing consulting work for several major corporations, none of which build nuclear plants.

Harry Cameron, true to his word, didn't run for election to the Board of Commissioners, but he's at almost every meeting, giving them a conscience. They need it since Frederick Reinholdt has been re-elected chairman.

Dr. Leon Salikoff is still CEO of Stratford Electronics—and volunteer chairman of the board for Apryl's School for Peace.

Dr. Elliot T. "Doc" Boone, still hacking and coughing, left *Century* a few years ago to return to academics where he is now teaching database retrieval and information processing in the journalism department of a mid-sized college in Indiana.

Greg Diamond, who had wanted to sit by a river and talk with bass, and who had gone to college to avoid the military, earned a "B" average his first semester, and then found a path that led to a remote part of the Susquehanna in northeastern Pennsylvania where Apryl Greene and her friends were building a school that would teach peace. He eventually earned a B.A. in computer art graphics from UMass through a special program that allows non-traditional students to earn credits from life experience, testing, and on-line courses. He divides his time between Apryl's school where he helps teach children and adults about the wonders of wildlife and *Century* where he is one of our page designers.

MaryBeth Martinez and Karlen Aroian left *Century* a few years ago to open their own publishing company. They publish art, photo, and travel books—and, every now and then, works of historical and cultural importance which they know won't make much money, but which they publish nevertheless. Of course, they don't need any of the other books to give them a profit because their *Singles Guide* series supports the other titles.

A couple of years after the School for Peace was built, Bernie Abrahams, newly married to a social worker, left *Century* to complete a Ph.D. in sociology at Boston College. He's now teaching the sociology of mass communications and contemporary social issues courses, challenging students and messing up the minds of professors who place a greater affinity for internal politics and manipulation than they do for the love of teaching and scholarship.

Sylvia Bachman, after swearing she'd never *ever* again live in California, moved to one of the hundred L.A. suburbs. She has an hour's drive to get to her office studio on the MCA lot where she now produces feature films, and is working on her third husband.

Dahn St. Michaels became managing editor when Sylvia left, and then left five years later to become an independent and well-compensated public relations counselor for several non-profit agencies.

Rheumatoid arthritis stole Ruth Weissmann's art career more than a decade ago, but it couldn't stop her enthusiasm for life and her passion for social justice. She still serves as Sam's and *Century*'s social conscience. The Whatever Room continues to be whatever is necessary at the time.

Sam, now well past the age when most workers retire, is still in charge of the nation's only true general circulation magazine with a liberal/activist philosophy. He spends less time in the office, but still writes about things that need to be said to a world that now says it doesn't care. And once a month, sometimes more, he and Ruth spend a day working at a homeless shelter; and once a month, they bring a single long-stemmed rose to their daughter's grave.

As for me—I returned to *Century*, as almost everyone knew I would. Got married again. Got divorced again. My full-time mistress, a demanding lady known as journalism, pretty much doomed this marriage as it had my first one. During the past few years, I have written two more books, but I never completed my story about Apryl Greene/Rachel Greenberg. Each day I knew her, I learned more facts; each day, the truth became more nebulous. The last parts I learned would become the first parts to her life. Maybe one day when I finally decide that the excitement and joys of journalism no longer compensate for the stress it takes from your mind and body, and I finally decide to leave Boston and find something a little quieter like, maybe, college teaching, I might dig through what's left of my yellowing clips, rummage through my notes about Apryl, and try to understand just what happened to my generation of activists, why many of us deserted our dreams, and why Apryl Greene didn't.

Kashonna, Apryl's floppy-eared extra friendly Shepherd constant companion for almost 13 years, never lost her puppy-like enthusiasm for life, keeping it even into her death two years after the school was built. On part of Apryl's School for Peace is the Kashonna Preserve, a place for abandoned dogs, named for Kashonna, herself named for one of Apryl's friends who was killed in an urban war in Miami in May 1980.

Apryl's gained a little weight. Her black hair now streaked with gray is shorter, and she needs reading glasses. But, she still has the most beautiful blue eyes I have ever seen. Now and then, she and I talk on the phone or send e-mails; now and then we get together—for a few hours, for a day or two. Boston. Marshfield County. Sometimes on the Cape or the Jersey shore. And always we find there is still something that binds us, which makes us one.

The County Ordinance of 1851, Pennsylvania's Home Rule Charter of 1935, and Section 691 of the Pennsylvania Code, upon which Apryl hung most of her arguments to reclaim her land and stop a nuclear waste plant, are still part of Pennsylvania law.

Oh, one other thing. Apryl's book? The one about the princess and the knight? It was published a few years ago. It's an allegory for children, but most of the sales seem to be to adults who still need to know there is a hope for peace and a concern for life in a world that may be racing to its own destruction in wars we can never imagine.

"The world is a dangerous place, not because of those who do evil but because of those who look on and do nothing."

—Albert Einstein

About the Author

Walter M. Brasch, Ph.D., is an award-winning syndicated columnist and the author of 16 other books, most of which fuse historical and contemporary social issues. He is a former newspaper and magazine reporter and editor, multi-screen multimedia writer–producer, and a retired professor of mass communications and journalism.

He is vice-president and co-founder of the Northeast Pennsylvania Homeless Alliance, vice-president of the Central Susquehanna chapter of the ACLU, and is active in numerous social causes. He was a Commonwealth Speaker for the Pennsylvania Humanities Council, and was active in emergency management.

Dr. Brasch is featured columnist for *Liberal Opinion Week*, senior correspondent for the *American Reporter*, senior editor for *OpEdNews*, and an editorial board member of the *Journal of Media Law and Ethics*.

He was president of the Pennsylvania Press Club and the Keystone State professional chapter of the Society of Professional Journalists, vice-president of the Pennsylvania Women's Press Association, and founding coordinator of Pennsylvania Journalism Educators. He is a member of the National Society of Newspaper Columnists, the Authors Guild, The Newspaper Guild (CWA/AFL-CIO), and the Online News Association. He is listed in *Who's Who in America, Contemporary Authors, Who's Who in the Media,* and *Who's Who in Education.*

Among his more recent writing awards are those from the National Society of Newspaper Columnists, Society of Professional Journalists, National Federation of Press Women, USA

Book News, Independent Book Publishing Professionals Group, Pennsylvania Press Club, Pennsylvania Women's Press Association, PennWriters, Pacific Coast Press Club, Press Club of Southern California, and the International Association of Business Communicators.

He was honored by San Diego State University as a Points of Excellence winner in 1997. At Bloomsburg University, he earned the Creative Arts Award, the Creative Teaching Award, and was named an Outstanding Student Advisor. He received the first annual Dean's Salute to Excellence in 2002, and a second award in 2007, and the Maroon and Gold Quill Award for nonfiction. He is the 2004 recipient of the Martin Luther King Jr. Humanitarian Service Award.

Dr. Brasch earned an A.B. in sociology from San Diego State College, an M.A. in journalism from Ball State University, and a Ph.D. in mass communication/journalism, with a cognate area in language and culture studies, from The Ohio University.

He is married, has two children, and is surrounded by dogs, a Vietnamese pot-bellied pig, and the rural beauty of northeastern Pennsylvania.

To learn more about Dr. Brasch, visit
http://www.walterbrasch.com

A NOTE ABOUT THE TYPE

The text of *Before the First Snow* is set in Century Schoolbook, a modified typeface of Century, which was designed by Linn Boyd Benton for The *Century Magazine*. Century Schoolbook was designed by Benton's son, Morris Fuller Benton.

The type family was developed following extensive research on readability. The Supreme Court of the United States requires, "The text of every booklet-format document, including any appendix thereto, shall be typeset in Century family."

Before the First Snow was typeset by
Creative Freedom (Danville, Pennsylvania)